LUST AT LARGE

'Excuse me.' The blonde was standing right in front of Gavin, on the other side of the counter. 'Hot, isn't it?'

Gavin was thunderstruck. Her yellow halter-neck was moulded to her body, tightly encasing her voluptuous form. Her protruding nipples were dark points beneath the cotton.

'I can tell you like my figure,' she said in a low voice. 'Would you like to see some more?'

Not waiting for a reply, she pulled the garment to her chin, exposing two stunningly proportioned breasts. They quivered in front of Gavin like ripe fruit.

It was a moment before he noticed the gun.

In a tone no less intimate, she added, 'While you're looking at my tits, put the money in the bag...'

Also available from Headline Delta

Lust on the Loose
The Lusts of the Borgias
Love Italian Style
Ecstasy Italian Style
Rapture Italian Style
Amorous Liaisons
Lustful Liaisons
Eroticon Dreams
Eroticon Desires
A Slave to Love
Amorous Appetites
The Blue Lantern
Sex and Mrs Saxon
The Wife-Watcher Letters
In the Mood
Fondle on Top
Fondle in Flagrante
Fondle All Over
Kiss of Death
The Phallus of Osiris
High Jinks Hall
The Delicious Daughter
Passion in Paradise
A Man With Three Maids
A Man With More Maids
Exposed

Lust at Large

Noel Amos

Copyright © 1994 Noel Amos

The right of Noel Amos to be identified as the Author of
the Work has been asserted by him in accordance with the
Copyright, Designs and Patents Act 1988.

First published in 1994
by HEADLINE BOOK PUBLISHING

A HEADLINE DELTA paperback

10 9 8 7 6 5 4 3 2 1

All rights reserved. No part of this publication may be
reproduced, stored in a retrieval system or transmitted,
in any form or by any means without the prior written
permission of the publisher, nor be otherwise circulated
in any form of binding or cover other than that in which
it is published and without a similar condition being
imposed on the subsequent purchaser.

All characters in this publication are fictitious
and any resemblance to real persons, living or dead,
is purely coincidental

ISBN 0 7472 4329 8

Phototypeset by Intype, London
Printed and bound in Great Britain by
HarperCollins Manufacturing, Glasgow

HEADLINE BOOK PUBLISHING
A division of Hodder Headline PLC
338 Euston Road
London NW1 3BH

The girl is wearing white shorts. They cling to the swollen curves of her buttocks like a second skin. The boy can't keep his eyes off them as he walks behind her, struggling to keep pace as her long brown legs bound up the hill. He longs to stop and catch his breath but the cotton-clad rounds of her sumptuous behind draw him on.

At the top she points to the village far below. The buildings are tiny, made insignificant by the vast carpet of meadow and moorland beyond. On the other side of the valley, distant peaks beckon against an ocean of cloudless summer sky.

The girl leads him down to a spring which bubbles from the rock. The water is clear and pure and she splashes it over her face and neck. It runs into the turquoise fabric of her T-shirt, turning the blue to black, moulding to the contours of her heavy breasts.

The boy drinks his fill, guzzling from cupped hands. He strips off his shirt and exposes his body to the sun. The girl gives him a curious look as she considers his lean pale frame. He catches her glance and grins. They have known one another for less than a day.

She wants to sunbathe and asks if he minds. She doesn't wait for his answer before pulling her top over her head and dropping it on the grass. He stares in wonder at her big bare breasts. They are brown, like the rest of her, and they sway as she moves to sit beside him on the bank.

She smiles when she sees the hunger in his eyes and makes no protest when he kisses her. Her mouth is hot and wet and the soft pressure of her bosom on his chest makes him dizzy. For a moment he is blinded by accomplishment and then he remembers he is a man with a mission. Before he can live again, Gavin Bird must lay a ghost – a ghost of flesh and blood.

He bends to his task and, as the girl's hand finds the belt of his jeans, he takes a raspberry-sweet nipple between his lips . . .

One
STORM IN A D-CUP

1

The big city was in the grip of a summer heatwave. As they sweated in traffic jams and sweltered on commuter trains, life for the average work-person was hell. It was a special kind of purgatory for the necktied and besuited male as he strap-hung next to his female counterpart on bus or subway train. He was imprisoned in yards of unnecessary cloth, she wore scarcely anything at all.

So began the worst day of Gavin Bird's life. Across the aisle of his carriage sat a curvy blonde, her hair teased upwards only to cascade down in delightful ringlets across her bare, bronzed shoulders. All she appeared to be wearing on her succulent body was a candy-pink vest-top with a scooped-out neck, a black micro-skirt and a tiny pair of white cotton briefs now revealed to the ogling Gavin as the girl crossed her legs. An expanse of shapely thigh was spread out in front of him and he marvelled at the delicate texture of the golden skin. He longed to plunge forward and trace with his tongue the inviting path from the tip of her knee up past the hem of her skirt and into the vee of her thinly pantied crotch.

Gavin wondered whether it was simply Josie's absence that made his sexual hunger so acute. They had been sleeping together for almost a year and he took their regular lovemaking for granted. She had been gone for three weeks now and he felt about ready to explode. Mind you, he couldn't picture Josie Twist doing to him the things he really fancied. The things he wanted the girl opposite to do to him.

He imagined strap-hanging in front of her, his loins on a level with her pretty, heart-shaped face. She'd smile up at

Lust at Large

him and then unzip his fly to slip her tiny fingers inside and free his aching cock. She'd pull it out, balls and all, and it would swing there right in her face and her mouth would open in a perfect O of wonder before she'd greedily suck it in, as deep as she could, between those pouting lips. He'd look down, through the tousled curtain of her blonde hair, into the cleavage beneath her flimsy top and feast his eyes on the bob and shift of her bulging breasts as she worked on him with mouth and hands, urging him on to a crescendo that would fill her sulky mouth with foaming spunk . . .

Gavin tore his gaze from the girl's full pink lips. He couldn't allow himself to think about sex. Not yet. Not here. Not at eight thirty in the morning, for God's sake. He turned his head away. In front of him now was a tall teenager, leaning against the window, the sun silhouetting the profile of her large breasts through the thin silk of her blouse. *I wonder if she's wearing a bra?* thought Gavin, he couldn't help it. The girl shifted her position, sending ripples through her superstructure. Beneath the fragile material it was obvious she wore not a stitch. Gavin closed his eyes.

By mid-morning he was alone in the front of the office, sitting at his work station, waiting for the next patron of the Kent Kindly Building Society. A plastic tag on his lapel read G BIRD, Trainee Manager. Gavin, a first-class English graduate with a half-written thesis on the lyric contemporaries of Keats to his credit, considered this the ultimate insult. Trainee Tea-maker would have been a more accurate description of his role.

Behind the door to his right, the female members of staff sat out the lull before the lunchtime rush. As a rule, Gavin enjoyed their company but today he was happy to mind the store. Maybe it was the heat, maybe it was Josie's absence, but today he couldn't bear being closeted with Janice Melting and her pals. Janice knew his weaknesses too well. Earlier she'd sent him to fetch a Coke from the next-door newsagent's fridge. She'd deliberately thrust the can into the vee of her blouse and rolled its icy coolness across the plush brown skin bulging over the lacy edge of her bra cups. She'd laughed at him when he'd stared at her with transparent hunger.

'Shame on you, Gavin,' she'd said, 'you're almost a married man.'

He wished now he'd never told Janice that he and Josie were engaged. She was always asking him about the wedding, offering advice and making jokes about the honeymoon. The truth was, he wasn't into this whole wedding-culture bit. He and Josie had simply agreed they would be married some day. It was more of an intellectual commitment, one to make them feel better now Josie had got this job which had landed her in Wales. To be honest, he wasn't sure about marriage. Not when he felt like he did about that blonde on the train this morning. Or even when he considered Janice and her can of Coke . . .

'Excuse me.' The young woman was standing right in front of his desk. Another gorgeous blonde. The world was full of them. This one was smiling. She held open the flaps of her light summer jacket. 'Hot, isn't it?' she said.

Gavin was thunderstruck. Her yellow halter-neck top was moulded to her body, tightly encasing her extravagant and voluptuous figure. The dark points of her protruding nipples were clearly visible through the thin material.

'I can tell you like my tits,' said the woman in a low, mellifluous voice. 'Would you like to see them properly?'

Without waiting for a response, she pulled the hem of her top to her chin, exposing two large, naked and stunningly proportioned breasts which quivered in front of Gavin like ripe fruit.

Then, in a tone no less intimate, she said, 'While you're looking, put the money in the bag.'

Gavin dimly realised that a plastic carrier bag was on the counter. He ignored it and stared at the wondrous, dangling glories in front of him, at the full curves of their undersides, at the way the flesh dragged ever-so-slightly to the side so the heavy rounds pulled away from the centre of her chest. He was mesmerised by the vivid scarlet of her nipples, standing out proudly from the crinkled haloes of her areolae like exotic berries. He could almost taste them.

'Hurry up, darling,' she said, 'or this will be the last set of jugs you'll ever see.'

Then Gavin became aware that beneath the adorable right breast, clasped firmly in an elegant hand, was a metal object of a distinctly unfriendly nature. Gavin's eyes flicked backwards and forwards, from tits to gun, and back again. *This is some surreal movie*, he said to himself. *And I'm in it!*

'Quick, you little twerp. Put the money in the bag!'

And that's what he did. Nearly £4000, that's what they told him later, though the papers said it was ten. When he'd finished filling the bag and had handed it back, she jiggled her fabulous bosom at him with a shake of her shoulders and blew him a kiss. Then she was gone. It had taken less than a minute.

2

'Are you a tit man, Monk?'

'I beg your pardon.'

'I mean,' said Superintendent Hatter turning from the window to face the man sitting opposite his desk, 'in the hit parade of feminine attributes, what is your number one?'

Inspector Archibald Monk stared at his superior and said, 'I don't quite follow you, sir.'

'Don't be bloody obtuse, Monk, you know just what I'm getting at.'

'I presume you are referring to this,' said the other, leaning forward and tapping the front page of the *Daily Rabbit* which lay on top of a pile of newspapers on the Super's desk. In letters an inch-and-a-half high it screamed: BRA-LESS BRENDA STRIKES AGAIN.

For a moment Monk's long lean face cracked into something that might have been a smile. 'I have been keeping an eye on developments,' he said. 'Like the rest of the country, I must confess to being mildly amused.'

Hatter sat down heavily in his chair and stared at him. 'From now on, Monk, I guarantee you won't find it so bloody funny.'

'What's it got to do with me? I'm condemned to exile among the paper-pushers for the rest of my days. You sentenced me yourself. Sir.'

The final word was an undisguised insult. Monk had no time for this fat flanneller, just as he had little regard for any of his senior colleagues. In his eyes, most of them were soft and poisonous, like jelly fish.

In Hatter's view, Monk was an obstinate, pig-headed, Scottish git incapable of rubbing along with his fellow man, who had the inconvenient habit of shining a spotlight on the force's own transgressions. There had been a recent and embarrassing incident. Which was why Monk was currently sidelined on a report about the efficacy of residents' parking schemes in the inner cities.

It was unfortunate that Monk also happened to be Hatter's best thief-catcher: brave, incorruptible and shrewd, a man who lived without the distractions of friends or family and devoted himself day and night to the task in hand. A man with ice-water in his veins. Immune to temptation. Just the man to handle the hottest potato on the books.

'I'm letting you out of jail, Archie,' said Hatter. 'I'm giving you Bra-less Brenda.'

It was not strictly true that Monk was a man without love. His passions were private and ran deep. There had been women. One had even walked up the aisle with him and into his bed for nine wild and wonderful months. But bonny Hannah McFee had left him for a double-glazing manufacturer with a BMW, saying that Monk could wear a hair shirt all his life if he wanted to, she preferred silk and cashmere with a dash of Christian Dior, thank you very much.

There had been friends, too. For a few months after Hannah there had been room-mates called Johnnie Walker and Jack Daniels, until Monk decided he had better live without them if he wanted to live at all. After that, apart from the vicissitudes of Partick Thistle, there had only been his cases. He'd gone after the killers, con-merchants and racketeers with all the single-minded devotion of a great lover. And he'd succeeded, his conquests were legendary – yet his zeal had left him unappreciated, unsatisfied and unloved.

And now came the case of Bra-less Brenda.

'Look at this,' muttered an ill-tempered Hatter, thrusting that morning's *Daily Dog* into Monk's hands.

'WHAT A PAIR OF CHARLIES,' he read. 'Two blushing bobbies were yesterday left grasping thin air as bare-breasted robber Belinda the Bosom once more waltzed off with a record cash hand-out from a high-street building society. Her intentions stuck out a mile, claimed witnesses who saw her enter the Grisewood branch of the Norwich Nicely. But still the local boys in blue failed to lay a finger on her. What's up with the nation's finest? You'd think every red-blooded copper on the force would be dying to place this little lady under close arrest!'

'Belinda the Bosom – that's a new one,' said Monk.

'That's what they're calling her today, last week it was Naughty Knockers Nina, next week no doubt we'll have Tina the Topless Tealeaf. The gutter press are loving every minute of this, the whole country is having a laugh at our expense and I'm getting it in the neck from upstairs. All because some silly tart is flashing her tits at spotty erks in building societies.'

'And pointing a gun at their heads and stealing thousands of pounds in the process,' added Monk. 'It's a serious business.'

'Precisely. I knew you would appreciate the true nature of this pernicious affair. I want some fresh thinking on this case, from someone who won't be sidetracked by the daft remarks and smutty innuendos of the press, the public and, I regret to say, his colleagues.' Hatter's large, jowly face spread into a menacing grin. 'She's all yours, Monk. Go and bring her back alive. And with clothes on.'

3

The phone rang at an inconvenient moment for Josie Twist. She was in a hurry to change and meet Gwen at The Plastered Prop, but first she was on her way to the kitchen. She was starving.

'Oh, Gavin,' she said with as much enthusiasm as she could muster, 'I'm in a bit of a rush at the moment, can I—'

But Gavin was in no mood to be fobbed off and Josie's heart sank. A part of her felt disloyal for she *did* love Gavin, in her own way, but things were changing in her life now that she had this new job.

He was telling her about his day at that bloody building society and she had to fight hard to keep her mind off her empty stomach. He was upset, that was obvious, but what was new about that? Anyone would be upset slogging away at the Kent Kindly, where nothing ever happened – if you discounted the shameless behaviour of that cow, Janice Whatsit. And then she realised what Gavin was saying.

'Good God, Gavin – are you all right?'

He wasn't sure. He was OK physically, he said, but his mind was screwed up.

'It would be,' said Josie, genuinely sympathetic. 'Anyone would be freaked out if they'd been threatened with a gun.'

It wasn't just that, the robber was a woman.

'So what? It doesn't matter if it's a man or a woman if you think they're going to shoot you.'

But there was more to it and as Gavin blathered, unable to come out with the precise circumstances of his humiliation, the truth dawned on Josie. Gavin had been mugged by the Topless Raider. The lads at The Prop had been

Lust at Large

joking about the Raider for weeks. Only last night they had taken a vote on which girl would make the best titty-robber and Gwen had won because hers were by far the biggest.

Josie didn't know whether to laugh or cry. Whether to ask for all the juicy details or face the horrible fact that her Gavin could have been shot dead. She listened to the whole saga in stunned silence. She was in shock herself, which was why what happened happened – or so she rationalised it later.

She was sitting on the living-room sofa, half out of her work clothes; her white blouse was still buttoned to the neck, but her bottom half was clad in just a pair of black tights. As she listened to Gavin she began to unbutton her blouse, conscious that she was running late. Her hand had just opened the third button down when she heard a sound and looked up to see Ivor, Gwen's boyfriend, standing in the bathroom doorway.

Apart from a large white bath-towel slung carelessly around his hips, Ivor was naked. His dark hair was plastered to his head and beads of moisture glistened on his broad pectoral muscles. His coal-black eyes were fixed on Josie's sprawling legs.

Josie smiled at him nervously and he acknowledged her with a nod of his head. Ivor always made her feel ill at ease. He said little and his gaze was so fierce it seemed to burn into her, stripping away her defences and challenging her in a very basic fashion. He was also the most beautiful man she had ever met.

There was another reason he made her uneasy. A few days after she had moved into the flat she had surprised him and Gwen on the very sofa on which she now sat. She had taken to bed early, had woken up after midnight and gone to investigate the strange noises in the living-room. If she hadn't been half asleep she would have known at once what was going on. Convinced that Gwen was crying out in pain, she had burst into the room and found the pair of them in the crucial stages of a vigorous fuck.

Gwen was lying on her back across the sofa with Ivor kneeling on the floor in front of her. Her bum overhung the seat and her legs rested on Ivor's shoulders as he thrust in and out between her legs. He wore an unbuttoned shirt and she wore black suspenders and stockings and a coffee-coloured camisole that had been pushed up around her neck.

From her position in the doorway, Josie could see the intimate collision of their bodies in every detail. Ivor's cock drove into Gwen like a thick white wand, stretching wide the outer lips of her pink pussy. He had one hand spread across her belly, his fingertips at the top of her slit, probing and nudging her clit. His other hand was out of sight beneath Gwen's bottom. Whatever he was doing to her, it was highly effective, for she was twisting her head from side to side, whipping her long red hair across her large juddering breasts.

Josie had withdrawn swiftly and she and Gwen had laughed about the incident the next morning. But Josie had never discussed it with Ivor and every time she saw him the image of his slim hips and long white cock sprang to her mind.

Now he was smiling at her as he unslung the towel from his waist and began to rub the moisture from his chest. The length of towelling fell down between his thighs, still concealing his groin – though Josie fancied she could see the bulge of his genitals beneath the swaying material. As Gavin continued to drone into her ear, Josie's eyes were glued to Ivor, to the smooth pale skin of his long flanks, to the muscles in his shoulders and to the scooped-out hollows of his buttocks as he turned to one side.

He was teasing her, there was no doubt. The towel flicked backwards and forwards over his crotch and her breath caught in her throat as she glimpsed again that pale finger of flesh that so fascinated her. Then he was drying his back, sawing the towel across his shoulders, and his whole body was on view. His penis was erecting, she could see. It pointed downwards from a knot of black hair at the base of his belly but, as she watched, it seemed to swell and jerk upwards. Now it was pointing straight out from his body and she felt as if she, like Gavin earlier, were staring down the barrel of a gun. The pale foreskin had peeled back to reveal a pink and glistening head as the cock swung up to full erection.

Josie's need for food was forgotten. Right now she felt a different kind of hunger.

Gavin was still talking as Ivor walked towards her and stood with his big penis on a level with her face. He folded his arms over his chest and bumped his hips so his cock waved in front of her. She looked up to see him grinning at her without shame. He ran his tongue over his lips in obvious suggestion. Josie couldn't help herself, she reached out and took hold of him.

His prick felt hot in her hand. It seemed to pulse with life and urgency. She ran her fingers up and down its length, tentatively at first, then boldly, rolling the foreskin right back to reveal the broad head, now reddening under her touch.

'I'm going to have to go now, Gavin,' she said firmly, dipping her hand between Ivor's legs to cup his furry balls. 'I've got lots of things to do.'

But she couldn't get rid of him that easily, there was a ritual to their conversations and she had to indulge it.

'Darling, I miss you, too,' she said, adding – as she knew she must – 'and your cock.'

That set him off. She knew he looked forward to talking dirty to her on the phone and up till now she'd felt rather prim about it. But at this moment, with Ivor's throbbing erection in her hand, it was undeniably exciting.

He was telling her how badly he wanted to ravish her – to throw her on a bed and rip her panties off her arse and thrust his bursting prick deep inside her until she screamed for mercy and then screamed for more!

'Oh yes!' Josie cried as Ivor's hand suddenly dived between her legs and began to probe her sodden cunt through her tights.

Gavin was expanding on his theme, describing his urge to spunk all over her body, in particular to thrust his cock between her breasts.

Ivor's busy hand had now found a tiny hole in the seam of her underwear and, in one fierce movement, he ripped away the material covering her crotch.

'Oh God!' wailed Josie as a thick finger was thrust inside her.

Gavin was still on about her satin-smooth breasts and

how he longed to wrap their bulging contours around his aching member. Josie knew he was jerking off as he talked and she was feeling so hot herself the idea thrilled her.

By now, Ivor had three fingers inside her and his thumb was rubbing her stiff little clit. She humped her bottom up off the sofa to meet his thrusts. Her juices were running down the inside of her thighs and somewhere in her head she realised she'd leave stains on the cushions – but then there must be plenty of those on the sofa already.

She reached forward and did what she had been dying to do all along – suck that beautiful dick into her mouth as far as it would go. God, it tasted wonderful! Salty but clean, a rich man-taste. She gobbled deeply then slid her mouth backwards and forwards, pumping with her hand on his shaft, rubbing the fat head on the roof of her mouth.

Gavin was getting close, she could hear it in the breathy tones of his voice and the way he kept repeating himself, saying the words 'big wobbling tits' over and over and—

Her mouth was suddenly flooded as Ivor's prick jumped and pulsed in her hand and shot a thick wad of semen down her throat. *God, this is obscene*, said Josie to herself, *but it's fantastic!* And then she came too, wriggling in ecstasy on Ivor's fingers.

'Goodbye, Gavin,' she said, her throat thick with spunk, and replaced the receiver.

'Well, well,' said Ivor, 'what a randy little piece you turned out to be.'

But she wasn't listening. It had only just dawned on her – Gavin wasn't drooling over her tits at all. It was that horrible Topless Raider!

4

Twenty-four hours after their first meeting Monk returned to the Superintendent's office. For once, Hatter greeted him with enthusiasm.

'How are you getting on, Archie? Any leads?'

Monk avoided a direct response.

'I've been studying the incidents, looking for the common denominators in the crimes.'

'I would have thought they were pretty obvious.'

'Indeed. Our perpetrator pitches up in a small branch of a building society, one which hasn't got the most sophisticated security. She waits till the place is empty and targets a young male cashier. Then she flashes her charlies, whips out her shooter and tells him to put the cash in a plastic carrier bag. She's softly spoken, very sexy, and gives the boy a real eyeful. She's out of the place in seconds.'

'It's a joke.'

'It's got a point to it. The breast-baring is obviously a distraction, designed to shock and to keep attention away from more easily identifiable portions of her anatomy, such as her face. So far it seems to have worked. Witnesses are sketchy on facial description. She's been clever in selecting young men who are completely overwhelmed by her behaviour and their statements only describe one thing. Two things, actually. As for the women who have seen her, their observations indicate that this lady has a variety of disguises. She must have an array of wigs, contact lenses, spectacles, fingernails and so on. And, of course, she's ringing the changes with her clothes and make-up. Given the resources at her disposal she's capable of looking entirely different from one day to the next.'

Hatter, whose initial optimism at Monk's appearance was draining away fast, ruminated on this information. 'Sounds just like my daughter. Or my wife. Or any bloody woman I know if they put their mind to it.'

At that moment the telephone rang. Hatter answered it without enthusiasm, his bejowled face a picture of dejection. Within seconds all had changed. As he listened, his eyes lit up and the dewlaps wobbled with joy.

'They've got her!' he cried, thumping the phone back into its rest and leaping to his feet. 'They caught her in the Bristol Bountiful with her blouse open and an imitation pistol in her handbag. She's downstairs now.'

'The Bristol Bountiful,' said Monk as he followed Hatter out of the door en route to the stairs, 'the papers will love that.'

Euphoria was short-lived. Monk knew at once that the suspect was not his girl.

When they arrived she was being attended by four policemen. Others milled around in the corridor trying to get a peak inside the interview room.

'Hi, guys,' she said as Hatter and Monk squeezed inside. 'Just how many of you are needed to take care of one little girl?'

She spoke in a high-pitched voice that, to Monk's ears, said 'low-class tart' and he fixed her with his Mad Monk stare. It was his speciality.

The suspect blew him a kiss. 'Oooh, that one's sexy,' she squealed, adding, 'You'd better not leave me alone with him!' as Hatter ordered the other officers from the room.

'It's not her,' said Monk.

'What do you mean?' shrieked the woman. 'I'm Brenda, Brenda the Bra-less Robber. It's a fair cop, you rotten bastard!'

Hatter ignored her and spoke directly to Monk.

'What are you on about?'

'Don't you see? She may be a thief but she's not the one we're looking for. This is copycat crime.'

'You swine!' shouted the object of their conjecture, her bracelets rattling with rage as she fumbled with the buttons

Lust at Large

of her blouse. 'Here's your bloody proof!'

With these words she yanked open her shirt and displayed herself from neck to navel, intruding into the conversation two pink and shiny rounds of flesh which sat high and immobile on the broad expanse of her chest.

For a moment there was silence.

'Well,' she cried in triumph, 'what do you think of those?'

'I think,' said Hatter to Monk, 'that you are dead right. Let's get out of here and nick the real Naughty Nora.'

Upstairs in Hatter's office, the Superintendent was philosophical. 'I suppose it was too good to be true, her turning up like that out of the blue. You knew at once, didn't you?'

'So would you have done if she had arrived five minutes later. I was about to discuss the video evidence and the one aspect of Brenda's appearance that she can't disguise.'

'The breasts themselves?'

'When you study the pictures from the fixed cameras you can see at once how Tiny Tits downstairs could never pass herself off as the real thing. Quite apart from the fact that she's really Dickless Dora straight off the boat from Casablanca.'

'A sex change, you mean?'

'Exactly. Didn't you notice the shoulders and the hands? She probably used to work on building sites. Of course, the real giveaway was the silicone job – those knockers wouldn't have shifted a millimetre if you'd asked her to stand on her head.'

'Oh hell,' said Hatter.

But Monk did not hear him. He was spreading a pile of black-and-white photographs across the surface of the desk.

'Now, look at these. This is the real thing. It's the photo sequence from last week's raid at the Gloucester Generous. Here's our girl in one of those halter-neck jobs. It's very handy for her purposes, it means she can yank the material up with her left hand and go for the gun with her right, all in the same movement. See, here and here. She gets in close for the hit, makes it very intimate between the cashier and her body. Gets all her guns to bear on him, as it were.'

'What does she say to them?'

' "Do what I say or this is the last pair of tits you'll ever see." She said to one of them, "Take a good look, lover, I want you to die with a smile on your face." '

'Nice,' muttered Hatter.

'That's what they say afterwards. All the tellers agree that hers are a Grade-A, number-one, first-class set of bazookas, and they share a sense of privilege at being invited to ogle them. There is concern that some of them may be traumatised for a while as a result of this experience.'

'Huh, it doesn't take long for them to cough up the cash.'

'If you ask me, it's the psychology of the carrot and the stick. And the fact that most British males under the age of thirty are mother-fixated.'

'You mean, they are all big babies and the sight of an overblown pair of breasts makes them compliant?' Hatter obviously did not consider this much of an excuse.

'It's a line of thinking that sells a lot of newspapers.'

'Don't mention *them*. We'll never keep the lid on that fiasco downstairs.'

'Maybe not but I have an idea that the papers could be of use to us.'

Hatter narrowed his piggy eyes and shot Monk a look loaded with suspicion.

'I'll need your permission,' continued Monk, 'but here is what I intend to do.'

Hatter listened intently and as he did so his fat face settled into a mask of gloom.

5

Robyn Chestnut burst out of the editor's office in a rage. Her colleagues in the newsroom of the *Daily Rabbit* smirked to themselves as she stamped back to her desk. The American girl lost her cool on a daily basis and it was usually very entertaining.

'What's today's drama, sweetie?' asked the diary editor.

'Fuck off, Crispin.' Robyn had upended her handbag on her desk and was pawing through her things, an unlit cigarette dangling from her wide curvy mouth. 'Just tell me what it is with you Brits and tits.'

Crispin produced a light and Robyn took a deep drag.

'I mean,' she said, 'I took this job on the basis that I would deal with proper women's issues. I know it's a tabloid paper but that means you can be more direct, show the human face, go straight for the guts.'

Crispin cut her short, he'd heard all this before. 'Let me guess, he's put you on Brenda.'

'Of course he's put me on Brenda. There isn't another story on this entire paper. It's twenty-eight pages everyday about a woman and her tits! It's un-fucking-believable.'

'Don't knock the breast, darling. It's our entire editorial philosophy. It's politically balanced, too. You see, there's a left one and a right one.'

'Oh shut up!' But Robyn grinned all the same. She couldn't stay pissed for too long.

Her phone rang.

'Robyn Chestnut,' she announced sharply. Then, as she listened, her look of impatience disappeared. She put the phone down a few moments later and began to gather up her belongings. Crispin raised his eyebrows.

'I just got a break,' she explained. 'An inside line on Brenda that might even please the Big Bastard – if I can bear to talk to him after what he said to me.'

'What was that?'

'He told me that just because I wore an A-cup I shouldn't be jealous because this Brenda woman took a double D. He said a true professional would not let her own physical deficiencies get in the way of a good story.'

And, with that, she uncoiled her slim six-foot frame from her chair and strode angrily out of the office.

In fact, Robyn did not despise her editor or even the story she was forced to work on. She could think of one or two angles on this topless-robber thing well worth exploring. But she did seem to be operating on a very short fuse these days and she knew the reason why. It was sex – she wasn't getting enough of it. Though it wasn't for want of trying.

The night before, she'd turned up at Alistair's unannounced. It was outside their arrangement but, where her hungry pussy was concerned, why make an appointment? He'd not been at home, Wednesday being one of his TV nights, so she'd waited for him to return from the studio. She'd dressed up for him or, rather, dressed down in his favourite costume of white blouse, short pleated grey skirt, blue serge knickers and white ankle socks. She'd put her long black hair in bunches, painted freckles across the bridge of her nose and placed the riding crop on top of the television set. While she waited for him to arrive, she watched his programme.

Alistair Needle's professional life had changed radically in the two years Robyn had known him. They had met as staffers on a dull sociological monthly, *The Pill*, for which Alistair had covered financial and home affairs. He'd worn rumpled corduroy suits and Hush Puppies, played rugby for the Old Boys on Saturdays and slept alone, still brooding over a long-dead, childless marriage. Robyn had changed all that – once she'd discovered a way through his defences.

The Needle was much sought after by the females on the magazine but none of them had the chutzpah that Robyn did. A few hours of beery conversation at the pub near the office revealed that Alistair had the hots for the Princess Royal, loved traditional English country pursuits and every year took his two nieces to schoolgirl hockey internationals. Before pouncing, Robyn had tested her theory. She'd worn jodhpurs and riding boots to the office once and had seen his eyes light up. She'd inveigled him into a walk past the local girls' school playground during a netball match and gauged his interest. After that it was easy.

The costume she wore tonight was the one that she had revealed to him an evening almost two years ago. The sight of her long long legs and tight bottom then had him glassy-eyed. She'd brazenly eased his big tool out of his corduroys in the hall of her flat and after that there had been no stopping him. They'd called in sick to the office for the next two days and had humped their way all round her small apartment. And, though she had paid a heavy price in carpet burns and minor bruises, she had never regretted it. As they'd said at *The Pill*, she'd got The Needle, all right.

Within weeks the corduroys had hit the dustbin along with the rugby boots and she'd turned the threesome at England v Scotland into a foursome – which was a deadly way to spend an afternoon but a blissful way to pass the following night. Just at the point when she had sharpened up The Needle's wardrobe to include some smart designer suits and had shown him the way to the local dry-cleaners, he had landed a reporter's job on a heavyweight TV news programme. He'd been an instant success. His laid-back public-school arrogance had pricked a few politicians' bubbles and suddenly he was a name, with a late-night show of his own.

Sometimes Robyn regretted it. If she'd left him in his stained corduroys she might have been able to keep him all to herself. But these days she was not sure if that was what she really wanted. As she waited for him to return she kept glancing at the whip she had placed on top of the television. Knowing that she was going to get her bum whacked gave her a thrill, there was no doubt, but only because she would enjoy a hard penis between her legs afterwards.

She fell asleep before Alistair returned home. He found her curled up on the floor, her small round posterior thrust cheekily towards him. He smacked it.

'Hey,' shouted Robyn, instantly awake, 'that's not fair!'

'Naughty little girls who turn up unannounced deserve everything they get,' he drawled, picking her up and draping her over an armchair.

'What about "Hello, darling, what a marvellous surprise"?' she protested as he peeled her knickers down her long thighs.

'How's this for surprise?' he replied and thrust his cock without ceremony into her spread pussy.

'Christ, Needle, you're some romantic. Aren't you even going to whip me first?'

'Later,' he said, lunging into her at full bore, stuffing his bony tool with brute force deep into her juicy hole. 'Then I'll fuck you all over again, just the way you hackettes on the *Bunny* like it.'

But he hadn't, he'd fallen asleep on top of her and in the morning they'd had a row about her turning up when she wasn't supposed to. Now, as Robyn peered through the gloom of The Frog in a Bucket looking for her mystery caller, she reflected that there had to be an easier way for a girl to get her rocks off.

6

Josie cupped her left breast and weighed it in her hand. It wasn't big but she could hardly be called flat-chested. It was average, pretty much like the rest of her, she reflected. Average face, average height, average tits. Lots of boys had said that she was ravishingly pretty but that was because they wanted to stick their cocks in her average pussy. Most of them were pretty average themselves. Except for Gavin. And Ivor.

She began to squeeze her nipple as she thought of Ivor, teasing it out into a perky pink stub. Most of her life had been average. Swotting at school and university to keep up. Working overtime at this research job in this boring bit of Wales.

Except that what had happened the other night with Ivor had not been average. That had been brilliant. It shone like a diamond next to all the other dull episodes in the chain of her limited sexual experience. Even her times with Gavin weren't thrilling in the same way. With Gavin there was always a hidden agenda, a burden of emotional need that detracted from the sheer pleasure of sex.

Whereas, on the sofa with Ivor, there had just been the feel of his cock in her mouth, the squirt of his juices down her throat and the tingle of his fingers in her pussy. And after she'd put the phone down he'd done just what she'd wanted him to – fucked her like he'd fucked Gwen that night. With her arse half off the seat and her legs around his waist, he'd shagged her long and hard. He'd pulled open her blouse, pushed her bra up over her breasts and had gone wordlessly to work between her thighs.

Just as he had with Gwen, he'd placed a hand on her

belly and toyed with her clit, while the other roved beneath her, over her pliant buttocks and into the crack between. When he'd pushed a finger firmly into her anus she'd come off with a scream. His dark eyes had bored into her, drinking in every detail of her soft slim body as she writhed in ecstasy beneath him. It had been delicious.

Her hand was in her knickers now as she thought about it. Her pussy was dripping with excitement, just as it had been for days. *Oh God*, she thought, *I'm going to have to wank again.*

'Hey, Josie,' said Gwen, sailing into the small bedroom without bothering to knock and then freezing as she took in the half-naked girl lying on the bed. 'Oops, I'm sorry, were you asleep?'

'It's OK.'

'I've brought you a drink to buck you up. Is red wine all right?'

'Who says I need bucking up?' said Josie, taking the glass nevertheless.

'With your boyfriend far away hallucinating about big-titted blondes, of course you do. Cheers.'

Josie had told Gwen about Gavin's babbling phone call and his fixation with the busty raider. She had omitted her own activities during the course of the call.

'If you ask me,' said Gwen, 'you need a man closer to home to keep your morale up.'

Josie gulped her drink and said nothing. Gwen had turned into a good friend but she may not remain one if she found out about Ivor.

'Why don't we go down to the rugby club? I fancy a little action myself.'

'What about Ivor?'

'He may be my home fixture but who says I can't play away from time to time?'

'Gwen, that's shocking. Do you really?'

'Every chance I get. So what about it some night?'

'I don't know. Anyway, it's the off season, isn't it?'

'Not for kind of game I'm talking about.' She laughed and drained her glass.

Josie followed suit and said, 'Can I ask you a personal question?'

'Anything, darling.'

'Do you think my boobs are big enough for titty-bonking?'

'What?'

'Don't look so surprised, I really want to know. If Gavin's getting so worked up about doing it over that woman's chest I suppose I ought to make myself available. But mine don't seem substantial enough. Look.' And she squeezed them together with her hands.

Gwen sat next to her on the bed and peered closely at her friend's delicate rosy bosom.

'I see what you mean. You're wondering whether there's enough flesh to go round. A prick might just flatten them out.'

'Yes, what do you think?'

Gwen picked up a tube of moisturiser from the bedside table and pushed it experimentally into the thin line of cleavage. 'Hmm. It sits on top a bit rather than sinking in. And most dicks are a bit bigger than this.'

'*Most* dicks! You've done a survey, have you?' Josie was beginning to feel a bit hysterical. And tipsy, Gwen had been topping up the glasses with a heavy hand.

'Look at it this way,' said Gwen, 'you might strike lucky and find a guy with a tiny cock. You'd be made for each other.'

She shook with laughter and peeled off her T-shirt. Her large tanned breasts were supported by a black bra with gauzy patterns that revealed the pale flesh beneath. Her freckled cleavage was deep and enticing. Josie felt woefully inadequate.

'Gosh, Gwen, they're gorgeous.'

'Well, yours are gorgeous, too, and you know it. Any guy with taste would adore to rub his knob all over those pretty little boobs. I just want to demonstrate how things work for us large-scale girls.'

By now she had shrugged off her bra and her great brown knockers were swinging free, their weight pulling them downwards ever so slightly. Taking a big tit in each hand, she said, 'Put that tube in the middle.'

Josie did as she was told and the tube vanished for a moment as Gwen folded her breasts over it. Then it

Lust at Large

reappeared as Josie, entering into the swing of things, began to push it backwards and forwards in imitation of a rearing penis.

'That's it,' said Gwen. 'It's usually best if you lie back and the guy straddles you. Or you can kneel in front of him. Some oil on the tits helps and you've got to give him a good gobble on the upstroke – they all love that.'

'You are rude, Gwen,' said Josie and pantomimed a dick in orgasm, thrusting the tube up and down in little jerks.

'What's very important is to rub the come all over your titties when he's finished. It helps get the feller going for the next round – which, Josie, I guarantee you'll be dying for.'

'Gwen, I am dying for it this very minute.'

There was a knock at the door.

'You're in luck then, girl. That'll be the boys.'

'What?'

'Stay here and don't panic.'

'Gwen!' But she was gone, her big boobs swinging as she left.

Josie slammed the door shut behind her, her heart pounding. From the hall she heard laughter. Male laughter. And cheers – Gwen had obviously opened the door half naked. Josie didn't know what to do.

The noises and whoops grew muffled, they must have gone into the kitchen or the living-room. Now there was silence. Josie made herself take deep breaths. She began to calm down.

She pulled on a thick sweater and a skirt and sat on the bed, breathing deeply. Five minutes went by. What were they doing? Surely Gwen wasn't so shameless as to start fucking on the living-room floor? Who could say? There must be at least two of them. The thought made her feel funny.

There was a tap at the door.

'Who is it?' said Josie.

Ivor stepped into the room, a look of concern in his big black eyes.

'Are you all right?'

'Go away, Ivor.'

'I thought you liked me.'

'Oh, I do.' It came out rather too quickly. He smiled and sat on the bed beside her.

Josie shrank away from him. 'What about Gwen?'

'She's talking to Terry. Are you hot?'

'No.'

'Well, I am.' And he began to unbutton his shirt.

Josie watched, mesmerised, as he bared his broad chest, then stood and unbuckled his belt. He shucked his jeans and underpants off in one movement and stood in front of her stark-naked. His penis was fully erect.

Josie began to giggle, she couldn't help it. 'Is striptease your only seduction technique?' she asked.

He picked her bodily from the bed and she clung, laughing, to his neck. Her earlier excitement had returned. He was going to fuck her once more and she couldn't wait.

They kissed hungrily, his tongue probing her mouth with a tenderness that surprised her. His hands were under her sweater and palming her breasts, pinching her nipples, then pulling her to him to press her naked flesh against his. She wasn't laughing now.

He pushed her skirt up to her waist and pulled the gusset of her panties to one side. She was sopping wet. He grunted his approval as he tipped her backwards onto the bed and positioned himself over her.

'Oh yes,' she whispered as he pressed the fat head of his tool into her crack, 'put that big thing in me. Shove it right up me. Hurry!'

His eyes were blazing into hers as he thrust home and she pushed her tongue into his mouth and sank her nails into his buttocks as she took the weight of him. She came at once. It was bliss.

He stayed motionless inside her as she calmed down and then began a more relaxed thrusting. She gloried in the feel of his strong hard body on top of hers. She loved the fact that he hardly spoke, he just appeared in her life and fucked her. She'd never had a relationship like it. They said it was what men really wanted from women. She could understand why. It was perfect.

He was doing his clit-tickling, bum-probing trick. It was obviously a speciality of his, he was bloody good at it. She came again, a slow, lingering orgasm this time that left her satisfied for the moment.

'Get off me,' she said. 'I want to do something.'

He obeyed and allowed himself to be positioned as required. He grinned, his white teeth flashing in the half-light as she smoothed ointment over her breasts.

Kneeling between his legs, she held his stiff organ between her tits, trying to envelop him in her cleavage. She kept him there by lacing her fingers and pressing her breast flesh inwards with her wrists. Held captive, his wet prick pressed into her bosom, the red knob-end just inches from her lips.

'Go on, Ivor,' she said, 'fuck my tits.'

He needed no urging, plunging his cock into the slippery hole made by her breasts and fingers. The head thrust up and down, getting redder and redder, the eye in the tip seeming to wink at her as he poked.

'Lick it, Josie,' said a voice behind her, 'give it a good suck.'

Gwen was standing in the open doorway and by her side was a boy Josie had seen with Ivor once or twice. Gwen was naked, her big breasts thrusting out proudly, her pubic bush a wild profusion. The boy – Terry – had his hand between her legs with two fingers hidden inside her. He was fully dressed but his flies were open and Gwen was holding his cock in her hand.

For a moment this extraordinary sight had Josie bewitched and she stopped her lewd movements. Then she did as she was told, dipping her head to capture Ivor's member between her lips, flicking at the glans as it thrust up and then retreated.

Suddenly Ivor groaned as if he had been struck and, on the up-stroke, a bolt of semen shot from his tool, inundating Josie's face and neck.

'Good God,' said Terry, 'that's the horniest thing I've ever seen.'

'Fantastic!' said Gwen and placed her free hand over Terry's fingers, pressing them further between her legs.

Josie said nothing but basked in the approval of her squirming flatmate as she began to rub Ivor's come into her tits.

7

'So, Ms Chestnut, what do you think?' said Archibald Monk to Robyn in the dingy snug of The Frog in a Bucket.

Between them on the scarred and beer-ringed pub table lay a large brown envelope. Robyn picked it up.

'Are these the pictures? May I look?'

Monk nodded but Robyn had already reached inside and extracted a dozen black-and-white photographs. There was no one near them in the deserted back room but she instinctively held them close to her body, safe from prying eyes.

'Oh wow. These are fantastic!'

'I thought they might appeal to you.'

Robyn shot him a sudden look.

'Not you personally, of course, Ms Chestnut, but your readers.'

'Call me Robyn, for Christ's sake. Yeah, these are just the kind of thing our ten million punters love to drool over. What's the catch?'

'There is no catch. We must find this woman and we need help from the general public. By making these photographs available in your newspaper we hope a reader will recognise her and come forward.'

'A nationwide womanhunt led by the *Daily Rabbit*. We'll be deluged. The post office will need a forklift truck.'

'I can set up one man on a special hot line, that's all we can spare. You'll have to deal with the calls and mail that come to you. Most of it will be worthless but someone must know who she is.'

'You bet,' said Robyn, examining a shot that showed the half-naked robber reaching to grab a plastic bag of money. 'You'd expect a pair like that to stick in the mind. They're unforgettable, wouldn't you say?'

'If you like that sort of thing.'

'Don't you?'

'I wouldn't admit to it while I'm on duty.'

Robyn eyed the tall Scotsman with interest. Did he have a sense of humour? She found it hard to tell.

'Tell me one more thing, Inspector—'

'Archie.'

'Why haven't you given this to the *Dog*? You did say we had this exclusively?'

'We are going to ask for cooperation from both of you. But the *Daily Dog*'s leader this morning decided us in your favour. They suggested that my superior, Superintendent Charles Hatter, and the men at his command were not motivated to catch Brenda because she was the wrong gender.'

'I don't get it.'

'The headline read ARE THERE FAIRIES IN THE MAD HATTER'S GARDEN? He is very upset.'

Robyn arrived two hours later for dinner. She thought that was pretty good going considering the amount of work she had put in at the office redrafting the next day's edition. The editor had been ecstatic and had completely remade the first half of the paper. He'd chucked out the intended glamour-girl spread on page three, saying that Brenda made her look like a grade-B slag. It was true, the grainy scene-of-the-crime shots from the security videos had a power all of their own. The robber's curvaceous body and flowing limbs made a vivid image on the page. Robyn had to admit it, she was damned sexy.

DO YOU KNOW THIS BODY? shouted the page-one headline next to a cut-out photo of Brenda in profile. 'The Bunny joins forces with the boys in blue to track down the country's most wanted woman. Be a Bunny Boob-Hunter – ring the Brenda Hot Line today!'

It was hardly Woodward and Bernstein, she had to admit, but they were going to sell a hell of a lot of papers. She'd left the office on a high.

She did not intend to share her euphoria with her dinner

Lust at Large

companions, however. She was a guest of Wanda Sherman, Alistair's producer, and The Needle did not approve of Robyn discussing her work in public. He would have preferred it if Robyn had done almost anything in the world but work for one of the nation's most notorious tabloids. Now, seated beside the empty chair that had evidently been waiting for Robyn all evening, he shot her a look of pure venom before turning his attention once more to an exotic Brazilian beauty on his other side.

The others were not so disapproving, however. They were making inroads into the brandy and were eager to hear of Robyn's exploits. As she attacked her dried-up salmon, they pressed her for details.

'I can't say,' she protested. 'It's a hot story but you'll have to wait till the paper comes out.'

'Come off it,' spat Alistair. 'Who here would dream of picking up the *Daily Rabbit*?'

'Actually,' said Barry Cresswell, a TV news editor, 'it's an essential tool of my trade.'

Boos and guffaws greeted this remark and Diana Ardent, the novelist, said loudly, 'It's only because you want to look at the naked boobies.'

'And read about Bra-less Brenda,' added Wanda Sherman. 'It's the biggest story around and the tabloids have got it all to themselves. Are you sure she's not on your payroll?'

Robyn laughed and poured herself another glass of wine, she had a lot of catching up to do.

'I wouldn't mind seeing Brenda's boobies,' said Barry, 'just to check out what the fuss is all about.'

'Buy tomorrow's paper,' said Robyn without meaning to.

'What? You've got her in the *Bunny*?'

'Well, as a matter of fact . . . none of you work for the *Dog*, do you?'

'Don't be stupid,' muttered Alistair, his face like thunder.

'So what's she like?' asked a fair-haired man called Nick.

'Fabulous. I hate to say it, but she's a real knockout. We've got pictures from security cameras and we're running an appeal to see if anyone recognises her.'

'No chance,' said Barry. 'There are only three kinds of breast – big, little and saggy – what do you say, ladies?'

Lust at Large

'I think,' said a voice which had not so far been heard – Mercedes Birch, the Brazilian – 'that every bosom is individual, like a fingerprint.'

'Really?' said Nick.

'I will prove it,' said Mercedes and got to her feet. She was a tall young woman whose curvaceous figure was encased in a plunging scarlet sheath dress. She turned her back to Alistair and said, 'Pull down the zip, please.'

The Needle hesitated for a moment then did as he was asked. Robyn was certain his hand shook as he did so.

Without obvious artifice, Mercedes turned to face the assembled company and slipped the shoulder straps down her smooth bare arms. The dress slithered to the floor in a whisper of silk, leaving her clad in just a pair of tiny black panties cut high on the hip. Her body was a uniform *café au lait* in colour, luscious in contour and texture. Her breasts were perfectly proportioned and shook ever so slightly as she turned from side to side to display herself. She was all but naked, even so she looked expensively dressed.

'Now you, Diana,' she said, pointing to the lady novelist.

Diana hesitated for a moment. Though it was well known she had never been reluctant to exhibit her formidable charms, Mercedes was a hard act to follow.

'What is the purpose of this?' said The Needle in his best interrogatory fashion. But no one took any notice, for Diana was already unbuttoning her blouse and shrugging the garment off her shoulders to expose a large white brassiere, the satin cups shiny like armour plating, the deep shadowy cleavage between revealing an acre of lush milky flesh.

Diana unclipped the bra and allowed it to fall under the weight of her big breasts. They seemed to tumble into the room, the large globes shifting of their own volition, the saucers of the areolae pink and ridged, the nipples sticking out like thumbs. Diana smiled with satisfaction at their stunned reaction and pointed her wobbling glories at Barry.

Wanda, as hostess, was keen to keep the party going and had already pulled off her thin cashmere sweater to reveal a surprisingly full bosom with tiny pink nipples.

Lust at Large

All eyes were now on Robyn.

'No,' she said, 'I'm American. We're prudes. We don't even sunbathe topless.'

'You're only half American,' said Alistair.

'Get 'em off,' shouted Barry. 'Reporters on the *Bunny* are duty bound to show what they've got.'

'Ignore the men,' said Mercedes, 'this is for the women. We're making a point.' And suddenly she was behind Robyn, slipping the light cotton jacket off her shoulders and unfastening the blouse at her neck.

Robyn wore no bra, she never did. Her breasts were small and high and, to her embarrassment, her disproportionately large nipples were fully erect.

'You see?' said Mercedes, a note of triumph in her voice. 'We are all completely different. Diana has big melons, Wanda has plump pears and Robyn has little pomegranates. I have dark hard nipples, look' – she was rolling her teat between thumb and forefinger – 'like a nut you could crack between your teeth. Robyn has long red sexy ones that stand to attention like little soldiers.'

To Robyn's utter amazement she felt Mercedes' fingers on her chest, pulling and stroking at her nipples as she illustrated her words. A lick of flame stole over her belly.

Barry lowered his head and pushed as much of Diana's right breast into his mouth as he could take. She let out a little sigh and ran her fingers through his thick dark hair.

'Every bosom is unique,' continued Mercedes, her hand still absent-mindedly stroking Robyn. 'I'm sure your robber can be identified from her breasts alone.'

'Why don't you two just get on with it?' barked Alistair and Robyn started guiltily. But The Needle was referring to Diana and Barry whose embrace was becoming complicated.

'OK,' said Barry and began to pull off his clothes.

'Fabulous,' said Wanda, 'I've always wanted to host an orgy,' and she turned to Nick and put her hand on his crotch.

Robyn was frozen to her seat, acutely aware of Mercedes standing just behind her and of the rigid disapproval that emanated from Alistair on her other side. She turned to look at him. His jaw was set firm and she could see a pulse beating in his temple.

Barry was on top of Diana on the carpet, his lean bare bottom almost hidden by her vast white thighs which were wrapped around his middle as he rose and sunk on her opulent body. Robyn could hardly believe what she was seeing. Could he really have his cock in her? He could indeed, she realised, as she discerned a thick prong of flesh, balls hanging below, poking into the pink crack at the opening of her legs.

Wanda and Nick were kissing open-mouthed. She had pulled his penis free of his trousers and its purple head reared from her slender fingers. She took her mouth from his and bent to take his cock between her lips. As she did so Robyn found herself staring directly into his eyes. He grinned at her as if this were the most natural thing in the world.

Robyn turned to Alistair. 'Let's go,' she said. 'Right now.'

'No,' said Mercedes in a low voice. 'You cannot go, Alistair, before you have satisfied the hostess.'

The Needle stared at her blankly. Mercedes indicated Wanda whose head was bobbing in Nick's lap, her inviting rear outlined in a pair of skintight designer jeans. Her rump was broad and full. Robyn reflected that it was just made for the saddle – how could The Needle resist?

'Go on, then,' she heard herself say, 'go and fuck her, if you must. She's your producer after all.'

But Alistair was already on the move, slipping to the floor behind Wanda, reaching round her waist to unfasten her jeans.

Mercedes tugged Robyn to her feet and their tits jostled together. Robyn shivered with unexpected pleasure.

Mercedes laughed, a low wicked chuckle. 'Just look at him unwrapping that ass,' she said with relish.

Alistair had Wanda's jeans partway down her rump. Half of her white bottom was on display, overflowing from the blue denim like rising dough. Then her jeans were down to her knees and her panties strung across the divide of her firm thighs. Alistair reached beneath her bulging cheeks to delve into the thick beard of hair and push a finger between her wet cunt lips.

'OH!' cried Wanda at this sudden invasion, her cry muffled by Nick's big cock. She thrust her arse back onto Alistair's hand, hungry for more.

Robyn didn't know what she felt as Mercedes led her to a sofa in the far corner of the room. One thought sprang into her head – 'Good career move, Needle' – as Mercedes' mouth closed over hers and she found herself snogging as passionately as she had ever done in her life. She heard the smack of hand on buttock from across the room and pictured Wanda receiving the bum-whacking treatment. Then with relief she opened her legs to allow Mercedes' clever fingers access to her soaking sex.

'Please make me come,' she heard herself say. 'Promise you'll diddle me and finger-fuck me and suck me off, all night long. Please.'

'I promise,' said the Brazilian. Then her mouth was on Robyn's hungry pussy, licking and flicking and sucking, and Robyn found herself soaring into the first of many orgasms.

8

Josie lay awake listening to the comforting hum of Ivor's breathing. It was the first time she had shared a bed with a man since she had last slept with Gavin, over a month before. Ivor had his back to her and she gently ran her hand from the nape of his neck down his spine to the crease of his buttocks. He was hairy there. His bum was hard and firm and she squeezed the flesh between her fingers. He grunted, then resumed the throaty exhalation of sleep.

He lay on his side with his top leg bent at the knee, his thigh thrust out at right angles. Her fingers crept over his hip then dipped beneath the curve of his buttock into the fork of his body. His balls protruded towards her, the skin of his scrotum drawn taut, and she cupped them tenderly. She searched further, seeking out his limp sticky penis. How small it seemed now. How funny. She tickled it lightly, finding the bulbous head, thinking it would be fun to make it spring into life again. *Am I turning into a nymphomaniac?* she thought, *I'm insatiable*.

For a moment his cock did indeed seem to lengthen and grow fat in her palm and then he cried out in his sleep and jerked his whole body away from her. She pulled her hand from his flesh. He now lay flat on his face, his breathing deeper, the noise more insistent.

She got up and pulled on a T-shirt. She was too wide awake to sleep. In the kitchen she put on the kettle by the light of the streetlamp shining through the curtain. As it boiled, she rinsed a mug and found the coffee jar.

'I'll have one of those,' said a voice from the door and Josie's hand jerked, spraying coffee granules across the worktop. It was Terry.

'Christ, you made me jump,' she said, automatically reaching for a mug on the draining board.

He shut the door behind him and came towards her. He was stark naked.

'White?' she said. He nodded.

It was surprising how light it was really. She could see the wisps of blond hair on his forearms. And the darker line of belly hair that ran from his navel into the forest of his groin. He was circumcised. The dark head of his penis swung back and forth as he moved to her side.

'What about Gwen?' she said.

'She's asleep.'

'So's Ivor,' she said. Which solved that problem.

He was almost standing on top of her. He was much taller than her and slim, not like Ivor. His cock was long and slim too, though it appeared to be thickening. She was very conscious that her T-shirt barely reached to the top of her thighs. So was he. His cock was definitely getting fatter.

'Josie . . .'

'Yes?'

'You're a sexy witch.'

'Am I?'

'You're the horniest woman I've met in years.'

'Me?' She was genuinely bemused. They were standing very close now, facing each other, but he hadn't laid a finger on her. Yet.

'When you were rubbing Ivor's come into your tits – that was fantastic.'

What was that touching her hip through the cotton of her vest? His finger? His cock?

'And the way you looked at me . . .'

There was warm pressure on her other hip now, definitely his hand, inching the hem of her shirt upwards.

'I knew you'd arrange something. I've been lying awake for hours, waiting for you.'

'Oh,' said Josie as a prying finger slipped into her bush and found her runny slit.

'You see, you're wet for me already.'

There was no point in denying it. Her cunt was bubbling over. Old juices were mingling with new. She was going to get laid in the kitchen while her lover snored next door and her flatmate slumbered across the hall and her coffee got cold. What the hell.

He was a very good kisser, better than Ivor. He licked the corners of her mouth and sucked on her lower lip, as if he really wanted to savour her. Ivor was too bull-at-the-gate, she decided. Maybe it was because he was so handsome. He kissed as if he was doing you a favour.

Terry had his hands beneath her T-shirt now, squeezing her breasts gently, rubbing his thumbs over her nipples so that they stiffened. Then he took his lips from hers and lowered them to her teats, mouthing first one breast then the other. She held her shirt up with one hand so he could get at her easily, with the other she held on to his long neck.

He picked her up and laid her on the kitchen table, pushing her knees back into her chest. She was spread wide open for him, her cunt crack fully exposed in the orange glow from the street. He licked her once, twice, bobbing his head and running his tongue from the nub of her clit to the whorl of her arsehole and back again. Then he was in her, bollock deep, and she was coming already, shouting silently into his mouth.

Above her, Terry stopped his rhythmic thrusting.

'Did you say something?' he panted.

'I said, "Give me your spunk. Make me wet for Ivor."' And she reached between his legs and circled the base of his cock.

His body jerked convulsively and he shot a bolt of semen deep into her, long before he had intended.

'You bloody sexy witch,' he muttered.

Oh, Gavin, she said to herself, her fingers stroking the balls dangling against her upturned bum cheeks, *this is all your fault*.

9

Now she was in the editor's good books, Robyn was free to pursue another angle to the Brenda story – one which she personally considered more worthy of her capabilities. With every post bringing a sack of responses to the *Rabbit*'s Boob-Hunter appeal and the Brenda Hot Line ringing off the hook, Robyn was only too happy to leave the office and head for the dreary suburbs of North London. She intended to write an article on 'Brenda's Boys', those building-society clerks so traumatised by the Topless Raider that they had filled her bags with cash while ogling her charms. According to Archie Monk, these luckless lads had been suffering traumatic repercussions.

First on her list was Gavin Bird, Trainee Manager at the Wenchmore Wood branch of the Kent Kindly. She'd got his address from a colleague at the building society, a nosy female called Janice who had already given Robyn some good stuff about Gavin's fragile state of mind before the robbery. 'I blame his fiancée,' she'd said. 'That Josie kept him short, I reckon, and then she went off to play the field in Wales. He was so sex-starved he could hardly look at a woman without blushing but his eyes were all over your body, if you know what I mean. Give him my love, if you see him. Tell him all the girls can't wait to have him back.'

Gavin had a room in his brother's house, a stone-clad terraced affair in a street full of satellite dishes and half-dismantled motorbikes. The brother hardly glanced at Robyn as he directed her up the stairs. 'It's the room with the RSC poster on the door,' he said. 'Tell him I'm off to work.' He stopped as he was half out of the front door and said, 'Just tell me why my wimpy baby brother gets all the

Lust at Large

good-looking birds running after him.' So perhaps he had looked at her after all.

Robyn knocked softly. There was no reply. She knocked again, louder this time. The door opened at her touch and swung wide enough for her to look into the room.

She saw a bed and the body of a man lying with his back to her. He was leaning up on one elbow, reading the paper. He appeared to be naked beneath the bedclothes, which came up to his waist. His body was pure white, without a blemish across his pale shoulders and his blond hair flicked up in babyish curls on the nape of his long slender neck. *He's just a boy*, thought Robyn.

She was on the point of coughing or otherwise announcing herself when she became aware of sounds of rustling and panting. Then she noticed the movement of his elbow and the surprise was such that her brain had only just worked out that this poor mistreated lad was beating his meat fit to bust when he turned onto his back and threw the covers from his writhing body.

He was indeed naked and, fully revealed, he was all man where it counted. He had a boner fit to poke your eye out and his hand jerked on his penis like a barman shaking a banana daiquiri. His long slender cock was an angry puce, as if it had been flayed for hours.

On the other side of the bed, no longer obscured by his body, lay the newspaper which had inspired this frenzy. Robyn recognised it at once. It was that morning's *Daily Rabbit*, open to yet more photos of Brenda in action.

The boy on the bed beat at himself faster, pummelling his flesh, battering his abused organ until he reached an orgasm that seemed to be dredged from the depths of his soul. As he came he shouted out and a small dribble of moisture filled the eye in the centre of his empurpled glans. His body twitched and convulsed, then he fell back on the bed like a puppet with severed strings.

As she carefully retreated down the stairs Robyn was severely disturbed. Was it possible to wank yourself to death? What a typically English way to commit suicide, she reflected as she opened the front door and placed a finger on the bell.

It took the best part of five minutes to rouse her quarry but eventually Gavin Bird appeared at the top of the stairs fumbling with the belt of his jeans, his hair sticking up in uncombed spikes.

'Sorry to wake you up, Mr Bird,' said Robyn cheerfully, 'but your brother said you wouldn't mind.'

'My brother?' Gavin was puzzled.

'He let me in, said to tell you he'd gone to work.'

Up close he was as tall as Robyn and she found herself looking straight into eyes of milky blue. His mouth opened but no sound came out, obviously he was still miles off, spilling his seed over the bosom of Belinda. Her heart went out to him. This boy needed mothering.

'Point me to the kitchen, Gavin, I'll make you breakfast.'

He gestured down the hall and followed obediently as she led the way. It wasn't till she had the eggs in the pan that she told him who she was.

BRENDA'S BOYS
by Robyn Chestnut

While the nation laughs at the exploits of the topless robber who has bagged a windfall of cash up and down the land, spare a thought for her victims. No, not the fat cats who run the building societies but the little lads who serve in them. The hapless chaps who sit behind the counter have been so gobsmacked by Bra-less Brenda that they have simply handed over the boodle. And then they've had to face the fury of their employers, the ridicule of their mates and the outrage of their girlfriends.

Where Are They Now?

Of the counter clerks who have coughed up, only one has returned to work so far. After three weeks back at the Nottingham offices of the Gloucester Generous, Rod Skimpole has been transferred to Aberdeen 'at his own request' – according to the company. Of the five others the Rabbit tried to trace, one is on an extended holiday abroad, two are on sick leave and the fourth has been remanded in custody on charges of arson and assaulting a police officer.

A Right Tit

Only dreamy Gavin Bird, sandbagged by Bouncing Betty last week, was prepared to talk about his ordeal. Over a mid-morning breakfast of eggs, he revealed the pain and agony of a life that has been suddenly scrambled. He confessed that he spends most of each day in bed, replaying in his mind the moment when an unknown beauty walked up to him and flashed her boobs. Lucky old him, some might say, but the reality is different. Since then he has been obsessed by this woman's image and by his betrayal – as he sees it – of his employers. Gavin is intelligent, hard-working and dishy-looking (a six-foot, blue-eyed blond, ladies) but his world has just fallen apart. To cap it all, his fiancée has run off to Wales leaving him to face this ordeal on his own.

Our Verdict

The Bunny says we look forward to the time when sensitive lads like Gavin Bird can repair their shattered lives. And that day will only come when this wobbling witch and her mercenary mammaries are safely behind bars. Or should we say bras?

10

'How are you doing, Josie?' Gwen's voice was a mischievous gurgle in the dark.

'She's doing just fine,' said a rich baritone voice in reply. 'She'd say so herself if she could talk.'

Which was true. Josie *was* having the time of her life. Correction – was still having the time of her life, the time that had begun the night Ivor interrupted her phone conversation with Gavin. And the reason she couldn't speak right now was because her mouth was full of cock.

'She's got wicked little lips, this friend of yours,' said the baritone, whose name was Dewy. It was Dewy who owned the large and comfortable BMW parked up the hill from the rugby club where they had spent the evening. It was as well the car was large as there were four of them stretched across the seats and Dewy himself was six foot six. He had been the Dibble Dragons' best line-out jumper in living memory and now boasted that he was the club's best cocksman. But, of course, claim to that title was less easy to substantiate.

Josie slurped happily at the large knob in her mouth. It felt like a warm apple stretching her jaw wide. She had both hands on his genitals, stroking the solid shaft and playing with the slack of his scrotum, rolling the big balls gently in her fingers. She wondered if he would come in her mouth and just how much he would shoot. Buckets, she expected. Lovely.

She heard a gasp and a squeal from the back seat. She wondered what Dewy's friend was doing to Gwen but didn't want to leave the task in hand to find out. Dewy solved her problem.

'What you doing to her, Gerald my old mate?' he asked.

'Just getting her tits out into the open,' said Gerald. 'She's got some pair.'

'Let's have a look,' said Dewy, craning round to look into the back of the car. 'Oho, I see what you mean, boyo. Give us a feel.'

Josie felt Dewy lurch in his seat as he thrust a long arm into the back of the car and, presumably, made contact with Gwen's opulent charms for there came a yell of protest.

'Get off,' cried Gwen.

'Come on, girlie, you've got plenty to go round,' said Gerald.

There was a scuffling sound and a smack of hand on flesh. Josie tried to raise her head to come to her friend's aid but found herself pushed back firmly onto Dewy's rampant cock.

There came another smack and a hiss of indrawn breath.

'Hey, look at those tits swing! Like chapel bells, man,' shouted Gerald.

'You're a pair of right crude bastards,' muttered Gwen.

'But you love it, don't you?' said Gerald cheerfully. 'Now, let's have your knickers off.'

'Fuck you!'

'That's the idea, girlie.'

There came further scuffling sounds but Gwen's protests were cut off, Josie guessed from the following silence, by Gerald's mouth on hers.

A rhythmic thumping began to rock the car and the noises of fucking filled the small space. Josie heard and felt the slap of flesh on flesh from the back seat as its occupants became more excited. The hot rod in her hands seemed to grow even harder and longer as Dewy, too, was swept up in the thrill of the moment.

Now came sticky, sucky noises as of a moist cock burrowing eagerly in and out of a wet pussy. Josie relished the thought that Gwen was getting shafted in the back seat while she was sucking a penis in the front. God, how incredibly rude. Josie could hardly credit that she was doing it, let alone enjoying it. How things had changed since she had left London!

Lust at Large

'Look at this arse, Dew,' came Gerald's voice in the dark, thick with lust. 'Have you ever seen anything like it?'

The cock in Josie's mouth seemed to expand as she heard Dewy exclaim, 'God, Gerry, that's incredible!'

'Put that light out!' came Gwen's voice.

'No chance, darling. Wiggle it about. Show us all you've got. Oh, that's grand!'

What the hell was going on? Josie wondered as she gummed the swollen glans in her mouth and teased her fingers up and down the throbbing barrel of Dewy's tool. It felt monstrous as it rubbed urgently against the soft skin of the roof of her mouth. His great hands were twined in the coils of her hair urging her head down into his crotch. The grunts of onrushing male orgasm were in her ears and Josie made as big an O as she could with her mouth and prepared to receive—

A deluge. The thick salty liquid gushed from Dewy's penis as her face was pressed against the hard muscle of his hairy belly. She swallowed and almost gagged, then swallowed again, determined to drink in all of this teak-hard Welshman whom she had no desire to ever see again. She had come out tonight intending to behave like a slut and she was revelling in it.

'God,' said Dewy, 'how I needed that.'

The energetic thrusting from the back seat had now stopped and harsh male panting filled the small space. A female curse split the air.

'You haven't come, have you?' said Gwen.

'Sorry, love,' muttered Gerald. 'You stay right there while I go and have a slash.'

The car lurched on its suspension as one of the back doors opened and Gerald got out.

'Take five, girls,' said Dewy as he unravelled himself from Josie and clambered out of the driver's door.

The two women watched in silence as the bold rugby players strode off into the gloom to relieve their other needs.

'Is the key in the ignition?' asked Gwen.

'Yes.'

'Right then, I'm driving.'

'Gwen!'

But there was little point in protesting. And no time to do so for Gwen was in the driver's seat in a flash and firing up the engine. As the big car swung round in a U-turn on the edge of the hillside, Josie turned to look out of the rear window. For an instant she thought she could see the trouserless figure of Gerald, his mouth open in a shout of protest, then he was lost in the darkness.

Gwen screamed with laughter as she bounced the powerful motor at speed down the rough track.

11

Robyn divided the responses to the *Rabbit*'s Brenda appeal into categories. Leaving aside the cheerfully rude – as in the many 'she can pinch my deposits any time' letters – she was left with two other significant kinds of reply. There was the 'that's the slag I used to go out with two years ago' pile and the 'she's the tart he was two-timing me with last year' collection. Most were accompanied by names and addresses, photos even, and about half of them were signed. These the police took more seriously and enquiries were made, as they say. Few, if any, genuine suspects emerged and they all turned out to have perfectly good alibis.

That left the cranks and the polemicists (the far left of the Women's Movement had naturally taken Brenda to heart) and a small pile of responses that identified not a person but a place.

'Archie,' said Robyn as they reviewed the situation at their table in The Frog in a Bucket, 'have you ever heard of Blisswood-in-the-Dale?'

Monk shook his head. 'Where is it?'

'It's a small town in the North Grinding. We've had three letters and two phone messages telling us to search there for this woman. Look.'

She laid the letters in front of him, adding, 'I don't think they can be from the same source. The letters are from Sheffield, Bournemouth and Barnsley and the calls came from Manchester and here in London.'

Monk picked up a thick bundle of Basildon Bond and scanned through the wobbly script that covered the blue paper. He read snatches of it aloud in a flat monotone without emphasis of any kind.

'Them are Blisswood titties I swear and I should know as I was brought up on 'em. My Ma was a Blisswood girl and swore she fed me on those bosoms till I was nearly two. When I was sixteen I first went to the Midsummer's. I can still see all the girls in the barn, their hair flying loose, their cheeks rosy red and their feet thundering as they danced. And their bare titties wobbling and bouncing in the candle-light. Afterwards in the moonlit fields they made a man of me.'

Monk paged through the letter to the end. Then he picked up another and read:

> 'We like the Blisswood lassies
> Even though they're shockers
> We like their pretty sparkling eyes
> And love their great big knockers'

He paused for a few moments before continuing, 'We used to chant this piece of doggerel on the way home from school when we were boys. But it held a germ of truth in it as I found out later in life. My wife was born and bred in Blisswood-in-the-Dale and I can swear to you that, in her youth, she exactly resembled the woman in the paper. Her combination of slender frame and high full bosom with the distinctive "strawberry peaks" is only to be found in women who come from this part of the world.'

Monk laid the page down and turned his attention to the last letter. It said simply: 'If the authorities have any sense they will concentrate their search on a small town in the North Grinding called Blisswood-in-the-Dale.'

'What about the phone calls?' said Monk.

'One's from an old duck in Barnsley saying all the girls from Blisswood have got busts like Brenda and she was born there so she should know. The other is from some professor's secretary telling me to make an appointment as soon as possible to discuss the fertility rites of the North Grinding in connection with the topless robber.'

Monk said nothing.

'So, Archie?' said Robyn. 'What do you think? There's something in this, isn't there? I can feel it.'

His mouth turned down at the ends and he sighed. 'I don't want to dampen your enthusiasm, Ms Chestnut, but you've either got a collection of letters from misty-eyed old cranks or someone is playing a little joke.'

'But these people all live in different parts of the country! They've given their names and addresses! Why else would they be on about this funny place that hardly anyone has ever heard of?'

Monk considered the point while Robyn fidgeted with her empty wine glass and regarded him critically. He was handsome but infuriating. She had the urge to give him a good kick, just to speed him up.

He was returning her stare now and it was just possible there was a hint of amusement in his eye. Was her impatience so obvious?

'Who is this professor?' he asked.

'Dalrymple hyphen somebody. I'm off to see him this afternoon.'

'Hugo Dalrymple-Ripley? I thought he was dead.'

'You've heard of him?'

'He's a famous old boy. Used to march with the CND alongside Bertrand Russell. An English gent – just your type.'

'What do you mean?'

Monk did not reply, he was getting to his feet and gathering up the letters.

'You tackle the professor, Ms Chestnut, I'll handle the rest of your star informers.' And he disappeared into the gloom of The Frog, leaving Robyn feeling vaguely insulted. For once the mother had been fast on his feet.

Robyn's taxi driver stopped at the top of an unmade road on the edge of Hampstead Heath and pointed in the direction of a clump of vast and gloomy horse chestnuts.

'Down the track there, love, mind how you go. You shouldn't really have worn those high heels, should you? That'll be seven pound thirty. Oh, a tenner. Very kind. I don't think I've got any change.'

Robyn came up with the exact money from the bottom of her purse and set off down the path to the sound of the

Lust at Large

cabbie's moans. She skirted a large puddle carefully. No, she shouldn't have worn heels and a short skirt but this was her professor-slaying outfit and spectacular legs in silk stockings were guaranteed to win over an ageing Brit. At least, they had never failed yet.

To her relief she found the house at once and made her way to the front door down an overgrown garden path behind an untrimmed yew hedge. As she waited on the doorstep and stared at the solid but worn wooden door she felt the first spots of rain on her cheek.

She was admitted by a square-jawed and sullen-faced woman who took in her skirt, her legs and her scarlet lipstick at a glance and sniffed.

'You're the journalist from the *Daily Rabbit*,' she accused Robyn in cut-glass tones. 'The Professor is waiting for you.'

Robyn was led down a narrow uncarpeted corridor, the sound of her heels echoing off the wooden floor. Disapproval rose like steam from the woman ahead, whom Robyn took to be the Professor's secretary. From the rear she was surprisingly attractive, with a slim waist, rounded hips and slender calves set off by a plain silk blouse and a charcoal-grey pencil skirt. Robyn decided to try out the business-efficiency look on Archie Monk. There had to be some way to get change out of that tight-arsed Scot.

Robyn was admitted to a room lined with books that gave onto a glass conservatory filled with high spiky greenery and a selection of cane tables and chairs. A cluttered desk dominated the foreground of her vision, piled high with papers and computer paraphernalia. An intricate Oriental carpet covered the floor and a fire burnt low in the rich mahogany fireplace, taking the chill off the damp summer's day. It was a delightful room – comfortable and welcoming, unlike the rest of the house.

But the chief surprise for Robyn was in the figure who rose to greet her and kiss her on both cheeks in an enthusiastic fashion. This was no decrepit old academic two steps from the grave. This was a man she had met in embarrassing circumstances just a few nights earlier at a memorable dinner party. A man who had cheerfully allowed the hostess to pull his prick out of his trousers and suck him off while he appraised Robyn's naked breasts.

'Hello, Robyn,' said Nick, thrusting a glass of something cold and fizzing into her hand and ushering her towards the sofa, 'I'm so looking forward to resuming our discussion about Bra-less Brenda's tits.'

12

'You can't just leave them there,' said Josie, as Gwen steered the BMW into the rugby club car park. It was empty but for Gwen's small Renault.

'Why not? They won't come to any harm. It'll only take them a couple of hours to walk down.' She was scrabbling in her handbag in search of something.

'You haven't lost your keys, have you?' Josie was struck with panic. The sooner they were out of this car and this place the happier she would be. The thought of Dewy and Gerald's revenge was terrible.

'Aha,' said Gwen in triumph and held up a lipstick, 'here's my pen. Now, what's my message, I wonder?'

Josie climbed out of the car. She didn't know what her friend was on about, she just wanted to go home. 'Come on, Gwen,' she called over her shoulder as she made for the Renault.

But Gwen was busy. She was leaning over the bonnet of the BMW, writing on the windscreen with her lipstick.

'Gwen!' cried Josie but all the same she retraced her steps to read: DEWY IS A DICKHEAD AND GERALD HAS A TWO-INCH DICK.

'Oh Gwen,' she said, 'that's brilliant!'

'It's also illegal,' said a male voice from behind them, freezing the laughter in their throats. 'Defacing stolen property, I imagine. Unless, of course, you can prove that you are driving Dewy Bishop's car with his permission.'

The torch beam was shining directly into Josie's eyes and so she had only a vague impression of the presence behind it. But he was big and he was close. Josie was paralysed with fright.

Lust at Large

'Who the fuck are you?' said Gwen, taking a bold step towards the torch bearer.

'Police sergeant John Buckler, madam.'

'Why aren't you in uniform then?' Gwen had a point; the torch beam had shifted and now Josie could see that the tall figure in front of them wore a civilian shirt and trousers.

'Because this is my night off. But, as a member of the club's management committee, I make it my business to keep an eye on late-night security.' The voice was firm and authoritative. 'Now, would you care to tell me whether you have permission to drive Mr Bishop's car?'

Gwen dropped her aggressive posture and switched to another tack. 'Ooh, officer, you're not going to take down my particulars, are you? If so, you're out of luck.'

'Why is that?'

'Because I'm not wearing any. Look.' Gwen turned and lifted the hem of her short dress to reveal a pale and shapely buttock quite unencumbered by underwear of any description. 'You see, my friend and I went for a quiet drive with Dewy Bishop and his friend Gerald and Gerald stole my knickers.'

Gwen pulled her skirt up to her waist and thrust her bum out in the gleam of the torch. The globes of her cheeks were smooth and full in the harsh white light, the valley between them deep and inviting.

The policeman said nothing but the sound of pennies dropping in his brain was almost audible.

'If you ask me,' continued Gwen, 'the real offence was committed by them. Gerald spunked off all over my bottom while Dewy watched and pawed my titties without permission. Here—'

Josie was mesmerised as Gwen took the policeman's free hand and thrust it into the shadow between her plump cheeks.

'There, feel that. It's all wet and spunky, isn't it? There's your evidence, all up my bum crack.'

Sergeant Buckler's fingers now began to palpate the firm flesh in his grasp and there was a chuckle in his voice as he said, 'Are you intending to press charges against Mr Bishop and his friend?'

Lust at Large

Josie realised that her fear had disappeared, to be replaced by a raging desire. All her previous frustration had returned in a rush and the *frisson* of danger in their present predicament only heightened her desire to fuck.

'If we did press charges,' continued Gwen, 'we'd have a good case. They took us both up there for a good shagging and we never came once. Frankly, officer, if that's not an offence it bloody well ought to be.'

The policeman had been openly fondling Gwen's bottom and now he slid his fingers between her legs. She bent over and leant across the bonnet of the BMW, thrusting the hairy purse of her pussy into plain view. Josie drank in the sight of the policeman's fingers probing between the wet pink lips and wished he was doing it to her.

'It's all true,' she found herself saying. 'I sucked Dewy's cock and swallowed all his sperm and he never even touched me up. Those men took their pleasure and left us high and dry. It's disgraceful!'

'I can see the club's honour is at stake,' said Officer Buckler, switching off the torch and placing it on the ground. 'I can't let two lovely lasses like you go home thinking the Dibble Dragons aren't up to it.'

Suddenly Josie was seized in a powerful embrace and kissed comprehensively, his tongue exploring her mouth with purpose. Next, her dress was pulled to her waist and she found herself lying face down on the bonnet of the car by the side of Gwen. She pushed her bottom backwards and felt the warm night air play over her bum cheeks as large male hands swiftly pulled her panties to the ground.

'Well, well, he said, evidently savouring the sight of two nude and wriggling female arses in the moonlight, 'what a pair of hungry cunts. Where shall I begin?'

'Fuck me first,' said Josie, shameless in her excitement. 'At least Gwen's had some fun, I never even had his thing up me.'

'You horny bitch. You weren't like this when you arrived from London,' muttered Gwen.

But Josie couldn't hear, all her sensations were concentrated in her pussy as she felt a stiff warm penis nose its way between her labia.

Lust at Large

'Oh,' she cried as the cock drove into her, all the way up her well-juiced passage in one thrilling strike. 'Oh God, yes! Fuck me, fuck me, please!'

Beside her, Gwen gasped as a strong hand descended on her fat white bottom with a resounding smack. Then she grunted as the hand delved into her crotch and his fingers sought out her aching clitoris.

Sergeant Buckler's prowess on the rugby field is not recorded but he turned out to be a skilled and courageous player of the games of lust. With pumping cock, teasing fingers and an inventive line in whispered indecencies he brought both girls to the brink at the same time.

As he did so, the headlights of a car lit the sky as it swung into the driveway.

'Who's that?' cried Josie, her buttocks trembling against the hard muscles of the policeman's stomach.

'Relax,' he said, not slowing his short rhythmic shafting. 'My brother always picks me up at this time. Just wait till he sees you two.'

Fantastic! thought Josie and came once more all over his spunking cock.

13

'Nick! What the hell are you doing here?'

Robyn wasn't displeased to see the fair-haired man who had greeted her so warmly but she was suspicious. She remembered the way Nick had ogled her at Wanda's. She smelled a setup.

'Where's the Professor?'

Nick's grin grew broader. 'That's me. Take a seat, quaff the bubbly – or would you prefer something else?'

'I'd prefer to know what you're playing at. Where's the old boy, Hugo Dalrymple-Ripley?'

'Up the road in Highgate cemetery. Dad's been dead for ten years. Your appointment is with Professor Nicholas Dalrymple-Ripley. Me.'

Robyn subsided onto the sofa and killed off her glass in one gulp. This put a different complexion on things.

'Don't worry,' said Nick, taking a seat beside her, 'this is a genuine attempt to help in your search for the topless robber. I was very interested in our discussion the other night about the female breast being as individual as a fingerprint. And when I saw the photographs of the girl in your newspaper I knew I had to talk to you.'

He refilled Robyn's glass and continued. 'In fact, this really is about my father. Apart from the philosophical work for which he was famous, he was a great countryman. He published many books about country lore and activities.'

He pointed to one of the shelves in the bookcase by the fire. Robyn read along the cracked, leather-bound spines: *The Cry of the Curlew*, *Down Among the Dalesmen*, *A Hummock for My Head* – there were a good half dozen.

'All written in the twenties, of course,' said Nick, 'before

Lust at Large

he went to Japan and returned with the theories that made him famous. And the real reason he went to Japan was because he had become infatuated with a small area of the North Grinding, a place called—'

'Blisswood-in-the-Dale,' said Robyn.

'Precisely!' said Nick. 'Obviously you're on the same track. Yes, in his youth my father spent a lot of time there. He always said it was the making of him. It inspired in him his love of the countryside and set him on the road to evolving his famous Japanese Precepts. His biographies tell you all this but they don't tell you the real reason why he fell in love with Blisswood and why he fled from there to Japan.'

'And why did he?'

'Because the women of Blisswood have the most fabulous breasts – round, flawless, satin-smooth, shapely. And with very distinctive nipples that distend, when aroused, to form the shape of a small strawberry.'

'Strawberry peaks.'

'Exactly. That's how connoisseurs refer to them.'

'And your father went for these fruit-salad boobs in a big way, I suppose.'

'He couldn't get enough. He spent five years there writing topographical books and researching the local history.'

'And boffing the local bimbos.' The champagne had gone straight to Robyn's head but Prof Nick did not turn a hair.

'One day he realised he had to get away. If he stayed he would never have the energy to do anything else in life. He just couldn't exist any more surrounded by women with such perfect breasts. And so he chose the one place where he knew he wouldn't find any. Japan.'

'Fascinating. So I take it you think that Brenda has a pair of these Blisswood tits.'

'Definitely,' he said and poured the dregs of the champagne into Robyn's glass.

'But how would you know, Nick? Even if all this is true about these women with these special bazookas, your father had his fun seventy years ago. Your theories have got a lot of dust on them.'

'Not exactly.' Nick's eyes had a gleam of triumph as he

Lust at Large

leaned forward, his face just inches from Robyn's as he said, 'I can offer you proof! My father wrote about the phenomenon before he left for Japan. I want you to look at the manuscript in a moment. It's all there: drawings, photographs and his private papers of the time. But first . . .'

He leapt to his feet and marched to the door. 'Joyce!' he bellowed down the corridor and, in an instant it seemed, the smart but sulky figure of the secretary appeared in the doorway.

'Come in, Joyce, and take off your blouse.'

The green eyes behind the heavy spectacles flickered with surprise.

'Hurry up, woman,' commanded Nick. 'Don't just stand there like some bug-eyed rabbit.'

The thin mouth set in a stern line and the big eyes flashed briefly before, to Robyn's amazement, the secretary lifted her hands to the button at her throat.

'You've met Joyce, haven't you?' said Nick as she began to unfasten the buttons over her bulging chest. 'She was my father's last secretary before he died and, like all his female staff, she was recruited from the North Grinding. Weren't you, Joyce?'

'That's correct,' said the woman, pulling the blouse from her waistband and sliding it off smooth dimpled shoulders. 'I was born in Blisswood-in-the-Dale and joined the old Professor straight from school. *He* was a proper gentleman,' she added as, without being asked, she pulled her camisole over her head to reveal a matching pink brassiere embroidered with rosebuds and heavy with a formidable load of flesh.

'But that didn't stop the old boy gobbling your goodies till the day he died, now did it?' Nick was behind her, his fingers on the hooks of the straining undergarment.

'The Professor was a wonderful man,' said Joyce directly to Robyn. 'He used to say that it was my figure that kept him so young at heart.'

'The randy old bugger had her tits out every day till he was over ninety. Still, you can't blame him, can you?' said Nick as he slipped the straps of the bra down Joyce's arms and revealed her naked bosom with a flourish.

They were a stupendous pair, there was no denying. Big but shapely, their weight making them swing and tremble, Joyce thrust them out with pride, happy to display her greatest assets even to a tabloid journalist.

'Wow!' said Robyn, her reaction not faked, her professional interest quick to spot the similarities to the photos of Bra-less Brenda. There were differences but, as Joyce was in her forties and the robber was probably twenty years younger, it was really only age that distinguished between the two bosoms. Lusher, heavier, lower though they may be, Robyn had to acknowledge that Joyce had a beautiful pair of breasts.

Nick was enthusing over their finer points.

'Look,' he said, rolling a thick pink nipple between thumb and forefinger, 'see how the tissue is erecting. It's like a little balloon swelling up!'

'Really, Nicholas,' muttered Joyce in distaste. Nevertheless, Robyn observed that she was leaning back against Nick and that his right hand had slid up to cup and support her other boob. The nipple in question had grown till it was a thick red bud, broad at the base and rounded at the tip. In a curious way, it did resemble a strawberry.

Robyn had a sudden flash of Mercedes Birch's pebble-hard buds in her mouth. She leapt to her feet on unsteady legs. It had to be the champagne.

'Impressed?' asked Nick, now cupping both of Joyce's breasts in his hands as she swayed in front of Robyn, her green eyes narrow slits behind her glasses.

'Yes, indeed,' said Robyn. 'Look . . . thanks for everything but I'd better get back to the office.'

'Oh no. Not before you've looked at my father's material.'

'Well, I'm not sure I have time . . .'

'Please.' The hand on Robyn's arm was Joyce's. It gripped her tightly. 'I went to a lot of trouble to dig it out.'

And so Robyn found herself directed to a small room that lay just off the main study. She sat at a small walnut table and confronted a stained and ageing box file. From where she sat she could see into the main room. Nick and Joyce were out of her sight but she could hear the low murmur of their voices. Joyce's blouse and slip still lay

Lust at Large

across the seat of a straight-backed wooden chair.

With an effort, Robyn turned her attention to the yellowing papers in the file. There was a lot of handwritten material, the penmanship immaculate and clear despite the pale sepia ink. It looked like a diary. She flipped to the bottom of the pile and discovered some drawings in pencil. They were of hills and moorland vistas, trees and birds – and naked women. There were far more naked women than anything else, sitting on chairs, lying on beds and reclining by river banks. Some were quick sketches, that was obvious, but in all of them the breasts had been drawn in great detail.

From next door came the sound of voices at odds. Robyn thought she heard Joyce say, 'I've never been so humiliated' followed by a whisper 'ssh' from Nick. Robyn tried to concentrate on the papers.

There were photographs amongst them, small and brown but with clear images of hearty country lasses *en déshabille*. Again the camera focused on the breasts, on strawberry nipples erected three-quarters of a century in the past and still standing sweet and proud.

There were rustling noises from next door and Robyn saw that a charcoal-grey skirt and a man's pair of bleached jeans had been added to the pile of clothes on the chair. She took out her notebook and began to make notes as she flipped quickly through the pages of the diary.

6 August 1920. A red-letter day! Martha J and her blonde friend took me up the hill to the tarn and allowed me to sketch them as they bathed. Of course they knew that I really wanted to taste their little fruits (Eleanor had told them of our Sundays, I discovered) and they were only too keen themselves. It is a puzzle though, Martha is such a strapping lass and Chloe a little slip. Yet both have the same shaped titties. Such wicked, delicious girls!

26 June 1922. I am hardly yet recovered from the Midsummer's Festival. What a night! Did ancient Rome ever stage such a debauch? If I believed in God I would pray for an extra pego to do myself justice next year. I've changed my plans. I cannot possibly leave here now.

10 November 1923. I am in paradise but I fear for my sanity if I stay. I only remain in this backwater, betraying my intellect and my ambition, because I am a slave to the flesh. Oh, sweet Rosie and Martha and Mrs H and Dolly M and all you others – you have robbed me of my senses. How can I break free? I don't think I could live without my daily spunking between the round titties of my Blisswood belles . . .

From the next room came a high-pitched squeal, an intake of breath, then a moan that reverberated round the small side room. Robyn put away her pen and stood up. She was damned if she was going to calmly read some dead guy's sex diary while next door two people she hardly knew were having it off. She was getting out of here to get laid herself. At least Needle wasn't working tonight.

As she made her way to the study door the sight before her stopped her in her tracks. Nick was stretched out on his back on the rug in front of the fire with Joyce squatting on her haunches on top of him, wearing just a pair of black-seamed stockings and suspenders. From Robyn's position by his feet his face was obscured and only his chin was visible, peeping out from beneath the wild confusion of Joyce's thick black pubic hair as he licked and tongued her snatch. Robyn could hear the slurping sound of his lips on hers as he ate her out.

Joyce looked up and smiled smugly at Robyn. Her hands were in the crotch of the nude male spread beneath her, toying with the beefy erection sprouting from the hair of his belly. His fat balls lolled obscenely in the fork of his legs, moving to the pull of her fingers on the skin of his scrotum. The smell of cock and cunt was thick in the air.

'Had enough have you?' said Joyce, waggling the fleshy stick from side to side. Her hair lay mussed and unfettered across her shoulders but the severe spectacles were still in place.

'Yes.'

'Very wise. I imagine you'd like to say goodbye to the

Professor but, as you can see,' and she shifted her big bottom squarely on top of Nick's face, 'he's otherwise engaged.'

Robyn could hardly tear her eyes from the bulging pink sausage being squeezed and moulded between Joyce's fingers. The secretary noticed Robyn's interest and speeded up her manual stimulation, slicking the tunnel of her hand back and forth on the stiff shaft. The purple penis head winked at Robyn out of its one eye.

'What's he a professor of?' she asked.

'Sexology,' said Joyce, the cut-glass accent now gone, replaced by flat northern vowels. 'He's the world's leading expert on Differential Mammary Responses in Double D-Cup Females.'

Her hand speeded up and the winking eye suddenly spat a volley of cream through the air, leaving a sticky trail across the carpet to Robyn's high-heeled shoes.

'Oops,' said Joyce, 'nearly missed you. I'm *so* sorry.' And she dipped her finger in a blob of juice and began to rub it dreamily into a swollen strawberry-shaped nipple.

Outside the rain was bucketing down. It washed the spunk off Robyn's shoes though it did nothing to quench the fire raging in her tiny soaking-wet panties.

14

Janice Melting blamed her sister. She'd shown Tina the article in the paper about Gavin, and she'd drooled over his photo.

'Cor, you never told me he was such a dish.'

'He's not. He's a bit wet.'

'Oh come on, he's dead cute. You've been keeping him all for yourself.'

'Well, he wouldn't fancy you. He's got a degree and you're not exactly the sophisticated type.' Which was true. Tina was all push-up bras and fuchsia-pink lipstick though, secretly, Janice didn't doubt that Gavin would be easy meat for her man-eating little sister.

'I think it's a great shame you haven't been round to comfort him in his hour of need,' said Tina. 'If you don't feel up to it, I'll go.'

Which was why Janice was now ringing the doorbell of Gavin's house, her bare brown legs and white sandals splashed by the sudden cloudburst. The door was opened by a man who was not Gavin but who looked remarkably like him some five hard years down the track.

'You must be Phil,' said Janice, stepping smartly inside. 'Is Gavin at home?'

'No, he's not.' The man was still holding the door open, obviously intending this unexpected visitor to clear off, back into the rain.

Janice was having none of it. She shut the door behind her and chucked her wet umbrella onto the doormat. Unbidden, she removed her denim jacket to give Gavin's brother an early glimpse of her slim full-bosomed figure in tight white top and blue denim skirt. She shook out her softly curled mass of brown hair and flashed him her best cheesecake smile.

'I'm Janice Melting, Gavin's boss in a manner of speaking. I've been meaning to come for ages.'

'Well, he's not here.'

'I'll wait.'

'There's no point. He's gone away.' The brother's eyes narrowed as he considered the curvy brunette in front of him. Recent experience had taught him to closely scrutinise gift-horses, especially female ones with big brown eyes. Nevertheless he said, 'Come and sit down,' and led the way into the front room and pointed to a black leather sofa.

Janice took the seat, not making much of an attempt to stop the denim riding up her lean brown thighs, and looked around. She was not impressed. Apart from the leather suite and a glass-and-metal coffee table, there was a dearth of furniture. She observed the gaps on the wall, the abundance of cardboard boxes, what looked like a car battery being recharged and a complex stereo system that trailed wires around the edges of the room. She also noted the framed photographs of a lanky female with big gormless eyes and stringy black hair. Even if she couldn't see Gavin, this was turning out to be quite interesting.

'Drink?' asked her brother, waving a bottle of supermarket whisky at her. 'I've got brandy, if you prefer.'

Janice did prefer and knocked back half an inch in one. She helped herself to a refill.

'So – where is he, Phil?' she asked.

'Up north. Walking the moors, so he said.'

'Will he be all right?'

'Oh yeah. Best thing for him. He wasn't doing much good moping around here. I told him if he wasn't going to get back to work he ought to take a holiday.'

'Is Josie with him?'

'She doesn't even know he's gone. She's bloody impossible to get hold of on the phone. Frankly I think she's as much of his problem as this daft robbery.'

Phil poured himself another drink, a big one. He was like Gavin in more than looks, Janice decided as she considered the cross-legged figure on the floor, though in his case the extra years had made him defensive and suspicious. He looked at her as if she might bite. And so she might.

'Is that Josie in these photos?' said Janice, knowing full well it wasn't.

'That,' said Phil in heavily ironic tones, 'is my very dear ex-wife and former business partner. Dear in the sense of expensive,' he added in case Janice wasn't following him. If he only knew, Janice was way ahead of him.

'The price of love,' she said.

'Love has nothing to do with it,' he muttered bitterly.

'Then why have you got her picture plastered around the place? I was engaged once, till my intended decided he fancied someone else. I took all his photos and letters and wrapped them in a sweater he'd given me and stuffed them down the S-bend in his loo. He had a horrible flood and I never gave him another thought. Let the silly cow go, that's what I say.'

Janice beamed at him and helped herself to more brandy before continuing, 'I reckon you and Gavin are very similar. On the surface you're smart, intelligent, educated, sensitive – all of that. But really you're stupid.'

Phil's jaw dropped and he quickly gulped at his Scotch but otherwise there was no reaction.

'You see? You don't know me from Fanny Fruitcake on the corner but I walk into your house and call you stupid and you do nothing. Never mind, just listen, it's very simple. Both you and Gavin are wasting your lives, pining for things you can't have. Gavin's going soft over some bird who waggles her whatsits at him in the course of a robbery and you're feeling sorry for yourself because your wife's scarpered and cleaned out your joint account. Am I right?'

'Well . . .' Phil took a breath but Janice cut him off. The question had been rhetorical.

'And meanwhile my sister Tina and I are living up the road just dying for the company of a couple of intelligent, good-looking fellers who can talk about a bit more than what's under the bonnet of a Ford Capri. Do you get my drift?'

In truth Phil did not know whether he did. There had been a shift of emphasis somewhere and the whisky was

Lust at Large

beginning to take its toll. However, he was aware that once more he was being challenged.

'Gavin is engaged to be married,' he said.

'I know that.' Janice was scornful. 'I also know he can't keep his eyes off my tits. Like you. Though maybe you prefer my legs, you've been trying to look up my skirt for the past half an hour.'

'I—'

'Go on, admit it. I'd be upset if you hadn't, to be honest. It's just as well Tina didn't come with me because her legs are just fabulous. Though mine aren't bad, are they?'

She stretched out on the length of the sofa and raised one golden limb, toe prettily pointed, high in the air. Phil's eyes followed the flowing movement with fascination.

'You're lovely,' he said awkwardly.

'Lovelier than your wife?'

To her surprise he burst into tears and for a moment she didn't know what to do.

The long evening was now at an end and in the near darkness the sobbing figure at her feet looked almost exactly like Gavin. Janice slipped the white summer top over her head and threw it to the floor.

'Come here, Gavin's brother,' she said softly, reaching out for his curly blond head and pulling it face forward into the warmth of her naked breasts.

15

Robyn was soaked by the time she arrived at Alistair's apartment. She let herself in with her own key and dashed for the loo in the hallway to grab a towel. She entered the lounge pulling her wet blouse from her body with one hand and rubbing the rain from her thick dark hair with the other.

'Sorry to barge in on you, Needle,' she said, 'but I've had the most peculiar— Oh my God!'

Frozen to the spot in the doorway, she saw the back of a brown curly head that was unmistakably Alistair's resting on the seat of the sofa. Above him, her head bent to the recumbent man's lips, was a sinuous coffee-coloured brunette clad in thigh-high glistening leather boots and a scarlet basque open to the crotch to reveal a strip of black fur.

'Hello, Robyn,' said Mercedes Birch. 'I've been wondering when you might turn up.'

There was a moment's silence. Robyn continued to dry her hair like an automaton, her mind racing. Seeing Mercedes was a shock – all the more so since her stomach had flipped at the sight of her and the memory of her mouth on that wiry pubic bush was suddenly sharp. And to catch Alistair with her was – confusing. She didn't know quite where to focus her jealousy.

'Good evening, Robyn,' said Needle, not even turning his head in her direction.

'Be quiet, Alistair!' barked Mercedes, jumping to her feet. 'You are not permitted to talk.'

It was then that Robyn realised that The Needle hadn't turned towards her because he couldn't move. He was trussed like a mummy in white gauze bandages that bound his legs together and his arms to his side. Now that

Lust at Large

Mercedes had risen to her feet, Robyn could see that, apart from his bonds, he was quite naked. His big straining cock stretched from his hairy belly to the well of his navel in a state of formidable excitement. The swollen plum-coloured head, unsheathed from the ruff of his withdrawn foreskin, glistened before Robyn's eyes like a mouthwatering lollipop.

'Well, darling, I believe you've caught us in flagrante,' said Mercedes. 'Why don't I help you out of those wet things while you decide how upset you are going to be?'

'You bitch,' said Robyn. 'You conniving, manipulative cow. What the fuck do you think you are playing at?'

'Very good.' Mercedes had swiftly stripped her to her stockings and panties and now placed her hand firmly over Robyn's throbbing pubis. 'Express your anger out loud, it will make you feel much better.'

'Take your hand off my cunt,' Robyn hissed but at the same time her feet seemed to move apart of their own accord. Already Mercedes' fingers were prising apart the moist lips of her pussy.

'Alistair, do something,' implored Robyn. 'She's got her fingers up my twat!'

'Oh shut up,' muttered Needle. 'You weren't complaining when she did it to you the other night.'

There was no denying that Mercedes knew how to handle a woman. It was as if she made no attempt to communicate with Robyn's brain but connected directly with her body. And her body liked it. Loved it, in fact, as the Brazilian's knowing fingers rimmed her aching clit. Robyn couldn't help herself.

'You bloody witch, you're going to make me come!'

And come she did. The combination of her recent experiences at Professor Nick's, the sight of The Needle's twitching tool and the pressure of Mercedes' magical fingers soon had Robyn boiling over. The Brazilian held her close as she threshed in orgasm and bent the tall American's face to hers to slip her pointed tongue into the other's slack mouth.

When it was over, Robyn collapsed into a nearby armchair.

'Oh my God,' she wailed, 'what's happening to me?'

'Nothing that you don't really want,' said Mercedes.

'I never used to do things like this. I never used to go to orgies or let women seduce me.'

'Huh.' Mercedes was contemptuous. 'You *norteamericanos*, you are as repressed as the British. I thought you had more spine than that fool over there.'

'Hey,' cried Alistair, rising to the bait.

Mercedes jumped to her feet and grabbed an object familiar to Robyn – her lover's riding crop. She smacked it down with frightening force across The Needle's hip leaving a candy-coloured stripe on the white flesh. 'I told you to keep quiet,' she said, 'or else I shall gag you. And that would spoil our fun, wouldn't it, Robyn?'

Robyn didn't know what this madwoman was on about. The sudden violence had filled her with concern for Alistair's wellbeing and she rushed to his side and began to pluck at his bonds.

Mercedes observed her with a wry smile. 'I wouldn't bother, darling, that's not what he wants.'

Robyn slowed in her attempt to unravel the bandages and bent to plant a kiss on his lips. As she did so, he whispered, 'Do as she says.'

Mercedes heard him. 'That's right. Don't you realise? This is what he likes. Look at his penis. No wonder you two are washed up.'

'What do you mean?'

'He likes to be pushed around. He's a bully himself but he needs a bigger bully. He needs me.' And Mercedes flicked the crop across The Needle's belly making his drooling cock leap and quiver.

'It's true,' he croaked. 'I'm sorry, Robyn.'

The Brazilian grinned and shrugged her delectable shoulders. 'You see. Now, let's not get sentimental, let's have fun.' And she slipped the thin straps of the basque down her arms and shrugged her perfect breasts into the light.

Robyn was frozen to the spot. This was unreal. The big love affair of her life was in ruins and yet she had a powerful impulse to run her tongue around the saucers of Mercedes' areolae, to suck the hard pebbles of her nipples into her mouth, to —

Lust at Large

'Come,' said Mercedes, taking Robyn's hand and leading her to the trussed form of Alistair, stretched out on the big couch. 'Just because you are washed up doesn't mean you can't enjoy him.'

Robyn watched in mounting fascination as Mercedes positioned herself across the recumbent Needle, her knees on either side of his body, her arse over his head, and settled her exposed crotch heavily on his upturned face. Robyn was unnerved. It was the position Joyce had adopted on top of Nick Dalrymple-Ripley.

'Eat!' commanded Mercedes and pulled the silk of the basque clear off her pubis. Robyn stared at Needle's chin poking from between the Brazilian's smooth and elegant thighs and saw a wet flicker of pink as he went to work with his tongue.

'Mmm,' murmured Mercedes, 'he's not bad at it – did you teach him?'

'No,' said Robyn, suddenly angry. The bastard was showing the domineering Brazilian more affection than she had enjoyed for months. There were tears in her eyes and she turned towards the door.

But Mercedes had her by the hand and her grip was strong. She pulled Robyn down hard and held her in a fierce embrace, her tongue wriggling into Robyn's mouth, her fingers in her hair.

'Stay,' she said as she broke the kiss. 'Let's have him together.'

'How?' Robyn heard herself say.

The answer was obvious. Alistair's stiff penis sawed hungrily at the empty air, the engorged tip purple with desire, a vein pulsing on the underside of the shaft. Robyn slid her fingers round the familiar tool. It felt bigger and harder than ever before. She realised she needed it inside her more than anything in the world.

Mercedes helped Robyn settle her long limbs across Alistair's loins and held the sticky pole away from his belly as she slotted the head between her pussy lips.

'Ohhh!' Robyn shouted as she slid down upon the hard flesh, stuffing the entire length up her in one movement. 'Oh, my God, that's fantastic!'

Lust at Large

The two women balanced themselves on the supine body beneath them, laughing now and revelling in the sensation of simultaneously fucking the same man. Then Mercedes pulled Robyn's mouth to hers and the laughter stopped. Tongue to cunt, cunt to cock, mouth to mouth – the circle was joined and the sensations ran between the three of them like an electric current.

Robyn felt out of control. Snapshots of the licentious happenings of the afternoon and evening ran through her mind as Alistair's cock speared into her belly and Mercedes' tongue thrust into her mouth... Joyce's big, heavy breasts with their swollen strawberry buds... Hugo's pencil sketches of lush lolling lasses... Nick's beefy sausage of a prick jetting spunk over her shoes... Alistair's tongue probing Mercedes' black strip of cunt fur... the Brazilian's glistening *café au lait* skin and beautiful dark-nippled breasts...

And beneath it all, running like an underground stream through the chambers of her mind, was the knowledge that it was over with Needle. They had failed each other somehow and this wild woman in her arms, with her silky tits and clever tongue, was manipulating them both and Robyn didn't care.

'Oh, ohh!' she moaned as Mercedes' fingers delved into her bush and found her clit. The prick in her pussy seemed bigger than ever, thrusting up into her like an iron bar. Mercedes was trembling and panting as she hung round Robyn's neck. Beneath her, Alistair was straining against his bonds and his cock leapt inside her as it fired its first shots.

'OH, OHH!' Robyn couldn't hold back any longer. This was the most indecent, most agonising, most exquisite moment of her life.

The three of them came off together.

16

Hotfoot off the early train from Wales, Josie was surprised by the changes in the Bird household. For a start, Phil was cheerful and animated in a way she'd never seen before. Then there were the bags of rubbish in the kitchen. She poked inside one and came across some women's clothing and lots of torn-up letters. And those ghastly photos of Deirdre had disappeared from the sitting-room.

Josie didn't comment, she was too concerned about Gavin.

'Why didn't you ring me earlier, Phil?'

'I tried.'

'Not very hard. You could have left messages. You could have rung the office.'

'Well, you could have rung too. You're meant to be engaged but he's been gone a week and you haven't been in touch.'

There was silence for a moment. Both parties sipped their coffee without tasting it.

'I'm sorry, Josie, I've been letting it all slide. I can't get that bloody woman out of my head.'

'Phil, that's all in the past.'

'So I realise. I'm cleaning up my act at last – look.' And he indicated the rubbish sacks.

'Deirdre stuff?'

'All of it. Letters, photos, clothes, the lot. Out with the old and on with the future. I'm determined.'

'Good for you.' Josie felt a rush of affection for him. He was so like Gavin sometimes. She kissed him on the cheek in a sisterly fashion.

'So where did he say he'd gone?'

'A funny-sounding place up north. He wrote it down for me – Blisswood-in-the-Dale.'

'Never heard of it. Why there?'

Phil shrugged. 'He wanted to get away from London and the whole mess. Get away from the reporters.'

'What do you mean?'

'Since the *Rabbit* did that article with his picture they've all been after him.'

'What article?'

'My my, Josie, you *are* out of touch.'

Upstairs in Gavin's bedroom Josie surveyed the scene with amazement. Newspapers and dirty takeaway food trays littered the floor. The bed was a jumble of muddy sheets and discarded clothes. The wardrobe doors hung open to reveal Gavin's work clothes hanging untidily and a pile of shirts and ties lying on top of his shoes. Letters, some of them unopened, were piled high on the table in the window and the rug beneath it was strewn with discarded envelopes and balled-up notepaper.

Above the bed the entire wall was covered with newspaper cuttings featuring the Topless Raider in action. The headlines seemed to leap out at Josie: BIG BOOBS BRENDA STRUTS HER STUFF... YOU PINCH MINE AND I'LL PINCH YOURS... NAUGHTY NORA KNOCKS 'EM OVER... DON'T POINT THOSE THINGS AT ME!...

'Good God,' said Josie, angry. 'He must be ill. Why didn't you do something?'

Phil shrugged and said nothing.

Josie peered closely at the newspaper photographs. 'She's a fat cow,' she said.

Phil chose not to disagree.

'What are all those letters?'

'They were sent on from the paper. After the article appeared he started getting a lot of mail.'

Josie picked up a sheaf of papers and read:

Dear Gavin – I'm writing to say how sorry I was to read of your terrible ordeal. Obviously you are a man who appreciates the voluptuous female form and as I myself have often been told I am 'all-woman' in

Lust at Large

the bosom department I wonder if I can be of assistance . . .

Ooh, Gavin, you hunk – you can weep over my three-pennies any time. Just call 081 . . .

My husband and I run a small amateur video business and I'm always on the lookout for new talent. Having seen your picture in the paper and read of your experiences, I wonder if you would care to recreate them for the small screen. I can guarantee that my own 44-24-36 figure will not disappoint a discerning 'tit-fancier' such as yourself . . .

'Bloody marvellous.' Josie threw the letters onto the floor. 'They are all from little tarts. No wonder he buggered off.'
'Well,' Phil looked embarrassed, 'I hate to tell you this, Josie . . .'
'Oh no. He didn't go off with one of them, did he?'
'Not exactly. But there was one letter in particular . . . It just said, "Sorry!" and it had a big lipstick kiss on it, you know, the imprint of a mouth. Gavin thought it had come from her. That's why he went.'
'Where?'
'I told you – Blisswood-in-the-Dale. That's what the postmark said.'
'Christ!'

The diary editor took the call because Robyn was still nursing her hangover in the loo.
'There's a Josie Twist waiting for you in reception,' he said as Robyn dragged herself back to her desk a few minutes later. 'My, you had quite a night of it, didn't you?'
If only you knew, thought Robyn. The Needle's reserves of single malt were to blame, she supposed, but it was the thought of what she had done with Mercedes and Alistair that really made her feel bad. She hadn't realised guilt could turn a person green.

'I don't know any Josie Twist,' she said.

'She says she's Gavin Bird's fiancée. And she's not going away till she sees you.'

'Oh shit.'

'Sounds like more Brenda copy to me: "My boyfriend can't get it up now he's gazed on the knockers of Nora." You do it so much better than me, of course.'

'Oh, fuck off, Crispin.' Nevertheless Robyn rose slowly to her feet and headed for the door.

Robyn had not given the missing fiancée any thought while contemplating the plight of Gavin Bird. She hadn't given Gavin much thought, either, since her piece about him. In any event she wasn't prepared for the beady-eyed party in red leggings and Doc Martens who came at her bristling with rage.

'Are you the slag who wrote this?' demanded Josie, waving a page of newspaper print in Robyn's face. 'It's inaccurate, insulting and bloody damaging.'

'Sit down, Josie, take it easy.'

'No, I won't. You don't know the trouble you've caused, you thoughtless bitch.'

'Well, I need a seat. You can please yourself.'

'I bet you fucked him, didn't you? You're all tarts on papers like this. You don't care who you screw to get the lies you print.'

'Come off it, Josie.' Robyn was not inured to this kind of abuse, though she had come across it once or twice. 'You know I'm not his type.'

Josie threw herself into a chair beside Robyn, scraping the feet on the wooden floor. By good fortune there was no one else in the reception area, though the uniformed porter at the desk was staring at them without pretence.

'And why did you write that stuff about me leaving him to face his ordeal by himself? That's just not true. It happened after I'd gone.'

'I'm sorry.'

'So you bloody well should be. If anything happens to him you'll be responsible.'

Robyn looked at Josie with interest for the first time. She was a pretty girl with loose curly brown hair and full lips.

Lust at Large

The big liquid eyes still blazed with fury but at least she had stopped shouting.

'Come on,' said Robyn. 'Let's go to Umberto's across the street. If I've got to grovel I need decent coffee.' And she made for the door.

As she ate the froth from her cappucino off a spoon, Josie told Robyn about Gavin's fan mail. 'It's all from women. Offering themselves to him, telling him they can cure his obsession with that Brenda cow, saying I'm no good for him. Making every kind of obscene suggestion they can think of.'

'And the *Rabbit*'s been sending it on, I suppose,' said Robyn. 'I didn't realise. What does Gavin think about it?'

Josie explained that Gavin wasn't around to express an opinion. He'd vanished over a week ago. After he'd received a particular letter.

'His brother says he was convinced it was from the robber herself. It wasn't like the others, it just said "Sorry" and was sealed with a lipstick kiss. That might identify her, mightn't it? Like a fingerprint. I haven't got it though, Gavin must have taken it with him.'

'So you think he's gone to find her?'

'Yes.'

'Where?'

'Aha.'

There was a silence. Despite the distant grumble of her headache Robyn was alert. This could be a red herring, of course, but she was alive to all sorts of possibilities.

'Where's he gone?' she repeated.

'I'm not going to tell you. He doesn't need the tabloid ratpack on his trail. This time I'm going to look after him.'

Robyn shrugged. 'You haven't got an address, have you? Just a postmark. How are you going to find him?'

'I'm quite capable, thank you.'

'I'm sure you are, Josie, but just think of the resources the *Bunny* can offer.'

'Such as?'

'Train fares, hotel bills, help with day-to-day subsistence. And if he's completely bonkers when you find him, a lump sum for medical expenses might come in handy.'

'Oh.' It seemed that none of this had occurred to Josie. She chewed her lower lip. 'What would I have to do?'

'Give me the exclusive story of your quest to rescue the man you love from the clutches of an evil woman.'

'And in the meantime I lead you to the topless cow and solve the biggest manhunt this country's had for years.'

'Boob-Hunt, darling, it's unique in the history of crime. We'll be famous. Anyway, I have a hunch I know where Gavin has gone so your story just gives me another angle.'

Josie stared at Robyn in disbelief. 'What do you mean, you know where he's gone?'

Robyn took a felt-tip pen from her bag and wrote on a napkin. She laid it carefully beside Josie's empty coffee cup and the girl's jaw dropped as she looked at it.

'Blisswood-in-the-Dale,' she read. 'Christ, Robyn, how the hell did you find that out?'

Robyn grinned and picked up the menu. 'It wasn't easy. While I explain to you the mysteries of investigative journalism, let's have lunch. I could eat a cow.'

17

Later that day two phone calls were made from the first-class carriage of an express train heading north.

'Hello, Ms Chestnut,' said Archie Monk as he sat at his office desk surrounded by photographs of half-naked women. 'How was your professor?'

Robyn summarised events at Dalrymple-Ripley's, glossing over the precise details but laying emphasis on the diary and drawings.

'And so you're off to the North Grinding on the basis of a seventy-year-old memoir?' Monk was sceptical.

'Not just that. Gavin Bird, the Kent Kindly counter clerk, is missing. We think he ran off after he received a note from Brenda saying she was sorry.'

'Who is *we*?'

'Bird's fiancée, Josie. She tells me Gavin's brother saw the note and the envelope was franked "Blisswood-in-the-Dale".'

'That's precious little reason to go haring round the country. Your newspaper must think a lot of you, Ms Chestnut.'

'Come off it, Archie, it all fits – the response to the appeal, the professor's papers and Gavin's letter. Besides, I've got the fiancée in tow. Failing all else, I can get a woman's-page feature out of her.'

'I see.'

'No, you don't. I'm giving you the only lead you've got. Get off your bum and join us. There's only one place worth staying, The Blisswood Spa Hotel. They've still got vacancies, I've checked.'

'Ms Chestnut, I really don't think—'

Lust at Large

'Well, you'd better start, Inspector. You wouldn't want the *Daily Rabbit* finding your girl first, would you?'

Monk replaced the receiver with a pensive look on his face.

Phil Bird had trouble recognising the voice on the other end of the line. For one thing, there was a lot of interference – for another, he was bewitched by the sight of Janice Melting's scarlet lips ringing the end of his cock.

'Phil, it's me – Josie.'
'Oh.'
'Can you hear me all right? I'm on a train. I've never made a phone call from a train before.'
'Ah.'
'I'm glad I caught you. I thought you'd be at work.'
'No.'
'You're not ill, are you?'
'I'm fine, Josie. Never been better.'

Janice raised her head from his groin and slid from the bed, leaving his prick sticking out wet and red.

'I'm going after Gavin,' continued Josie. 'That reporter's with me. We're going to stay in Blisswood.'

'Which reporter?' Phil's eyes were on Janice as she strolled around his bedroom. In a see-through lace cami-top, suspenders and stockings, she was the picture of provocation.

'Robyn Chestnut. From the *Rabbit*. She says you met her.'
'Did I?'

Janice sat on the stool in front of the dressing table – another Deirdre reminder that would have to go, thought Phil – and pulled open the drawer.

'She's six foot tall with incredible legs, Phil. No man could forget her.'

'Oh, her.'

Janice was leaning forward now, writing on the mirror with an old lipstick she had found. As she did so, her slender back hollowed out, emphasising the creamy ovals of her naked arse. The firm cheeks spread wide on the small stool, the crease between them a mysterious shadow.

'What do you mean "oh, her"? She's gorgeous. Honestly, Phil, you've got to start looking at other women.'

Lust at Large

'Josie, believe me, I am.'

Janice's buttocks were now tilted up in the air, the pink-lipped purse of her pussy fully revealed, fringed by a halo of soft brown hair. And above the hanging pouch of her vagina winked the dark star of her arsehole. Phil's cock rolled and twitched on his belly in an agony of desire.

'Anyway, Phil' – Josie was still talking – 'we're staying at somewhere called The Blisswood Spa. The paper is paying, thank God. So if Gavin rings, tell him where I am.'

'OK.'

Janice's curly brown head had now slumped forward onto the dressing table top and Phil could read the message in lipstick written on the mirror. PUT CREAM ON YOUR COCK, it said.

'I'll call with the number when I get there.'

'OK.'

Janice had her hands behind her, spreading her cheeks even wider, baring every centimetre of her bum crack. In her fingers she still held the tube of lipstick and, in the glare of Phil's disbelieving stare, she began to circle the ring of her anus in fuchsia pink.

'And if my friend Gwen rings, tell her where I am.'

'OK.'

The blunt point of the tube had now disappeared into Janice's bumhole. She pulled it out a fraction and then thrust it inside herself with real purpose. As it disappeared from view Phil imagined he could hear her sigh.

'I'd better go now, Phil. Are you sure you're all right?'

'I'm fine,' said Phil reaching into the cupboard by his bed for a dusty tube of K-Y jelly. 'Honestly, Josie, I couldn't be better.'

Janice was moaning clearly now as she pushed the small tube in and out of her bottom. Her other hand was in her bush, plucking at the nub of her clitoris.

'Bye, then, Phil.'

'Bye-bye, Josie. Take care.'

Phil threw the receiver into its cradle and began to massage the cold jelly into his burning cock.

'Christ, Janice,' he said, lunging for her, 'you are the horniest bitch I've ever met.'

She took the shaft of his penis in her hands to guide the head between the full white cheeks.

'You mean your wife didn't let you do this?'

'Don't make me laugh. Oh!'

Somehow she had squeezed the big glans into the tight ring of her anus. He held it still as she slowly, sweetly, began to corkscrew her rear back along its length.

'I'm really surprised, Phil.' She was panting as she spoke. Her hands were now on his hips, pulling him into her, urging him into a rhythm that sent his tool burrowing out of control deeper into her tight passage. 'It sounds as if Deirdre couldn't do the simplest things to please you.'

'Fuck Deirdre!'

'Oh no, Phil. Fuck me. Fuck me hard. Fuck me as hard as you like. Shoot your spunk right up my arse! Oh my God, I think I'm going to come!'

It was Janice's intention to drive Phil's ex out of his head within a week. In fact, as she had already told Tina, she didn't think it would take that long.

Two
STRIKE ME PINK

18

'I'm sorry, Rodney, I don't like it. In fact, I absolutely hate it.' Julia Jarvis, manager of The Blisswood Spa Hotel, hurled the folder onto her desk with a crash.

The occupant of the armchair by the window regarded her with amusement.

'I love it when you get upset,' he said. 'Your cheeks go pink and your big blue eyes turn positively cloudy with grief. It's such a turn-on.'

'Don't!'

'Darling, look at my trousers, I'm stiff already. But we'll have to wait, business before pleasure and all that. It's a pity you don't approve of my new brochure but hardly a surprise. You haven't liked any new initiative I've taken since my father died, have you?'

This was true. In the six months since Sir George Holmdale's death there had been many changes and Julia had not welcomed any of them. The old boy had scarcely been boxed up and laid to rest before his son and heir had abandoned his recession-hit London brokerage and returned to Blisswood to run the family business. Rodney was City-slick and money hungry. He bristled with 'initiatives'. In Julia's opinion most of them were designed to turn the hotel into a brothel.

'Let me explain, sweetie,' said Rodney. 'We want the conference business. Most conference attendees are men. Most men like girls. We have some of the best-looking girls in the hotel trade. So we put them in our publicity material. Simple.'

'But, Rodney,' Julia tried to sound calm and reasonable, 'we have a reputation for style and excellence. Turning our

Lust at Large

marketing literature into a top-shelf men's mag will ruin our good name.'

Rodney laughed, a nasty contemptuous sound.

Julia blundered on. 'Besides, it's so out of step with the times. These days many key executives are women. Companies can't allow themselves to be seen as sexist employers. This is the age of equal opportunities. What are the mistresses of industry going to say when your brochure lands on their desks full of big boobs and bikinis?'

Rodney appeared to consider the matter. 'Good Lord, Julia, I believe you may have a point. You see, I don't just keep you on because of your delectable arse.'

Julia's full lips set into a thin line and her sky-blue eyes blazed with as much venom as she was capable of. Rodney noted the effect with pleasure and continued, 'I don't see why we can't incorporate a few strapping fellows into the spreads. There's that new Italian waiter with the smarmy grin and tight trousers. We'll tickle a few fancies on the distaff side, no probs.'

'But you can't, it's so *crude*!'

'Don't worry, sweetie. That's just my rough plan you've been chucking about. I'm getting Clifford Rush to design and photograph the real thing. By the time he's finished we'll have enough artistic white space and grainy flesh textures to put it on sale in Waterstones.'

Before Julia could protest further the door opened and a young woman entered with a small cafetiere of coffee and two cups on a tray. She walked slowly on three-inch pencil heels, her stride restricted by the tight black skirt which finished halfway down her stockinged thighs. Rodney slid lower in his chair to savour the sight as she bent forward to place the tray on Julia's desk.

'You're an angel of mercy, Mercy,' he said.

'I'm Melanie,' replied the girl.

'Ah well, it's a fifty per cent chance, every time, isn't it? Perhaps you and your twin should wear name badges. A discreet little tag on your left breast, maybe. Of course, considering the size of the breast, it might just as well be a big tag.'

'For God's sake, Rodney,' protested Julia.

'You're not offended, are you, Melanie Melons? I can say what I like to you, can't I?'

'Provided I can call you a dirty sod in my turn, sir, I don't much care.'

And she didn't look like she did as she turned to pour the coffee, presenting Rodney with an awe-inspiring view of her barely concealed bottom and a glimpse of milky thigh above her stocking tops.

'How are you liking the new uniform, Melanie? I'm pleased to see you are doing full justice to the regulation underwear.'

Melanie placed his coffee on the side table by his chair, untroubled by his obvious interest in the neckline of her blouse.

'It's a laugh,' she replied. 'And it's a big help with tips.'

'You see,' said Rodney to Julia, his voice thick with I-told-you-so, before saying to Melanie, 'How would you and your sister like to star in our new promotional brochure? After all, you are one of our USPs.'

'Eh?'

'Unique Selling Points. Clifford Rush will take some fabulous photos of you.'

'From what I hear, he's as much of a lech as you are, sir.'

'There'll be a fee.'

'If it's large enough, then you can plaster my USPs all over reception.'

Julia was fuming. She'd had enough of this. 'Get out, Melanie.'

The girl shrugged and closed the door behind her with a bang.

There was a silence. Julia was lost in thought, her coffee rapidly cooling by her elbow. Melanie and Mercy were her younger sisters but sometimes they seemed like aliens from another planet.

An ominous sound broke the spell, the metallic purr of a zip descending. Rodney had his cock out of his trousers. The blue-veined shaft looked huge in his hand.

'Talking of Unique Selling Points, Julia, why don't you take your tits out?'

'Please, Rodney!'

Lust at Large

'Come on, woman. I want to see if you are also complying with my new underwear regulations.'

'I won't do it any more, Rodney. I won't!'

'I see.' He sprawled back in the chair and played with his hairy scrotum, rolling his balls between his fingers. His fat staff waggled in the air. Julia couldn't take her eyes off it.

'I mean it, Rodney. I won't let you abuse me any more.'

'In that case, Julia, perhaps you'd be interested to hear that this morning I got another offer for that piece of land.'

'Oh God.'

'Very generous it was, too. I think they want to build a garage or a supermarket or something.'

'Rodney, you wouldn't—'

'Your mother could keep her cottage but unfortunately the donkey sanctuary would have to go.'

'You're a heartless bastard, Rodney Holmdale. That sanctuary is her life.'

'Don't get hysterical, Julia. You know she has first option on the land.'

'But how can she meet your crazy price? She's got nothing to sell and I can't raise that kind of money.'

'Yes, I know. We go through this every time. Just think of the use I make of your body as interest on a loan. You mortgage your beautiful ass to me and I allow your mother to minister to ugly asses on my land. It's a fair deal.'

'Oh God!' wailed Julia. 'I suppose I have no choice,' and she began to undo the scarlet bow at her neck. Her delicate fingers shook as she unbuttoned the front of her bulging blouse.

'None at all,' agreed Rodney and he rose to his feet. He pulled his belt from his waistband with a loud crack.

Julia stiffened at the sound.

'Please, Rodney, be gentle with me this time.' Her blouse was off her shoulders and her big breasts were quivering with distress beneath her coral-pink camisole.

'Be gentle,' he sneered. 'How boring. You deserve to have your arse walloped to wack the cosy clichés out of you. Now let's see your tits.'

Hesitant and shaking, Julia took the camisole by the hem and slowly raised the thin sheaf of silk upwards, baring the fine flesh of her slender ribcage. The material continued to rise, like a curtain on a stage, and Rodney watched with childlike wonder as the undercurves of her swollen breast globes swung into view. For a moment the striptease was suspended and the snowy mounds dangled there before him partially veiled. He itched to leap forward and rip the silk from her sumptuous body but this element of suspense, contrived or not, was one of the reasons he so lusted after her.

Then the slip was up and off, revealing her soft and shapely form to his famished gaze, the weighty rounds of flesh out-thrust and trembling, the nipples pink and swollen.

As if in a dream she pulled the skirt to her waist and turned to bend over the desk. Her rear was framed by pink suspenders and stockings, the thin straps drawn tight over the jutting curve of her buttocks. A wisp of transparent panty was tucked into the pocket of her bulging arse, leaving the alabaster cheeks bare of any protection. The perfect white moons were on offer to Rodney in open invitation, begging for the first caress of the strap.

In the corridor outside, Melanie shifted on her knees. Not that she was going to tell Hot Rod, but the new skirts made peeking through keyholes much less comfortable.

19

Not far from the corridor where Melanie crouched on her haunches, another woman squatted down in the cause of sex. Felicity Dodge – Fliss – was a woman on the verge of her thirtieth birthday and her best days still lay before her, so everybody told her. In any event, a few good years lay behind her and she felt that, by now, certain matters should have come to a head. Like the matter of Clifford Rush, on whom she was currently bestowing head as she knelt on the bedroom floor of the room directly above Julia's office.

In the past Fliss had not always been what is known as a good girl. In fact she had been a downright naughty one. Her curvy figure, full lips and big brown eyes had got her into a lot of mischief. Meeting Cliff, however, convinced her she should turn over a new leaf and stick to one guy. He was successful, rich and generous. In short, he was marriage material. Now, however, two years with him had gone by and she was staring down the barrel of the big Three Oh. As she saw it, this trip up north on Cliff's latest assignment was make-or-break time.

Right now Fliss was pleasuring Cliff in the way he enjoyed best. It was possibly the most unequal sexual activity in the book and one her liberated friends in London would not have approved of – but this was no time to be a killjoy. Especially as, according to him, she was so good at it.

They had christened the position the San Francisco Suck-off since they had done it in that city in the first flush of their romance. Stranded by fog in a hotel bedroom lined with mirrors, Cliff had become addicted to the reflection of Fliss's bouncing white posterior as she knelt on all fours

Lust at Large

between his legs and gobbled his prick. Then as now, its particular charm for Cliff was the image of Fliss's winking vagina displayed between the smooth lower cheeks of her shaking buttocks as she knelt before him.

They had been at it for a while, he sitting on the bed and she crouching before him, her bum thrust backwards, towards a carefully angled mirror. Up down, up down, went her mouth on his stiff penis, wink wink went her other mouth in the mirror. Her knees and arms were aching and so were her breasts because Cliff enjoyed slapping them from side to side as they dangled beneath her crouching frame. With her titties swinging, her arse wobbling, her head bobbing and her cunt winking, he was in seventh heaven. In his opinion, for visual and tactile stimulation this position could not be bettered. Fliss never volunteered her opinion. She usually had her mouth full at the time.

'Uh,' grunted Cliff and reached forward to land a smack on her upturned bottom. Her bum cheeks danced for his pleasure.

'Ooh, baby, that's good,' he muttered. 'Shake your fat little arse for me.' And he smacked her again, hard. This was a sign he was getting excited.

She accelerated the tongue action and brought a hand up to squeeze the base of his root. He had to come soon, surely. But he bent to kiss her head and whispered, 'Slow down, darling, let's make this last.'

Fliss wouldn't have minded so much if she hadn't discovered that Cliff had played the same game two months ago with her former best friend Betsy in a hotel in Palermo. (So, what cute little name for it did they dream up? The Betsy Bumdance? The Sicilian Swallow? The bastard.)

Suddenly an alien sound burst upon their ears. A shrill squeal. Then another, louder this time. And another.

Fliss raised her head. 'What's that?'

'It's a woman.'

'Where's it coming from?'

The cries were loud and regular. And between them could now be heard other noises: muffled cracks, low masculine grunts.

'What's going on?' said Fliss.

Lust at Large

'What do you think, sweetheart?' Cliff was grinning at her. 'That's the sound of a woman getting laid.'

'But she's in agony!'

'Oh really? Just listen.'

It was true, the sounds had changed. The voice was lower now and the cries had become moans and sighs. Some words could be discerned: 'Oh, you swine. Don't stop. Please don't stop. Oh! Yes, yes! God, I hate you!'

'You see.' Cliff laced his fingers through Fliss's dark curls and pushed her lips towards his straining member. 'Now, let's get back to business.'

Fliss did not protest. Indeed, she sucked the ruby red knob back into her mouth at once and swivelled her hips for him with a will. The sound of the unknown woman teetering between agony and ecstasy filled her ears. She imagined what the grunting man was doing to her. She'd bet he had a big cock, that he was ramming it up the woman's pussy while she screamed out, begging him for more. That's what she wanted too. A cock in her own hungry pussy. A thick red-capped stalk to fill the void between her legs. Oh yes! She thrust back hard, imagining a rock-hard male organ plugging her empty hole.

'Ooh, baby!' moaned Cliff, drinking in the sight of her gyrating bum cheeks.

'Aah! Yes, yes, do it to me hard! Fill me up! Oh you bastard!' yelled the other woman.

'Fat little arse indeed,' thought Fliss to herself in an agony of frustration as a very naughty plan took shape in her mind. It could backfire but it *was* make-or-break time after all. 'I'll nail you down yet, Clifford Rush,' she muttered but the words were drowned in a cascade of spunk as her lover finally shot his load and collapsed onto the bed.

Fliss sat back on her haunches and allowed his cream to bubble from her lips and dribble down over her pink and heaving tits. Just the way he liked it.

Between her legs, her empty pussy wept.

From below, the howls of a woman in orgasm rent the air.

20

The sounds of Julia Jarvis's orgasm travelled across the grounds of The Blisswood Spa Hotel as far as the adjoining donkey sanctuary. The plump and contented collection of asses foraging in the meadow registered the noise but did not let it disturb them. They were used to it. Gavin Bird was not.

'What the hell's that?' he said.

His companion, a pink-cheeked girl in cut-off denims and a blue gingham shirt, just giggled.

Julia screeched on, the sound echoing round the big barn they were attempting to clean in preparation for the forthcoming Midsummer's dance.

'What is it, Lucy?' repeated Gavin. 'It sounds like someone being murdered – shouldn't we do something?'

The girl stopped sweeping the floor and turned her big amber eyes on Gavin.

'I thought you townies were meant to be sophisticated. That's Miss Jarvis entertaining Hot Rod up at the hotel. She's a bit of a screamer.'

'Oh,' said Gavin, recognising the dying notes of a woman in the throes of lust.

This was a new Gavin. Stripped to the waist in the mid-morning heat, a pitchfork loaded with straw in his hand, he looked like any other healthy country youth. The burdens of a nine-to-five life had slipped from his broad and now-tanned shoulders. The pinched and pasty air of city-bred anxiety was gone from his face.

He began to laugh and Lucy laughed with him. She gave him the kind of look she'd been giving him all morning. The look that said, 'Why the hell not?' He put down the pitchfork and took the broom from her hand. Her big eyes grew wider as he slipped an arm round her waist and backed her towards a pile of hay bales inside the door. She could guess what was coming.

The new Gavin was a man with a mission. He knew Brenda was in Blisswood somewhere, he couldn't prove it but he knew it to be true. It was the letter that had convinced him – and the Blisswood women. They were all around, luscious laughing lasses with big breasts and swinging hips. She could be any one of them. He'd know it when she was naked in his arms. All he had to do was fuck every one – it was simple.

The girl on the hill had merely been the first. He'd been busy since then. The women of Blisswood had welcomed him with open arms, you might say. And now there was Lucy.

Her tongue slipped into his mouth as his hands eased the thin shirt from the waistband of her shorts.

'We can't do it here,' she said. 'Miriam could pop in at any moment.' Nevertheless he ignored her protests and she did nothing to stop him unbuttoning her blouse and pulling the cups of her bra up over her breasts. The soft flesh fell into his hands and he lowered his head to take a firm pink nipple into his mouth. Now was the moment of truth. He nuzzled and fondled the two globes, lifting each in turn to squeeze and lick the satiny skin. Gavin had suspected from the first that Lucy was not the Topless Raider – her tits were too pointy and pear-shaped – but he believed in being thorough.

She cradled his head to her bosom and stroked the blond curls on the back of his neck.

'Who's this Miss Jarvis?' he said, raising his lips from her bosom and undoing the button at her waist.

'Julia, Miriam's daughter. She's the manager of The Blisswood Spa. She looks a prim little miss but she fairly howls the place down when she gets going. God, you're a fast worker, aren't you?'

Gavin had her denim shorts off by now and her panties soon followed onto the wooden floor. She lay back on the prickly makeshift bed, making no attempt to hide her pink and nubile body from his searching gaze. Her legs lolled open to reveal a thick brown triangle of fur, trimmed neatly round the prominent lips of a pouting pussy. She was fired up already, he could see, and he trailed an experimental finger down the gentle slope of her belly and through her silky bush. It came up wet with her juices and, on impulse, he fell to his knees between her thighs and ran his tongue the length of her crack.

'Ooh,' she squealed, 'ooh, yes please' and swung her lithe brown legs up into the air, over his bare shoulders, thrusting her exposed pubis into his face. Gavin lapped her with an enthusiasm and skill he would never have imagined just a few weeks ago. He swirled his tongue deep inside her and sucked on the long scalloped lips of her labia. Then he pushed two fingers deep inside her and began to massage the sensitive inner walls of her cunt. As his mouth closed over the tiny finger of her clit she bucked her entire pubic delta against his face and launched into her first orgasm.

Gavin had done this to Josie, of course. But not often and not recently. He'd always worried that maybe she didn't like it, that she was only doing it to please him. In his previous life he had never fancied himself as a great lover. But now, with the Blisswood air in his lungs and this uninhibited country girl squirming on his tongue, tugging his head into her loins and whispering that he must never, ever stop and that she was coming, coming, *coming*! he felt he had been reborn in paradise.

Miriam Jarvis moved through life amused by the foibles of others, rarely jolted from her customary serenity. There were only three subjects capable of rousing her passion. The first was her donkey sanctuary. It was even more important than the second – her children – because the poor helpless asses needed her, whereas her daughters were intelligent young women able to look after themselves. Nevertheless, Miriam did worry about Julia, the most vulnerable of her brood, in the way that every mother does. Specifically, she wanted her married to a rich young man with a kind heart.

And so, had Miriam realised that the blistering screech

Lust at Large

which regularly rang out across the dale was the sound of Julia enjoying a man's cock she would not have turned a hair. More to the point, had she known the cock in question belonged to Rodney Holmdale she would have been thrilled. In her eyes, the young beneficiary of the Holmdale estate, who indulged her donkey refuge – as his father had done – without asking a penny in rent, was Prince Charming. And she nurtured a not-too-secret hope that her Julia might turn out to be his Cinderella.

She approached the barn with donkeys and Julia on her mind, then both were suddenly wiped away and the third passion of her life took over the entire focus of her attention.

Through a crack in the barn door her eye was fixed on Lucy Salmon, her regular helper, and the young man from London who had volunteered his services only that morning. And what services they were! She could see that he had Lucy on a journey to the stars simply by the use of his tongue. A pulse beat in the pit of her stomach at the thought. It had been a long while since she had had a fresh young face between her thighs.

One hand stole unconsciously inside her blouse to pinch a swollen nipple as she watched the lad – Gavin, she remembered – climb to his feet. He stood in front of the girl and stripped off his jeans, freeing his cock with pride. It was long and hairless with only a down of light fuzz covering his balls, but the staff was straight and the bulb was purple and Miriam thought that she had never seen anything quite so delicious in her life.

Lucy evidently felt the same for she bent her knees back to her chest and spread herself wide. 'Put it in all the way,' she said. 'And hurry up.'

Gavin held back. He savoured the sight of his new conquest squirming before him, offering herself without shame or reserve.

'I thought you were worried about Mrs Jarvis,' he said, stroking his cock, pulling the foreskin over the shiny glans and slowly easing it back again.

'She won't care. She'll be jealous I got to you first,' said Lucy. 'Don't tease me. Just shove it all the way up. Please.'

Turned on as she was, Miriam smiled at the reference to

herself. She toyed with the idea of intruding, of claiming that beautiful white staff for her own use. Lucy was a good-natured lass, she wouldn't hold it against her – they'd shared a travelling sales rep only two months ago. However, she wouldn't want to frighten the young man away.

He'd put it in now. Just the knob. And Lucy was wriggling her hips, trying to capture more of his length in her hungry hole.

'Play with your clit,' he said to her. 'Show me how you do it. Bring yourself off.'

'Must I?' she muttered and turned her crimson face to one side. But her fingers splayed open her crack and busied themselves at the apex of her slot. Eyes bright, he pressed his cock in another inch as she diddled herself into a frenzy.

By now Miriam had pulled her skirt to her waist and she, too, was knuckle-deep in her burning loins.

Lucy came once more with a sigh and jerked up and down on the bales making her long breasts bounce and judder. Gavin fell on her and drove his tool all the way home, his lean white buttocks pounding in pent-up longing between her brown thighs.

'Oh my God,' groaned Miriam, both hands busy in the wet thatch between her legs, bumping her hip heavily against the door as the first wave of orgasm shot through her. The door swung back slowly on its hinges with a loud creak, flooding sunlight across the dirty wooden floor and the naked bodies of the copulating couple.

As the light fell on Gavin's face, blinding him to everything but the sensations of the moment, his cock leapt and spurted inside the pretty girl beneath him. She took all he had with a shout of pleasure. *Paradise indeed*, was his only thought.

21

Julia Jarvis found the best way of coping with Rodney Holmdale was to pretend he didn't exist when he was not in her sight. Fortunately the running of the hotel threw up so many dramas which demanded her instant attention that this was just about possible. But Rodney did have a way of thrusting himself into her mind. His presence was everywhere.

Like now, in the sound of heated voices rising from the reception area. Rodney was elsewhere doing God knows what – Julia couldn't bear to think – but the altercation below was nevertheless his fault.

The girl on reception was at the centre of the dispute. She was a small disdainful beauty with jet-black hair cut smartly to her jaw revealing the delicate white tulip-stem of her neck. Her eyes were big and dark, her cheeks porcelain pale and her mouth a perfect pout of scarlet. She was French and Rodney's most recent appointment.

Julia had objected, of course.

'I thought you said we should make more of our local girls.'

'And so we will but we must also cater for a variety of tastes. Chantal is a sophisticated Parisienne. She adds a touch of class *et du mystère, n'est-ce pas?*'

'She's rude to every female guest and she looks like a tart! The only room number she knows is *soixante-neuf*!'

'And how, darling. She was very persuasive at the interview. Why, I do believe you're jealous . . .'

Of course there had been no point in arguing with Rodney. And now here was Chantal standing up to a slim brunette who towered over her by about a foot, while a younger woman in red leggings and clumpy shoes with a rucksack on her shoulder looked on.

'See here,' said the tall woman in a low voice with a transatlantic twang, 'I phoned you from London at two o'clock today. I booked a two-person suite and requested the use of a fax machine. I told you I didn't know how long we would be staying. I gave you a credit-card number and said there would be two for dinner. You confirmed it all. So what do you mean the suite is booked?'

'It's no longer available,' said Chantal. 'I may be able to find you two separate rooms in the annexe just for tonight.'

'But what happened to my booking?' The American was beginning to lose her temper.

'Please, *madame*, if you do not keep your voice down I must ask you to leave at once.'

Julia made her intervention not before time. 'What's the problem here, Chantal?'

The French girl turned to her and said, without lowering her voice, 'This Yankee woman and her scruffy girlfriend are on their own. They have no men and no luggage to speak of. They say they want a suite and dinner but it is eight thirty and the suite is being used. They are not desirable clientele in my opinion. Why don't they stay at the pub?'

'It's Ms Chestnut, isn't it?' said Julia quickly, seeing the American's face freeze into a mask of rage. 'I believe I took your booking earlier. We're delighted to see you. We've put you in the Holmdale Suite.' And she plucked a key from the board and indicated the way to the grand wooden staircase. 'I'm sorry we don't have a lift but Chantal will arrange to bring your bags upstairs.'

Josie set her rucksack next to Robyn's small overnight case and shot the Frenchwoman a look of triumph. Robyn followed Julia in a daze, hardly listening to her effusive apologies. As they ascended the stairs Chantal called out, 'Madame Julia, the Holmdale Suite is *occupé*,' but Julia ignored her.

As it turned out, *occupé* did not quite cover the situation. Julia led them first into a large and beautiful sitting-room which looked out of the front of the house down the long

Lust at Large

driveway flanked by fields of grazing sheep. As they appeared at the window, a scattering of rabbits fled for the trees, their white scuts twinkling in the golden light of the summer evening.

'Hey, this is fantastic,' said Robyn, the tension now gone from her face.

They were just as impressed with the first bedroom with its chaise longue and swagged curtains. Josie threw herself onto a bed the size of a billiard table, saying, 'This is more like it.'

She dragged herself to her feet to view the second bedroom and was glad she did for she would otherwise have missed one of the high spots of events to date.

This room was even more sumptuous, with high ceilings, delicate watercolours and an antique writing desk. But it was the four-poster bed that took the eye and, in particular, the blonde beauty reclining on a mountain of pink and lacy pillows, the cones of her breasts glistening in the glare from the lights erected around the bed. She appeared to be naked but for peach silk stockings and garters and an exquisite pair of matching satin shoes that waved in the air as her legs threshed, egg-beater fashion, over the form of a man kneeling between her thighs.

'Oh my God,' said Julia. 'Clifford!'

The great photographer raised his bushy head, revealing that the girl was indeed naked to all intents and purposes. Her pussy was pink and wet from his tonguing, a small knot of blonde hair providing no cover for the open split with its spread lips and yawning scarlet interior.

'Give me just one moment, girls,' said Cliff. 'I've got her just how I want her.' And he scrambled to his feet and positioned himself behind a camera on a tripod aimed directly at the nubile vision on the bed.

The spectactors were too stunned to say anything but Cliff was in his element and chatted away as the camera-shutter clicked. 'That's fantastic, my love, fabulous. Oh you're gorgeous. Toss your head from side to side. That's my girl.

'Just look at the way the light catches the hair on the pillow,' he said by way of an aside. 'And look at that pussy glisten. It's taken me half an hour to get her like this. She's dying for it. Just watch.

'OK, darling, think sexy. You're on the brink of orgasm, you've been tongued to the point of ecstasy and any moment now your lover is going to give you the benefit of his big cock. But you can't wait, you're going to have to give yourself a little feel. That's right, tweak that nipple, make it stand up, roll it between your fingers. Imagine that lovely Mario you told me about is going to suck it. Feel the excitement build in your belly, let it run right through you like an electric current, right down to your clit. Hey, I've really got you going now!'

And it was true. The girl on the bed was playing with herself without shame, one hand plucking and pulling at her nipples, the other delving into her crotch. Cliff was shouting out instructions and bouncing on the balls of his feet.

'That's it, baby, that's it! Spread those pussy lips for me. Let's see inside, open up your tunnel. Imagine that great cock. Think of it filling you right up. Picture him thrusting it in all the way! Now stroke your clit. That's it! Go for it! You're going to come soon, aren't you? You can't help it, you're on the brink! Here it comes, here it comes! Oh yes!'

'AAAH!' screamed the girl on the bed, her fingers a blur between her legs, her pelvis pumping in mid-air.

She flopped back on the coverlet, her limbs askew, her sex red, pouting and running with juice. There was silence, broken only by the clicking of the camera as Cliff took his final shots.

He turned towards the spectators and ran a handkerchief over his sweating brow. He looked as though he had just run ten thousand metres. 'Fantastic,' he said. 'Rodney told me your local girls were something special, Julia, and he was right.'

'Clifford Rush,' said Julia in a croak, her mind suddenly empty of anything appropriate to say. 'Clifford, this is Robyn Chestnut and this is—'

'Josie Twist,' said Josie, holding out a hand and gazing at Cliff in awe.

'Pleased to meet you,' he said, grinning and curious. 'Did Rod send you two along? It's possible I could fit you in tomorrow. I'm sure I could come up with something special for you, Robyn, your legs are just fabulous. And there's something rebellious and sexy about you, Josie. Those big brown eyes would be great for what I've got in mind. Unless,' he added, a brainwave striking, 'all of you would be game right now. I feel I'm on a roll and I could shoot some good stuff with all three of you on the bed here. You're such contrasting physical types. I know you've turned me down already, Julia, but imagine your beautiful peaches-and-cream tush spread out with this sexy twosome. It would be fantastic! I'm coming in my pants at the thought!'

'Cliff!' The shout from the bed brought this bizarre proposition to an end. 'Get those cows out of here and take your pants off. You can't leave me like this!'

Cliff shrugged apologetically at the three dumbfounded women. 'Duty calls,' he whispered as he ushered them out of the door.

Julia collapsed into an armchair and covered her face with her hands. Josie looked at Robyn and, to her relief, saw she was struggling to control her laughter.

'Did I tell you I was a national newspaper journalist?' said Robyn to Julia.

An unhappy noise rose from the armchair.

'And you know that complimentary bottle of champagne you mentioned?' said Josie. 'I think it might have to be a case.'

22

Monk was working late. He'd had a grim day and he was in a foul mood. The air in his office was like soup. He popped an indigestion pill in his mouth to settle the bile left over from his daily row with Hatter. For two pins he'd chuck it all in and retire to a Scottish loch to fish, except he hated fishing. But the thought of escape, of getting out of the foul heat of summer in the city, that soothed him. It would be balm for the soul and that's what he needed. However, he'd never run away from an investigation yet. Then he remembered his conversation that afternoon with Robyn Chestnut. Maybe there was a way to get out of town and to stay on the Brenda trail. He was about to dial Hatter's number when there came a tap on the door.

DC Stephen Fantail was not the most assertive member of Monk's team. He was tall and awkward and blushed at the smallest thing. Given the nature of the Brenda investigation he spent almost the entire day with a red face. However, he was young and keen. Monk liked him. He also acknowledged that he had a sharper eye for detail than any of his colleagues.

'I'm sorry to bother you, sir,' he said as he stood in the doorway hopping from one foot to the other. 'It's about Brenda and it's probably not important. That is, it could be but I'm not sure. Shall I come back tomorrow?'

Monk pointed to the chair facing him but Stephen did not take it. Instead he spread a selection of 12 × 14 black-and-white prints across the desk and stood looming over his superior. Monk could smell his excitement.

'See here, sir, and here.'

At first Monk couldn't grasp what was before him. The

Lust at Large

prints had been enlarged so much the shapes were indistinct. It was like looking at pictures of so-called UFOs in the trashy papers. Then the shadows resolved themselves into all-too-familiar configurations. These were no UFOs but Bra-less Brenda's breasts.

'This is from the most recent robbery, sir. You can see it more clearly here.' Stephen stabbed his finger at a blur which, as Monk peered closely, took on surprising detail.

'It looks like the wing of a butterfly,' he said.

'Yes, that's what I thought, sir.' The young detective was beaming.

Monk turned over the implications in his mind. 'You mean that our lady friend has tattooed tits?'

'Possibly, sir, but look at this one from the previous raid. You can see the underside of both breasts and here's the tail of the butterfly, it's just visible.'

'So?'

'Tattoos don't move, sir. This is her left breast but in the other photo the butterfly is on her right one. And she doesn't have them on both breasts as you can see.'

'Hmm. What are you suggesting?'

'It must be some kind of a transfer. You know, something you can stick on the skin.'

'Very interesting. Congratulations, Stephen, no one else spotted it.'

'Thank you, sir. I thought I saw something on the first set of prints but it wasn't till I did the blow-ups that I was sure.' Fantail was flushed with pride.

'I don't want to dampen your enthusiasm,' said Monk, 'but why does she do it? It can't be for effect, you can hardly see the damn things. And why would she move the butterfly from tit to tit?'

Stephen's face fell. 'I don't know, sir.'

'Nevertheless, it's good work. All we need now is a suspect with a selection of stick-on butterflies in her vanity chest. We'd better get to work on who manufactures butterfly transfers and how they are distributed. They're probably carried by every Woolworth's in the land,' he added as a gloomy afterthought.

'I doubt they'd use this particular butterfly, sir,' said Stephen.

Monk stared at him.

'I mean, this butterfly is very rare. If I were a cosmetics manufacturer I'd just use any old design for a butterfly. I wouldn't go to the trouble of copying a *Lepidoptera extasis*.'

'What!'

'You see, the irregular wing shape and bifurcated body do not correspond to the clichéd concept of the butterfly. I'm sure most young ladies would prefer a generalised pretty shape.'

Monk stood up and placed his face inches from that of the chattering youth. 'Do you mean to tell me, Fantail, that you can recognise the precise kind of butterfly this woman is wearing?'

'Oh yes, sir. It's a Moorland Martyr or *Lepidoptera extasis*. As I said, it's got a distinctive wing shape and the body is forked. You can just make it out in this photo here. It's a fascinating creature with a life span of only two days and it breeds in the high moorland in just one area of the country.'

'And what area would that be, Fantail?' Monk's voice was cold.

'The North Grinding, sir. It's just—'

But Stephen's wind was cut off as the inspector seized him by the throat and backed him up against a metal filing cabinet. Monk's eyes were like chips of ice as he glared at his spluttering victim.

'I've always thought you were clever, Fantail, but I never took you for a smartarse. You are going to be very sorry you tried to take the piss out of me and my investigation.' He slammed the young detective viciously against the cabinet and the boy slumped to the floor.

'Who put you up to it?' Monk shouted. 'Have you been talking to the press?'

Stephen couldn't answer for a moment. His eyes danced with fear as he tried to regain his powers of speech.

'I haven't talked to anybody, sir. You're the first to know about this. I can prove it, too,' he added ruefully as he clambered to his feet.

A few moments later Monk was staring in disbelief at the entry in *Butterflies of Europe*. It was all there, just as Stephen had said. The insect existed. Exclusively in the North Grinding.

Lust at Large

Monk was out of the habit of making apologies. 'You're a keen butterfly-fancier are you, Stephen?' he muttered.

'I prefer bird-watching, sir.'

'How appropriate. Pack your binoculars and turn up here at eight tomorrow morning. We're off to the country for a few days.'

'Sir?'

Monk smiled at him. 'Don't worry, Stephen. You've done brilliantly. The clean air of the North Grinding is what we both need.' And he shooed the young man out of his office with a cheery wave. The effect was terrifying.

Monk picked up the phone again and this time he did dial Hatter's number. As he did so, his mind was not on his carping superior but on how to handle a certain newspaper reporter. The *Daily Rabbit* might be quick off the mark but if Robyn Chestnut knew a butterfly from a bumblebee he'd be surprised – and he didn't intend to enlighten her.

23

Rodney Holmdale chuckled as Chantal recounted the arrival of the American woman and her scruffy companion. He particularly enjoyed the account of Julia leading them into a suite and interrupting a naughty photo session. Chantal enjoyed it too.

'I told Madame Julia it was being used but she wouldn't listen. When I went up with the bags I found her promising those women all sorts of things. One of them is a journalist. No wonder she has no manners. They are having dinner right now. On the house. I thought you ought to know, Mr Holmdale.'

Rodney smiled his approval. Chantal was a most useful girl in all sorts of ways and enjoyed keeping him up to date with the gossip. He suspected she loved bitching even more than she liked men – but who could complain about that?

His attention drifted, as it invariably did whenever Chantal paid these impromptu visits to his private annexe, to the scarlet swell of her lips. Lush, ripe and elastic, the lower curve was a tempting half moon, the Cupid's bow of the upper lip scarcely less full. There was something positively carnal about that mouth of hers. He couldn't look at it without longing to plunge his cock deep inside the pouting ring of flesh.

So far she had only sucked him off once, at the interview. Since then she had allowed him to kiss and paw her through her provocatively skimpy attire but she had withheld the further use of her bewitching mouth. Obviously she needed a little incentive.

'I've been thinking, Chantal.'

'Yes?' The big black eyes regarded him with amusement. She could guess what he had been thinking.

'Julia has rather a lot on her plate at the moment. The Gartertex sales conference starts tomorrow and there are certain aspects of it that need sensitive handling. I've been wondering whether we have anyone else on the staff who could help out.'

He broke off and strolled to the sideboard. He poured two glasses of sherry and offered one to Chantal. She took it but did not drink.

'Naturally, increased responsibilities would merit increased remuneration. However, I do need to be assured that the person I select has the right attitude.'

He touched his glass to hers. 'Drink up.'

She took an infinitesimal sip and he watched the imprint of her mouth on the glass with ill-concealed fascination as he waited for her response.

'Would this person have to report to Madame Julia?' she enquired.

'Not necessarily. Considering the nature of some of her duties it would be better if she reported directly to me.'

'So this person will be a woman?' She was teasing him. He had no option but to make matters crystal clear.

'Gordon Garter, Chairman and Managing Director of Gartertex, would not relish a man as his liaison officer. GG requires some very specific services. As I remember from your interview, you would be well equipped to take on the role.'

'How much extra?'

'I was thinking of another fifty pounds a week.'

She sank her sherry in one gulp and set the glass down on his desk with a tiny click.

'Two-fifty and five hundred pounds cash before I lay a finger on him.'

'Now, look here, Chantal—'

'Ssh.' She placed a slender forefinger on his lips, stilling his protest instantly. Her other hand fanned out over the crotch of his trousers. 'Say yes, *chéri*, and I give you a reminder of my attitude right now.'

'Oh yes,' he breathed and her knowing fingers began to trace the outline of his straining cock.

Fliss was so furious she could hardly eat. The trout on her plate stared balefully at her as she prodded it and her stomach turned over.

'Take this away,' she said to the waiter.

'Is there something else I can get you?' he asked.

'Another drink,' said Fliss. 'A very large glass of the most expensive cognac you have.'

She lit a cigarette and drew on it with gusto. The people at the next table stared at her crossly but she didn't care. They were the reason she was upset, so fuck them, she thought. The truth was, though, that Clifford was the real source of her unhappiness and the two women beside her were merely the unwitting bearers of bad news.

Dining on her own – she had waited long enough for Cliff and he had warned her he'd be busy – she couldn't help overhearing every word that passed between the tall American woman and the English girl. It hadn't taken her long to work out that they had stumbled on Cliff in mid-shoot. And it soon became clear that when her lover had said he would be 'up to his ears' in work he'd meant that literally.

'He really got her going, didn't he?' said the English girl.

'You thinking of taking up his offer?' asked the American.

'No fear.'

'If you posed for him there'd be a modelling fee.'

'Ooh, yes. I wonder how much.'

'Payment in kind, no doubt.'

And they'd dissolved into giggles. Fliss felt like throwing her food in their stupid faces.

She drank her brandy fast and called for another. Already this morning's plan, conceived as she knelt between Clifford's legs and shook her bottom for him in the mirror, seemed doomed. Then, charged up and randy, she had imagined pandering to his voyeuristic desires and capturing his affections once and for all. He was always egging her on, pleased whenever she flashed her panties climbing out of a car and urging her to bare her titties on the beach.

Lust at Large

To date, Fliss had always been reluctant to go too far. Maybe now was the time. Perhaps he'd like to see her really go wild. She'd get him to take photos of her masturbating. With a banana maybe or a big dildo. That would be just the kind of visual stimulus he'd enjoy. And how about other guys? She'd offer to fuck and suck as many as he liked and he could snap away. What did she have to lose? At least she might get a stiff dick in the proper place.

Another glass of cognac appeared in front of her and she looked up into a pair of soulful brown eyes that gazed at her with evident concern.

'What's your name?' she asked. It was funny how she sounded tipsy even though she didn't feel it.

'Mario.'

'You Italians know how to take proper care of a girl, don't you?'

'Are you feeling all right, madame? Can I get you anything else?'

Fliss knocked back her drink and got to her feet. 'I feel a bit squiffy. Where's the ladies?'

'It's just down those stairs and to the—'

'You show me.' She leant against him, pushing the soft mound of her left breast against his arm. She took his hand in hers. 'Come on.'

'But, madame—'

'Come on.'

He knew he should decline but the allure of this mysterious beauty was hard to resist. As she pressed her small curvy body against his side, her big liquid eyes implored, the shadow of her cleavage beckoned and her perfume seduced.

They descended the stairs quickly.

24

'Did you see what I just saw?' whispered Josie.

'Yeah. Little Miss Lonely has gone off with the waiter to screw. I think this place is a madhouse.'

Josie nodded and carved herself another mouthful of succulent fillet steak. She could hardly blame the woman. The waiter was a dish and she was feeling as horny as hell herself. Events at Blisswood had so far only served to remind her that she hadn't been laid for nearly a week. Not since that night with Gwen in the rugby club car park. And now she was dying for it – was she turning into some crazed nympho?

'What's the plan tomorrow?' she asked. 'I suppose I ought to scout about for Gavin.'

'Sure. Check the B&Bs and pubs. If he's here we ought to be able to trace him pretty quick.'

'I suppose so.'

'You don't sound very enthusiastic, Josie. Don't you want to find him?'

'Of course.'

But there was a little piece of Josie that secretly hoped she wouldn't, not just yet. Not now she'd seen that dishy waiter and been propositioned by the famous Clifford Rush. Despite her journey and her need to reassure herself Gavin was all right, a part of her dreaded finding her fiancé. *Face it*, she told herself, *you don't want to be monogamous just yet*.

In a stall in the downstairs ladies toilet, Fliss had no intention of ever being monogamous again. Not while there were cocks like Mario's to be had. It was thick, it was long and it was splitting her in two. God, she needed it.

She'd made him sit on the seat and she was riding him.

Lust at Large

She had her hands flat on his broad shoulders and she was pulling herself up and down on his rod. The first thing he'd done when they'd locked the door behind them was to slip the thin black straps of her evening dress from her shoulders and bare her succulent breasts. Now they jiggled and wobbled in front of his face as she rode him. It was heaven.

She grasped his head, plunging her hands into his thick black wavy hair, and pulled his mouth to hers. She swallowed his tongue like a starving woman, revelling in the feel of his hands which now palmed and squeezed her shaking bosom.

'Oh yes,' she said, 'squeeze my tits. Squeeze them hard! Pinch my nipples. God, I love it!'

She changed the rhythm, grinding her pelvis into his stomach, pressing her mound against his as she cradled his thick tool deep inside her. He knew what she wanted and dropped his hands from her chest, sliding them under her rucked-up skirt. One roved to the front and he wriggled a finger down into her pubic bush to stroke her clit. The other pried between the firm globes of her buttocks to tickle the puckered aperture of her anus.

'OHH!' she howled and bucked up and down in a small orgasm that served only to increase her need.

'You like that?' he said.

'Oh yes, Mario. Fuck me. Fuck me harder. Stick your finger up my bum, you dirty bastard!'

She came again and then again, her cries of passion echoing off the white-tiled walls.

Suddenly he stood up, holding her arse in his big hands, and she clung to him, her legs scissored tight around his waist.

'What are you doing?' she moaned but the feeling of being suspended on his cock was fabulous and when he pinned her against the wall and began to ram in and out of her like a bull she almost fainted from the thrill of it.

He shot off inside her in a frenzy and she came again, quivering and flopping on his spurting staff like a rag doll.

'I think I love you,' whispered Mario as they slithered

Lust at Large

down the wall and slumped into a heap on the floor.

Fliss said nothing, she just lifted her face to be kissed.

In the annexe, Chantal took the big bulb of Rodney's cock into her mouth for the third time that night. She wrapped the fingers of her right hand round the bottom of his shaft and began a gentle frigging motion. Her left hand cradled his furry balls, gently caressing them, rolling them back and forth, determined to make them yield their last vestiges of juice. Above her bobbing head she heard Rodney moan and she began her special sucking motion round the rim of his glans, pressing her soft plump lips into the meat of him with a technique she had honed to perfection.

For once Chantal was a happy woman. The evening had turned out to be very lucrative and she had a feeling the future would be even more profitable. Besides, she reflected as the cock in her mouth began to twitch and jerk in a familiar fashion, this was just the kind of work she liked best.

The penis in her mouth swelled and gushed, and Chantal swallowed every drop. She kept the spent member between her lips, enjoying its slow diminution, savouring the notion that she had her employer just where she wanted him. Finally she raised her head and regarded her handiwork. His once-swollen cock lay limp and drained, looking remarkably small in the half light of the bedroom. *How satisfying*, she thought. *Just let that blonde bitch Julia try and get something out of it tomorrow morning!*

Josie lay on her bed that night and stared up at the brocade canopy that covered the four-poster. She thought of the nude model she had seen earlier, sprawled across the same counterpane. She remembered the thresh of her legs as the dark mop of Clifford Rush's swept-back hair bobbed and jerked between those slim pink thighs. She imagined the photographer arranging her own limbs on the bed, spreading her legs wide and gazing close up at her open crotch. And then lowering his smiling face and tonguing her pussy until it glowed to his expert satisfaction.

She lifted her bottom from the coverlet and pushed down her leggings and knickers in one furious movement. Then, as the fantasy of her own photo session unwound in her head, she set about giving herself the kind of satisfaction she craved.

Next door, Robyn unpacked without thinking, her mind on other things. She was struck by images of the previous night, when her relationship with Alistair had finally ended in the threesome with the delectable but dangerous Mercedes. Already she realised she didn't care about losing Needle, he'd been no good for her. On the other hand, she wasn't sure about the Brazilian. And the sight of the blonde wanking on the bed while being photographed – well, she had to admit it had turned her on.

She walked naked into the bathroom and set about her regular cleansing ritual. She wasn't becoming a lesbian was she? Or was it just Mercedes? Josie was a remarkably pretty girl but she didn't fancy her, did she? Surely not.

She came out of the bathroom and turned down the cover on the bed. It was not as elaborate a piece of furniture as the four-poster but it was much bigger and more suitable for her long frame. The bedposts were carved mahogany and she examined them more closely. They looked like ornate wooden asparagus shoots. Or big, veiny cocks. Oh God, sex was everywhere here, it seemed.

A cry came through the walls. Robyn froze, her hand on the wooden knob of a bedpost. Then came another, softer this time but long drawn out. A cry of pleasure. And another. Josie was masturbating, there was no doubt about it.

Robyn listened closely, ashamed of herself but, nevertheless, bewitched by the gurgles of excitement. She realised her hand was caressing the wooden bulb in her grasp. It was warm and smooth, like a cock. God, how she wanted one inside her.

Josie squealed loudly and there came the rhythmic thumping of the bed. *She sure knows how to give herself a good time*, thought Robyn as, without ever consciously deciding to do so, she swung one long leg over the angle of the bed and lowered her pouting cunt over the bedpost.

She was so wet, it slid straight up.

In a small tent half a mile from The Blisswood Spa Hotel, Gavin Bird turned over in his sleep, images of silken-breasted warm-thighed nymphs spinning through his head. If he had known his fiancée and the reporter from the *Daily Rabbit* who had turned him into a national laughing-stock were on his trail he would have fled for the hills. As it was, he dreamed his sexy dreams in blissful ignorance, his erection burning a hole in his sleeping bag.

25

On the motorway, driving north, Monk laid down the law to Stephen Fantail.

'Son, this is going to be the hardest police work you've ever done. We're on our way to a renowned beauty spot in the height of summer to try and bring to book the most notorious criminal in Great Britain. She's a young woman of remarkable physical beauty whose most dangerous asset is a bosom she uses like a weapon. Our task is to uncover this lethal pair of breasts. They are approximately 38D and may or may not be decorated with a stick-on skin transfer of a rare butterfly. What's more, according to my information, this place is packed with nubile beauties with large chests. Do you think you can handle it?'

Monk's tone was heavily ironic but this was lost on Stephen. 'Yes, sir,' he gulped, concentrating hard on the road, determined not to let his misgivings show. For Stephen had considerable misgivings relating to the task in hand. It wasn't that girls were not his cup of tea, quite the contrary. Sometimes it seemed that thoughts of golden-limbed lovelies dominated his every waking thought. But Stephen had a secret – he was painfully shy with women. He was also a virgin.

'The hell of it is,' continued Monk, 'we can't even stay at the pub. Because of that reporter woman I feel duty bound to patronise The Blisswood Spa Hotel. We're just going to have to put up with five-star luxury, I'm sorry to say.'

Stephen missed the unusual sight of Archie Monk grinning from ear to ear because at that moment a caravan lurched without warning into the middle lane and he had

Lust at Large

to stamp on the brake to avoid it.

'That was close,' he muttered. But the reason his knuckles were white and his brow beaded with sweat was the thought of confronting the shadowy images on his blown-up photographs in the flesh. How he would ever summon the nerve to tackle the Topless Raider he could not imagine. His face would flush, his palms would sweat, his tongue would tie and he would quail before her, he knew it – it had happened before and those women had been pale shadows when measured against the glory of Bra-less Brenda. Compared to the ordeal that lay ahead, a motorway pile-up might just be preferable.

When they arrived at the hotel Stephen's worst fears were instantly confirmed.

The reception area was grand and intimidating. The mahogany counter gleamed and the glossy magazines on the occasional tables were fanned out in millimetre-perfect regularity. The cushions on the Regency-striped sofas were plumped to perfection, defying anyone to sit on them. These things dismayed Stephen, making him conscious that, out of uniform, he was nothing but an unkempt and unsophisticated oaf from Cricklewood. Posh surroundings and beautiful women – these were the things in life that unsettled Stephen Fantail the most.

They didn't seem to bother Archie Monk though, quite the contrary. He appeared unimpressed by the blue-eyed vision in a pink suit who booked them in. Stephen thought she was possibly the most gorgeous woman he had ever seen face to face but Monk muttered, 'Time to go to work I suppose,' and squinted down the front of her blouse as she leaned forward to enter their names.

At that moment a noisy group of people descending the staircase attracted their attention. A tall young man in a suit and tie began issuing loud instructions to two workmen as they set about stringing up a banner from the first-floor landing. A small dark-haired woman in a sunshine yellow jacket buzzed around making unnecessary suggestions in a French accent. Stephen stared at her open-mouthed, for the jacket scarcely reached to the tops of her thighs which were encased in black leggings. Could it be that she had left off her skirt by mistake?

Completing the party were two identical blonde girls and a man with a shock of swept-back dark hair and a camera around his neck. The blondes were tall, their hair piled high on their heads in an elaborate coiffure which displayed their long slender necks to advantage. Both wore silk wraps of peach and for a moment Stephen wondered if they were guests who had got lost on the way to the bathroom.

'What the hell do you think you are doing, Rodney?' said the vision in pink behind the desk, her pretty face now crumpled in a scowl.

'It's for the conference, Julia,' said the man in a suit. 'Chantal is helping me organise a special welcome for Gordon Garter and his team.'

The workmen had finished arranging the banner and it now hung down above the reception desk. Julia raised her eyes and read:

BLISSWOOD SPA HOTEL WELCOMES
LOUCHE LINGERIE!

A squeak of horror issued from her lips. 'What does this mean? What's Louche Lingerie?'

'Didn't I mention it? It's a Gartertex subsidiary line they are featuring at the conference. They are discussing their new collection.'

'But what *is* it, Rodney?' wailed Julia. 'It sounds disgusting.'

'Ah well, my darling—' and here Rodney included Monk and Stephen in the exchange by grinning playfully at them all '— you'll just have to wait and see.'

'They're here, Rodney,' cried the Frenchwoman who was now keeping watch at the door and, taking that as their cue, the two blondes slipped the wraps from their slim shoulders.

The physical impact of scarlet stretch lace on golden limbs, of pink silk stockings on legs that went on forever, of black chiffon edging the contours of dimpled cleavage hit Stephen like a blow to the stomach. The effect on Julia was almost as dramatic.

'Melanie, Mercy – what the hell do you think you're doing!' she screeched.

'Keep your hair on, Jay,' said one blonde.

'It's all in a good cause,' said the other.

'This is ghastly,' cried Julia. 'Put your clothes on at once! I'm so sorry, gentlemen,' she said to Monk and Stephen. 'Please don't judge us by these events, we're not like this at all. Rodney, stop this immediately!'

'Be quiet, you silly bitch,' hissed the Frenchwoman, 'they are here,' and she held the door open.

In strode a man who seemed to fill the doorway. He must have been six and a half foot tall and about as wide. He wore pin-striped trousers and yellow braces and carried his jacket over his shoulder. His face was red and jowly and tufts of hair bristled in his nostrils. Vertical lines punctuated the bridge of his nose, as if his expression was usually one of displeasure, but at present his grin was broad and his little blue eyes gleamed with pleasure.

And no wonder, for the blonde girls were busily kissing his cheeks, one on each side, standing on tiptoe to reach his face, pressing their scantily clad flesh into his bulk.

Lights flashed as Rodney strode forward to grasp a meaty hand; the photographer was at work capturing the moment.

'Welcome, GG,' cried Rodney. 'What do you think of our little reception?'

The big man barked out a laugh and punched Rodney on the arm. Stephen winced in sympathy but Rodney bore it with a smile.

'You don't miss a trick, do you, Holmdale?' said the newcomer. 'There's more of the salesman in you than there ever was in your old man. The sign's good and the fillies are even better – though I'm not sure about the togs they're wearing.'

He swivelled one of the girls round and thrust a huge hand into the top of her French knickers. 'Ooh,' she squealed but had the presence of mind to thrust her buttocks against the intruding paw and grin over her shoulder.

At that moment, however, Gordon Garter was not interested in her body.

'I thought so,' he said, 'made by one of our competitors.

Inferior materials, lacklustre design, not a patch on our stuff. Don't worry, my girl, we'll fix you up in some clobber that will really do you justice, won't we, lads?'

'You bet,' came a loud voice from behind him, echoed by other cries of assent. A group of besuited men, clutching square black cases and other luggage, had followed their leader into the hotel and were now asserting their corporate solidarity. The Gartertex team had arrived.

The small Frenchwoman now insinuated herself into the spotlight and Rodney set about introducing her. He urged the clothing manufacturer to consider Chantal Bellefesses as his personal liaison officer during his stay.

Gordon Garter loomed almost a foot and half above the French girl but she still insisted on greeting him in the Gallic fashion, with a kiss on both cheeks. Then, with her small white hands on his gigantic shoulders, she pressed the scarlet plum of her mouth to his and held it there for a moment.

Stephen was not the only one to note the flash of surprise that sent Garter's bushy eyebrows arching up his brow. He drew the same conclusion as Julia who, standing directly behind him, exclaimed under her breath, 'Good God, the little tart has got her tongue in his mouth!'

26

Josie and Robyn had enjoyed their morning. Though they had not got far in their search for Gavin, they had savoured a long lie-in, taken a leisurely breakfast and then strolled the streets of the village in the morning sunshine. It had been delightful.

'I just love this country air,' said Robyn as they stood on the arched stone bridge over the Bliss and contemplated the view across a lush meadow to a fringe of trees. She took a deep breath and exhaled slowly. 'This is probably the healthiest morning I've had in years. I haven't even had a cigarette.'

'Don't,' said Josie as Robyn, inspired by the thought, reached for her handbag. 'Come and have a drink instead. We could ask in that pub over there about Gavin.'

Robyn thought the landlord of The Cow and Kisses was a knockout. He had morning-blue eyes and thick sandy hair and, as he pulled Josie a pint of Spigots Special, she marvelled at the fine blonde hairs on his bronzed forearm.

'Do you let out rooms?' she asked.

He took a fresh lemon and put a slice in her gin and tonic before replying.

'Are you two ladies looking for a bed then?' he asked.

'Not for us,' said Josie, 'we're looking for a friend. We thought he might be staying here.'

'Oh,' he considered this information, leaning forward on the bar so his face was close to Robyn's. 'As it happens, I do have a few rooms to let out but I'm most particular who I let 'em to. And I won't let 'em to men.'

'Why not?' said Robyn.

He grinned and his eyes twinkled. 'Because I prefer the

ladies. And since the wife ran off with a paying guest three years ago I reckon I can please myself.'

'He's a bit of all right,' said Josie as they sat outside on a wooden bench and enjoyed another round in the sunshine. 'I wouldn't mind an hour in the snug with him one chilly night.' The Spigots had gone straight to her head and she didn't care. 'It was you he fancied though,' she added.

'What?'

'Go on, you know he did. He was giving you the glad eye while he was talking about his beds to let.'

Robyn was about to protest further when a shadow fell across their table. It was the landlord himself.

'Look,' he said, 'are you American?'

'Yes,' Robyn replied, struck by the way even a cheap denim shirt and worn jeans could look good on the right man.

'I had an American woman staying here recently and she left some stuff behind. Would you like to come and look at it?'

'Well . . .'

'It's no use to me. Come on.' And he turned back into the bar.

If it hadn't been for Josie, Robyn would have remained where she was.

'Go on, Robyn, here's your chance.'

'What? You must be joking.'

'Go on. You know you fancy him.'

'That's true.'

'Go on, then.'

'Only if you come too.'

The landlord was waiting for them, the hinged end of the counter raised to allow them through. Robyn and Josie managed to avoid meeting the smirking gaze of the boy behind the bar as they followed the man up a narrow staircase. He led them along a corridor and through a door marked Private.

'These are my quarters,' he said, ushering them into a small room with flowered wallpaper and a bed with a candlewick counterpane. 'No one is allowed up here unless they're invited.'

'And do you invite many, Mr . . .?' asked Robyn as he pulled a small leather suitcase from beneath the bed.

'Ted, please. No, I don't. In fact nobody since, er—'

'Since Charlotte Evans Peabody of Round Lake Hollow, Chicago, Illinois?' suggested Josie, reading from the luggage label on the case.

'Yes.' His face lit up. 'Do you know her?' He addressed this question to Robyn.

'Well, no.'

'I just thought, since you were American, that you might . . .'

'It's a big country, Ted, and I haven't been back in a while.'

'Ah,' he said. 'That explains it. Well, since you're here, maybe you could make use of some of these things.' And he flipped open the case and began to pull out a variety of female garments.

Josie giggled as Ted produced a bundle of flimsy underwear. He held up a brassiere that was no more than a wisp of material and turned to Robyn. 'Would this be about your size?' he asked.

Robyn was dumbfounded.

'Put it on, Robyn,' said Josie.

'Don't be ridiculous. Anyway, I never wear a bra.'

This fact was suddenly obvious to everyone in the room. Even Robyn lowered her eyes to her own chest. Beneath the thin top her nipples thrust as big as acorns against the cotton.

'How about this then?' said Ted, producing a cherry-coloured miniskirt about the depth of a curtain pelmet.

'Ooh, that looks good,' said Josie. 'You'd look fabulous in that.'

Ted offered it to Robyn who took it without thinking and held against her pelvis over her navy blue trousers.

'Go on, Robyn, try it on,' said Josie.

Robyn shot her a look of suspicion. She had the feeling she was being set up. She also had the feeling that she wanted to show off her body in front of this gorgeous man and the hell with the consequences.

'OK,' she said and undid her belt. Her trousers fell to

Lust at Large

her ankles in a whisper of silk and her stomach flipped. She had forgotten that her white panties were almost transparent. Her thick black pubic bush showed through the material as clearly as if she were wearing nothing at all. Ted and Josie – he standing and she sitting on the bed – stared hard at Robyn's legs as she hurried to pull the tiny skirt up her long thighs.

There was silence in the small room.

'So,' said Robyn and spun round to give them the full effect, 'what do you think?'

'Fantastic,' muttered Ted, his voice thick.

'I wish I had legs like yours,' said Josie.

Ted was scrabbling through the case, his hands shaking. 'Put these on next,' he said, holding out a black suspender belt and stockings.

'OK,' said Robyn but Josie stopped her.

'If he's so keen he can put them on you himself.'

Robyn opened her mouth to protest and then shut it again.

'Please,' said Ted, falling to his knees in front of Robyn. His eyes were great pools of blue. She knew she shouldn't but she felt like diving in.

'I think you should take her knickers off first, Ted,' said Josie, 'they don't match.'

Robyn giggled and then said sternly, 'OK but I'm not having him look straight up my pussy. You'll have to blindfold him, Josie.'

From the look on Ted's face it was as if they had offered him the Holy Grail. 'As you wish,' he said.

Josie produced a scarf from the case and knotted it round his eyes. Then he reached out with his hands to locate Robyn's legs and shuffled forward on his knees until his face was just a couple of inches from her crotch.

Though his hands were large and calloused, they were gentle. Robyn shivered as they slid up the backs of her thighs, under the tiny skirt and over the moons of her clenched buttocks to the waistband of her panties. He did it slowly, caressing the flesh as he went, savouring the feel of her. Already she had the gnawing pangs of desire in the pit of her stomach and her cunt was weeping, she knew.

When he pulled her knickers down, over her hips and arse cheeks and down the smooth slopes of her thighs, they snagged in the crevice of her crotch. He freed the wet cotton with his fingers, peeling the material from her moist folds. Robyn put a hand to her mouth and bit on the ball of her thumb to prevent herself crying out.

When she lifted her feet to release the fallen garment she had to steady herself on his shoulders. She let her hands rest there, feeling the bands of muscle beneath her fingers.

Now he had the suspender belt in his hands and he pushed the skirt to her waist to clip it on. As he lifted the material upwards, the smell of her excitement filled the room. He drank it in, his nose almost buried in her pussy hairs as he fastened the garment around her hips.

'I love the smell of a woman on heat,' he said. 'It's the odour of life. It's like the scent of baking bread or newly cut grass or fresh-brewed beer. The smell of ripe cunt. That's what a man lives for. Nature's perfume.'

'He's a poet,' said Josie, who was watching with a pounding heart.

'I'm a connoisseur of women,' said Ted, leaning forward to bury his nose in Robyn's bush, 'and I'm going to fuck you both senseless before you leave this room.'

'I can't wait,' said Josie, sliding a hand inside her blouse to roll a thick nipple between her fingers.

Robyn said nothing intelligible, she just grasped Ted by the hair and pulled his open mouth to her cunt.

27

'Where's that girl?' barked Gordon Garter almost the moment his entourage had left his sitting-room. Only one attendant remained, a lanky lad with thick spectacles who tugged nervously at the tight collar of his shirt. He wished he could make himself scarce for a moment like everybody else and find a cool beer. There wasn't much chance of that, however. He was Gordon Garter's son.

'Well, Graham? Don't just stand there like a gormless dipstick, go and find her at once.'

'Which girl, dad? There were lots downstairs.'

Garter sighed in exasperation. 'Don't be dense, lad. That French bit, the one that Rodney's handed over for my personal use.'

'Chantal. The hotel liaison officer.'

Garter gave vent to a filthy cackle. 'That's the one. I'm going to enjoy liaising with her. Get her up here.'

Graham did not have to look far. Chantal was already at the door of the suite having effected a quick change. She wore a floral summer frock which left her arms bare and was fastened down the back with large white buttons.

Chantal presented herself with a little curtsey and a demure smile as she asked, 'Is everything to your satisfaction, Mr Garter?'

'So far I'm moderately content, lass.' He eased his vast bulk further into the cushions of the chesterfield and looked her up and down.

'A few ground rules, my dear. I drink strong tea with three sugars, I do not observe no-smoking restrictions and you may call me GG or Mr Garter or Fatso but you must never call me Gordon. Only my dear departed Ethel—' and

Lust at Large

here he indicated a framed photograph of a square-jawed frump on the table by the window '—referred to me that way. By which a sharp little filly like you will have observed that I am a family man. This shambling oik here is proof of that. He's my son, Graham.'

Chantal favoured Graham with a dazzling smile.

'Unfortunately, Graham is my only son and it is about time he learned about the family business before his obese old man drops dead.' He smiled but, Chantal was quick to notice, his son did not. 'Which longed-for event would doubtless please many, including my devoted offspring, but would also doom the Gartertex empire to takeover by one of my many rapacious competitors. And so Graham has been removed from his self-indulgent studies at university and is by my side, observing my every moment so he can LEARN HOW TO RUN THE FUCKING BUSINESS!'

Chantal took an involuntary step backwards as Garter's benign expression turned to rage and he lurched forward and roared at Graham. Behind his glasses the lad's eyes blinked but otherwise his expression did not change. Garter slumped back on the sofa, his face puce. After such exertion he appeared to have a little difficulty breathing. He waved away the glass of water Chantal poured for him from the carafe on the table.

'Take that stuff away,' he said, mopping his eyes. 'I only drink water if it's got whisky in it, make a note of it. Now, where was I?'

'You were saying that I was on a watching brief, father, observing how you run the business,' said Graham.

'Right. So you, my little French maid, are to ignore this gangling idiot completely. He's invisible unless I say so, got it?'

'Yes, sir,' said Chantal.

'And there's one other thing you should know before we get down to business. When it comes to brass, I'm as tight as a nun's twat.'

Chantal was puzzled. Garter expanded on his theme with relish.

'Tight. Mean. Slow to put my hand in my pocket. I shall enjoy all the hospitality you have to offer and when I leave

Lust at Large

I'll pay the bill to the last farthing. No extras, no service charges, no tips. That's how I run my business and that's how I am. You can tell that to Rodney Holmdale.'

He smiled at her with considerable self-satisfaction and Chantal smiled back while she digested this information. Her chances of wringing a large bonus out of Garter as well as Rodney were obviously under threat. However, she was not down-hearted. Gordon Garter presented a challenge that she would overcome. From her observation he was nothing more than a peasant and she knew how to deal with them – she came from peasant stock herself. Already she was formulating a plan.

'Now that we understand one another,' continued Garter, 'why don't you take your dress off.'

'But GG—' she feigned surprise '—I don't see what relevance this has to—'

'Tut, tut, girl, don't worry. This is entirely professional and above board. I'm in the underwear business. I want to see yours.'

'Oh.' She tittered prettily. 'There's just one problem.'

'Yes? Spit it out.'

'I am not wearing any.'

Garter's jaw dropped.

'But if you'd like to look at my body that's no problem. Perhaps your son would give me a hand. I find these buttons very difficult.' And she presented her back to Graham whose face flushed beet red.

'Go on then, son,' shouted Garter. 'Help her off with her kit. I think I'm going to enjoy this.'

And so he did, what red-blooded male wouldn't when confronted by a curvaceous French girl with the face of an angel, the body of a pocket Venus and – it was obvious from her demeanour – no shame at all?

Graham's hands shook as he eased the soft material from the pale and dimpled shoulders. The dress fell to the floor in a flutter, exposing an exquisite rear view from slender neck to milky buttocks to taut calves and tiny feet with petal-pink polish on the toenails. He had never been this close to such naked perfection before.

His father's viewpoint was just as thrilling, more so

maybe. Apart from the high swollen breasts, the nipples like brown thimbles against the porcelain whiteness of her flesh, the dome of her belly curving into a knot of short curly hair at the base and the elegant sweep of her rounded thighs – apart from these obvious things that anybody would appreciate, there was the message in those big black eyes. Gordon Garter had had women from Hong Kong to Hartlepool and he knew a carnal challenge when he saw one. Chantal's expression said, 'I'll do whatever you want. I am unshockable. Are you still up to it?' Garter fully intended to be up to it, he had been as stiff as a poker since she had walked into the room.

'Beautiful,' he said, 'very lovely. It will be a privilege to clothe you in Louche Lingerie's new collection, won't it, Graham?'

But Graham could not talk. He was struck dumb by the sight of the nude Chantal pirouetting before his father, allowing him to ravish every inch of her with his beady eyes. Or maybe not *every* inch, for she held her hands demurely over her mound of Venus.

'And is that all you want from me, Mr Garter? Just to dress me up in peephole bras and polyester peignoirs?'

Garter's face flushed with anger but before he could protest Chantal cut him off.

'My instructions were to obey your every whim. To make each nook and cranny of my body available for your use. Don't you want to stroke my breasts and pinch my nipples? To smack my bottom and come in my face and stick your cock in my pussy? Wouldn't you like to do those things?'

From Gordon Garter's throat came a strangled mew of lust but no words. For once the wind had been taken from his sails.

Chantal folded herself elegantly onto the large sofa at the opposite end from Garter. She laid one foot on top of his meaty thigh and kept the other on the ground, spreading her firm thighs and thrusting her crotch towards her goggle-eyed audience.

A close-cropped moustache of black hair adorned the head of her slit but from the hood of her clitoris down the length of her crack she was completely hairless. The

Lust at Large

lips were long and succulent, a pretty fringe of furled flesh, madder in hue. And when she probed between them, opening the petals of her cunt to their disbelieving gaze, they could see the coral-pink flesh inside pooling with juice.

She pushed a finger up into herself and both men watched in awe as the mouth of her vagina closed around it.

'You see, GG, you are not the only one who is tight. I'm told I am very tight on the penis of a lover. Wouldn't you like to find out? Or would you prefer to fuck my mouth? I adore to suck a man's cock.'

Gordon Garter grunted, his mind seduced by the prospect of carnal delights with this extraordinary French girl.

'There's just one orifice you cannot have,' continued Chantal, lifting both legs so that her knees were pressed to her chest. It was an obscene posture but one that presented her bottom at its most uncompromising. The full white cheeks were spread wide and no mysteries remained in the valley between.

'See here,' she said as dispassionately as if she were showing them an architectural drawing. 'This is my special place, *mon trou secret*, my arsehole, I believe you say. It is pretty, is it not?'

They did not disagree. She circled the puckered whirl of flesh with the finger she had inserted in her vagina, highlighting it with a glistening trail of juice. She probed with a long pink nail and then sunk her finger in to the first joint.

'Ooh, that makes me feel so naughty,' she said. 'You can fuck me however you like, GG, but you cannot fuck me up my arse. I am saving my bottom for the man I marry.'

'Then I'll just have to make do with the rest of you,' cried Garter, picking her off the sofa as if she were made of feathers.

He made for the bedroom with his nubile burden while, heart pounding and palms sweating, Garter Junior looked on in disbelief.

'Is this a business meeting?' he called after his retreating father. 'What about my watching brief?'

By way of an answer the bedroom door slammed in his disappointed face.

28

Ted's massive penis slid into Robyn's pussy as sweetly as a key into a lock.

'Ooh,' she squealed as the column of flesh filled her up and the mat of his belly hairs covered the soft skin of her loins. She hadn't felt so thoroughly plugged since . . . since – she couldn't think for a moment such was the surprise and thrill of what he was doing. Then it all came back to her and she turned her head away and met the rapt gaze of Josie sitting on the bed by her side. Now she remembered exactly when she had felt like this before and a bubble of merriment surfaced in her throat which she had to stifle because she didn't want to offend Ted.

She had just turned seventeen and had lost her cherry to her first real boyfriend, Brian. And she'd been disappointed. 'Seventeen years of build-up,' she'd said to her best friend Maxine, 'and what a let-down. He slobbers over my neck and goes "Ugh, ugh, ugh" into my ear while he jumps all over me. Then he's stretched out on his back panting like he's done a marathon and I've got ick running down my legs. It's not worth waiting seventeen minutes for that, let alone seventeen years.'

Maxine had been sympathetic and had broken into her dad's liquor cabinet. She'd then confided some real intimate details of her new relationship with Scott Wingo, who was a school hero because he was on the football team. And after three hefty bourbon and cokes she'd gone to the kitchen and brought back a cucumber which, Maxine said, bore more than a passing resemblance to the mighty Wingo wang.

Robyn remembered all this in an instant as Ted lowered

Lust at Large

his head to nuzzle a perky nipple. She remembered the chill of the cucumber on the flesh of her upper thigh and the way Maxine had looked at her, all wicked and sly, as she coated the thick green skin with cream. But most of all she remembered how it felt sliding up her cunt, stretching her wide, touching her in places she didn't know she had. She'd looked down in wonder at her spread pussy mouth as it gorged on the glistening green monster and listened to Maxine's exclamations of wonder that she could take so much. And she recalled the orgasm she had had, her first real filled-up-pussy orgasm, as her naughty friend had thrust and twisted the great green limb within her and she herself had wanked her pink and swollen clitty in a drunken frenzy.

Robyn found herself laughing as all this came back to her. Josie's eyes were on her face and she too was laughing. And then Robyn's cries took on another note as Ted really began to put it to her. She was moaning now and giving little high-pitched squeals, digging her fingernails into the meat of his broad back. He grunted as she pierced the skin but she didn't care and she dug in harder as the first wave washed over her.

He took his prick all the way back now and slammed it in, again and again, powering the big tool into her as if he wanted to skewer her to the mattress.

'Oh God!' she wailed and the long-buried memory of her session with Maxine, the intensity of this big stranger's passion as he rode between her thighs and the thought of Josie watching her every twitch and wriggle – all these things combined and she was swept into an orgasm that, for a moment, robbed her of her senses.

When she recovered she found her head pillowed on Ted's broad furry chest, which rose and fell in the aftermath of his exertions. Across his belly lolled his penis, still half hard and sticky with juice. She reached for it and squeezed gently.

'Mmm,' she murmured, 'it feels like you're not finished.'

'He's not,' said Josie, peeling her T-shirt over her head, 'but you are.' Her pretty pink nipples were puckered with excitement and her breasts bobbed as she leant over to replace Robyn's hand with her own. 'It's my turn now.'

On the hillside opposite The Cow and Kisses, the birdwatcher cursed as his binoculars fogged up once again. He quickly wiped the lens and clapped the eyepiece to his brow. His hands were shaking as he readjusted the focus.

Stephen Fantail was a keen student of the natural world but he had never before seen anything to match his observations of life in Blisswood. After he and Monk had lunched on a sandwich in the hotel bar, his superior had instructed him to familiarise himself with the lie of the land. 'Get out there and eyeball the birdies,' he had said, 'and I don't mean the feathered variety.'

Stephen had begun close to home, strolling out of the front of the hotel and across a field into a nearby fringe of trees. From there he had surveyed the hotel buildings, admiring the Georgian manor house that was the focal point of the complex. He squinted through his binoculars, trying to pick out his room and realising at the same moment that he couldn't possibly see it as it faced towards the swimming pool on the other side of the house. Nevertheless he looked along the line of first-floor windows, some thrown wide open, the curtains billowing in the breeze. It was then he saw the first naked woman.

She leapt into the frame of his vision, slipping between the window and the curtain, obviously intending to hide herself from whoever was in the room. In doing so she revealed a delicious swoop of naked back and two plump white buttocks that bulged delightfully as she pressed them against the sill. She was frozen there for a second and Stephen marvelled at the sweetness of her curves and prayed for her to turn around so he could commit her face and other salient points to memory. This, after all, was the purpose of his mission.

Then came a flurry in the curtains as a pair of masculine arms encircled both material and woman. A man's head appeared and buried itself in the crook of her neck. There was a shriek of laughter – Stephen could hear it clearly across the field – and the woman lifted her hands to the man's head and twined her fingers in his long dark hair. They kissed, the open-mouthed snog of two lovers hungry for each other, and under her raised arm Stephen could clearly see the swollen white globe of a full breast.

The clinch came to an end and both disappeared into the room, leaving Stephen breathless and unsatisfied. Though her hair was dark and curly Stephen knew that was not significant. This could be Bra-less Brenda – the glimpse of bosom from the side indicated that she was of the right proportions. He had to see more.

Stephen worked his way back through the trees to the point where they were closer to the building. This gave him a better angle, too. If only he could get higher he could see right into the room. And he could get higher by climbing into the branches of the old oak that faced the building. Stephen was good at this kind of thing. He was up the tree in a flash.

Inside, there was action of the kind that set his heart pounding. The woman still had her back to him; the man was sitting on the bed facing the window and she was on his lap, her legs around his waist, her arms around his neck, her mouth glued to his. But it was the position of his hands, one on each white buttock, that gave Stephen the shivers. The man kneaded, fondled and spread the creamy flesh in his grasp and she writhed under his touch. Then Stephen realised, as she rose higher and then slumped back, that she was impaled on his lap. She was sitting on his cock, jiggling up and down – good God, they were doing it right in front of him!

Stephen reflected that this undercover police work provided a special kind of challenge. When he'd joined the force no one had warned him that one day he'd be perched up a tree peering through sweaty binoculars trying to see a woman's breasts as she bounced on a man's prick.

They were at it for a long time in that position and Stephen had no choice but to stay and watch. It was hell but it was also instructive. He hadn't realised that a woman could like it so much. For she did like it, he could tell. She moaned and yelled and threw her head back and tossed it from side to side, the brown curls dancing on her creamy

Lust at Large

shoulders. The man had lowered his head out of sight and Stephen guessed he was licking and kissing and sucking the breasts that Stephen was so anxious to observe – for professional reasons of course.

An astonishing thought popped into the young policeman's brain – if he seduced the woman himself then he could see those breasts at first hand, right up close!

The notion was so disturbing that the binoculars slid down his sweaty nose and it took a few seconds for him to rearrange them. When he did so the scene had changed. The man and woman were still there but matters had obviusly come to a conclusion. He lay stretched out on the bed and she sprawled in a heap at his feet. Stephen was mesmerised by the wild profusion of black hair in the man's groin and the bulging, glistening genitals that hung in the fork of his thighs. He fancied he could see the steam rise.

Then the woman sat up and, for the first time, turned towards the window. She reached for something just out of sight and Stephen sucked in his breath as her breasts swung into clear view. Was this – could this be – the pair all England sought?

It was hard to say. Shapely and delectable as they were, thrilling though it would be, Stephen knew, to have them bounce against your chest as she rode your cock, there was no telling from this distance whether these were the fabled tits of Bra-less Brenda. Stephen made a careful note of the position of the window. This woman merited further investigation.

She was only the first naked female of the afternoon. In the window next door but one Stephen observed another. This girl was curvy but small, white-fleshed and exquisite, and displayed the grace of a ballet dancer as she twisted and turned on top of a fat man lying on the bed. Stephen had been unable to tear his eyes away even though he soon realised who this was and, indeed, the identity of the prone party whose unworthy body was being so honoured. This was the lovely French girl called Chantal whose warmth of welcome Stephen had already witnessed earlier in the hotel lobby. And the prone party, of course, was the fat man whom she had welcomed.

Lust at Large

Chantal could not be the Topless Raider, Stephen had no doubt. For a start she wasn't tall enough, the breathtaking O of her mouth was the wrong shape and her high saucer-curved breasts with the chocolate-brown nipples didn't correspond to the photos. Nevertheless Stephen remained where he was, fixed to his uncomfortable perch, unable to tear his eyes from every adorable wriggle and lewd caress of the shameless French girl as she pleasured the mountain of gross and hairy male flesh beneath her. It was as well to be absolutely certain, after all.

Now, some thirty minutes after the Frenchwoman's magnificent exhibition had come to an end, Stephen was sitting on an outcrop of rock on the other side of the river from The Cow and Kisses on a level with the bedroom window. Though the window was not as large as those of the hotel, the action taking place on the bed was clearly visible to the goggle-eyed policeman. There were two women and a man. The tall woman with spectacular legs had just been comprehensively poked by the man and now the smaller woman was peeling off her clothes.

Neither of them were Bra-less Brenda, that much was obvious, but Stephen was resigned to that. He knew police work was long and arduous. Many suspects would fall under the microscope before a big case like this one was sewn up. What a thought! Before this investigation was over he might see thousands of breasts jiggling and bouncing, thousands of pert little nipples twitching in the air, thousands of legs spread to receive thousands of thrusting twitching pulsating cocks!

Just look at that girl now, he said to himself. *She's got it in her mouth. She's got one hand under his balls and the other feeding his shaft into her mouth. Look at the way her head bobs and the way she sucks it all down! And now it's sticking up big and red in her hands and she's grinning at him – probably begging him to shove it up her pussy and make her come.*

'Oh God,' groaned Stephen out loud, scrabbling in his fly with one hand to liberate his aching cock, the internal monologue continuing to run through his head as he drank in the lewd scene before him.

Now she's climbing on top of it, he's making her do all the work. It's so big it won't go in. Good Lord, the other woman's helping her, she's holding it up and pushing the head into her slot. That's obscene! Oh, they've managed it. Just look at it go in! That must feel like heaven. Ooh, she's sitting on it, she's swallowed it all in her cunt and now she's wiggling around with it right up her. She likes it. Look at her talking to the other woman while she does it. For goodness sake, the tall one is playing with herself while she watches! Look at her fingers go in and out. Now she's put the man's fingers there. Fancy doing that — aren't they embarrassed? I couldn't do that.

Oh yes, I could. I could do all of it. I could do it with the short one or the tall one. I could do it with that first one with the big tits or the French one. I could do it with any of them. Oh Lord, please let me do it with one of them!

And as Robyn approached orgasm on Ted's fingers and Josie jerked in ecstasy on his loins, the sperm shot from Stephen's lonely cock and splattered onto the dusty ground.

29

Clifford Rush was happiest when he was working. Considering that his work involved luxurious locations and beautiful women dressed in very little this cannot be considered surprising. His ideal working situation also involved a third ingredient, namely, a *deal*. Large fees and under-the-counter favours could be taken for granted, of course, but a little something extra, another *angle*, made life perfect. And at the moment life for him at The Blisswood Spa Hotel was indeed perfect.

To the dismay of some of the guests, he had commandeered the swimming pool which glistened, blue and inviting, in the afternoon sunshine. He had disarmed the disgruntled swimmers, however, by persuading the women to pose for some jokey shots and allowing the men to spectate while his models cavorted for the camera. He had also arranged for a few drinks to be provided. Quite a few drinks in fact, courtesy of the hotel, not that Rodney would complain. 'After all,' he said to one buxom German tourist as he emptied a bottle of fizz into her glass, 'we need a few empties as props.'

Right now one of Rodney's girls, a fantastic blonde called Melanie or Mercy (one of the twins – he couldn't tell them apart), was floating topless on a red and yellow sunbed. She wore wrapround green shades and held a champagne flute in one hand. Her hair was wet, slicked back off her forehead and droplets of moisture glistened on the slopes of her full and fabulous breasts. Cliff wanted to eat her and reflected that he probably already had, last night, gobbling her on the four-poster just as those dishy females turned up. Of course, it could have been her sister on the bed, he wasn't sure and he didn't care. It made this shot all the more exciting not to know whether he'd had the model yet or not.

And the *angle* that added spice to all this was that he was doing five jobs at once, all of which would be very profitable. There was the brochure for Rodney, of course, plus an undercover series of shots for Rodney's personal use of, as Rodney put it, a 'raunchy' nature. There were also the photographs that Gordon Garter had asked him to take of the new Louche Lingerie collection. He'd be using Melanie/Mercy for those too, which made it easy. Then there was a calendar he was working on which featured top hotels throughout the country. And finally there was what he considered his serious work, for which the hotel and grounds provided a perfect location. The work in question was his private portfolio of erotic photographs, each a personal vision and, in his opinion, a work of art. 'Move over Helmut Newton and Robert Mapplethorpe,' he had once told Fliss, 'here comes Clifford Rush!'

The icing on the cake had come just that morning in bed when Fliss had looked up from her breakfast cup of coffee and said, 'Would you like to take photos of me fucking other guys?'

That had got his nose out of the newspaper all right. He'd stared at her with suspicion but it seemed she'd been sincere.

'I've been thinking, Cliff. I want to contribute to your real work. I want to give something of myself. And my tits and arse are all I've got to give – if you want them, that is. It doesn't have to be guys, of course, it's up to you, you're the artist. I just thought I'd let you know I'm not as inhibited as you think. I'll make it with girls if you prefer. I'm quite partial to a sniff of pussy – you didn't know that, did you?'

Cliff didn't but the idea of Fliss's ripe body in the arms of, say, the luscious blonde now in front of him had turned him on so much that he had abandoned breakfast and fucked Fliss amongst the jam and croissants there and then.

Now he turned to the matter in hand, adjusting the erection in his swimming trunks and not caring who noticed.

Lust at Large

In his line of work, a hard-on was simply a litmus test of creativity.

'I've got a great idea,' he said to the blonde. 'Take your bikini bottoms off, we'll put the champagne bottle between your legs instead. That'll blow Rodney's mind.'

There was a ripple of applause from the male spectators at this suggestion and a buzz of disapproval from some of the women. Nobody left the poolside, however.

Clifford waded out to the girl and helped her rearrange herself. It was no easy matter to remove a bikini bottom while afloat and the girl didn't try, she let Cliff do all the hard work. When he had finally slipped the scrap of material from beneath her he positioned the champagne bottle in her crotch, its broad base obscuring the blonde thatch of her pussy hair, the neck pointing towards her feet.

'Oh,' said the girl, 'don't you want it up the other way? Then you could stick the neck up my twat.'

Sometimes women amazed him. They had dirtier minds than men, in his opinion. She was right, of course. It would be a great shot for Rodney's naughty file even if it didn't make it into his personal portfolio. And if he turned the bottle round so the label showed he might even do a deal with the champagne distributor.

'You're a genius, darling,' he said to the floating woman. 'Why don't you open your legs?'

She obeyed without question. Life was perfect. No doubt about it.

30

Rodney made Julia walk ahead of him up the winding footpath to the upper pasture where the horses were grazing. He loved the rear view of a shapely woman in skintight riding trousers and few came more shapely than Julia. He knew for a fact that she wore not a stitch beneath her caramel-coloured jodhpur-style leggings. This was not the first time he had invited her to go riding.

As she strode ahead, her broad buttocks stretching the thin material at every step, she gave vent to a litany of complaint.

'Why didn't you tell me that you were planning a welcome ceremony for that ghastly Garter man? It makes me look such a fool in front of the staff. I am supposed to be the manager after all.'

She stopped to tackle a stile and Rodney observed her technique with admiration.

'You *are* the manager, Julia, and a very good one too. Nobody is trying to undermine your position.'

'Huh! You could have fooled me. That Frenchwoman is, for a start. To think you've actually promoted her, Rodney. She's rude and incompetent and downright bolshie.' She strode on up the gradually increasing gradient, her knee-high leather riding boots kicking up dust from the bone-hard ground.

'Why did you do it, Rodney? You should get rid of her, not make her responsible for our most important business client.'

She turned to face him, her cheeks pink with anger and effort, her chest rising and falling beneath her high-necked cream blouse, a stray strand of blonde hair escaping from her riding cap.

'You look gorgeous,' he said.

'Cut that out, you bastard, you're not going to fob me off.'

'You don't know how to take a compliment, Julia.'

'And she does, I suppose. That dirty little Frog will take anything that comes her way.'

'There you are, you've answered your own question. She's just the kind of girl to handle Gordon Garter. He'll be putty in her hands. Now give me a kiss.'

'Oh Rodney!' she cried in exasperation but she allowed herself to be pulled into his arms and her mouth opened to allow his tongue access. 'You're not . . . seeing her, are you, Rodney?'

'I see Chantal every day, darling, and so do you.'

'You know what I mean. You don't really fancy her, do you?'

'Well . . .' Rodney ran the edge of his thumb round the nipple of her left boob; her flesh felt hot and firm through the thin material. 'I must say she has a magnificent mouth, it's so full and lush. But not—' and here he dropped his other hand to fondle her rear '—as full and lush as your bottom.'

'Rodney!'

'So why don't we proceed with our perambulation, my dear? You carry on ahead of me and make sure you jiggle that pretty bum of yours as we go.'

She shot him a complicated look which encapsulated her mixed feelings about him and turned to resume her progress. Rodney grinned at her wiggling posterior, he knew just what she was thinking. In her eyes he was a manipulating, devious, handsome, irresistible swine. And she was spot on.

The path had now levelled out and ahead of them, at the end of an avenue of trees, stood a five-barred gate. It gave way onto a field and it was here that Rodney usually kept his horses.

'I don't see them,' said Julia as they approached the gate.

'You won't. I asked one of the lads to move them to the river paddock, it's cooler down there.'

'But we're here to go riding!'

'No, we're not.'

Lust at Large

'You mean you've dragged me all the way up here in my riding gear for nothing!'

'Not at all. Those jodhpurs do wonders for your arse and I promise you we're going to do lots of things now we're here. We're going to have some fun. Like last time.'

'No, Rodney.'

'Yes, Rodney, you mean. There's no point in protesting, Julia. We're going to do it my way. Just like we always do.'

'No,' she yelled at him, her face red with anger. 'No, no, NO!'

'OK, Julia, but I hope you remember this moment on the day the concrete-mixers begin to pave over your mother's precious donkey sanctuary.'

Her mouth opened and shut again without uttering a sound. Then, as her big blue eyes filled with tears, she began slowly to unbutton her blouse. She pulled its hem from her waistband, slid it from her shoulders and threw it in his face. For a moment the material blinded him, clinging to his features and ravishing his nostrils with the sweet smell of her. Then the silk shirt fluttered down into the dust and she stood before him naked to the waist, her wondrous breasts shaking with emotion. The tears in her eyes left snail tracks down her dusty cheeks.

'I hate you,' she said.

He smiled at her with unalloyed pleasure, his cock an iron bar in his breeches, the riding crop sweaty in his palm.

'Bend over the gate, Miss Jarvis,' he said, 'and take what's coming to you.'

Her heart thumping in anticipation, Julia did as she was told. Doubled over the gate, her feet on the bottom rung and her hands clasping the strut from the other side on a level with her knees, the semi-nude Julia Jarvis was a sight to rouse the dead. Her rump, suspended in the air and arched over in breathtaking fashion, filled out the tight jodhpurs like a balloon inflated to the point of bursting.

Rodney was on the point of coming already but he was determined to make the most of this delicious moment. He took a full minute to savour the sight of Julia's swollen arse offered up to him for his personal pleasure. The fact that it was offered under protest made it all the sweeter.

The whip made a satisfying Thwack! as it smacked into the caramel oval of her left buttock. Thwack! it went again, on her right cheek this time. As yet Julia had made no sound but Rodney knew it was just a matter of time. The whip whistled through the air and landed a full cut across both cheeks. And again. Whack! Whack! Oh what an incredible sight to see that magnificent bum dance and flinch!

Julia exhaled and noisily gasped in air, determined not to cry out. But Rodney was intent on making her do just that. Down came the whip again. And again. 'Oh,' she cried, 'OH!' and shimmied her buttocks before Rodney's delighted gaze.

Then she was off, yelling and moaning, her cries echoing around the hillside. Rodney slowed down his bum smacks, tantalising her with the delay between strikes, savouring the jerk and bounce of her hips under the lash.

When he judged that he had her nicely warmed up and could curtail his impatience no longer, he fell to his knees and pressed his face to her twitching rear. Ah, the glorious feel of her bountiful flesh beneath the stretched material of her riding trousers! He pressed his face hard into the pliant flesh of her twin moons and inhaled the sweet smell of her. It was glorious! The sun shone and the birds sang and the tanned arse of a beautiful woman jerked and throbbed against his face – to Rodney this was bliss.

With a growl he snagged a square of material between his teeth and bit down, jerking his head backwards. Julia gave a shriek as her trouser seat tore and then his fingers were in the rent, ripping the thin covering up the back seam, from crotch to waist.

The compressed flesh of her beautiful *derrière* was revealed through the torn cloth like the billowing cleavage of a Hollywood glamour queen. Rodney thrust his fingers into her exposed bum cleft and forced wide the breech, delving between her legs to explore the furry treasure of her pussy. As he had suspected, she was sopping wet.

'Oh God, Rodney, please don't!' she cried.

He laughed like a stage villain and ran his tongue the length of her bottom crack.

Lust at Large

'Oh please, please!' came the cry as he pushed his thumb deep into her pussy tunnel and began to strum her clit. She came at once, her arse cheeks twitching and shuddering in his face at the mercy of his licking, probing tongue. With deliberate care he wet the winking brown knot of her bumhole, jabbing the tip of his tongue into her circlet, making her jump and twitch further.

With the sound of her orgasmic howls still ringing in the trees, he reached for the crop and, without ceremony, inserted its stout wooden handle between her pussy lips.

'Oh God!' she yelled as she felt its thickness stretch her cunt and, 'Oh no!' as she felt something else, just as stout and stiff, pressing against the puckered whirl of her exposed arsehole.

'Oh yes!' cried Rodney in triumph as his big tool sank into the tight ring of her rectum. 'This is what you like, my darling. Don't pretend otherwise.'

'Oh please,' she yelled, 'please, please, PLEASE!'

'Please what?'

'Please fuck me! Fuck me hard! Harder, you swine! Fuck me harder!'

It was just as well, Rodney reflected later as they walked back, that he had moved the horses. They could have been badly frightened at the sight of two half-naked humans buggering and fucking on top of a five-barred gate and screaming out their passion at the top of their voices.

As for him, there was no doubt life had taken a turn for the better once the old man had shuffled off the mortal, allowing him to make free with Blisswood Spa. He marvelled once again at the sight of manageress Julia Jarvis walking ahead of him down the path, her torn trousers affording a tantalising glimpse of her flushed pink bum cheeks as she went, his own spunk leaking from her arse and soaking into the tattered material.

'You'd better buy some more pairs of those jodhpur things, Julia. You seem to go through them rather fast.'

Julia did not reply but strode on ahead of him, her smooth and perfect buttocks quivering at every step.

31

The atmosphere in the hotel's ground-floor meeting room was stifling. It had been a long afternoon for the Gartertex team and the air was thick with the blue fug of cigarette smoke. Some dozen people sat facing inwards at three long tables arranged in a U shape. In this fashion they could observe both the screen ahead of them and a procession of models, garbed in the latest Louche creations, patrolling a small catwalk set in the jaws of the U.

The meeting had started in ill humour as Gordon Garter had berated all the agents for missing their sales targets the previous quarter. Some of the bolder spirits had fought back, turning their fire on the quality of the last collection and, in particular, on the work of designer Jason Quiff.

'Face it, Jason,' said one, a granite-faced individual from Humberside, 'how the bloody hell are we expected to get fifteen quid for see-through knickers in green netting? A man sees enough fish in Grimsby without expecting one to turn up in his bed on a Friday night.'

'Too right,' cried another. 'Give us some stuff to breathe a bit of life into the missus, not things that make her look like she's died already.'

'Fucking Philistines,' replied Jason wearily – this was not a new experience for him.

'Now now, girls,' said GG, 'let's all think positive.' Having stirred the hornets' nest he was quite happy to play the peacemaker. 'Bring on the new collection.'

And so the latest offerings from Louche Lingerie had been paraded back and forth on the lithe backs and ample fronts of a selection of local maids supplied by Rodney. Some were shy and some were awkward and some were

Lust at Large

breathtakingly fuckable but the impact of their nubile bodies on the assembled company was negligible.

These men were as hardboiled as shoe leather and when it came to business they left their libidos outside the door. In the bar later they would all be pushovers for a winsome smile or a demure flutter of long eyelashes but now, sweating it out in conference under the despotic eye of Gordon Garter, things were very different. A half-naked woman with open thighs and pouting bosom on show was of no more interest than a tailor's dummy.

Graham Garter was flabbergasted. He alone was stirred by this display of tempting female flesh and, though he tried to concentrate on the complexities of price points and special offers, of hook-and-eye versus shoestring-ribbon fastening, of reinforced gussets and underwiring, he could make no contribution to the cut and thrust of debate. *Mine's a watching brief*, he reminded himself and in those terms he more than fulfilled his remit.

His eyes feasted on slender legs in keyhole stockings, on bulging pussy mounds in stretch-lace thongs, on creamy breasts spilling over strapless boned bustiers. And, as his cock vibrated in his plain white Y-fronts like a tuning fork, he revised his opinion of his father's firm.

For as long as he could remember, Graham had hated the family business and had resisted all efforts to make him take an interest in it. Encouraged by his mother, he had thrown himself into his schoolwork and, though not tough enough to rebel completely, he had resented being dragooned into his current role at the expense of his university career. But now, as he ogled a pair of pert bum cheeks tantalisingly revealed by a figure-hugging bodyshaper in black lace, he thought, *What a bloody fool I've been all these years!*

There was a lull in proceedings as the last girl exited and no one took her place. Men yawned and stretched. 'Is that it then?' said Ray from Humberside loudly. 'I could do with a pint.'

'Too right,' said other voices with more enthusiasm than had been heard all afternoon.

'Sit down,' shouted Gordon Garter, the voice of

unquestioned authority. 'We've not bloody well finished yet. Go and see what's holding things up,' he added to Mitzi Bluitt, the Press Officer and only female member of the Gartertex crew. But before she could make her way through the swing doors to the impromptu dressing-room beyond, a model who had not so far taken part in proceedings stumbled into the room.

She could scarcely have been past her sixteenth birthday and her white flesh gleamed with unsullied purity. A corona of midnight black curls framed her pretty face and her eyes were pools of azure anxiety. Her body was lush beyond her years, made coltishly graceful by her height, and rendered more naked than nudity itself by a garment that was plainly inadequate to contain her bountiful charms. The white satin halter-neck was slashed to her waist and non-existent at the back apart from a thin G-string which disappeared between the divide of her gloriously rounded buttocks. Two gold chain links held the front together over the bulging mounds of her breasts but, as she tottered towards them on four-inch-high spike heels, the material was pushed aside by the weight of the flesh and her left nipple thrust itself into view – 'like the pink snout of a newborn puppy seeking his mummy's teat' as Ray, moved to poetry, later put it over a large Bell's.

An awed silence fell on the cynical gathering. Graham was torn. Part of him wanted to throw his jacket over her exposed innocence and rush her from the room. The other part wanted to rip the stupid garment completely from her body and ravish her on the floor. He guessed everybody else felt pretty much the same.

But not Jason, of course. Though he had spent his entire working life inventing ways of showing off the female form he himself was susceptible only to men in tight jeans.

'Well, dearie,' he said in exasperation, 'I don't know where you sprang from but a size ten you'll never be. Tuck your tit in, for God's sake.'

The girl gulped and prodded unsuccessfully at her errant bosom. Some twenty-odd hands itched to help her but only the indifferent Jason was able to reach over and adjust her straining cleavage.

'Ooh, I'm ever so sorry,' said the girl. 'I've never done owt like this and I'm right nervous.'

'Don't you worry, love,' said Barry from Scotland, 'you look absolutely cracking.'

'Right, lads,' announced Jason over the hum of comment, 'you are now looking at Suky the Ultimate Playsuit and *pièce de resistance* of the new Louche Lingerie collection. It's as raunchy as Ravel's Bolero and as saucy as steak Bernaise—'

'Cut the crap, Jason, and put the poor girl out of her misery,' said Ray.

'Oh don't worry about me,' piped up the young model, 'you can look as long as you like, I don't mind.'

'You're a game lass,' said Tony from Wales and the girl smiled, with breathtaking impact.

'OK,' said Jason loudly, 'let's keep our minds on the job. One of the main sales points of the Playsuit is the unique Velcro crotch release which gives the wearer's partner instant access to her you-know-where. There are no frustrating buttons or poppers to fiddle around with. Just one teensy tug and the little lady's defences are down and joy is at your fingertips. All for twenty-nine ninety-nine.'

'How do we know it works?' said Gordon Garter, voicing the question in everybody's thoughts.

'I'm about to demonstrate, GG,' said Jason, slipping to his knees and turning to the gleaming white triangle of satin that concealed the girl's prominent pubic bulge.

'My,' exclaimed Jason as he surveyed the target area, 'you are a hirsute young lady.'

It was true. Thick tendrils of jet-black pubic hair overhung the edges of the gusset and curled across the tops of her creamy thighs.

'I'll give her a bikini wax any time,' muttered Don the Marketing Director, which prompted a dig in the ribs from Mitzi at his side. She was only half amused by the turn of events.

'All an admirer has to do,' continued Jason, 'is to reach between the legs for the tiny flap and—'

There was a small scratching sound as his long fingers delved and pulled and suddenly a veritable forest blossomed into view. The girl swivelled around on parted legs so all could see the effect. And the effect was spectacular, for in the centre of the forest was a clearing, so to speak, and her long pink vaginal lips, prettily scalloped and daintily furled, were fully revealed. The watching men were speechless.

The silence was broken by the girl. 'Is everything OK? Mr Holmdale said he'd give me twenty quid if I didn't do nothing wrong.'

'Don't you worry, love,' came a chorus of reassurance.

'You're the best model we've ever had,' shouted Barry.

'Can I have a try at that crotch release?' asked Ray.

'Ooh, go on, then,' said the girl. 'But you'll have to help me do it up first.'

'Here, let me,' cried Tony, jumping to his feet.

'This is getting out of hand, GG,' hissed Mitzi.

The fat man shot her a sly grin. 'What you are seeing is the birth of our next bestselling item, my dear. I guarantee these lads will bust their targets on Suky after this.'

There was no doubting the enthusiasm for the new product amongst the sales force as they broke ranks to surround the girl and try for themselves the intricacies of the new crotch flap.

'Ooh, that tickles,' the girl called out as Ray thrust his stubby paw into her bush. 'It makes me go all weak at the knees.'

'What's your name?' asked Tony as her legs buckled and she clung to him for support.

'Mandy.'

'How about a little overtime, Mandy? Me and the lads will throw in some extra if you'll let us try out the bodice fastening too.'

A flurry of hands reached for wallets and suddenly a pile of banknotes appeared on the table. At about the same time, Suky the Ultimate Playsuit parted like the Red Sea down the front of Mandy's precociously ripe young body.

'I think I'd better just supervise,' muttered Don, rising to his feet, but sharp fingers dug viciously into his arm through the cotton of his shirt.

'Oh no, you fucking don't,' said Mitzi in his ear. 'You lay a finger on that fat trollop and I'm telling your wife.'

Lust at Large

'Ah.'

'On the other hand, if you take me upstairs right now I'll think about that weekend in Brighton.'

Don disengaged her fingers from his arm and pulled her quickly to her feet. 'Christ, she has got you going, hasn't she?' she said as he hustled her out of the door.

In the centre of the room the action was hotting up.

'How about a kiss for your Uncle Ray?' said the man from Humberside to Mandy but someone else was already snogging her thirstily. Tony was licking a thick button-bright nipple as he hefted her weighty left breast and Barry was easing a long red erection out of his trousers. Without appearing to look in his direction, Mandy folded her fingers around his stalk and began to pump.

In the shadows at the back of the room an amazed and fascinated Graham looked on, frozen to his seat. A meaty hand suddenly descended on his shoulder and he looked up into the grinning face of his father.

'Welcome to the world of haute couture, my boy. It's all about stiff dicks and sexy knickers and making a few bob on the side. What do you think to that?'

'I think it's incredible, dad. Fantastic. But will she be all right? They're eating her alive.'

Gordon Garter laughed out loud. 'Don't you worry about her, she's going to clean up tonight with what she gets from them and the bonus I promised her. She's the best little actress I've seen in years.'

For a moment Graham tore his eyes from the spectacle of Mandy on all fours on the table, accommodating a penis at both ends. He gazed at his father in awe.

'You mean you set it up?'

'An old trick, son. Always get a conference off with a bang. Now where the bloody hell's Chantal? My dick needs sucking.'

Three

THE CARNAL QUEST

32

'There have been developments, Fantail,' said Monk, accepting a glass of mineral water from Stephen as they sat on the terrace of the hotel in the early-evening sunshine. 'Significant developments.'

Stephen thought back on the variety of erotic scenes he had observed that afternoon and took a long draught of his pint. In his terms there had also been developments but he did not intend to reveal them to his superior.

'There's been another robbery.'

'A Brenda robbery?'

'Yes, indeed. At Flintwhistle, it's forty-five minutes' drive away. I've just got back.'

'What happened?'

'The usual. At four thirty this afternoon, with one counter clerk on duty at the Flintwhistle Philanthropic, our girl walked in and did her act.'

'Did she get much?'

'Seven and a half grand, apparently. She struck lucky.'

'Any witnesses?'

'Well . . . there's the wally on duty, but he's not much help. Told me in great detail about this cut-off vest she was wearing. He was struck by her belly button winking at him before she even unveiled her big guns. And when she pointed the little pistol at him as well he just kept piling the cash into her bag. I think he rather enjoyed it.'

'Did he say anything about her, er, her chest?'

'He said that you didn't get many like that to the pound, that he'd always dreamed of nobbing a pair that size and that his girlfriend was going to do her pieces when she found out. All things considered, it seems Brenda lived up to her reputation.'

'Did he mention tattoos? Did he say anything about the butterflies?'

'He did not and I had no desire to plant the notion in his tiny noddle. He went on about her swollen pink nipples and the way her titties wobbled when she grabbed the bag of cash. He requested an hour alone with her when we finally made an arrest.'

'You don't sound very impressed with him, sir.'

'Frankly, the Flintwhistle Philanthropic deserve to lose their money if they put idiots like him in charge of it. Even their security camera was on the blink.'

'Oh.' Stephen was puzzled, by all accounts Monk should have been downhearted and he wasn't. He was looking pleased with himself. Stephen soon discovered why.

'Fortunately not all the locals are oafish youths with their brains in their pants. We have an eyewitness. An elderly party called Agatha Finch who saw a dark-haired woman in a cherry-coloured top and tight jeans enter the building society empty-handed and emerge with a full plastic carrier bag just two minutes later. She followed her into the supermarket across the street which has a rear exit to a car park. She saw the woman drive off in a small red hatchback which she thinks is a Peugeot 205 because her son's got one.'

'Did she get the registration?' asked Stephen, excited at this breakthrough.

'Not entirely. She thinks it might have an S in it and a 5.'

'That narrows things down, I suppose. Mind you, they are bloody popular cars. There were two of them in the hotel car park when we arrived. Oh . . .'

'Precisely, Stephen. There are two of them there now, one has an S and the other has a 5 on the numberplate.' Monk smiled. 'Bearing in mind that an S and a 5 probably look similar to an eighty-six-year-old lady at thirty yards I think we can consider them both as possibly belonging to our girl.'

'So who owns them?'

'Let me get you another, Stephen. I can see you have a powerful thirst.'

Lust at Large

'No, sir, don't leave me in suspense. What does the computer say?'

'That one car belongs to the manager of this hotel, Julia Jarvis, and the other to a local hire firm. I got the garage owner at home and he told me he'd rented it yesterday to one Felicity Dodge who turns out to be a guest here.'

'Good Lord. That's marvellous. Two suspects sitting right in our laps, so to speak. What do we do next?'

'We'd better have a word with them, Stephen. I suggest we split up, I'll take La Jarvis.'

'She's the woman who checked us in, isn't she? The one who was getting all hot and bothered when that Garter bloke turned up.'

'Correct. And to make your life easier, I can tell you that Felicity Dodge is staying in Room 17 with a photographer called Clifford Rush.'

Stephen took in this information and then its significance hit him like a blow to the stomach. Room 17 was the first room he'd observed that afternoon, where the woman had sat in her lover's lap and bounced up and down on his prick. The one he'd marked down as worthy of further investigation. And now he was going to have to carry out that investigation.

Stephen felt his armpits fill with sweat and the colour rise in his cheeks.

'Can I have that drink now, sir?' he said.

33

'Haven't you finished yet?' Pamela Perch asked Gavin, squinting at him out of the corner of her wide green eyes, for she dare not turn her head. She sat on a tree trunk by the edge of the tarn, her pretty face turned to the grey limestone cliff that overhung one end of the pool. Her burnished red hair hung down her back almost to her waist and her bare white breasts, firm and jutting in profile, were splashed with the honeyed light of the summer evening.

Gavin considered his hastily made pastel sketch. He'd caught the glinting copper of her hair and the creamy billow of her bosom and he was pleased with the thrust of her thigh along the log, with its rucked-up swirl of pale blue gingham skirt. Considering this was his first effort for over a year it was pretty good. And as a means of getting girls to shed their clothes it could hardly be bettered.

'Can I have a look now?' said Pam, one of the daughters of the farmer who was allowing Gavin to camp in his field. She had been only too keen to lead him up to the local beauty spot known as Maiden's Pool and there to doff her togs and pose.

'Here you are then,' said Gavin, getting to his feet and holding his drawing out so that she could see it.

'Ooh, that's brilliant!' she cried. 'You've made me look all sexy.'

'You are sexy,' he said.

'Go on with you,' she protested and laughed, setting her shapely breasts jiggling. Her nipples were small and round like cherry stones and Gavin knew she wanted him to slip one into his mouth and suck. And though this girl could hardly be the one he sought – Brenda could not possibly

Lust at Large

have disguised all those freckles, could she? – he wanted it too. In any case, from the way she was looking at him from beneath her long fringed lashes, he doubted if he was going to have much choice.

'The sun's still ever so strong,' she said, taking hold of his hand. 'Feel.'

So he felt, allowing his fingers to be placed on the milky strip of skin beneath the bulge of her right breast. Her body was hot to touch.

'You're on fire,' he said.

'Yes. Feel here.'

His hand slid up onto the silken swell of her tit, where the heat from her simmering flesh seemed to flow into him.

'You'll burn. You should have said.'

'It doesn't matter. It's in the cause of art, isn't it? No, don't take your hand away, it's soothing.'

'Is there anywhere else that hurts?'

'Here.' She put his other hand on her left breast and it warmed his flesh like a hot coal, the stubby nipple spiky in his palm. He bent his head to nuzzle the side of her neck and the glowing flesh of her shoulder.

Her mouth was like a furnace, seeming to burn his tongue as she sucked it in. He wallowed in her scalding embrace, stroking and feeling her soft hot breasts and drinking in her juicy kisses.

They fell onto the pebbly beach at the edge of the water.

'We should have brought a blanket,' he said.

'I don't care,' she said. 'We can lie on our clothes.'

She had the shirt off his back already and his jeans halfway down his thighs. Then she stopped and lowered her face to his crotch, her hair hanging in a copper curtain so he could not see what she was doing. But he could feel, and the touch of her warm little hands had him rigid with anticipation. He lay back, gazing up at the edge of the cliff outlined against the blue vault of the sky, as she prised his cock from his underpants and stuffed it into her burning mouth.

It was so exquisite he thought he would squirt down her throat at once but she seemed to sense his excitement and ran her lips along the length of the shaft to mouth his balls.

She had done this before, he could tell. The thought made him even hornier.

'Turn round,' he said. 'I want to put my face up your skirt.'

She lifted her head and the copper curtain parted. Her eyes were alive with mischief as she looked up at him past the big sticky staff rearing from his belly.

'Yes,' she hissed as she swivelled round, still clutching his cock. 'Suck me through my panties. I love that.'

Her skirt made a satisfying tent over his head, shading his face from the brilliance of the light, enclosing him with sl n pale thighs and a pair of tight, elastic-fleshed buttock moons already spilling out of white cotton panties. He reached for the cheeks of her arse and pulled her onto his face, his mouth wide open to receive the bulging gusset of her briefs. They were wet already and he could feel the curls of her hair beneath his tongue as he mouthed her. His nose was wedged between the rounded cheeks of her bum and he drank in the odour of her. She smelt of pussy on heat, rich and ripe. He felt intoxicated.

He sucked and probed with his fingers, kneading the pliant flesh of her arse, finding the nub of her clit through her knickers and making her moan. She slicked his foreskin back and forth across the head of his cock and wormed the point of her little tongue into the eye of his helmet.

When she enclosed her lips around the end of his knob and began to pump rhythmically on the shaft he knew he was not far off coming and went to work in earnest.

He pried the damp cotton of her panties from her crack and ran his tongue around her steaming honeypot. She was gluey with sex juices and her bottom was trembling with desire. He sucked her labia into his mouth and gently, insistently, stroked the perfumed flesh at the top of her crack, titillating her twitching clit till she was at bursting point. When he pushed his tongue deep into her pussy she came, grinding down on his face and crying out.

But her cries were muffled as, with one, two, three, strokes of her cunning fist and a feather-light caress of her tongue on his bulging glans, he exploded in her mouth.

They remained stuck together for a long and happy

moment, his spunk trickling down her throat, her love juice drying on his lips. They unstuck themselves with regret.

She lay in his arms with her skirt around her waist and her freckled bosom comfortable against his chest. The sky was just as blue and cloudless up above.

'Did the earth move for you?' she asked with a chuckle in her throat.

'No, but I think the hillside just did,' he said. 'We're being watched.'

34

It had not taken Chantal long to work out how to pull the strings of Gordon Garter's desires. Whether those same strings would open up his purse was another matter. But she was working on it.

During the afternoon session on his bed she had allowed him to satisfy his basic lusts and had manoeuvred over and under his vast bulk with nimble grace. Given his age and size there was obviously a physical limit to his exertions. After his second climax – a life-threatening missionary poke which had her fighting for air – he had dismissed her. This had annoyed her but she had gone quietly enough. Though not before putting a hand between her legs and simulating a dramatic climax.

'What's up with you, girl? Have you gone short?' he had said, regarding her performance with surprise.

'I am sorry, GG,' she said, 'when I am with a bull like you I can never get enough.'

Now, after Mandy's display at the sales conference, Garter was all over her the moment he entered the bedroom.

'*Non, non,*' protested Chantal as he lunged for her with one huge paw and ripped open his trousers with the other.

'Suck it, you little French tart,' he roared, pushing her to her knees in front of him and attempting to force his thick prong between her lips.

She took hold of the waggling member but she had no intention of complying with this brutish request.

'OW!' he cried as she gave his cock a vicious twist, cutting off the blood supply. 'You little bitch!' And he took a clumsy swing at her which passed harmlessly over her head but left him sprawling on the bed, his limp cock dangling uselessly from his flies. 'What the fuck did you do that for?'

'To teach you a lesson, you great *rosbif*. And to give you more pleasure, if you care to believe it.'

He stared at her with confusion in his piggy eyes.

'Look at me, GG. I have been here waiting for you to come back from your horrible business meeting so we can make passionate love and you wish to treat me like a fifty-franc whore. If you simply want to shoot your spunk off then I can find you a box of Kleenex.

'On the other hand, do you not observe what I am wearing?'

Garter looked at her properly for the first time since he had entered the room. He took in the midnight-blue silk tie-waisted peignoir (Petula, £49.99) which she was already slipping from her slender shoulders. And the stretch lace bodyshaper in white which was moulded to her curves, hugging the pert saucers of her breasts and cutting in from her hips in a long swooping vee, concealing and revealing as it went. He knew only too well that the garment fastened down the back with a tantalising row of hooks and eyes and that the rear of the panty was a G-string thong, bootlace thick, worn between the naked buttocks. This was La Serenissima (£29.99), a perennial favourite or 'a cock-stiffener for every season, duckie,' as Jason invariably put it.

La Serenissima worked its magic once more, breathing immediate life into the fat man's abused penis which now sat up and gazed one-eyed at the small dark shadow of pubic hair clearly visible at the base of Chantal's taut belly.

The Frenchwoman turned slowly to present her rear view which was as breathtaking as Garter had known it would be. She stood on high pencil-thin heels which seemed to force her onto tiptoe, emphasising the full unblemished cheeks of her beautiful *derrière*. Gordon Garter stared at this pretty behind goggle-eyed. It filled his vision.

'So – what do you think of that, Mr Bull-at-the-gate? Is it not better to appreciate a woman's beauty before you decide how to take your pleasure? Especially since these lovely clothes are your own creations.'

Chantal had assumed that Garter had more than a

Lust at Large

professional interest in women's underwear and that he would, at the very least, be flattered if she dressed this way to please him. But in choosing this particular garment she could not know how successfully she had hit the bull's-eye of his obsession. It was dear to his heart because he had virtually designed it himself. 'Can't you combine a basque and a G-string?' he'd said to Jason in a flash of prurient inspiration. 'I want to see a lot more arse hanging out.'

And now there was La Serenissima modelled as never before, exclusively for him.

'It's incredible,' he croaked. 'It's just as I first imagined it.'

'You are a very naughty man to sell such sexy clothes, I think,' she said, continuing to flaunt her shapely bottom before his eyes. 'It gives a girl such wicked thoughts.'

'You're a witch, Chantal. The most beautiful witch I've ever seen in my life!'

'So, GG, you are not such a brute after all. Tell a woman she is beautiful and she'll let you do anything. How would you like to have me? My mouth, my tits, my cunt, my bottom – tell me quick. I can't wait any longer.'

'I'll have your arse!' he cried, jumping to his feet, his trousers round his ankles, his cock quivering with expectation.

'Yes!' she said then clapped a hand to her mouth. 'Oh dear, what did I say? You cannot, I am sorry.'

'What do you mean? You just offered me your bum, Chantal, and I mean to have it!'

'Is this a proposal of marriage, GG? Remember, I told you this morning I am saving my bottom hole for the man I marry.' And she laughed at the absurdity of it all, a flirtatious gurgle that even in his frustration Gordon Garter found enchanting. 'Never mind, GG, you can have my behind in a very special way. I will show you.'

And so Gordon Garter allowed himself to be manipulated into a deed that fired him with lust and emptied his balls but which left him wanting more – much more.

She bent forward over a chair and thrust her rear backwards on a level with his loins. And then, to the beat of her lewd directions, Gordon Garter embarked on an act he had not contemplated since he was nineteen and walking out

Lust at Large

with Mavis Armitage – buxom Mavis of the buckteeth who was so paranoid about the potency of male sperm that he had had to jerk himself off at a distance of six feet while she displayed to him her naked breasts.

At least Gordon Garter got a little closer this time to the objects of his desire, the perfect thrilling buttock halves of Chantal's creamy bum, swelling in a delicious curve from the tiny circlet of her waist and bisected by a glistening white lace thong that ran the length of her bewitching arse-crack. When he thought about it later Garter wondered why he hadn't simply torn the strip of material from her secret divide and plunged his cock into her anus. But he had spoken the truth earlier, she was a witch and she had him enchanted.

'Go on, GG, wank your cock for me. Look at my bottom, it's pretty, is it not? Let me shake it for you, does that look good? Imagine your penis between my buttocks, sinking deep inside my channel, driving in and out between my cheeks. Oh God, it would be so heavenly to have you there! Maybe I'll let you anyway, maybe next time. And you can drive your big cock up my little passage. I'll be tight for you I promise. *Mon Dieu*, I think I'm going to come at the thought. Oh yes, I can't hold back much longer. Come with me, my sweet. Shoot your juice all over my bum! Spunk all over my arse cheeks! Do it now, please. I'm coming! Oh YES!'

Outside the bedroom, in the sitting-room of Gordon Garter's suite, she found Graham standing in the grand bay window, shifting nervously from foot to foot.

She threw herself onto one of the two large sofas with a sigh of fatigue and surveyed the poor lamb.

'So, Mister Invisible,' she said, 'are you still on duty or can you drink some champagne with me?'

Graham tore his eyes from her milky thighs, half bared by the careless drape of her blue peignoir, and looked at the door she had just closed behind her.

'Don't worry, he is sleeping. He told me to wake him in an hour. It's been a hard day, yes?'

'Yes,' said Graham emphatically. Hard described it

precisely. He still *was* hard, his mind full of images of Mandy taking it fore and aft and now of Chantal who was making no attempt to hide the seductive body that was his father's exclusive, if temporary, property.

'There's a mini-bar in that corner,' said Chantal, waving a slender arm in imperious command. 'You'll find champagne in there and you needn't worry, Rodney says it's on the house.'

'Like you, you mean,' said Graham as he fetched a dark green bottle and two glasses.

She decided to let the remark pass. After all, the poor boy must be feeling a little left out.

'If you don't know how to pop the cork,' she said as he fumbled with the bottle, 'I'll do it.'

'Don't worry, mademoiselle, I know how to pop a cork even if I haven't mastered your sophisticated techniques,' muttered Graham through gritted teeth just as the bottle appeared to explode in his hand and fountained creamy foam all over his trousers.

Chantal didn't try to stifle her laughter. Maybe it was the release of tension now she was off duty or the sight of this gawky young man struggling with a tricky cork and a flagrant erection at the same time, at any rate she laughed until she was close to tears.

He hit her sharply across both cheeks and then handed her a glass of bubbling liquid which she drained in one gulp. He refilled it, making no attempt to avoid looking at her half-exposed breasts, the dark points of her nipples pushing through the thin white mesh.

'You didn't have to hit me so hard,' she said.

'You were becoming hysterical.'

She looked up at him, the red marks of his hand stark on both cheeks.

'You're so beautiful,' he said, 'I'd never hurt you, believe me.'

'Not even with that iron bar you have in your pocket?'

His face coloured and he turned his head away. A naughty idea was taking root in Chantal's head. To be accurate, the naughty idea had been there from the first but only now did Chantal allow herself to recognise it. She finished her second glass of champagne and thought to herself, *Why not? Surely I deserve some pleasure of my own?*

'Graham—' she pronounced it Gray Ham – he had never heard it said like that before and he thought it enchanting '—does that door lead to your bedroom?'

35

'This is Rosie,' said Pamela, 'and this is Jon. They said they'd look out for me.'

They'd done that all right, thought Gavin as he nodded hello to a tall grinning youth and a chubby-faced blonde with grass stains on the cushions of her denim-clad behind. They'd slithered down the hillside the moment Pam had called out to them. From the amusement in their eyes he guessed that they'd seen everything he and Pam had been up to. Well, if she didn't care – and she obviously didn't – why should he?

'Let's see your masterpiece then,' said Rosie and before Gavin could say anything Pam had picked up his drawing and passed it over.

'Cor,' said Jon, 'he's made you look right tasty, our Pamela.'

'It's great,' cried Rosie. 'Will you draw me too?'

Funnily enough, it didn't seem an odd request. Blisswood was that kind of place.

'Why don't you do 'em both together,' suggested Jon. 'If it's any good my dad will buy it and put it up in the pub.'

'Well . . .' said Gavin but the notion was entertaining. He could see the two contrasting types side by side, the slender freckled redhead and the blooming puppyfat blonde. He was erect again at the thought.

'Hang on,' said Pam, 'why don't all three of us pose for him? Unless you're not up to it, Jon. I don't see why it's always the women who have to strip off.'

There was no arguing with that and, within a few moments, Gavin was arranging the three of them on a grass bank.

Lust at Large

'You don't really have to take your clothes off,' he said and was met with a chorus of protest.

'Why not? I did,' said Pam.

'It doesn't bother me,' said Jon.

'That's the whole point, isn't it?' said Rosie, reaching behind her back to unclasp a black brassiere which was straining to contain a pair of large and sumptuous breasts. As she did so, the breath seemed to catch in Gavin's throat. Could these be the fabulous mammaries that had changed his life? Rosie seemed to him too plump and too short to be the Topless Raider but this was the acid test.

Her massive orbs swung into view, thrusting outwards from the centre of her chest, the big pink nipples surrounded by the salmon-coloured saucers of her areolae. They were twin pulsating udders of flesh, bountiful and creamy, open invitations to lust. But they were not the tits of Bra-less Brenda. Gavin's disappointment echoed in the pit of his stomach even as his cock leapt in his jeans.

'So how do you want us then?' said Pam who had discarded her skirt and panties and wore just an unbuttoned shirt as protection for her pale skin. The chestnut curls of her bush glinted in the sunlight.

Gavin the artist did his best. He had never drawn more than one model at a time, let alone three. He knew the sketch would be no good, his hand was shaking so much. Besides, the three of them would not stay still. They couldn't. Gavin watched with mounting excitement as Jon, a girl on either side of him, kissed first one, then the other.

Gavin's pencil flew over the paper. He concentrated on Jon's crotch, where his long thin penis was now enveloped by Pam's small fist. It was a skilful fist, as Gavin well knew. He tried to capture the rounded end of the boy's knob as it emerged between the girl's slim fingers but he was distracted by another hand – Rosie's – which was now palming Jon's furry balls.

'That's not fair,' said Jon, 'you're turning me on too much.' It seemed an accurate observation. Pam's hand was pumping his shaft and the eye of his cock was an angry blood-gorged purple as she toyed with him.

Lust at Large

'Why don't you fuck me then?' she said and pulled him on top of her.

Gavin's pencil slid off the paper as he watched Pam's long legs swing up in the air to present her crotch to the eager probing of Jon's stiff stalk. For a moment his prick jabbed blindly at the pink gash at the fork of her body, then the head found the open notch and slid straight between the pouting lips of her pussy.

'Oh that's heavenly,' sighed Pam, her ankles hooked around Jon's waist, her loins thrusting up to meet his. Gavin could hear the slap of flesh as their bellies came together, then the rude sticky sound of cock in cunt as he began to ride and probe her. Jon's buttocks hollowed and his balls shook with each thrust.

Gavin felt a warm hand on his arm and looked up from the intoxicating spectacle in front of him into the milky-blue eyes of Rosie. Her huge tits were on a level with his mouth.

'They look great, don't they?' she said. 'I always like to watch, don't you?'

'Yes,' he gulped, though in fact this was the first time he had ever seen two people make love. He knew he should laugh and say it was comic, that they looked silly. That was the sophisticated response. But Gavin didn't feel at all sophisticated. He felt as horny as hell.

He put his arm round Rosie's waist and she seemed to melt into his embrace. She was a big little girl, a solid armful of flesh whose touch was both tender and urgent.

'Ooh yes,' she said as she unzipped him and found his fierce erection, pulling it free of his jeans and delving in further to draw out his balls.

His hands were all over her, cupping and weighing her glorious boobs, roaming over the curves of her hips and sinking into the twin pillows of her pliant bum cheeks. Her skin was soft and silky and her hair smelled of grass and strawberries. Between the legs she was slick and buttery and when he licked around the bowl of her belly, from the whorl of her navel down into the browny-blonde mat of hair at its base she pressed his head hard into her crotch.

She tasted differently to Pam. She was honey sweet where

her friend was salty and pungent. Was there a science in this? Gavin wondered as he tongued her. Could you distinguish a woman by the taste of her privates? If Brenda the Robber had forced him to kiss her pussy instead of ogle her breasts would he now be roaming the land with the tang of a myriad cunts upon his lips like some exotic wine taster?

'OH!' His bizarre reverie came to a swift conclusion as Rosie's thighs clamped shut around his ears and her fingernails raked his bare back. She was coming, coming with the full vigour of a strong and enthusiastic young woman and Gavin fought for survival as she writhed and bucked on his tongue.

She let him up at last and he rolled onto his back, gasping for air.

'Not bad, is he?' said Pam, a wicked grin on her face as she lolled in Jon's arms, her legs spread wide in a sticky vee.

Gavin was conscious that he was the only one of the four who hadn't had a climax. His cock was a stiff truncheon sticking up from his belly.

By his side Jon said, 'Our Rosie's a grand tit-fuck, if you like that kind of thing.'

Gavin didn't know whether he did or not. But he fully intended to find out.

36

Fliss looked at the clock on the bedside table and was surprised to see that it was almost seven. She must have dozed off. There was no sign of Clifford and the thought of eating on her own again did not thrill her. In any case, she didn't feel hungry and it was still too brilliant a day to contemplate sitting in that stuffy dining-room. She fancied an evening stroll. Preferably with an attractive man by her side to help her work up an appetite. Unfortunately Mario was on duty.

She got out of bed and padded on bare feet to the window. In the car park in front of the hotel, next to Cliff's white Porsche, was the little Peugeot he had hired for her. The mean sod wouldn't let her drive his flash motor so she'd insisted she had some means of getting about when he was busy.

Perhaps she'd go for a drive.

As she stood there she saw a man approach her car. At first she thought he was checking out Cliff's glistening willy-wagon but he ignored the Porsche and circled her small red hatchback. He laid a hand on the bonnet, palm down, as if testing for something and peered through the windows. This was odd behaviour in anyone's book.

As he prowled around the car Fliss noted his cheap functional clothes: off-the-peg jeans, scruffy trainers and a blue-and-green-check shirt rolled to the elbows. She also noticed that he was tall, broad-shouldered and thin as a rail. The sun caught his thick thatch of blond hair and Fliss admired the trim taut buttocks that stretched the faded denim as he bent – why? – to examine the tread of her front tyre.

That settles it, she said to herself as she pulled a white sleeveless T-shirt over her bare breasts and reached for her purse, *it's time for an evening spin.*

Stephen was aware he was only putting off the evil hour. He knew he should stroll confidently up the stairs to Room 17 and engage the curvaceous brunette in a subtle dialogue which would reveal her whereabouts at four thirty that afternoon. He himself could vouch only too vividly for her presence in her bedroom until half past two but that didn't get her off the hook. She could have been in the Flintwhistle Philanthropic within an hour of quitting the arms of her lover – who had not been Clifford Rush the photographer, Stephen could vouch for that as well.

All in all, the young policeman was in a turmoil. The flagrantly sexy brunette he had seen cavorting naked with a man that afternoon could easily be the most wanted criminal in the British Isles. Maybe he was the man destined to bring her to justice – and to condemn her to years in some ghastly prison where her beauty would fade and her capacious desires leave her at the mercy of sadistic warders and predatory lesbians.

For a moment he wallowed in fantasy. He would confront her. She would fall at his feet and confess. 'Take pity on me,' she would say, 'I am utterly in your power. I'll be your sex slave forever if you keep my secret.' And then he could enjoy those sumptuous breasts himself, drown in the honeyed sweetness of her grateful kisses and thrust his aching virgin cock into the carnal mystery that lay between her legs . . .

A small perfect foot in a white open-toed sandal stepped onto his hand as he knelt on the gravel of the car park. 'If you don't tell me what you are doing with my car,' said a soft woman's voice, 'I shall fetch the police.'

When viewed from close up she was even more luscious than he could have imagined. He looked at her from his kneeling position, up the slender thighs and curvaceous hips revealed by her figure-hugging white cotton slacks, over the scoop-necked vest that clung like cellophane to the twin fruits of her breasts, to the wide pink mouth and chocolate-coloured eyes that were fixed firmly on his as she

Lust at Large

waited for an answer. He was rendered quite speechless. Not that it would have been easy to explain that he was taking samples of grit from the tread of her tyres in the hope they might match the gravel of the Flintwhistle supermarket car park.

'I've been watching you,' she said. 'You've been acting most suspiciously. You're a thief or a vandal or both.' She increased the pressure on his hand as he tried to stand and he remained there, mouth open and heart pounding, struggling to cope with the very presence of her. Two dark saucer shapes were clearly discernible beneath her white top and the pegs of her nipples pushed out the fabric. Stephen had never seen anyone so desirable in his life.

A car key plopped onto the gravel by his foot. 'Get in the car,' she said. 'You drive while I decide what should be done with you.'

With his free hand Stephen picked up the key.

Like Fliss, Josie was also faced with the prospect of dining alone. She had opted for the bar and now nursed a half of strong cider as she wolfed a bowl of peanuts and wondered just how long it would take Robyn to cover developments in Flintwhistle.

The *Rabbit* had rung Robyn at six, just as she was complaining for the umpteenth time that Josie was not suitable sob-story material.

'I thought you were a one-guy gal. That you were on a mission to find your missing fiancé and nurse him back to sanity. Another piece of human wreckage left bobbing in Brenda's wake. Instead you turn out to be a shameless slut who doesn't care who climbs on board.'

'Come off it, Robyn, you bonked the guy first. You loved every minute of it. I don't see what you're complaining about.'

'I'm complaining, Miss Wet Knickers, because you haven't got Gavin, I haven't got a story and I've got a copy deadline in – oh God – now!'

At that point the phone had rung and Robyn had turned ashen. Her relief as the call unfolded was palpable.

'The good life is ours for another day,' she said as she

Lust at Large

hunted for her shoes. 'The Brenda bimbo has turned over a business in a nearby shitheap called Flintwhistle and I'm off to interview the survivors. Be a sweetheart and get the desk to magic me up a taxi in thirty seconds.'

Magic it probably was but it only took five minutes and Josie bundled her into the car and then wandered aimlessly into the bar to contemplate the rest of the evening. Which was where Clifford Rush found her.

'It's fate,' he proclaimed. 'Here am I, exhausted by a long day's photographic labours, troubled by a sudden shortage of delectable females for the morrow's endeavours and here are you, the answer to my prayers. Let me get you a decent drink, you can't survive on that horse piss.'

'You can get drunk on it though,' said Josie, draining the last drops from her glass. 'I'll have another and a refill of the nuts.'

He made a face but did as she requested.

'Where's your equally gorgeous friend this evening?'

'She's working. She's a reporter on the *Rabbit*. Bra-less Brenda's struck again and she's covering the story.'

'Really? That's the titty-flasher, isn't it? I wouldn't mind getting her in front of my lens.'

'Tell me, Clifford, is there any attractive woman you wouldn't mind zooming in on?'

'Probably not.' And he guffawed with laughter. Josie found it impossible not to warm to him.

'I'm serious about you, though. You'd make a damn good model. You've got a good face.'

Josie smirked into her glass. 'You'd appreciate my face, I suppose, when I was lying flat on my back with my knickers off and my head under a pillow like that girl yesterday.'

'That's not what I've got in mind for you.'

'Isn't it, Clifford?'

Fliss gave Stephen directions as he drove out of the hotel grounds and took a small lane that led up the dale to the top of the moor.

As he concentrated on the winding road he was able to assess his situation more clearly. What was she up to? It was like some psychological game: he was the naughty schoolboy and she was the mistress with the whip in her hand. The thought was somehow delicious provided it *was* a game. If she really were Bra-less (well, there was no doubt about that) Brenda and she had somehow discovered he was a policeman, then he could be in real trouble up here alone on a deserted hillside with such a desperate criminal . . .

'Stop here,' she said as they crested the rise and he parked off the road on a long rectangular layby overlooking the valley.

She got out of the car and walked to the edge. He followed her. A slight breeze whispered over them both, caressing the brown cascade of curls that lay on her bare shoulders. He suddenly realised the top of her head only reached to his chin.

She stretched her arms out wide and held her face up to the sun. 'How wonderful,' she said.

He said nothing, still bemused by the turn of events.

'So what were you doing poking around my car?'

He had to say something. 'I saw a beautiful woman in a Peugeot like yours this afternoon. When I spotted the car in front of the hotel I had to check it out. I thought I might find out who that beautiful woman was.' He was surprised at his own eloquence.

She turned her big toffee-coloured eyes on him and said nothing.

'I did. It was you.'

'You're trying to sweet-talk your way out of it. I wasn't in the car this afternoon. I was sleeping.'

Stephen looked at her keenly. She showed no signs of guilt though half of what she had said was certainly a lie. She smiled at him and her eyes sparkled. She really was beautiful, he realised, with a pointed heart-shaped face and lips which snaked upwards at the ends, wicked and enticing.

'I'm sorry,' he stammered. 'I was curious about you but I didn't have the nerve to approach you directly. I'm shy.'

She laughed out loud. 'Come off it, you cunning bugger. You've picked me up by letting me do all the work and now I suppose you're going to get me to seduce you as well.'

Stephen's mouth fell open.

'I don't care,' said Fliss, 'it makes a change. Shall we take our clothes off now or will you kiss me first?'

'How about another? Or would you prefer something proper to eat?'

'Well . . .'

'Come on, we've both been stood up so let's slum it with each other.'

'No.'

'You don't like my company?'

'It's not that, it's my clothes.'

'Ah.'

'The dining-room's a bit posh for me. I can't wear what I had on last night and I haven't got anything else.'

'We can soon fix that. I'll lend you some of Fliss's.'

'Is Fliss your wife?'

'Er, no. She's a dear friend who's invaluable to me on these shoots. We often travel together. But she doesn't seem to be around at present and she's got tons of clothes upstairs. Come on.'

'Won't she mind?'

'Fliss? No. She's the soul of generosity. Always happy to help young people.'

Fliss was certainly happy to help the young person who at that moment was clasping her tight to his broad chest and gorging on her lips like a starving man.

Up close, he was much younger than she'd first thought and, unless he was faking it, he didn't really know what he was doing. In Fliss's opinion, the man prepared to pretend he was a clumsy kisser did not exist.

But although this boy was inexperienced he was passionate and his lean hard flesh trembled at her touch. After the ease with which Mario had manoeuvred her body that afternoon – as if he were the choreographer and she some puppet of a dancer – there was a freshness in his clumsy technique that touched a place deep inside her.

He stroked her hair and planted wet gentle kisses in the hollow of her neck, all the time muttering that she was beautiful, incredible, magnificent. He even sounded like he meant it. As Fliss basked in this puppyish adoration it occurred to her that she had become used to being taken for granted.

Suddenly she wanted something more than innocent adoration. She took one of his big hands and slipped it under the hem of her vest, up to aching breasts that yearned to be squeezed and palmed and fondled.

His touch was tentative and awkward but also electric. His hot fingers roamed the hills of her bosom as if they were uncharted territory. He took a heavy teat in his hand and squeezed it gently.

'Ooh yes,' she said, 'do that harder. Don't worry – you won't hurt me.'

'Like that?'

'Oh God, yes! Mmm, that's great. Now I want them sucked. Lie on the grass and let me dangle them in your face.'

She pushed him flat on his back and sat astride his waist. His eyes were wide and incredulous as she took the hem of her top in her hands and pulled it up and over her head. Her marvellous breasts burst forth, full and round, and danced before him in all their pink and wobbling glory.

'Oh God,' he moaned as the weighty mounds descended on his face and then his lips fastened around a stiff and turgid nipple and he sucked as instinctively as a baby.

Fliss shivered with pleasure and pressed her bosom to his head with a tenderness that was almost maternal.

Almost.

37

'What about this?' said Clifford, pulling a cream linen suit from the wardrobe and holding it out to Josie.

'Oh no, I couldn't—'

'Or this?' He held up a yellow and black sheath. 'Too dressy perhaps and I have to say she's a bit bigger in the bust so . . .'

'Let's forget the whole thing, Clifford.'

'Nonsense. Consider it payment in advance for all the modelling you're going to do for me tomorrow. Here, try this on.'

It was a little black cocktail number, a classic, beautifully cut. Josie hesitated.

'Come on, take your things off. Don't be shy.'

She shrugged and began to unbutton her denim shirt. He was a big-deal photographer, after all. He'd seen enough tits to last a lifetime.

He took no notice of hers which was, she had to admit, something of a disappointment. He was more concerned with helping her on with the dress. It was a silk wrap-around with puff shoulders and a square neckline cut low over the bosom.

'Not bad,' he pronounced when he had finished with her, 'but we've got to tackle that bust.'

He searched inside a large red box with LOUCHE LINGERIE emblazoned in gold on the lid. Triumphantly he held up a black lacy brassiere. 'I'm told it's one of their most popular numbers,' he said as he helped her on with it and retied the dress at the waist. 'It simply adds to what nature has bestowed. They call it The Paddington Bare. Oh my, that's better.'

Lust at Large

It was indeed. Aided by the miracle bra, Josie's breasts now pushed out the front of the dress in two plump rounds.

'Well, I never, I've got a cleavage,' she said in amazement.

'Absolutely,' he agreed. 'Now, off with those ghastly leg things.'

Josie obeyed without thinking, pulling off her leggings and panties in one go as he selected for her a matching black suspender belt and sheer silk stockings.

Now he's going to make his move, she thought as his skilful fingers fastened the belt and smoothed the stockings up her trembling thighs. But he didn't. He seemed to take no notice of her brown-haired pussy which she made no attempt to hide. Indeed, as his hand fastened the stockings at the very top of her thigh, she had to resist an impulse to move it over two or three inches and push his fingers into her bush.

Instead he made her stand in front of the wardrobe mirror, the skirt smoothed down over her naked charms, while he rummaged in the bottom of the wardrobe for a pair of shoes, emerging with a pair of black high heels with cross-over straps. Finally, he placed a gold heart-shaped pendant round her neck to complete the effect.

'Darling, you look fabulous,' he said.

And she did, she had to admit it. The pretty scruff had been transformed into a chic beauty. A chic and randy beauty.

'Let's go,' he said.

'I'm not hungry, Cliff.' *Not for food anyway*, she thought.

He grinned at her, his eyes twinkling, and picked up a camera from the top of the chest of drawers. 'I thought we might have a bit of fun first. Are you game?'

Josie nodded and, bare-arsed beneath the swishing silk of the pretty frock, followed him out of the room.

Stephen had kissed half-naked women before, had fumbled with their breasts and sucked their nipples and pressed his straining loins against theirs as they had squirmed together in a hot clinch. But he had not done it often. He had not done it with any expectation that it might lead to The Real Thing. And he had never done it like this.

Lust at Large

In his arms, Fliss was so much more a woman than any other he had held. She was rounder and softer, fuller and riper, sweeter to the senses in every degree. Compared to the thin-lipped blue-stockings he had chased to date, she was like fine claret to weak tea. Not that Stephen had any more experience of fine claret than he did of women but he had his ambitions.

His ambition of the moment, once he had had his fill of the luscious tit globes offered without shame or reluctance to his hungry lips and inquisitive touch, was to rip the pants off this sex goddess and finally *do it*.

Despite this, of course, he was determined not to neglect his duty. To lick and maul and fondle her heaving breasts was quite justifiable considering the nature of his mission. Indeed, Stephen made a point of examining her free-swinging mammaries with a view to eliminating her from his enquiries. He lifted each boob to scrutinise the undercurve for signs of butterfly transfers. He licked deep into the perfumed undercrease, where the swollen tit-flesh met the silky skin of her ribcage, in search of tell-tale sticky patches – and found nothing but sweet woman-flesh. He was very thorough.

'Mmm,' said Fliss in appreciation. 'What a boob-lover you are. It's heaven.'

Stephen couldn't have agreed more.

Clifford did not lead Josie downstairs to the dining-room but headed up two flights to a long gallery that ran the length of the house. One side of the corridor was punctuated by doors which, presumably, opened onto the rooms of the upstairs guests; the other was made up of windows which overlooked the front of the hotel.

The sun poured in, lower in the sky now but still hot and bright, bleaching out the golds and reds of the carpet and illuminating swirls of dust motes like dancing clouds of flies.

'Here we are,' said Clifford. 'I love this weird light. We'll get some gorgeous effects.'

Josie was nervous but excited. Clifford had got her all steamed up by treating her body simply as a clotheshorse. She became even more worked up as she was made to pose in the patches of fierce light while he clicked away.

The underwear she had on stimulated her. The bra lifted and constricted while the filmy itch of the stockings and suspenders just served as a reminder that her arse and cunt were quite bare.

'Open the dress,' said Clifford and his words ran through her like an electric shock. Her fingers automatically went to the bow at her waist.

A door opened to her left and a tall paunchy man in a pin-striped suit emerged.

'Carry on, Josie,' said the photographer.

The paunchy gent pulled his door shut and stared curiously at the two of them as he made his way past.

'Hurry up,' came the next command and Josie pulled the bow loose.

'Open the dress.'

The man had reached the top of the stairs and as he began to descend he turned for one last look. She was holding the dress wide open with both hands. There was something about the look on his face – disbelief mixed with naked desire – that made Josie's stomach turn over. She stared back at the man with as much disdain as she could muster as his face disappeared from view.

'That's fabulous, darling,' purred Clifford. 'You're a little jewel. Now walk towards me.'

As she did so, she felt a pearl of juice begin to trickle down the inside of her leg.

Fliss had always like screwing in the open air. Sometimes there was nothing to beat planting your bare bum up against a tree, or rolling naked in a pile of grass cuttings, while a man waved his big hard-on in your face and said he was going to fuck you silly no matter who came strolling round the corner. And when people did turn up that only added spice to the moment. She savoured the time when she and an admirer had earned a round of applause from a group of walkers while celebrating the ascent of a tricky hill in the Lake District. There had also been an occasion when she and her lover of the day had had to run like fugitives when they were spotted in a field by a group of Brownies at camp.

The pack leader had made for a nearby phone box and called the police.

Right now, however, Fliss could not have cared two hoots if Brown Owl herself had come over the hill. She was going to see what this gauche but adorable young man had to offer. It was time to get matters out into the open.

She slid down his body to sit across his thighs. He looked at her with open-mouthed wonder. She placed a small hand across the big bulge in his loins and pressed. He gasped. It felt like a solid block of wood. She grinned and began to unbuckle his belt. It was party time and Fliss loved unwrapping presents.

The gift she laid bare looked just her size, some eight – maybe nine, she'd have to measure – inches of hard pulsing flesh with a cute furl of foreskin that was slick and wet with obvious excitement.

'Oh my,' she said as she peeled the skin back and forth across the shining pink bulb of his glans. The cock leapt in her hand like a frightened fish.

'What's your name?' she asked.

He didn't answer, his brain bewitched by the sight of this half-naked beauty bending over his long-neglected tool, her breasts swaying as she fondled him with obvious relish.

'You have to tell me,' she continued. 'It's one of my rules.'

'It's Stephen,' he gasped, his hips thrusting urgently as she worked on him. 'What rule is that?'

'Not to put a man's cock in my mouth until I know his name.'

'Oh.'

'I'm glad you told me, Stephen.'

'OH!'

He came the moment her plump curling lips closed over the head of his penis and he shot the accumulated frustration of twenty-two virgin years into her mouth.

Rodney found Clifford Rush and a model he didn't recognise on the second-floor gallery. It was not a chance discovery, he had overheard some members of the Gartertex sales team enthusiastically discussing the frosty-faced little number who was showing off her bare fanny upstairs. They were not complaining, indeed the Gartertex chaps were positively beaming.

Rodney was eagerly anticipating his first full report from Chantal *vis à vis les affaires Garter* but that wasn't scheduled to take place until midnight in his bedroom – provided Chantal's new responsibilities allowed, of course. And since the afternoon's stroll with Julia had primed rather than exhausted his sexual capabilities he made it up the stairs two at a time.

The girl was reclining on a chaise longue at the end of the corridor. Clifford had placed her so that her torso was propped against the arm of the chaise, her face turned into the yellow shaft of sunlight from the window. The toes of both shoes touched the floor but bore no weight and her slim legs and taut thighs in sheer black stockings curved upwards enticingly. The hem of her skirt was clasped in her hand and held tight to her ribcage, leaving the gentle swell of her flawless belly completely exposed from the dimple of her navel to the pink petals of her vagina. Rodney's cock throbbed with hunger at the sight.

'Just in time, Rodney,' said Clifford. 'I need a man in these shots. Go and sit down next to her. And take your plonker out, there's a good fellow.'

'What!'

'You don't mind, do you? It'll make a stunning image for my next exhibition. But you've got to pretend you don't know each other.'

'We don't,' said Rodney and sat down.

'We can soon change that,' said Clifford. 'Josie!'

Without turning her face from the sun, she reached over and unfastened Rodney's fly.

Fliss was naked beneath thin white summer slacks that were now stained with dust and dirt. But the dry-cleaning was not on her mind as she pushed the material over the delectable rounds of her bottom and down her thighs. The spunk was still wet on her throat and breasts. Nevertheless, at the sight of her flowing hips, plump pussy mound and pretty knot of pubic hair, Stephen's cock was already lengthening along his thigh. He still lay where she had put him, flat on his back with his jeans around his knees. It was as if he was her toy to play with. She rather liked that.

She stood over him, one sandalled foot on either side of his head, letting him look up into the fork of her body.

He gaped at her as she opened herself up, fingers fore and aft, spreading herself in a vertical smile. He was fully erect now as she stepped back and lowered herself in a squat across his loins. He made no effort to help her but she didn't care, she wanted it that way. She took his tool in her right hand and placed the fat head in the moist notch of her pussy.

'Oh yes,' she said as she sank down, her left hand spreading herself, the slippery flesh stiff and unbending as she pushed it into her tunnel.

Balancing on the balls of her feet, her eyes closed, her hands on his hips, she let herself go. She fed the hungry mouth of her cunt with his prick, savouring its length and thickness, riding on it vigorously until her first orgasm washed over her. Then she continued with no regard for him, plucking at her stiff little clit and wanking her long pink pussy lips until she came again with a full-throated groan.

She opened her eyes to see Stephen staring at the junction of their bodies as if in shock. She dragged a finger up through her bush and sucked the juice off it noisily.

'Do you think I'm awful?' she said.

'You've got no shame, have you?' he said.

'No,' and she fell on top of him and pushed her tongue into his mouth.

What followed took her by surprise and, on reflection, was quite wonderful even if it did spoil her illusion of being in control.

With one arm wrapped round her waist like a steel band and his cock buried deep within her body, he suddenly rolled her over. Then, with a buttock in each hand, his lips locked to hers and his chest squashing down on her big soft breasts, he fucked her.

It was a long, hard shafting. A comprehensive hump. A good old-fashioned shag. Except that, for Stephen, there was nothing clichéd or old-fashioned about any of it. This shafting and humping and shagging, thrusting his tool deep into the sexiest woman he had ever encountered, was all he had dreamed of for ten years. He was glad now that Rachel and Penny and Monica and the rest of those bony-arsed girls at home had refused and humiliated him in the past. What better way was there to lose your cherry but on a sun-dappled hillside with a mysterious beauty with brown eyes and incredible breasts and no inhibitions whatsoever?

'I love you,' he shouted and pumped his soul into the warmth of the welcoming split between her soft-skinned thighs.

'Of course you do,' whispered Fliss into his ear as he crushed her to him in his final spasms. It was what Mario had said to her as he had finished fucking her in the hotel toilet the day before. This time though she was almost prepared to believe it.

'No more,' said Josie. She was sitting on the chaise by Rodney's side. She had one hand wrapped around his meaty penis which was poking rudely out of his neatly pressed cavalry twills. The other still held her skirt to her waist. She was so on heat she'd have diddled herself but Rodney already had two fingers buried in her cunt.

'Come on, darling, you're doing well,' said Clifford, snapping away on his knees in front of them.

'No more photos,' repeated Josie. 'I want a proper fuck. Give me some real cock, the pair of you.'

'Just hold it a bit longer,' said Clifford but Rodney, too, had had enough. Or not nearly enough, to his way of thinking.

He took Josie's legs and pulled her entire body onto the chaise. She spread them wide as he climbed between her thighs and howled with pleasure as he thrust his rock-hard boner deep into her wet pussy.

'Oh shit,' muttered Clifford to himself, getting to his feet. He wasn't entirely unhappy, however, he'd got some fantastic stuff.

A hand reached out and grabbed him by the belt, yanking him towards the figures on the couch.

'Aha,' cried Josie, pulling down his zip and thrusting her hand inside, 'the great photographer's dick. At last!'

And she plunged its angry red tip between her lips and began to suck as, between her thighs, Rodney worked his staff deep into the sweet depths of her dripping honeypot.

At the head of the stairs, the Gartertex sales force looked on in awe.

'No doubt about it,' said Tony from Wales, 'this is the best fucking sales conference we've ever had.'

38

Mercy showed Archibald Monk to Julia's office just after half past eight, her blue eyes full of concern for her sister. To be precise, Julia was her step-sister – she and the twins being products of two different liaisons of Miriam's. But though Julia was the elder by five years, sometimes it appeared to all parties that she was the least mature of the three.

That afternoon, after the interlude with Rodney, Julia had collapsed on her bed in her room, which was where Mercy had discovered her. The only reason Julia was now sitting at her desk, freshly groomed and smiling bravely at her visitor, was thanks to Mercy who had bathed her, rubbed ointment into her abused bottom and listened to her troubles.

Now Mercy ushered Monk towards a chair, shot him a warning look and stopped just short of ordering him not to tire her patient. Then she left.

The entire performance was wasted on Monk.

'I must tell you, Ms Jarvis,' he began, 'that my companion and I are here under false pretences.'

'Oh?' Her pretty face was blank. Her mind was still half on Rodney and the pressure of the chair on her tender buttocks was a constant reminder of the events of the afternoon. She squirmed uncomfortably. Monk continued with his prepared speech.

'I am an inspector in the Metropolitan police force and together with my colleague, Detective Constable Stephen Fantail, I am here in connection with a series of robberies.'

'Oh dear, is the hotel under threat?'

'Not the hotel as such, Ms Jarvis, but we have reason to

believe that our principal suspect is based in this area.'

'Good Lord!' Julia appeared genuinely shocked.

Monk was struck by the acting ability of the statuesque blonde facing him. Of course, he could expect nothing less from Bra-less Brenda.

'You say you're from the Met?' said Julia. 'Aren't you a bit off your regular beat?'

Monk smiled, a sight which did nothing to allay Julia's growing sense of unease.

'I'm heading an investigation into a sequence of crimes that have been perpetrated nationwide, including several in the London area. The most recent, however, has been on your own doorstep.'

A flash of understanding stole over Julia's features. She had listened to the news while recovering in the bath.

'You don't mean that topless woman, do you?' she asked. 'Bra-less Beryl?'

'Brenda is what they call her in the tabloid press, Ms Jarvis.'

'And you think she might be here in Blisswood?' Monk was impressed by the note of incredulity in her voice. Impressed but not convinced.

'That's preposterous!' continued Julia.

'Is it?' He leaned forward, fixing her with a penetrating glare, and was gratified to see the smile freeze on her face. 'If I told you the suspect was a beautiful young woman with considerable cunning, few morals, large breasts and undoubted exhibitionist tendencies could you truthfully say there was nobody of that nature in this village?'

Julia blanched. If she were honest, that description summed up just about every nubile young woman in Blisswood. Excluding herself of course.

She did not voice this opinion.

'We have reason to believe,' said Monk, 'that such a person might even be residing in this hotel.'

Julia tried to prevent a smile rising to her lips. She did not entirely succeed.

'If you intend to pursue your enquiries here, Inspector, may I ask that you do so discreetly? We wouldn't want the hotel to suffer any unfavourable . . .' Her voice tailed off as

Lust at Large

two thoughts struck her simultaneously. The first was that Rodney Holmdale would jump at the opportunity of free publicity – however unfavourable. The second was that a tabloid journalist was already on the spot, lap-top booted up no doubt, raring to dish the dirt for the *Daily Rabbit*.

'Quite so, Ms Jarvis,' said Monk, lending his own interpretation to the look of concern on Julia's face. 'But you must understand I have a public duty to perform.'

'Oh yes, I see that. Naturally, we'll do all we can to render assistance.'

'Very good.' Monk gave her a reassuring smile. 'In that case do you mind accounting for your movements this afternoon from, say, three thirty onwards.'

Julia stared at him in horror.

'Me?'

'Yes.'

'But I thought you wanted to question the guests?'

'Some of them, maybe. I'd also be interested in talking to members of staff. Like you, for example. You *can* account for your movements this afternoon, I take it.'

'Of course, I—' Julia's cheeks flushed a bright pink and her heart pounded against her ribs. Monk admitted to himself in a moment of rare sensual appreciation that he had never had such a fetching suspect under the cosh.

'I went for a walk,' she blurted out, 'up the hill, to see the horses grazing. It was such a fine day.'

'Alone?'

'Er, yes. Quite alone.'

'When did you get back?'

'I'm not sure. About six.'

'Did you see anybody after your walk?'

'My sister, Mercy. The girl who showed you in here. She came home after I'd got back.'

'So that would be after six?'

'Oh yes, more like six thirty when I got in, it was so hot . . .' Julia was aghast at how she sounded. She found it almost impossible to lie but she couldn't bear to tell this terrifying inquisitor about Rodney because then he'd ask her precisely what they'd done. She was panic-stricken at the thought.

Lust at Large

'I believe you have a red Peugeot 205, do you not?'

'Yes.' Julia was perplexed by this sudden change of subject but nevertheless relieved.

'Registration number F204 SMK?'

'Yes.'

'Are you sure you didn't drive it this afternoon?'

'Certainly not.'

'I see.'

There was silence. Monk gave her the benefit of his Mad Monk stare – a stony, inscrutable look from unflickering limestone-grey eyes that had been known to crack the toughest nuts of London's gangland.

Julia shivered under this basilisk glare and wriggled her sore bottom on the lumpy padding of the chair. Her big blue eyes pooled with water and two fat tears began to meander over the plush contours of her unlined cheeks. Even to a granite-hearted misogynist like Archibald Monk she looked like an angel.

Admit it, Archie, he said to himself as he offered her a large blue handkerchief from his breast pocket, *she's as bonny a lass as you'll ever see – and as guilty as sin.*

39

Rodney was still chuckling to himself when Chantal let herself into his bedroom at midnight. A tearful Julia had kept him on the phone for nearly half an hour and he was still savouring the conversation.

'You won't let him arrest me, Rodney, will you? You will come forward and say I was with you this afternoon.'

'Julia, you could have told him that yourself.'

'I know but I didn't dare. I was so flustered. What if he'd asked what we were doing?'

'You should have told him, Julia. There's nothing to be ashamed of in having your arse smacked on a sunny afternoon. You could have proved it, too. You could have dropped your knickers and showed him your big red bum.'

'Oh Rodney!' She'd burst into hysterical sobs at that point and he had elaborated on the scene for his own amusement.

'I tell you what, Julia. I'll give Cliff Rush a ring and get him to take some photos of your tush before the bruises fade. We can get a few people to sign and date them so they can be submitted as proper evidence.'

'You're such a bastard, Rodney. Just promise me that if necessary you'll say you were with me and we were discussing business.'

Rodney chuckled. 'I'd love to, darling, but it would never wash. To convince him you were with me I'll have to tell the truth, otherwise why did you lie? I'll have to tell him all about your torn jodhpurs and describe the way you hung your pretty bottom over a five-barred gate.'

'Oh!'

'You might be able to persuade me not to mention that

Lust at Large

you weren't wearing panties. I'm sure that would be very prejudicial in the eyes of a jury.'

'I hate you.'

'I'd better let him know what a noisy fuck you are, though. Then the coppers could interview everyone in a five-mile radius. "Excuse me, sir, did you happen to hear a woman having an orgasm at four thirty on the afternoon of June the twentieth?" You are positively deafening when you get going, you know.'

'Shut up!' she screamed, adding before she slammed the phone down, 'I bet this is really turning you on, isn't it?'

That much was true and Chantal's heart sank when she saw Rodney lying naked on the bed with a rock-hard erection thrusting rudely across his belly. The last thing she felt like was a fuck. Instead she asked him why he was grinning at her like that.

'You want to hear something funny? The police think Julia Jarvis is Bra-less Brenda.'

It took Chantal a moment to realise what Rodney was saying but even she, a Frenchwoman whose contempt for domestic British news was profound, had heard of the Topless Raider. And the notion that such a spineless lump of pink *blanc-manger* as Julia could be mistaken for a bank robber was indeed mildly risible. More than that, it was hysterical.

She allowed herself to be pulled onto the bed and Rodney's hands to rove companionably beneath her plain white T-shirt – nothing glamorous, she intended to return to her own bed as soon as possible – while he laughed and told her of Julia's predicament. He did not go into the details of his own involvement.

'But the whole thing is so stupid,' she said. 'It is typical of you British. You are mad about big titties. A woman shakes her melons at a spotty boy behind a counter and he hands over all the money. If only I had fat udders like that stupid Julia I could make a fortune in this country, no problem.'

This was, of course, a cue for Rodney to lift her shirt to her armpits and to shower praise on her delicately curved

195

bosom and plant gentle kisses on her pretty brown nipples which, despite her best intentions, began to stiffen between his lips.

'Rodney,' she said, her hand brushing by chance against the hot pole of flesh that thrust from the junction of his thighs, 'I am very tired.'

'Me too,' he said, nuzzling into the pale stem of her neck.

'That Gordon Garter is an exhausting man.' More to the point, so was his son. It was Graham whom Chantal was thinking of as her fingers curled around Rodney's cock.

'As long as he's a happy one,' said Rodney. 'Mmmm, that's nice.'

'He is very happy, believe me. I have taken care of Garter real good.' It was just as she thought, Rodney's penis was big but Graham Garter's was even bigger. No wonder she was feeling exhausted. Pleasantly exhausted, however.

'Chantal, would you mind most awfully if I just lay back here while you made your report.' Her fingers were working on him with purpose now and the big mushroom cap of his tool was beginning to turn a deeper shade of red.

'But, Rodney, I don't really have anything to say.'

'That's OK. Just use your lips anyway, sweetheart.'

And she did as she was told. For the moment, Rodney Holmdale was still paying her wages.

40

Gavin trudged slowly up the path from the Perch's farmhouse to the field where he had pitched his tent. He was weary but happy. And though no nearer his goal of finding the woman who had robbed him, a part of him secretly hoped that this carnal quest would never end. The marvel was that the part in question seemed to have an unlimited appetite for the search. Over supper, sitting at the big wooden table in Farmer Perch's kitchen, he had scarcely been able to drag his eyes from the daughters of the house. Despite the furious pace of events by Maiden's Pool, his prick still yearned for pussy and his hands itched for the soft weight of Pamela Perch's freckled bosom.

He had no torch but by now the path was familiar. The stars were brilliant in the velvet sky and a warm breeze whispered in the hedgerows. It was a glorious hot summer night.

He pulled his clothes off and crawled naked on top of his sleeping bag. He did not bother to close the tent flap but looked out at the indigo triangle of night.

He was just drifting off to sleep, jumbled images of Rosie's plump titty flesh in his mind, his cock stiff with reminiscence, when the patch of sky and stars ahead of him was blotted out. There was a rustle of clothing, a whispered, 'Hi, Gavin, it's me,' and suddenly there were two of them in the tent.

Gavin drew the obvious conclusion, wrapped his arms round his visitor and kissed her hard. After a moment's resistance her mouth opened to swallow his tongue and a hand slipped onto his waist and downward to massage the firm cheeks of his bum. It was only then that Gavin realised that the woman in his arms was not Pamela.

'My,' she said when they came up for air, 'you know how to make a girl welcome.'

'Cleo?'

'Who did you think it was?'

Gavin didn't answer with words, it was simpler to kiss her again and absorb the information that Pamela Perch's younger sister was enthusiastically fondling his naked arse.

Cleo was an olive-skinned brunette with high cheekbones and unfettered breasts whose tips had jostled the cotton of her candy-striped blouse all through supper – Gavin had noticed. He had also noticed the wide smile and the slim thighs that were just like her sister's and the small dainty hands that were now exploring his rampant cock and balls. She had the knowing touch of Pamela, too.

'I knew you'd be ready for it after an afternoon with my prick-teasing sister,' said Cleo. 'I thought I was going to have to seduce you.'

'But—'

'Shh, lie back and let me do all the work. I've always wanted to stumble across a naked man in a field and hump myself to heaven under the stars. Can we go outside and fuck on the grass?'

Gavin allowed himself to be dragged out into the open. She pulled off her shirt and pressed her bare chest to his, the hard little points of her nipples burning into his skin.

'Cleo . . .?'

Her skirt was off now and he could see the faint glow of her panties as she slipped them down her thighs.

'How old are you?'

By way of an answer she pushed him down onto the grass and laid the warm length of her nudity on top of him. She thrust her tongue into his mouth and he could feel the tender skin of her belly on his.

'I'm old enough,' she replied at length. 'You're lucky you've got me out here, I'm the hot one of the family. My sister's a virgin and my mother might as well be. Can we put it in now? I want to fuck you silly.'

There was no point in arguing, so Gavin didn't. She wriggled down his body and he felt the kiss of her wet pussy on the head of his straining cock. He put his hand between

Lust at Large

their bodies to play with her cunt. It was juicy and eager, sucking in his finger to the joint. He'd never felt such a small, almost hairless, pussy. She squirmed on his finger and stuck her tongue into his ear.

'Let me put it in, Gavin, please. I can't wait.'

He wondered how she was going to manage but it didn't take her long. It was a tight fit but a delicious one and she moaned with pleasure as she eased his length up her sticky passage.

Then, true to her word, with the pair of them naked in the grass in the warm night air, she fucked him silly.

Afterwards he crawled back into his tent and fell asleep at once. He was woken by a hand on his shoulder and a flash of light.

'Gavin.' It was a woman's voice but not Cleo's nor Pam's. 'I've brought you a nightcap. I don't like to think of you lying out here on the bare earth catching your death.'

'Mrs Perch—' Gavin automatically took the glass that was being pressed into his hand, his sleepy brain suddenly alert as he calculated the significance of this latest visitation. He put the glass to his lips and the stimulating aroma of rum enveloped him.

'Do you always sleep naked, Gavin, or are you just travelling light? One of the boys could lend you some pyjamas.'

A torch was in her hand. She played its thin pencil beam down his body. It came to rest on the outcrop of pubic hair at the base of his stomach – and on the pale finger of flesh that Gavin was amazed to see was once more standing to attention. The beam held steady as the penis rapidly came to full erection. Then she shut it off.

'I'm sorry, Gavin. That was naughty of me. But you are a delicious young boy lying naked on my land. It makes me feel almost feudal. As if I own you.'

Gavin was not surprised now to feel yet another set of Perch fingers wrap themselves around his genitals. The genitals themselves did not mind and a shiver of pleasure ran up his belly. There was no doubt where the Perch daughters had gained their digital skills. It was in the genes.

'Get your knickers off, Mrs Perch,' said Gavin, the rum going straight to his head.

'Take them off yourself, you bad boy.' And she giggled

Lust at Large

when he put his hand under the hem of her dress and found she wasn't wearing any.

She was very hairy, with a soft and perfumed rug of fur that ran from the crack of her arse to halfway up her belly, and she was dripping like a tap. Her large breasts were like fabulous balloons, warm and silky to the touch and full of puff. He fastened a rubbery nipple to his mouth and ran his hands through the fleece between her legs. She muttered soft obscenities in the dark that set his mind buzzing with filthy thoughts.

'Do you lick pussy, Gavin? Do you like a juicy cunt in your mouth?' she said and took his head and placed it between her butter-soft thighs. He sucked in her juices like a drunk, his senses spinning as his hands ransacked the pillows of her bottom and she came off in one long mounting crescendo of moans and cries.

They weren't finished yet and they both knew it. But as he lay on the heaving swell of her comfortable chest, his cock butting a hole in the swell of her hip, he said, 'What is it about this place? Why are all you women so damned sexy?'

She laughed and pulled him between the vee of her firm fleshy thighs. 'It's Midsummer's, Gavin. Blisswood's a special place at Midsummer's. None of us can get enough.'

There was no doubt about that, he thought, as he held the knob of his cock to the thick stem of her clitoris and listened to the gurgling in her throat as she heaved her flanks against him.

'Put it in, Gavin, put it in,' she pleaded and she tugged at his root with her strong countrywoman's fingers.

He thrust deep into her, determined to satisfy her utterly, to quell the storm that raged in her, and found himself swept along in a current too strong for him to resist.

She wrapped her legs around his back and took charge, heaving up at him in a frenzy, her hands squeezing, pinching and pulling his flesh, forcing him to fuck at her pace.

The soft valve between her legs threatened to swallow him whole. It gorged on the length of his prick like a mouth, sucking and swallowing him up. It was furious and sweaty and possibly the most fantastic fuck of his life.

'Oh yes!' she squealed. 'Fuck me! Fuck me! Give me everything you've got!'

She slid a long index finger between his bum cheeks and into the dimple of his arse. Gavin yelled and ejaculated the very last dregs of his balls deep into her capacious cunt.

The moment she left him he fell into a sleep that was like a drug-induced coma. He woke from it once, driven by a sense of self-preservation, to grab his sleeping bag and stumble across the meadow.

He found a welcoming patch of grass two fields away from his tent. And, as he began to crawl unsteadily into his sleeping bag, he was certain he could hear Pamela Perch calling his name seductively in the night.

Four
SHAFTED

41

Midsummer's Day dawned hot in the North Grinding. It had not rained for weeks, the fields were parched and those who lived off the land were grumbling.

So too was Robyn Chestnut, though for different reasons. Her trip to Flintwhistle had not been entirely successful. She had returned late to the hotel and had tossed and turned all night, wrestling with the heat and the problems likely to be posed by her editor. Nothing was going quite right and now, at seven in the morning, she was sitting on the terrace devouring a cigarette by way of breakfast.

'Well, well,' said a familiar voice, 'if it isn't Robyn from the *Rabbit*. I wondered when we might resume our little dialogue.'

Robyn looked at Archibald Monk with some interest. He seemed more relaxed than when she'd last seen him. The open-necked shirt and casual cords suited him better than the dog-eared grey suit she had seen him in before. A little itch in the pit of her stomach reminded her she found him bloody attractive.

'I was right, wasn't I, Archie?' she said as he folded his lean frame into a white metal chair upwind of her cigarette smoke. 'That Flintwhistle job confirms that Brenda's on the loose round here.'

'Maybe.' He nodded in his usual noncommittal style but he wasn't fooling Robyn.

'You're on to something, aren't you? I didn't know you Scotch buggers could look cheerful.'

'The investigation is proceeding satisfactorily, Ms Chestnut.'

'Come off it, Archie, you owe me more than that. I'm the reason you're here, after all.'

'Not entirely, though I don't mind telling you we are following leads to yesterday's robbery provided by a witness who saw the suspect leaving the building society. She is Miss Agatha Finch, a well-known Flintwhistle character.'

Robyn angrily ground her cigarette into the stone flagging of the terrace. 'Thanks a bunch, Archie. I spent half of yesterday evening listening to that old bat. She'd have the entire female population under thirty behind bars if she had her way. Apart from anything else, she can't see her nose in front of her face.'

'She can see perfectly well in her new spectacles, Robyn, and she was wearing them yesterday afternoon.'

'Oh yeah. So how come the local police say the witness saw a dark-haired woman? Brenda's blonde, we all know that.'

'There are such things as wigs.'

Robyn did not look convinced and lit another cigarette.

'You might be interested to hear of the conversation I had last night,' continued Monk. 'A reporter from the *Daily Dog* rang me.'

'What!'

'He asked if we were going to hold a topless identity parade.'

'Hell.' Robyn jumped to her feet. She was wasting time here, she had to do . . . something. How could she have been so foolish as to think she had the field to herself?

'Who was it, Archie?'

'Maxwell Shaftesbury. He said he was arriving in Flintwhistle this morning to cover the case.'

'Oh shit,' wailed the intrepid hack from the *Bunny* and fled for her room on the run, almost knocking the tall figure of Stephen Fantail into the bushes as she did so.

'Who was that?' said Stephen as he took a seat next to Monk. There was a dreamy look in his eyes and a nick on his chin that oozed a claret-coloured dribble of blood. He was ten minutes late for his briefing with his superior but he couldn't care less.

'That is one of the leading ladies of the press getting her knickers in a twist,' said Monk with some satisfaction.

'Knickers,' echoed Stephen, the word conjuring up images of recent pleasures.

'So, Stephen, how did you get on with Miss Dodge?'

Stephen blushed from his throat to the tips of his ears as he said, 'She's clean, sir. That is, she's not Brenda, I'm certain.'

'She has an alibi for yesterday?'

'Ah. She told me she was resting in her room and I know she was because I saw her through my binoculars.' His voice dropped as he added, 'She was with a man.'

'*All* yesterday afternoon?'

'Well, the first part certainly. Anyway, I know she's not the robber.'

'How?'

'Her breasts, sir. They are the wrong shape. I've examined them.' Stephen's face was a deep shade of beetroot but he held Monk's eye as his superior gazed at him thoughtfully.

'How did you manage that, Stephen?'

'She – she asked me to, sir. I couldn't very well refuse. Was it the wrong thing to do?'

'Oh no, Stephen.'

'Just for the purpose of eliminating her from the enquiry, sir.'

'Quite,' said Monk. 'Excellent work, detective.' He smiled at his young colleague with satisfaction. He had certainly justified his inclusion on this jaunt.

Upstairs, a restless Robyn was pacing Josie's bedroom turning the air blue in a variety of ways.

'Must you smoke in my room?' asked Josie when Robyn's tirade had finally burnt itself out.

'Who the fuck do you think is paying for it, you useless little tart?' was the reply, followed by, 'Oh God, I'm sorry, Josie. I'm just pissed off in case that bastard, Bonker Shaftesbury, screws me up.'

The story, as Josie understood it, was that last night Robyn had been rebuffed on the doorstep of the house of the Flintwhistle Philanthropic clerk who had been the victim of Brenda's latest outrage. The rebuff had been delivered by a teary-eyed and skinny girl who had claimed to be Craig Gammon (the clerk's) fiancée. In an almost incomprehensible local accent she had shouted at Robyn and told her to 'fook off' – that part was clear, so too was a reference to 'real mooneh'. Robyn had left a note with a phone number but now was in a turmoil in case the *Daily Dog* reporter got to Gammon first and bought his story. And she couldn't ring him herself until the fiancée left for work which, according to a neighbour, wasn't for another hour.

All in all, thought Josie, Robyn was jumping around like a turkey in need of stuffing. Which gave her an idea. She reached for the phone.

'Rodney, it's Josie. We met last on a chaise longue. No, I didn't think you'd forget. Remember I promised to introduce you to my friend, the reporter on the *Daily Rabbit*? She's with me now and I think you should come up. It's an emergency.'

Stephen listened, enthralled, to Monk's account of his interview with Julia Jarvis. He was mightily relieved that suspicion did not appear to point any longer at Fliss. After the events of the evening before they would have had to lead Fliss to the cells over his dead body.

'I didn't want to go in too hard first time out,' said Monk. 'I often find that letting the guilty stew a bit works wonders. I'm due another little talk with Ms Jarvis this morning.'

'Do you want me to be present, sir?'

'No, son. I'd like you to put on your bird-watching gear and check out her mother's house – that's where she's living. My guess is that there's enough evidence in there to nail her. Take a note of the comings and goings. Keep a special eye open to see if she's shifting stuff out. After I've talked to her I'll see about getting a proper warrant to search the place.'

'Yes, sir.'

'Go carefully, Stephen. There's no call to go *examining the evidence* like last night.'

Stephen laughed along with Monk, his face once more a distinctive shade of scarlet.

42

Rodney Holmdale was in fine fettle on this bright Midsummer's morning. His days as a City yuppie in the go-go Eighties had accustomed him to early rising and so, despite the exertions of the night before, he was game for whatever Josie had in mind as he entered the Holmdale Suite. He was not prepared, however, for the six-foot-tall vision in scarlet stretch pants and knotted silk blouse who scowled at him through a cloud of cigarette smoke.

'This is Robyn Chestnut, ace reporter for the *Daily Rabbit*,' said Josie, looking pretty stunning herself in a pale blue thigh-high kimono, tied at the waist and with – Rodney would have put money on it – a Louche Lingerie label on the inside. 'Meet Rodney Holmdale, the owner of Blisswood Spa.'

'You told me he was a masseur,' said Robyn crossly.

'He is, he gave me a brilliant massage last night, didn't you, Rodney?'

'It was my pleasure.'

'But is he properly trained?' asked Robyn.

'I learned my craft at the feet of the eastern masters,' said Rodney. This was true, up to a point. *Feelin' Fine – the Art of Sexual Massage* by Ken & Suzie Blo was one of the few books he had ever read from cover to cover.

'Allow me,' he said, stepping close to Robyn and putting the index finger of his right hand just above the bridge of her nose, in the gap between her thin black curving eyebrows.

'Hey—' she protested and tried to step away but his other hand held the back of her head and his pale blue eyes bored directly into hers.

'Don't fight it,' he said. 'Just let me press this little spot

Lust at Large

here and if you don't like it I promise I won't lay another finger on you.'

'Oh,' said Robyn as she focused on the pressure exerted by his fingertip. Then, 'Oh, oh, that's good,' as she felt her head suddenly clear of tension.

'Am I getting to you?'

'Ooh yes.' Her eyes were closed now and she was rubbing her forehead against his finger like a contented cat.

Josie looked on in awe. He had indeed given her a very successful massage last night after the photo session broke up. But the spot he had stroked so beautifully had not been situated between her eyes.

'Undress and lie down,' he instructed. 'Josie will help you.'

'Yes, sir,' said Josie but the gibe was ignored. Rodney was stripping off his jacket and rolling up his sleeves. Robyn was fumbling at the knot in her shirt.

Josie helped her strip down to a pair of tiny white panties which only served to emphasise the shadowy triangle of her pubic bulge.

'Put the bedspread on the floor and lay her face down,' said Rodney, his eyes all the time on those fabulous dancer's legs. Josie gave his crotch a friendly grope as she hurried to obey him. He was as stiff as a poker.

In the bathroom she found some aromatic skin lotion. And she took off her kimono. Though she intended to get her friend sorted out she could do with a bit of sorting herself.

Rodney took the bottle from her and raised his eyebrows at her fetching nudity.

'I think you should disrobe, O Master,' she said, unbuttoning his shirt, 'lest your celestial robes get sullied.'

Rod shot her a warning glance but Robyn appeared to have cast her fate entirely into their hands. She lay in silence at their feet, her head on one side and her face hidden beneath a cloud of dark hair.

Rodney knelt over her body, his bare knees on either side of her legs, wearing only a bulging crotch pouch. Josie thought he looked good enough to eat, which she wouldn't mind doing later. She was wet with mischief and anticipation.

Lust at Large

Rodney began by dribbling the oil along Robyn's spine and then smoothing it in with both hands, from the base of the neck down to the waistband of her panties. He rubbed systematically from one shoulder blade to the other and onto the pale skin between shoulder blade and spine, kneading the flesh and rolling his thumbs along the bone. Then he slid his hands down to her lower back.

He worked slowly, with concentration, and long before his fingers reached the smooth curves of her buttocks Robyn was moaning out loud. He grunted, too, with the effort he was putting in and it struck Josie that this thoughtful melding of flesh was already highly sexual.

Rodney's fingers pushed at the band of Robyn's panties and Josie pulled them over the beautiful white ovals of her small buttocks and down the length of her legs. Her thighs inched apart and in the vee between could be glimpsed the long pink split of her sex.

Rodney turned his attention to her legs, sitting below her feet and working on the firm flesh of her thighs and calves. He took hold of her feet and pulled, stretching the joints of the leg.

Then he turned her over, breathing heavily as he took in the long red nipples standing up like spikes and the full glory of her pouting pussy mouth visibly agape in the bush of burnt umber curls.

Robyn's eyes were open, gazing at his body and the sheen of sweat on the well-defined muscles of his chest. And at the swollen cotton pouch at the base of his flat belly.

Josie reached out a hand and pulled his briefs down to his thigh. His cock, stiff and thick and brutish, swung out like a boom.

'I think it's time for the full-frontal body rub,' he said with a catch in his voice.

'Oh yes,' said Robyn and held out her arms as he sank onto her.

Josie poured oil into the palm of her hand and reached between their bodies to slick it over his swollen tool. Her fingers found their way onto the open mouth of her friend's vagina and she let them remain there, revelling in the thrill of the moment.

But Josie was not primarily concerned with her own

Lust at Large

pleasure. Her aim was to settle Robyn's nerves and what better way than to see her well shafted?

She took the head of Rodney's firm dick and pushed it into the gash of Robyn's pussy lips. It lodged in the opening for a moment as if stuck, then he flexed his hips and Josie felt the solid meat of him slide through her fingers and into the waiting cunt. It was an extraordinary sensation to feel this intimate joining of two people. At any moment Josie expected one of them to push her away but they didn't. She felt lewd beyond measure as she ringed Rodney's big tool and felt it leap and thrust its way into Robyn.

Then a hand found her thigh and delved without ceremony between her legs. Fingers spread the outer lips of her pussy and dipped between them. An arm circled her shoulders and pulled her tight to the two bodies by her side. Rodney raised his lips from Robyn's and bent to kiss Josie. She took his tongue into her mouth and tasted Robyn.

Robyn was coming, the high-pitched squeals were unmistakable and her pelvis was shivering and shuddering beneath Josie's palm. Josie slid an intruding finger higher, onto her clit, and the cries of orgasm echoed round the room.

Rodney's cock pounded on, thrusting into Robyn in a steady, irresistible rhythm. All three were grinning at each other now, bound together in a rude tangle of limbs.

'Fantastic!' said Rodney.

'I'm going to come again,' muttered Robyn.

Josie saw that Rodney had a hand on Robyn's breast and an arm round her shoulder. She realised that it must be Robyn's fingers in her pussy and came herself in an orgasm that set the others off all around her. There was such a delicious, shattering eruption of sound and sensation that even after they had all subsided it took a moment for them to realise the phone was ringing.

Josie got to it first, breathing hard. It was Craig Gammon.

'Time to go to work, Robyn,' she said, holding out the receiver. 'If you can bear to take that man out of your pussy.'

43

An urgent rapping at the door roused Chantal from her fitful slumber. For the duration of the Gartertex visit she had been allotted a spare room on the top floor and the unfamiliar bed and the usual night-time disturbances of a hotel had not allowed her much rest.

'*Merde*,' she muttered as she stumbled out of bed. 'What do you want?'

A bespectacled face gazed at her in adoration through the crack in the door.

'Gray Ham,' she said, her anger draining away. Then it surged through her afresh as she guessed the reason for his presence. 'You can tell your father to fuck off. It's too early.'

'I've brought you breakfast,' he said, pushing at the door with the tray he was holding. 'My father knows nothing about it.'

With a show of reluctance, Chantal stepped aside to allow him entry. She regarded him with interest as he laid the tray on the small table by the bed and drew the curtains. He arranged two large white china cups and began to pour. The aroma of coffee suddenly ravished her senses.

'Croissant?' he asked, turning to her for the first time, his eye on her nipples through the cotton of her T-shirt. She curled up on top of the bed exposing her thighs almost to her rump and grinned at him.

'You know, Graham, I like you very much. You give me champagne and coffee and croissants. For an Englishman that is impressive.'

'I can give you more than that,' he said. 'I'm in love with you.'

'*Oh la la!* It's eight o'clock in the morning and he talks

of love.' She laughed and bit into a croissant.

'There's no need to make fun of me, Chantal. You may think I'm a milksop, like my father does, but these few days have opened my eyes. I know what I want. I want to make Louche Lingerie the Rolls-Royce of underwear. And I want you.'

Chantal drank her coffee and said nothing.

'My father's not going to go on for ever, you know. He's so fat he could keel over at any moment, God forbid. And when he does, the fate of Gartertex will be in my hands. I'm going to need all the help I can get.'

'Is this a proposal of marriage, Graham?'

'Well, er, yes. I suppose it is.'

'*Formidable*. It's so nice to start the day with a declaration of love. You are a sweet boy.' She put down her coffee cup and stretched one leg high up in the air, toes pointed prettily, thus exposing the bewitching expanse of her naked belly to his hungry gaze.

He accepted the unspoken invitation and fell to his knees by the side of the bed, plunging his face into her crotch. She folded her leg over his back and carefully removed his spectacles as he covered her soft and scented skin with tender kisses.

'What you say is very interesting, Graham. I promise I will think about it seriously.' That was true, her brain was already buzzing with possibilities.

'You will?' He raised his head and gazed at her earnestly. Without his glasses his eyes were misty pools of azure. His jaw was firm and his cheekbones sharp. Chantal pushed a thick black lock of hair from his brow and lifted her hips. 'Kiss me,' she said.

For a lad without much experience of women he did it well, she thought. 'You are a naughty boy, Graham, the way you tease my *chatte*, my little pussy. You mustn't get me too excited. Your father would not be happy.'

'Sod my bloody father!' cried Graham, pulling away and leaping to his feet. Chantal watched with surprise as he began to rip his clothes from his body.

'*Non!*' she cried but she made no attempt to close her legs and the moist petals of her vagina were whispering a very definite *oui*.

Naked, he was no awkward lad. There were muscles in his arms and shoulders and though his flesh was white and unbronzed it was trim and firm. From the black hair of his belly sprang a long curving weapon that glowed with anticipation. Chantal looked at it with pleasure and alarm.

'Put that big thing away, Graham,' she squealed. 'Your father must not see I have been with another man. You must not – ooh!'

He sank the stiff tool into her in one smooth thrust, all the way in until it seemed to touch the very bottom of her. His mouth devoured hers, his tongue filling her up, as his hands lifted her T-shirt to her neck and his broad chest crushed the soft rounds of her small breasts.

He rode her furiously but not without skill. He was strong and fast and urgent but he was not rough. She continued to protest but her cries of 'No' and 'Stop it' changed to 'Please, Graham' and 'Ooh yes' as his irresistible rhythm swept her away with the force of his naked desire.

Then she began to moan without calculation or artifice, begging him to fuck her, to fuck her hard, to keep on and on and – to her utter surprise she suddenly found she was coming. She listened to the sounds ringing round the room aware, for the first time she could remember, that this was the sound of her own untarnished pleasure.

Graham lifted his body off hers to watch the feverish clutch of her pussy on his plunging tool. As the writhing of her perfect flesh subsided he pulled his weapon from her cunt, leaving the flushed vaginal mouth empty and bereft.

To her eyes his cock looked huge. Red and sticky with their juices, it shuddered and twitched in the air and shot a bolt of spunk the length of her body, splashing her face and neck and breast and belly. She had never seen anything like it before.

'There,' he said through lips drawn back in a rictus of jealousy and lust, 'now all you've got to do is wash and you'll be as good as new.' And then he began to cry.

As Chantal hugged his shaking body in a gooey embrace she felt an emotion that she couldn't identify. She stroked his long neck tenderly and held him fast to her soft bosom.

44

Craig Gammon turned out to be a tricky customer.

'I think it only fair to let you know that we are already in discussions with another party,' said the voice in Robyn's ear, returning her swiftly to the sordid cut-and-thrust of massmarket journalism after the happy interlude at the hands of Rodney the masseur.

All the relaxation text books claimed that a satisfying workout would provide a long-lasting inner glow guaranteed to relieve the stress of business. But Robyn, sitting on the bed covered in oil and sex juice, found it difficult to conceal her irritation with the victim of the Flintwhistle Philanthropic. 'We' indeed! However, she was a professional.

'I presume you mean the *Daily Dog*, Mr Gammon?'

'Er, precisely. They have given us certain assurances as to the matter of our expenses and other incidental costs.'

'You've been talking to Maxwell Shaftesbury, haven't you?'

'As a matter of fact, I have and I'm very impressed. I've seen him on the telly.'

'Then you'll know what a smooth-talking bastard he is. I'd caution you not to be too easily impressed. I bet whatever he's promised you is worthless.'

'What are you on about?'

'You're the wrong sex, Craig. The man's a rabid lecher devoted to separating other men from their women. He'll buy you a ploughman's lunch and knock up your fiancée. Believe me.'

'I suppose he did say he wanted to meet Franny . . .'

'Don't worry, I've got a better idea.'

'Eh?'

'Come to the hotel this morning. We'll talk real terms.

And I promise you I'm much prettier than he is.'

'But what about the identity parade?'

'The identity parade?' This rang a bell – what had Archie Monk said?

'I had this idea for a photo in the paper. You know, with me looking at a row of suspects, all topless beauties like Braless Brenda. He thinks it's a great idea.'

'So it is,' said Robyn, desperate not to lose her advantage. 'We'll do it in the *Bunny*. Have you got a car?'

'I got a motorbike.'

'Good. Leave home right now and come straight here. Don't speak to anyone, don't answer the phone, just leave.'

She put the phone down with a groan. 'Oh God, now I've done it.'

A pair of strong male arms folded themselves around her body and tugged her down onto the bed.

'Don't worry,' said Rodney, 'we'll make a plan.'

'But how am I going to set up this bloody photo? I don't even have a photographer, let alone the models.'

'Don't be stupid, Robyn,' said Josie, nestling down on the other side of the agitated reporter and running a soothing hand along her thigh. 'This place is bursting with pretty girls and there's the best glamour photographer in England on hand, isn't there, Rodney?'

'Yes indeed.' Rodney's voice was muffled because his face was buried in Robyn's hair, nuzzling the back of her neck. 'Cliff Rush will love the idea. It's just up his alley.'

'Really?' The gloom fell from Robyn's face. 'Do you think he would?'

'Leave it to me,' said Rodney.

'You're fantastic!' cried Robyn and pulled Rodney's mouth to hers for a thank-you kiss that soon stretched into something more interesting. When Robyn came up for air she reached for Josie. 'You, too,' she said and kissed her.

Josie froze as Robyn's tongue pushed hesitantly into her mouth. The sensation was somehow more intimate, more forbidden, than the other woman's fingers in her pussy. Robyn was kissing her insistently now, the long tongue exploring, and Josie sucked on it, kissing her back. They broke away and looked sheepishly at Rodney whose cock was at attention and whose eyes gleamed with anticipation.

'I expect Cliff will need paying,' he said.

'Of course,' said Robyn. 'The *Bunny* always plays fair. We'll pay a fee.'

'If I know Cliff, he'll be more interested in a personal favour.'

'He wants you and me to pose for him,' said Josie. 'He said so last night.'

'You'd look fabulous together,' said Rodney, thinking of his private portfolio.

'Oh Christ,' muttered Robyn, though in truth, as her hand toyed with the firm nipple of Josie's pretty left breast, the notion was not unpleasant.

'Mmm,' said Josie, resting her head on the pillow next to Robyn's, 'that's nice.' And she began an exploration of Robyn's own flushed and perky bosom.

The two of them kissed again and this time their bodies entwined, the long slender American wrapping her limbs around the softer, smaller English girl. As Robyn's fingers caressed the silky swell of Josie's hip, a fleeting image of Mercedes Birch swam into her mind and she probed lower, over the creamy skin of Josie's belly.

Suddenly Robyn was rudely shocked out of her explorations as a hand descended on her rump. 'Ow,' she yelled and jerked open her eyes to see a grinning Rodney standing over the pair of them.

'Sorry, girls,' he said. 'There's no time for this kind of hanky-panky. Before your star witness turns up, Robyn, your other benefactor needs paying. So which one of you ladies would like to settle my account?' And he pointed to his penis, which was jutting from his loins in a flagrant display of male impatience.

Josie giggled at the sight but closed her thighs on Robyn's curious finger, pressing it to her pussy mound with her hand in a gesture that clearly stated her preference.

Robyn fought back an impulse to tell Rodney to jam his dick into a keyhole somewhere and instead found herself spreading her luscious legs wide open in invitation.

'Help yourself, lover,' she said. 'Like I said, the *Bunny* always plays fair.'

45

Max Shaftesbury stood on the doorstep of a terraced cottage on the outskirts of Flintwhistle and swore.

'The little bastard's legged it,' he said to the woman by his side. Her lovely mouth curved into a grin which, Max knew from long experience, did not necessarily mean she found the situation amusing. Adriana accepted the ups-and-downs of life without fuss, treating triumph and disaster with a sloe-eyed smile. Some people found this bloody irritating. Others thought she was stupid. Max knew for a fact she was neither.

'Let's try the neighbours,' she said and knocked at the next door along. There was no response. Max took over and thundered all his impatience into the agitation of the door knocker. This brought results of a sort. The door on the other side of the first swung open and a voice said, 'Knock all you like but she won't hear you. They buried her six weeks ago.'

The woman who spoke wore a well-filled purple housecoat and pink mules with bobbles on. Her hair was pinned up on her head in a brown tangle and her jaw was large and firm. She looked Max straight in the eye and challenged him to contradict her.

The journalist swung into action as if programmed. His face lit up as he looked at her, crinkling the laughter lines round his deep brown, soulful eyes. The voice was deep brown as well.

'Maxwell Shaftesbury of the *Daily Dog*,' he intoned, smoothly invading the woman's personal space, 'I'm delighted to meet you, Miss . . .'

'Mrs to you. Margot Scallion, with two ells if you're putting it in the paper.'

'We might, Mrs Scallion. You're our only hope.' His face looked plaintive. Get their sympathy right off the bat. It was a cardinal rule.

'How's that?'

'I had an appointment to speak to Mr Gammon and he's not answering his door. You don't know where he is, by any chance?'

'Aha,' she said, leaning against the doorjamb and searching in her pockets for a packet of cigarettes. She took her time placing one to her lush lipsticky lips and Max supplied the flame, leaning in close to shelter his lighter from a non-existent breeze.

'If you could tell me anything about Mr Gammon's disappearance, Mrs Scallion, it would be of considerable assistance to my paper. My editor would be shocked if I did not offer you some small token of our gratitude.'

On cue, Adriana produced a thick wallet from her handbag and peeled off six five-pound notes.

Margot Scallion looked at her and sniffed. 'Put away your brass and come on in, Mr Shaftesbury. The little girl can wait outside.' And she turned and disappeared through the door.

Adriana said, 'Attaboy, Max,' and retraced her steps to the blue Spacewagon parked on the other side of the road. Other women might have been insulted, Adriana gave no sign of it – it was one of the reasons she had kept her job for so long.

Max stepped into the tiny hallway, momentarily unbalanced by the swirly pink carpet and flower-patterned wallpaper. Mercifully, Mrs Scallion was in the kitchen where the linoleum was plain and there was a view of the tiny back garden. Three very large brassieres hung amidst other items of family apparel upon the washing line. A Charentais melon would fit snugly into each cup, Max thought.

'So,' began his hostess as she poured tea the colour of mahogany, 'you want to know what's going off with him and her next door.'

Lust at Large

'Tell me, Mrs Scallion.'

'Well, she – that's Franny Wintergreen as is supposed to be marrying Craig – she's in a right tizzy over what went on yesterday with him at work. They had a real set-to and she smacked his face and made him sleep on the sofa.'

'Why?'

'She said he shouldn't have been looking at that girl's chest and he said he couldn't help it what with her having a gun. She said he should have kept his eyes on her face so he could identify her and he should have stalled till the police got there. He said that was all right for those whose lives weren't in peril and if she, Franny, wasn't so flat-chested he'd never have been so gobsmacked by such a whopping great pair in the first place.'

'Oh dear.'

'Quite. That was when she hit him. My Brian and I were trying to watch the television but we decided the entertainment was better through the wall and we turned it off.'

Max took a reluctant sip of his tea which was noted by Mrs Scallion. She was a lady who missed little.

'Here,' she said, producing a bottle that looked as if it had once held disinfectant, 'let's freshen that up a bit.' And she poured a generous slug of brown liquid into both mugs.

'I suppose you'd like to know about the other reporter?' she went on.

Indeed he would, his disappointment at the news was tempered by the scorching pain of raw whisky in the back of his throat. Did Mrs S brew the stuff herself? he wondered.

'She fetched up about nine, after they'd had the big ding-dong. I heard her say she was from the *Daily Rabbit*. Franny told her to bugger off. She wouldn't let her talk to Craig.'

'Did this reporter have an American accent?'

'Most definitely. She was very tall with lots of dark hair. She knocked on my door after but I wouldn't let her in. Not like you.'

Max mulled this over. He wasn't personally acquainted with Robyn Chestnut but he knew all about her. He'd just love to pip her to this one. It was fortunate that firebrand

Franny had opened the door to her. He'd got Craig himself on the phone that morning and he'd sounded like your average avaricious prick who could be bought on the cheap. The girl sounded like a killer.

'So where is Craig now?' he asked. Maybe La Chestnut had him after all and he'd lost out. It wasn't a pleasant thought.

'Aha,' said Margot Scallion and looked at him significantly.

'So you *would* like some money?' Max said. He was not surprised. In his experience banknotes, along with drinks, were rarely scorned.

'No, I'd prefer your opinion on the new rug upstairs.'

He wished he hadn't been on the road since dawn. He couldn't seem to get his wits going today. 'I'm sorry?' he said.

Mrs Scallion laughed, a contemptuous high-pitched cackle that reverberated through Max's limber frame. 'Eeh, I am disappointed in you, Mr Shaftesbury. You're not living up to your reputation at all. Us ladies don't have etchings or stamp collections in our parlours but we do have shag-pile rugs on our bedroom floors. Do you get my drift?'

Max looked over her shoulder at the dangling melon traps on the washing line. He got the drift.

'It will be my pleasure, Mrs Scallion.'

'Margot, from now on, please,' she said as she got to her feet. 'You know you mentioned your editor was keen for you to offer me a small token of gratitude?'

'Yes?'

'It'd bloody well not be small or I'm never buying the *Dirty Dog* again.'

Max drained his spiked tea to the very dregs. All stimulation was welcome at this point. Then he followed her large purple bottom up the narrow stairs to bed.

46

'Mercy,' said Melanie as she looked out of the window of the bedroom she shared with her sister, 'do you see what I see?'

Mercy joined her twin and looked over the back garden, past the vegetable patch to a knot of trees by the river.

'It's a bloke with a pair of binoculars,' she said. 'So what? There are walkers and bird-watchers all over the place.'

'That one has been there for half an hour and he's not taken his bins off our house for a moment.'

'Maybe Mum's doing her exercises in the nude again. You couldn't blame him for peeping at that.'

'This is serious, Mercy. Don't you recognise him?'

'Is he at the hotel?'

'Room 31. Next door to his friend in 32.'

'Oh.' The grin faded from Mercy's pretty face. She had seen the occupant of 32 in action and Inspector Archibald Monk was not high on her list of favourite people. Not after the way he had treated Julia the night before.

The realisation that an associate of Monk's was spying on their house filled her with alarm. 'What shall we do, Mel?' she asked.

'Not bad-looking for a copper, is he?' said Melanie.

'A bit young.'

'Nice hair. Long legs. Tight bum.'

'You can't see his bum from here.'

'I've checked him out before.'

Mercy was not surprised. 'So what are we going to do?' she repeated.

'Teach the little bastard a lesson.'

'But he's a policeman!'
'No man would bring charges over what I've got in mind.'

Stephen Fantail was a conscientious fellow. He enjoyed his work, in particular the detail. What most of his colleagues considered to be tedious and bureaucratic thrilled Stephen the most. Files and paperwork, computers and databases, these were the things that gave his life meaning. Other aspects of police work, such as doorstepping the public and confronting witnesses face to face, appealed to him rather less. Until last night, that is. Until his hands-on interrogation of a woman suspected of being the country's most wanted criminal. Until he came face to face with Felicity Dodge.

He watched the big old farmhouse with unseeing eyes, his mind filled with breathtaking images of Fliss. Maybe his reflexes had been undermined by the loss of his virginity, maybe he was simply tired after his romantic exertions on the hillside but, trained observer that he was, he didn't see what hit him.

Crash! He thumped onto the ground as his legs were swept from beneath him and his head smacked into the rough bark of a tree. The ground was as hard as concrete and punched the air from his body and the binoculars flew from his fingers to land on his face.

Despite his strength and fitness, there was nothing Stephen could do about the weight on his chest which pinned him to the ground. Hands tugged at his clothing and he was aware that his legs and arms were being bound. In his imagination, when considering the possibility of being jumped by a villain, he had always seen himself dodging and parrying, his lightning reactions saving him from the thrust of a knife or the swing of a crow bar. Now he learned the truth. A victim of total surprise, he was as helpless as a captive toddler having his nappy changed.

This unlikely image entered his mind as he became aware that his jeans were being lowered and his loins bared.

'Get off me!' he protested and took a hefty smack on the ear. His skull rang with the impact and his eyes watered with pain.

'Shut up, you wanker,' hissed a voice. 'I'm going to show you what we do to Peeping Toms around here.'

The voice was female but his vision was fogged and he could only make out a shape in shiny scarlet bending over him. She was wearing something on her face, he realised, probably a stocking, and the features were distorted into a weird blurry mass.

'Mmm, that's nice,' continued the voice and a hand slid over his bared belly. He writhed and struggled but his arms were above his head, tied to something, and there was a soft but immovable weight on his knees.

The hand was between his thighs, at the fork of his body, cupping his twitching testicles.

'Don't worry, darling, if you're a good boy you won't get hurt.'

Fingers were on his penis now, tracing its flaccid length, teasing the furled knot of skin at the tip.

In his distorted vision the shape in scarlet resolved itself into a woman in a figure-hugging lycra leotard that left nothing to the imagination.

'Come on, baby,' she said, 'get it up for mama. Show me all you've got.'

At her neck the silver tab of a zip fastener glinted in the sunlight. Two fingers took hold of it and began to ease it down with a soft metallic purr.

Stephen's breath caught in his throat as the hills of a magnificent bosom soared into view, spilling from the sea of scarlet in a soft tumble. The swollen pink nipples swung over his face and he lifted his lips involuntarily, yearning for their touch despite his predicament.

'You like them, don't you?' said the voice. 'You're as stiff as a post.'

He was, too. He couldn't help himself.

The spectacular tits shivered and wobbled before his eyes, swaying just out of reach, the creamy rounds full and firm, the nipples big and berry red. Stephen was mesmerised. His head hurt with looking as the balls of flesh dipped and trembled. It seemed that there were two bosoms now – four breasts, four nipples – two identical pairs of lefts and rights dancing before his confused gaze.

His breath was coming hard as the hand in his crotch speeded up, pumping the barrel of his tool, slicking the juicy folds of his foreskin backwards and forwards over the bursting knob.

'That's right, big boy,' said the low sexy voice, 'keep your eyes on my tits. They really turn you on, don't they? I bet you're going to come soon.'

That much was true. His loins were out of control. He could no more hold back than uproot the tree he was tied to. But, as he gazed on the wondrous breasts in front of him and a river of spunk spat from his jumping prick, other images floated before his disarranged mind's eye. Grainy black-and-white images produced by photographic enlarging. Images he had pored over for hours. Photos of Bra-less Brenda's breasts.

47

Margot Scallion need not have worried. Maxwell Shaftesbury's token of gratitude was far from small, indeed it was bloody enormous – as Margot described it to her friend Dolores over a laced coffee the following morning. For now though, she clung on to the real thing and savoured every millimetre of its warm baby-smooth length. She had never before had such an object of beauty between her lilac blue sheets and she knew she never would again – she was making the most of it.

'Margot,' muttered Max through a mouthful of brown rubbery nipple, 'do you really know where Craig is?'

'Of course I do. You don't think I'd take advantage of you unfairly do you? I might be a woman with appetites but I wouldn't do the dirty on you, love.' She ringed his firm stalk in her big strong fingers and began to jiggle it up and down.

Max groaned and pushed business to the back of his mind for the moment as the perfumed flesh of her vast breast swamped his face. Her hot hand on his cock was as reassuring as a mother's touch and as knowing as a whore's mouth. This was not what he had expected when he had climbed the stairs.

Margot was indeed a woman of appetites. Beneath the purple housecoat she had been wearing peach-coloured French knickers and a brassiere that was a marvel of structural engineering. Tall and square-shouldered, with a cascade of chestnut locks now loose about her neck, she was a formidable-looking woman. But it wasn't just the obvious things – the bulging melons of her breasts, the violin-curve of her hips, the satin-creased outline of her pussy – that

Lust at Large

engaged Max's attention and shook him from his early-morning lassitude. It was the expression on her face. The firm-set mouth, the glistening black eyes, the straight nose that pointed at him like the barrel of a gun. This woman knew all about him and she wanted her money's worth.

Maxwell Shaftesbury's reputation was on the line.

He'd got on his knees and placed his mouth over her bush through the thin material of her knickers. He'd slid his hands up both legs of the satin bloomers, grasped a handful of bottom flesh and pulled the weight of her onto his face. Kneeling at her feet fully clothed, he'd pressed his mouth, his nose – his entire famous star-reporter face – into the hidden folds of her vagina until she was panting and clawing at his thick curly hair and begging him to put her on the bed and fuck her.

He'd done that too. First he'd released her quivering tits from the restraints of her mighty brassiere, catching the big pink beauties as they tumbled from the cups and licking and kissing the ridged brown pegs of her nipples which thrust, as hard as nuts, into his mouth. Then, throwing his elegant designer casuals onto the vile shag-pile rug, he'd plunged his ever-ready tool between her big white thighs, through the open gusset of her knickers and into the moist petals of her hungry cunt. When she came – and she had come quickly – she had squealed like a stuck pig and thrashed like a beached fish.

That had been Round One to Max but he was aware, as he nuzzled the intoxicating flesh of her bosom, that the bout was far from over.

'Come on, Margot, spill the beans. What's Craig Gammon up to?'

'He went off on his bike just before nine. Why don't you put your hand just a little lower? Ooh that's nice. We had a little chat before he left.'

'And?'

'He did mention he was off to meet the woman from the *Rabbit*.'

'Damn.'

'Don't stop, Maxwell. Eeh, you've got a right naughty pair of hands on you.'

'Did he say where they were going to meet?'

'Well, he were in that much of a hurry I can't recall exactly which hotel it was. He was all excited that she was going to put a photo in the paper of him looking at topless girls. You know, like in an identity parade. Mind you, I think he's mad. That Franny will kill him when it comes out. What's up, Maxwell? You look right poorly.'

'Poorly' didn't adequately describe the naked reporter as he squatted on his haunches above Margot, his face as stiff and red as the cock which stuck out from the flat muscles of his belly.

'That was *my* idea!' he shouted, his eyes blazing and his penis waving in the air between Margot's dimpled thighs. She folded a comforting hand around the fat shaft and pointed the head downwards into the dark forest of hair that covered her pussy – it was as well to put a dangerous thing like that somewhere safe.

'I spoke to Gammon about that this morning!' raved Max as his cock disappeared into Margot's moist tunnel. 'I've got a photographer with me, I've got quotes from the police, it's going to make a great spread!'

'Aye, it will,' agreed Margot, pulling the delirious man on top of her and folding her solid haunches around his hips. 'Pity you'll have to see it in the *Bunny* though.'

'But it was *my* idea,' repeated Max, his pelvis pumping as he responded to Margot's demands.

'Genius is rarely recognised in its own lifetime,' she said philosophically and shut him up by pushing her large plush tongue between his lips.

It had been a long road that had led Maxwell Shaftesbury to the rigours of Margot Scallion's bed. Australian by birth, he had become such a part of the British entertainment scene that few remembered his origins. The high point of his career had been his own TV chat show, whose success was based on the sexual chemistry between the good-looking, abrasive host and a stream of sporting female guests. It was set to run for ever until, as the station boss put it, Max had 'overcooked it'.

He'd been flirting harmlessly with Henrietta Suckling, a

cut-glass English actress whose carefully groomed beauty had improved, like good wine, with the march of time. Her cunningly managed career gave her an entrée to almost any kind of work, from drawing-room sitcoms to voice-overs for after-dinner mints to sitting on judging panels of literary prizes. The interview had been going well. Too well, as it turned out.

'I have a theory about you, Henry,' he'd said.

'How thrilling, darling,' she'd cooed in her famous breathy tones and crossed her long legs with a cock-stretching *swish*.

'I think you're the woman of every man's dreams because you come across like an intellectual whore.'

'Really?' A pencil-thin eyebrow arched upwards.

'I picture you sitting at home reading philosophy with no knickers on.'

'Darling, I do *lots* of things without knickers on.' *Swish, swish* went the legs amid much studio laughter.

'Such as appearing on TV chat shows?' Louder laughter.

'I'm not saying.' *Swish*. 'That's for you to find out.' There was a whoop of delight from the audience.

'Are you telling me, Henry, that if I put my hand on this adorable knee here and let my hand slide up beneath your skirt like this –' *Ooh!* from the studio audience. 'She's wearing suspenders, ladies and gentlemen, and has the smoothest, silkiest thighs . . .'

'I didn't know this was a consumer research programme, Max,' said Henrietta staring him coolly in the face, her full lips curled into a trademark smile that was pure sex.

In retrospect this was the point at which he could have retreated and still kept his job. But, with his hand halfway up her thigh and the audience egging him on, he needed a rebuff from her to get him off the hook. As he looked into her pale grey eyes he knew he had met his match, there would be no backing down from her. He thrust his hand right up her skirt.

A collective intake of breath came from all around, followed by a burst of applause. To his amazement she sat as cool as a cucumber while he explored.

'Well, Max, what's the verdict?' she'd said.

He'd not replied but, with one hand on the soft down of her pussy and the other round her waist, he had fastened his lips to hers and rolled her backwards onto the plump cushions of the studio couch.

The audience had roared and whooped and the station had pulled the plug on the show and Max's TV career. He'd often thought that the following few days he'd spent tucked up in bed with Henrietta at her sister's flat – to escape the newspaper ratpack – had made it all worthwhile. One thing was sure, the whole business had done nothing to harm Henry's prospects. He had mixed feelings these days every time he saw those damned commercials.

It was ironic that Max now found himself part of the ratpack. Only a sleazy rag like the *Dog* would take him on, of course, but they knew their market. The public still loved him and Max often consoled himself with that thought. The real public, that is, not the high-minded watchdogs of public morality who loved to lay every ballooning crime statistic and undesirable social phenomenon at the door of the media. He knew he had a following of people like Margot Scallion who even now, as she relaxed after her fourth orgasm on his redoubtable cock, asked him, 'When that Henrietta Suckling was on your show, was she, you know . . . ?'

'No, Margot. The hot bitch *wasn't* wearing any knickers.'

'By gum, that's disgusting!' She sat up in bed, her huge udders swaying dangerously.

'Absolutely,' said Max, eyeing the shifting of sweet pink flesh with a *frisson* of alarm.

'I'm never going to give Brian them mints again,' she said as she swung her legs across his supine torso and took hold of the brass rail of the bed head.

'Margot, where is Craig Gammon meeting that reporter from the *Daily Rabbit*?'

But her reply, if she made one, was lost in a whirl of perfumed motion as Max's ears were buffeted with a mass of breast flesh, like soft satiny sandbags smacking backwards and forwards across his head. Between his thighs, his prick rose to the carnal call of a titty-whipping the like of which

Lust at Large

the great cocksman of the *Dirty Dog* had never experienced before.

Margot Scallion climbed aboard his long curving prong, guiding the big banana up her pussy with a sigh of immense satisfaction. This was turning out to be the best morning of her life since she and Dolores had entertained that dishy plumber and his mate. Better, in fact. What plumber, after all, could give her the inside story on Henrietta Suckling's knickers?

48

Clifford Rush had leapt at the opportunity to work as a stand-in photographer for the *Daily Rabbit*.

'Just keep my name out of the paper,' he told Robyn, 'and I'm yours for the morning. Then you're mine for the afternoon. Agreed?'

'It's a deal,' said the reporter, lighting a fresh cigarette from the butt of her last. 'Get me through this and I'm yours for life.'

Cliff rushed off to prepare the room they were going to use for the shoot. It was a large and dingy storeroom with a tiled floor and once-white walls. Rodney had suggested it might make a suitably stark location and Robyn was only too happy to agree. She was also relieved that Cliff had volunteered to round up a selection of suitable models.

Rodney and Josie had disappeared in Rodney's car to Smegley, the nearest town, to buy a selection of Brenda-style T-shirts and halter-necks. Which left Robyn to handle the man of the moment, Craig Gammon.

He was dressed in motorcycle leathers and a grubby vest and wore it's-my-day-off stubble on his chin. It occurred to Robyn that the reason he had not shaved was probably to avoid running a razor over the left side of his face which was swollen and pink. His left eye was half closed and every minute or so he brushed away a tear which seeped down the side of his nose.

'I fell down the stairs last night,' he said as he lowered his big shambling frame into the chesterfield in the sitting-room of her suite.

'Did Franny push you?' asked Robyn.

'How do you know?' he asked, fixing her with his one good eye.

'I met her myself. I thought she was going to take a pop at me too.'

'Oh aye,' he nodded unhappily. 'She were right worked up yesterday. It weren't my fault that Brenda come in the bog shop and flashed her charlies while I were there.'

'Bog shop?'

'Building society – bee ess – bog shop. It is, too. I'm glad a little smasher like her got the money. I reckon she ought to bung a bit my way. I mean, it's all thanks to me, isn't it?'

'If you say so.' Robyn could hardly conceal her glee. This idiot was a gift.

He frowned. Something of the sort had also occurred to him.

'Here, all this is off the record, right? We haven't talked money yet.'

'Let's talk about it now then. What figure did you have in mind?'

'Five.'

Robyn frowned. Five thousand pounds for a one-off piece was a bit steep even if it did freeze out the *Dog*.

'Two,' she replied.

'Come off it!' He was indignant. 'This is my exclusive account of going face to face with the most wanted woman in the land. It's got to be worth four.'

'Three and we'll use your photo idea. My photographer is rounding up some beautiful girls right now.'

He thought about this for a moment. The mention of 'girls' had put a gleam in his one functioning eye.

'OK,' he said, 'three hundred and fifty pounds, that's my last word.'

Robyn could have leapt for joy. The guy was a certifiable moron.

'Done,' she said with a straight face and offered her hand.

He took hold of it by the wrist and yanked her towards him so that she almost fell into his lap.

'Three fifty and I get to shag the model I like best after the photo session.'

Maybe he wasn't quite as stupid as he looked.

Her hand had come to rest on the shiny black leather of his thigh. It felt hard and firm beneath the slippery material.

'I can't guarantee that,' she said, 'but suppose I suck your cock now and you make your own arrangements for later?'

He didn't reply in words, he just grabbed her shoulders and pulled her mouth to his stubbly face.

He tasted better than she would ever have thought and, as his tongue slipped between her lips, she relished the brutish rasp of his chin. A big hand suddenly yanked her skirt to her waist and he grabbed a fistful of pliant bum flesh.

'No,' she said firmly as she tried to stop his fingers ripping away the wisp of panty that covered her bottom. 'We do it my way or the deal's off.'

'I'll talk to Maxwell Shaftesbury,' he said, cupping her arse cheeks in both hands and probing for her crack. In another moment she wouldn't care if her clothes were ruined.

'Get off or I'll talk to Franny,' she replied with finality and shoved him backwards so he sprawled across the sofa.

He grinned at her sheepishly and she knew the threat of Franny had won the day. In some respects that was a pity but there was no time for anything more complicated. Besides, she relished what she was about to do...

She knelt between the spread vee of his leather-clad thighs and put her hands on the bulge in his crotch. He slid lower in his seat and surrendered to her fingers as she deftly pulled open his fly and delved inside for his penis.

It was thick and shiny and circumcised, as big as a billiard ball on top, and she almost gagged as she stretched her mouth wide to take it in. She pulled his balls from his trousers and held them in one hand while she went to work on his shaft with the other.

He grunted in appreciation and shifted his leather-clad pelvis to her rhythm.

Coming up for air, she took her lips from the steaming red helmet in her fist and smiled to herself. Such tasks there were in the pursuit of her chosen profession! Her hands masturbated him briskly and the smell and creak of leather assailed her as she exercised her considerable skills in the cause of journalism.

Lust at Large

She licked and kissed his burning knob and tickled the underside of his glans with the tip of her tongue.

'By Christ, that's good,' he muttered, his face as flushed as his tool.

'Yeah,' she said, 'I love the way your dick sticks out of the leather. It's wild. Pure Brando.'

'Yer what? If you don't want me to spunk all over your blouse, love, you'd better put it back in yer gob quick.'

Robyn did as she was told and swallowed every drop.

49

Stephen drifted in and out of consciousness. He couldn't shift the cords that bound his wrists and ankles and he was resigned to being discovered like this. Someone would come along sooner or later, he knew, and it was going to be most embarrassing when they did. He tried not to think about it.

The day was balmy and warm already, the grass beneath his half-naked body had long lost its morning dampness. Up in the sky birds flitted, close by insects buzzed. In some respects he was quite comfortable.

Just what had happened to him? Had it been one woman in a scarlet bodysuit or two? He had seen two pairs of breasts, there was no doubt about that, but had it been an illusion? Had the bang on his head so scrambled his vision that he had seen double? Everything about the women had been identical down to the tiny blonde hairs on the forearms and the pink puckering around the strawberry nipples. Everything was the same, except maybe . . .

He was distracted by sounds of a door opening and a warm contralto voice humming a tune. The humming came closer and Stephen lifted his head and strained against his bonds. He would rather not be rescued by a woman but what choice did he have? He called out.

Miriam Jarvis was feeling particularly cheerful this morning. And why not? It was Midsummer's, after all, and that was always a special day for a Blisswood woman. She had been on heat since watching Lucy and Gavin in the barn and tonight her fire was going to burn . . .

Nevertheless it was a surprise to find a half-naked man in her garden at ten o'clock in the morning – staked out

Lust at Large

for her pleasure, as it were, with his hands tied above his head to a large oak and his ankles lashed to a garden roller.

'Please untie me,' he said, misery in his voice and desperation in his eyes.

Miriam took stock of the situation, of the broad shoulders and long lean frame, of the jeans crumpled around the thighs and the exposed penis lying in a sticky pool of spunk.

Stephen took stock of her in turn. He saw a well-built, well-preserved woman of indeterminate years with thick fair hair and an expression he could not read. She wore a thigh-high Chinese silk wrap decorated with red and green dragons which revealed sturdy brown legs and bare feet. In her hand she carried a bundle of flimsy underwear evidently just gathered from the washing line.

'What do you think you're doing in my garden, young man?' The voice was low and musical.

'Untie me, please,' repeated Stephen. 'I've been attacked.'

'Oh yes?' She was sceptical.

'Two women jumped on me and tied me up. They pulled my trousers down and – and—'

'Raped you?'

'*Yes!* I've been indecently assaulted.'

'I'd better call the police then.'

'I *am* the police. I'm Detective Constable Stephen Fantail of the Metropolitan Police Force.'

'Can you prove it?'

It occurred to Stephen that he couldn't. His wallet was back in his room.

'I'm a guest at The Blisswood Spa Hotel.'

'Really?' Miriam came closer. He could see right up her legs beneath the hem of her wrap. 'My daughter is the manager. Let me ring her and ask her to come and identify you.'

'No, no! *Please* just untie me.'

She was wearing pale yellow panties and he could see the shadow of her muff through the thin cotton.

'How do I know you're not a pervert? I bet you get your kicks out of tying yourself up and exposing yourself to women.'

'How? Look at me.'

'I *am* looking and what I see merely confirms my suspicions. How do you explain *that*?'

In effect the explanation was simple, it was the result of a pair of long pretty legs and a bulging pussy mound on a febrile imagination. Stephen's cock was not inhibited by the situation. Newly introduced to the delights women carry between their legs, it had scented fresh cunt and was now sitting up and begging for more.

'God, I'm sorry,' moaned Stephen. 'I can't help it, you're just too – too . . .'

'Too what, you perverted youth?'

'. . . unbelievably gorgeous. It's impertinent of me to say it, I know. If you'd only let me go I could cover myself up.'

'And allow you to frighten the next defenceless female you come across? I would be failing in my civic duty, Constable Fantail, if I allowed that to happen.'

He stared at her thinly clad figure – bare brown legs, deep freckled cleavage and wickedly curving grin – in a turmoil. She lifted a slender foot and slid a scarlet-painted big toe along the crease of his thighs until it rested beneath his scrotum.

'As a policeman,' she said, 'you'll know of cases in which abused young women have been rescued and then taken advantage of by the men who have rescued them.'

Stephen's balls were now bobbing up and down on her foot. The effect was both terrifying and titillating. A strangled moan came from his throat. It was the only response he could manage.

'Here's my chance to reverse the process and take revenge for my sex.' Her foot pressed on the shaft of his blood-gorged penis, rolling it from side to side across the sticky plain of his belly. Stephen squirmed his arse into the grass, he was turned on – he couldn't help it.

'Take your foot off me,' he hissed in a vain show of authority.

'OK,' she said and replaced her foot with her hand, kneeling over him so that he could see her laughing face. She took a pair of silky peach panties from her bundle of washing and wrapped them round his shaft. She caressed him slyly, rubbing the soft material the length of his throbbing tool and plunging him into a fever of desire.

'Stop this at once!' he moaned.

'But I thought this was what you perverts enjoyed – don't you want to come in my knickers?' Her eyes bored into his as she manipulated him and then her full mouth twitched with sudden merriment. 'I suppose this is what you might call handling stolen goods.'

'Christ,' he muttered through clenched teeth, fighting to hold back the rush of excitement building in his loins, 'are all the women here sex mad?'

'Yes,' she said simply and straddled his legs. She pulled the gusset of her panties to one side and showed him the dark brown mat of hair beneath. Holding his stiff cock up from his stomach, she rubbed the ruby red glans against the plump and glistening flesh of her long pussy lips. 'It's Midsummer's Eve, Mr Policeman, and all we Blisswood women want to do is fuck. You're not complaining, are you?'

And, notwithstanding his humiliation, DC Fantail wasn't.

50

It took an hour and a half for Max to get the information he needed out of Margot. As Max emerged from the Scallion household, Adriana took hold of his arm.

'Where's Gammon then?' she asked.

Max had a distracted air and his hair was awry. Adriana's question seemed to bring him down to earth.

'At some snooty hotel called The Blisswood Spa being interviewed by Robyn Chestnut of the *Bunny*.'

'I see.' Adriana rebuttoned Max's shirt which had somehow become misaligned and set about brushing dog hairs off his jacket.

'What's more, the little bastard is getting them to shoot a topless identity parade.'

'Oh dear.'

'That was *my* idea. I ought to sue him for infringement of intellectual copyright.'

'No point. What would you do with a whippet and a collection of Motorhead records? That's about all he's got.'

'How do you know?'

'There are no secrets round here. I've been talking to the girls.' And she pointed to the Spacewagon whose interior seemed to be full of wild blonde hair, flowery print dresses and bare brown shoulders. High-pitched giggles could be heard from inside, punctuated by bursts of shrill laughter.

'Who the hell are they?'

'Models for the identity parade photo. I got most of them from the café round the corner. I suppose you're about to tell me the shoot's off.'

'Too right. The *Dog* doesn't copy the *Bunny* – even if the bastards have nicked our idea. Get rid of them.'

'That's a pity. They're all looking forward to meeting you. There's one that makes Dolly Parton look undernourished.'

Maxwell gave her a baleful stare. 'To tell you the truth, Adriana, I've had enough of large chests for a bit. Fortunately the woman we need now is as flat as a pancake.'

'Fiancée Franny?'

'Precisely. If we tell her that her beloved is eye-balling naked women at this hotel and offer her a lift we should be onto something. "Furious Franny wreaks revenge. In the aftermath of this latest robbery another human drama unfolds," etcetera. At the least we ought to be able to screw up the *Bunny*.'

'That's my boy,' said Adriana, pushing an errant curl over his ears and surveying him critically lest she had missed anything. 'Come and be nice to the girls while I pay them off. Then we'll go and pick up Franny.'

'You know where to find her?'

'Sure. She's the office manager for Whitewash and Dross, the solicitors in the High Street. Marilyn used to work there.'

'Who?'

'The girl with the footballs under her vest who is ogling you from the nearside window.'

'Christ!'

'What's up with you, Max? I thought you Australians were keen on sport.'

Max had always been an independent fellow. He'd left home at sixteen, lost touch with his parents when he'd moved to England and he'd never been wed. But now he was beginning to wonder if he shouldn't marry Adriana. He'd not laid a finger on her in lust, had never even kissed her, but without her he knew he'd be lost.

She probably didn't fancy him, he knew that. She had observed him too closely for him to hold any romantic mystique in her eyes. But to his mind that was a perfect recommendation. As for sex, hanky-panky was too much a part of his work ethic for him to attach any importance to it after hours. He looked at Adriana's small capable hands on the wheel of the big vehicle as she drove down the High Street. A sexless marriage. It sounded like bliss to him. He wondered if she'd go for it.

'Shall I go in and get her?' asked Marilyn.

They had dismissed the other girls but kept Marilyn because of her connection to Franny. Sitting in the rear, she thrust her elfin face with its crown of yellow curls between the two front seats. Her skinny vest-top was moulded to her strapping frame, clinging to every breathtaking contour of her twin peaks.

Despite himself, Max was already picturing her naked. Would those gigantic breasts fall to her waist as she unclipped the black lace bra whose straps kept sliding into view? Or would they jut straight out from her chest buoyed up by the elasticity of youth? With the memory of Margot's satin melons still imprinted on his face and lips and hands, he wondered how Marilyn's marvels would compare.

'Well, Max?' said Adriana. It was obvious from her expression that she could read his mind. 'Aren't you going in to talk to her? I think Franny needs the star treatment, don't you?'

'Eeh, I think he's lovely,' said Marilyn as Max walked from the Spacewagon to the office door. 'It must be wonderful working for him like you do.'

Adriana smiled at her kindly. 'Fetching and carrying for Maxwell Shaftesbury is not particularly glamorous, you know.'

'I wouldn't mind. If I asked him nicely, do you think he'd let me fetch some things for him?'

Adriana stared at Max's retreating back and for once her serene smile was not in place.

'No doubt about it, Marilyn. He'd love it.'

51

Miriam rang Julia at the hotel in a state of contentment. The unexpected fuck in the garden had started off Midsummer's with a bang and she was determined it was going to continue in the same vein. But, for the moment, her new lover was in the bath and she had time to satisfy her curiosity.

'What is it, mummy?' Julia was in no mood for conversation. Before long, Monk would be knocking on her door and she was already sweating with fear.

'Do you have a young man staying at the hotel called Fantail?'

'Yes.'

'Detective Constable Stephen Fantail of the Metropolitan Police?'

There was silence.

'Julia? Are you there?'

'Yes, mummy. Why are you asking?'

'No special reason. I've just bumped into him in the garden, that's all.'

'In the garden?' Julia was stunned. Monk had his spies after her. They were surrounding her home, harassing her family. 'Mummy, are you all right?'

'Oh, absolutely.'

A warning bell rang in Julia's head. She knew this naughty-me tone of old.

'Mother, you've not ... *done* anything with him, have you?'

'Don't pry, Julia. I have simply met a pleasant young man out enjoying the countryside and I wondered if you had come across him at the hotel.'

Julia was in a panic. She had not told her mother about the interview with Monk – how could she? – but the last thing she needed at the moment was her own mother chumming up to one of his colleagues.

'Look, mummy, I don't think you should talk to him or let him in the house or – or anything.'

'Why not? He's a policeman, after all. Between you and me, he's rather a pussy cat. How he ever catches criminals I can't imagine.'

As he lay in lukewarm water in Miriam Jarvis's bathroom, Stephen couldn't imagine catching criminals either. It was becoming clear to him that since he had arrived in Blisswood he had fucked up royally – and literally.

Last night he had been kidnapped and seduced by a prime suspect and this morning he had been tied up and assaulted by one, or maybe two, half-naked women. Now he had been raped by another suspect's mother and, to cap it all, he was held a virtual prisoner in the bath because she had disappeared with his clothes.

On the other hand, there was a positive side to recent events. His undercover work had enabled him to eliminate Felicity Dodge from the enquiry and now his adventures had placed him inside Julia Jarvis's house in an excellent position to snoop around for evidence. It would be necessary, of course, to keep the mother sweet. Such hardships there were in detective work . . .

In the garden, Miriam had ground his arse into the dry lawn as she had ridden his prick. She had bitten his tongue and scratched his nipples and squeezed his balls, all the while plunging her warm weight up and down on his loins. He had been helpless and she had been rough and he had loved it. He had shot his spunk up into her like water from a geyser and they had shouted in unison as they came.

Now he eased his abused body out of the water and wrapped himself in a large fluffy towel. It was soft and perfumed and he was grateful she had left him something to wear. He set off along the corridor.

He opened the first door he came to. It was a woman's bedroom – he presumed it belonged to Julia. There were clothes lying in a heap on the unmade bed and on the floor. A river of shoes flowed out of the wardrobe and the dressing table was a muddle of cosmetics and perfumes and other aids to feminine beauty. Stephen found it hard to imagine the immaculate manager of The Blisswood Spa Hotel leaving her bedroom in such a mess.

'Are you out of the bath yet, Stephen?' Miriam's musical tones rang out along the corridor and he jumped backwards in answer to her summons. As he did so, he knocked over a cardboard box by the foot of the dressing table. He bent to set it upright and a wig of thick chestnut curls fell into his hands.

'Stephen!'

He quickly put the wig back in the box, pushed it under the dressing table and found himself staring directly into the half-open top drawer. It was full of old lipsticks and tweezers and mascara brushes – and dozens of butterfly-shaped transfers scattered like fallen leaves.

For a young man only recently acquainted with the full glory of the female form, Stephen's view of Miriam as he stood in her bedroom doorway was breathtaking. She lay on her bed on her stomach with her silk wrap drawn up to her waist. A pillow lay beneath her hips, thrusting her spectacular white buttocks up in cocky invitation.

'Come here,' she said, 'I've got a wicked idea.'

Stephen stepped to the bed, his loins on a level with her face.

'What have you done with my clothes?' he said.

She ignored him and pulled the towel from his waist. It fell to the floor and his half-erect prick swung inches from her lips. She closed the distance and swallowed him till her nose was buried in the curly brown hair of his belly. Then she went to work.

She licked his cock from root to tip and back again and skinned the hood to wiggle the point of her tongue under the rim. His organ was massive in her hand, the head a gleaming blood red.

Though the room was stifling, both of them were shivering like flu victims.

Lust at Large

'Slap my bottom,' she said.
'What?'
'Slap my cheeks hard. Don't you want to?'
Of course he did. The generous white ovals were a tempting target, upturned and begging for a firm hand. He applied it.

'Ooh!' She sucked in her breath. 'Do it again. Go on! That's it. Harder!'

Then he needed no more urging. He stood by the side of the bed, his tumescent penis in her mouth, looking down her body as her great white cheeks turned pink then red under his open-palmed slaps. The rounds of flesh wobbled and quivered beneath the rain of blows and in the exposed valley between the shifting hills could be glimpsed the brown whorl of her anus and the gash of her pussy.

He pushed his fingers deep into her split. She was gummy with juice and the smell of her excitement was thick in the air. She took her mouth from his cock and said, 'How would you like to fuck my arse?'

The words shot through him like an electric current and struck him dumb.

She took his silence for agreement or, more likely, she was in no mood to take no for an answer. She rubbed thick white cream into the head of his tool and along the shaft. It felt cool and thrilling. Stephen's heart was pounding in his chest. His sexual education was taking an unexpected turn. Did every woman expect this? he wondered.

Her bum was big but firm, broad but shapely. He climbed between her backthrust thighs and savoured the dimpled contours of her outspread rear.

'Just hold it steady,' she commanded. 'Let me get it in,' and she reached behind to place the head of his cock against her anal ring.

Stephen didn't think it would work. He didn't see how the broad helmet of his glans could penetrate the tight pucker of her rectum. But he held his shaft steady and she rubbed the top of his stalk into her arse, deliberately relaxing her muscles as she pushed back. Suddenly he was in the breach and he gasped as the tight warmth enveloped him. He thought he was going to come just at the sight of his cock disappearing into the hole between her large pale buttocks.

'Oh God,' she muttered between gritted teeth.

'You're so tight,' he breathed.

'You're so big.'

'Oh, Miriam—'

'Now bugger me!' she commanded but there was no need. His well-greased truncheon was already pistoning up her bum to the manner born. In his zeal for this new assignment, there was no stopping Fantail of the Met.

52

'What's *she* doing here?'

Franny Wintergreen sounded cross. She looked cross, too. Her pale lips were set in a thin line and two vertical creases furrowed the flesh above her nose. Her mass of dark curly hair shook as she spoke and her black eyes flashed. The shoulder pads of her navy blue business suit positively bristled with aggression.

Max had formed the immediate impression that dissatisfaction was Franny's permanent state of mind. She had treated Max with suspicion, examining his NUJ card in minute detail. She had even rung the *Dog* in London to ensure he was not an impostor. As he had explained what her fiancé was up to and watched her eyes narrow with fury, he was surprised to feel a pang of sympathy for Craig Gammon. Franny's vengeance would not be pretty – on the other hand it should make good entertainment for readers of the *Daily Dog*.

Everyone in Franny's office had jumped to accommodate her once she had decided to take the rest of the day off. Her boss, the sheepish Arnold Dross, had fallen over himself to assure her that they could manage without her, given the circumstances.

Now her anger had fallen on the luckless Marilyn.

'What's she doing here?' Franny repeated, subjecting Max to the full glare of her disapproval.

Adriana answered for him. 'We needed some help with the local liaison. Marilyn kindly agreed to help out.'

Franny almost exploded. 'Liaison! She can't bloody well spell it, let alone do it.'

'Oh, Franny,' wailed Marilyn, 'you're so mean.'

Lust at Large

They were driving out of town and Adriana did not take her eyes from the road as she said, 'I'm sure you can find Mr Shaftesbury a coffee when we get to the hotel, Marilyn, and help him carry his bag.'

'Ooh yes,' said the girl. 'I'm ever so grateful, Mr Shaftesbury.'

'Call me Max,' he said, turning in his seat and marvelling at her formidable rounds of breast flesh bouncing with the motion of the vehicle as it sped down the narrow rutted road.

By her side, Franny Wintergreen sat ramrod straight and looked out of the window, her mouth as tight as a purse.

Nobody knew what happened at a real identity parade – at any rate no one admitted to such knowledge. So Robyn let Cliff have his head in setting the scene for the photo session. The result may not have been authentic but it was bound to bring a smile to the faces of *Daily Rabbit* readers and that was the point of it all, everyone knew that. Everyone apart from Craig Gammon, it seemed.

He watched the photographer arranging the line-up of girls with his mind in turmoil and a funny look on his face which was interpreted by all as naked desire.

Such an expression was entirely appropriate, given the personnel Cliff had assembled.

From the waist down, Mercy and Melanie wore their waitress uniforms – black mini-skirts, stockings and high heels – but Mercy had slipped a thin camisole strap down her arms to reveal the whole of one quivering breast and Melanie had allowed Cliff to pull both of her tits out of her bra.

Lucy Salmon had been summoned from the donkey sanctuary. She still wore her jodhpurs but had been given a sunshine yellow T-shirt which Cliff had carefully arranged so that it sat in a roll above her pouting pear-shaped breasts as if she had just yanked it up in a moment of violent exhibitionism.

And sixteen-year-old Mandy, keen to follow up her sensational appearance as a Gartertex model, wore a pair of scarlet hotpants and a cut-off T-shirt so tight and tiny that her nipples stood up like knobs on a hat rack.

It had been easy to persuade these four to take part but four fake Brendas was not considered enough. 'We need at least six,' said Robyn and Cliff had thought hard.

The result was suspect number five, a curly-haired brunette with toffee-coloured eyes and a heart-shaped face. Her full creamy breasts were cradled by an underwired half-cup brassiere from the Louche Lingerie collection which thrust them out as if to say 'help yourself'. When reminding Fliss of her promise to pose for him, Cliff had expected howls of protest at the circumstances. But Fliss, who had hardly said a word to him since breakfast the previous day, had simply nodded and muttered, 'OK.'

At that point, Cliff would have settled for five girls but Robyn wasn't happy.

'Get your clothes off, Josie,' she'd said, 'you're in the line-up.'

'What!'

'Please, Josie, we need six women.'

'I can't. Suppose Gavin sees it.'

'He'll be proud of you. He'll come out of hiding to marry you and if he doesn't he's not worth it. Don't argue.'

And Josie hadn't, believing that she had to support her friend.

'You're the prettiest of the lot,' whispered Cliff as he helped her on with a rhinestone-studded denim shirt, which was all she wore above jeans cut off at mid-thigh.

'I feel out-titted,' she said.

He arranged the shirt so it fell open, revealing one shallow-scooped breast with an upturned nipple. He pinched it gently between finger and thumb and it stood up, cherry pink and perky.

'Well, he likes you as you are,' he said, indicating an open-mouthed Craig Gammon. 'He looks like he's going to cream his leathers.'

'I don't think he's looking at me, Cliff.'

It was true, he wasn't. His eyes were flicking from Melanie to Mercy and back again, devouring their golden bodies, their ripe curves, their identical swollen tit globes . . . It was *her*, he was sure of it. Yet which her? There

Lust at Large

had only been one yesterday and, anyway, the robber was hardly going to turn up here for a press photo was she? He must be going a bit soft in the head . . .

'He's got a sodding great hard-on,' muttered Melanie to Mercy.

'Mmm, yummy,' said Mandy who had overheard.

'I love the leather,' said Lucy, pointing her bazookas at him.

Clifford clapped his hands. 'OK, girls, give us your best. Let's start. I don't need you yet, Craig, so you just relax.'

Craig didn't think he'd ever be able to relax again. In his leathers, in this small room under the fierce lights, he was a mass of sweating tumescence. But he'd not have left for ten times what he was being paid. Twelve pretty breasts swivelled and pointed in his direction. The pain in his cheek faded away. If one of them was the real Bra-less Brenda then good luck to her, he wouldn't have missed this for the world.

53

Monk was late for his appointment with Julia. This was not, as she assumed, a deliberate ploy but the result of an ill-timed telephone call. And so, when he took his seat on the other side of her desk, she was a nervous wreck and he was hopping mad.

The call had been from Superintendent Hatter whose own anger was ill-concealed. 'You've got twenty-four hours, Monk. Nail that woman down by tomorrow morning or you're back in Traffic.'

'That's unfair, sir. I'm close to a breakthrough but I can't guarantee an arrest to a deadline.'

'Tough. I'm the one who decides what is unfair. And in my book that's the hotel bill you and Fantail are racking up at the taxpayer's expense. Not to mention the insults I am exposed to every day in the gutter press. The press with whom, I believe I am correct in saying, you appear to be hand in glove.'

'Sir?'

'Or should it be hand in knicker? I'm told that Robyn Chestnut of the *Daily Rabbit* is also a resident of this country-house hotel for the randy rich.'

'Superintendent, I can assure you that my relations with Ms Chestnut have been entirely professional.'

'If that means you're paying for the pleasure of her company just don't put it on expenses.'

'Sir, I protest—'

'Don't bother. If I were you, Monk, I'd make the most of the next twenty-four hours. That's if you don't want to be counting traffic cones for the rest of your career.'

So it was no surprise that Monk's face was grim as he

waved away Julia's offer of coffee and laid his notebook on the table. He gazed at the woman on the other side of the desk, his face like thunder.

It was the allegation of sexual impropriety, more than anything, that so upset him. It was well known that he was no womaniser – he hadn't so much as kissed one for fifteen years. And the notion of a liaison with Robyn Chestnut was a joke. Make love to that Yankee ball-breaker? Preposterous. If he were going to fall for a girl she would be the opposite of Robyn. Warm and submissive, soft and feminine, someone who would respect his rough edges and aim to please. No tall dark skinny chain-smokers for him. He wanted a curvy blonde with pink pouting lips and huge sky-blue eyes . . .

'Inspector?'

The red mist in his mind cleared and he looked into a pair of huge sky-blue eyes. His eyes feasted on Julia, checking her attributes against his requirements. She fulfilled them all, and then some.

'How can I help you, Inspector?' She was shifting unhappily in her chair. She looked vulnerable and, he couldn't deny it, *very* desirable.

Monk shook aside inappropriate thoughts and began to question her. Julia Jarvis was his number-one suspect. Her car had been spotted at the scene of the last robbery. She had no alibi for yesterday afternoon. And there was no doubt she looked the part. What's more, if he could crack her, she was his passport to glory. The fact that he found her physically disturbing was irrelevant.

'Ms Jarvis, can you tell me what you were doing on these particular days?'

He pushed a piece of paper across the desk. On it he had written some half a dozen dates spanning the previous two months. Monk did not say that these were the days on which Brenda crimes had been committed. He did not need to.

Julia checked them against her desk diary, frantically searching for an entry that would prove her innocence. Surely, amongst the myriad notes about Rotarian dinners and staff holidays and ladies nights at the health club, there was *something* that would dispel suspicion? If she could just prove that she was on duty when one of the crimes was committed then she must be in the clear.

'I was here on May the eighth,' she said. 'It was Mrs Clegg's silver wedding and there were eighty-five for dinner. They had salmon en croute and the young Cleggs got drunk and pushed each other into the swimming pool.'

There was a pause in the interrogation. Monk had become distracted by the play of sunlight on the side of her face. Her complexion was flawless, he noted.

'What time did you start the preparations?' he said at length.

'I came on duty about four. The kitchen staff were at it all day, of course.'

He was finding her perfume distracting. It invaded his senses and lured his thoughts from the matter in hand. Was this some cunning ploy to throw him, literally, off the scent? If so, it wouldn't succeed.

'What did you do before that?' he asked.

'I – well – I can't remember exactly. I should imagine I went for a walk then had a bath. I generally rest before a late night.'

He said nothing and she realised she hadn't helped her cause.

'Are you sure you can't recall what you did? You didn't go for a drive, for example?'

Her eye fell on a pencilled note in the column headed May 8 and she said firmly, 'Oh no, I couldn't have done that because . . .'

She stopped and suddenly began to page through her diary comparing entries.

'Because?'

There was a strange expression on her face, as of someone counting the pennies as they dropped.

'Perhaps I did go for a drive.'

'Where to?'

'I really can't say.'

Monk was puzzled. He changed tack. 'Get around the country much, do you, Ms Jarvis?'

'Not really, I don't have time.'

Lust at Large

'Just the odd trip, then. Like the one you took to Bristol on the twenty-sixth of May.'

Julia turned the pages.

'If you say so,' she replied.

'That would account, then, for the Bristol car-park sticker of that date which is still adhering to the windscreen of your car.'

She smiled and lifted her chin high, it wobbled slightly but her voice was firm as she said, 'Quite.'

Monk closed his notebook. He knew just about all he needed to know. She could have done the robbery in Skipton on May 8 and driven back in time to go on duty at four. She hadn't denied being in Bristol the day the Clifton branch of the Bristol Bountiful had been turned over. She hadn't come up with one alibi. The case was in the palm of his hand. So why didn't he feel elated?

He stood up. 'Thank you, Ms Jarvis, that will be all.'

'All?' The sun streaming in the open window lit up her golden halo of hair. To Monk she looked like an angel – a beautiful and plucky angel staring her fate in the eye. A thrilling realisation struck him: here stood the master criminal of his dreams. He felt significantly affected and the effect was indeed significant – his penis was burning a hole in his trousers.

She walked to the door as if to show him out. Then she turned to face him.

'You'll need to examine my breasts, I suppose. I mean, given the nature of these robberies.'

'Please don't worry about that, Ms Jarvis. We have the most sympathetic female officers. I'll make sure it is dealt with as discreetly as possible.'

'No!' Her blue eyes suddenly flared violet and her cheeks flushed pink. 'This is between you and me, Inspector Monk. I want you to examine me. Now.'

'Ms Jarvis, please. That's not necessary. Please don't—'

But Monk's protests were already being ignored. With one hand, Julia was pulling her blouse from the waistband of her skirt; the other was unbuttoning the starched white cotton at her throat, her shiny pink nails slipping the tiny buttons free of their constraining holes.

Lust at Large

Monk watched as if paralysed, his mouth making noises as ineffectual as the buzzing of the honeybees on the roses outside the window. The action of those precise and slender fingers had him transfixed. He knew that this was his sternest test as a policeman – Bra-less Brenda was about to unveil her weapons.

The plain cotton blouse fluttered to the floor, unveiling a boned white bustier which enhanced rather than concealed. The flesh of Julia's wondrous breasts glowed through the lace and the discs of her nipples thrust against the cups like the outlines of ten-pence pieces. She reached behind her back for the fastening.

Then the garment was gone and Julia's delicious orbs were finally revealed. Full and round and trembling, their impact on Monk was like a blow to the chest. He sank into a chair.

Julia took a step towards him and the big tit globes shimmied in the brilliant sunlight with a motion all of their own. The nipples were a flaming pink, swollen like ripe strawberries. Monk longed to taste them.

She came closer, her breasts undulating inches from his face. He couldn't help himself. Fifteen years of abstinence had not wiped from his memory the ecstasies of the flesh. As he touched her those fifteen barren years might never have been.

'Oh yes,' she said as she surrendered her bosom to his hands and mouth. Then, 'Oh yes, yes!' as she caught his fever of desire.

For Julia, fear was the ultimate aphrodisiac and she liked her loving rough. Despite her complaints she needed what men like Rodney Holmdale could do for her; she thrilled to Rodney's arrogance, his selfishness, his bestial requirements. Now she revelled in the firm handling of another man of authority, whose power over her was even stronger than Rodney's, for he held her liberty in his grasp.

Fifteen years of self-denial had left Monk a hungry man and, even as he crammed his mouth with tit flesh, his fingers were beneath Julia's skirt tearing away her defences. In seconds her flimsy panties were shredded and her skirt was round her waist.

Lust at Large

'Oh my God!' she cried as the policeman laid her over the desk and spread her firm white thighs. 'No more, please!'

Monk paused with his rampant cock at the mouth of her vagina. For a second it seemed he might regain control. But Julia was too quick for him.

'No, no!' she cried, wrapping her legs around his waist like a boa constrictor around its prey – and jammed his long-neglected cock deep into the recesses of her hot wet pussy.

'Oh God, this is dreadful!' she cried at the top of her voice, already halfway to orgasm.

Like riding a bicycle, there are some things a man never forgets. Monk rode Julia's succulent and sturdy body as if never out of the saddle. And when the journey was over, when he had shot a gallon of spunk into her soft white belly and torn his face from her heaving breasts, he ran from the room with a groan of anguish.

Julia lay crushed against her desk, her legs in the air and her diary in the small of her back – wherein lay the key to her self-sacrifice. She wondered when the inspector might want to question her again.

54

On reflection, Fliss didn't know why she had agreed to do this. Posing topless with a lot of other women had never been her ambition – particularly when the competition was so strong. She could swear the girl with black curls had helium in her tits, they seemed to be floating without visible means of support. But then, she was probably half the age of Fliss.

Given her declaration to please Cliff at whatever cost she could hardly have refused to take part. But now, as she caught the gleam in his eye as he fussed around the models, she wondered if he was worth it. Did she really want a future with a man obsessed with photographing other women? Perhaps she'd be better off with someone obsessed with *her*. Like the boy with the hot breath and trembling hands up on the moors last night . . .

Standing by the side of Fliss, Josie felt rather differently about posing half naked for the readers of the *Daily Rabbit*. She had to admit, it really turned her on. She knew it was tacky, standing there with her boobs hanging out amongst a crew of other half-dressed females, yet it appealed to some place inside her – a place she had only recently discovered. She was playing a game, just as she had been since the evening Gavin phoned her in Wales with the news of the robbery. The evening Ivor had emerged from Gwen's bathroom and showed her his long white cock.

'That's it, darlings,' shouted Clifford from behind his camera. 'I want you all to think naughty thoughts. Just like Josie.'

Josie blushed and glared at him with a rueful, caught-with-my-pants-down expression that he immediately captured on film. How the hell did he know what was in her head? She supposed it was the same sixth sense that made him such a brilliant photographer.

With so many mouthwatering models at his disposal he was in his element. The main shots of the pretend line-up had been over in a flash. Then he had manoeuvred Craig and the girls into some unscheduled poses – 'Just for fun,' he had said to Robyn.

From the outset Cliff had complained that Craig looked more like a Hell's Angel than an office clerk. Now he produced a collar and tie and asked Craig to examine the girls' boobs through an outsize magnifying glass.

Craig spent an age peering through the glass at Melanie's tits, then he turned to Mercy.

'Look at him,' muttered Fliss by Josie's side, 'he's going to eat those blondes for lunch.'

'Unless they eat him first,' said Josie seeing Melanie's hand slip inside his borrowed shirt.

Things might have developed from there – Mandy and Lucy were crowding round Craig and the promise of indiscreet behaviour hung in the air – had not the door swung open and a small dark-haired woman in a business suit rushed into the room.

Without a word, she headed straight for Craig, spun him round and kicked him in the crotch with the full force of a black patent size-four shoe. Small though the foot was, the effect was devastating and the horny building-society clerk doubled over in soundless grief. Then the woman hit him with her fists and applied her feet to his recumbent body. Franny Wintergreen had arrived to reclaim her man. But first she was going to walk all over him.

Clifford was horrified. His cunningly orchestrated photo shoot was in ruins.

'For God's sake, woman,' he cried, 'what the hell do you think you're – oof!'

Franny was probably the kind of woman who practised kicking men in the crotch. At any rate, her aim was deadly. She disabled Cliff with the speed of a striking snake and, for a long moment, the two men rolled on the floor, faces crimson, eyes popping, watched by an audience of stunned and silent women. Then came a howl of rage from Robyn and the girls, and Franny was buried beneath a vengeful avalanche of half-naked flesh.

Adriana's photographs in the following day's edition of the *Daily Dog* immortalised the entire sequence of events, from Franny's entrance to the free-for-all. She even captured the moment when the *Dog*'s own Maxwell Shaftesbury nervously broke up the fight and emerged with Franny wriggling and spitting in his arms.

'Ooh, isn't he *fantastic!*' squealed Marilyn in Adriana's ear. Adriana did not respond but focused her camera on the stricken features of the tall female who was shouting into Max's face.

'You bastard, Shaftesbury – you've wrecked my photo session! I'll fucking sue!'

'As it happens, you're the one who needs suing – you've infringed my intellectual property rights.'

'Bullshit, you asshole!'

'You're an artist with words, Ms Chestnut. You speak with the true voice of the *Daily Rabbit*.'

'It's better than that shit sheet you work for.'

'No doubt that accounts for our extra half a million readers.'

'Stolen from us, you scumbag . . .'

This elevating exchange might have continued for some time had Craig not let out an ear-splitting howl of agony. Franny threw herself to the floor at his side and, with a tenderness that surprised everyone present, cradled his battered head in her arms. 'Eeh, Craig love, I never meant to hurt you,' she whispered and burst into tears.

Adriana rushed forward to record the affecting moment and Robyn, competitive to the last, wrestled the camera from the groaning Clifford's neck and clicked away at the blubbering twosome.

'I've had enough of this,' said Fliss, buttoning a silk shirt over her mouthwatering charms.

'But what about Cliff?' said Josie who had long ago worked out that Fliss was more than just the photographer's travelling companion.

Fliss looked at Cliff, who was being eased into a seat by a

blonde girl with frizzy hair and very large breasts that were barely contained beneath a skinny pink T-shirt. This remarkable bosom appeared to move independently of the girl's body and offered itself as a soft and convenient pillow for Cliff's head. With sure fingers, the girl began to undo his trousers, announcing to no one in particular, 'I've got to get it in the open before the swelling starts.'

'I think he's in good hands,' Fliss said. Under her breath she added to herself, 'And what's more, she's welcome to him.'

55

Stephen saw Monk from a distance as he returned to the hotel. Recognising the figure sitting on the terrace, he injected a spring into his weary step and ran a handkerchief over a mouth still smarting from Miriam's ardent kisses. He was fucked out and he was sure he looked it too. On the other hand, his scars had been won in the heat of battle and he had important information to impart.

There was an empty glass by Monk's elbow and, for a moment, Stephen thought he caught a whiff of alcohol. Surely not. Monk was the only teetotal Scotsman on the force, it was well known.

'I've had a result, sir,' he announced as he took a seat.

Monk did not acknowledge his presence.

Stephen tried again. 'I think we've got her, sir.'

Monk slowly turned his head. 'Got who?' he asked.

'Bra-less Brenda, sir. That is, Julia Jarvis.'

'Julia,' muttered Monk. 'The bonny Julia.'

'Precisely, sir. I found—'

'Do you like poetry, Stephen?'

'Not much, sir. But my mum used to be a Pam Ayres' fan.'

'Don't be stupid, lad. I mean real poetry: "My love is like a red red rose that's . . ." Stephen, what's the date today?'

'June the twenty-fourth, sir.'

'Precisely! "A red red rose that's newly sprung in June!" Amazing!' He gazed over Stephen's shoulder, his mind engaged elsewhere.

Stephen tried again, shock tactics this time. 'I went into her bedroom, sir.'

That got his attention. 'Julia's?'

'She's got a dark brown wig, sir, and a drawer full of

transfers. *Lepidoptera extasis.*' There was a long silence so Stephen added, 'You know, the butterfly.'

'Of course I bloody well know, Fantail.'

'Sorry, sir.' Funnily enough, this display of irritation made Stephen feel better. He didn't know where he was with an inspector who spouted poetry. His relief did not last long.

'Between you and me, Stephen, I shall probably be resigning in twenty-two hours' time.'

'What?'

'I've got a gun to my head. Only twenty-two hours left in which to catch Brenda.'

'But surely it's Julia Jarvis? How did your interview go?'

'She's got no alibis for any of the robberies.'

'Did she confess?'

'Not in so many words.'

'Well, now you know about the wig and the transfers why don't you arrest her?'

Monk picked up his empty glass and sniffed the dregs. 'Stephen, a man has a dreadful thirst after fifteen years.'

'Would you like another, sir?'

'Indeed I would. But before you get it, tell me why a woman would want to stick butterflies all over her chest.'

'It is a puzzle, sir. I can't help thinking it's to cover up an identifying blemish. Like a mole.'

'Take it from me, Stephen, Julia Jarvis has perfect breasts. Quite, quite flawless.'

'I see, sir.'

' "How sweet unto that breast to cling and round that neck entwine!" '

Stephen stood and picked up Monk's glass. He couldn't stand any more of this poetry business.

'Get me a very large Glenmorangie, Stephen, and leave me to ponder this knotty problem. You look exhausted, I suggest you go to bed.'

And Stephen did just that. But even in his dreams he could not escape. The women of Blisswood came back to haunt him all over again: Fliss with her hot warm mouth on his cock; Miriam with her broad white bottom thrust high in the air; and, spilling out of skintight scarlet bodysuits, two pairs of beautiful strawberry-tipped breasts. Beautiful but not flawless. Their loveliness marred only by two round moles, like chocolate buttons, nestling in the undercurves of their near-perfection.

Julia sat in her office waiting for Melanie and Mercy – which gave her plenty of time to rue her conduct. She shouldn't have thrown herself at the policeman like that. After all, it wouldn't prevent him arresting her, he could deny it ever happened. Her allegations would be construed as a crude smokescreen to get herself off the hook.

So why had she done it? She asked herself the question over and over, even though she knew the answer. It was the way she always reacted when a man had a hold on her. It was why Rodney abused her so freely. She must be a masochist. Besides, she had seen the hunger in Monk's slate-grey eyes. It had been irresistible.

The phone rang. It was the man she least wished to hear from at that moment.

'Hello, darling,' said Rodney. 'Fancy an early-evening stroll to a certain five-barred gate?'

'No!'

'Oh dear, I sense insubordination. I shall have to take you in hand once more, I can tell.'

'Rodney, please!'

'That's better, a pathetic plea for mercy. I can picture you on your knees already.'

'Sod off, Rodney. You've taken advantage of me for the last time.'

'Oh yes? May I remind you that I have an offer of fifty thousand on that land.'

'I don't believe you. It's not worth ten. No one will lend me the money on it – I've tried.'

'Poor Julia. I don't see the problem. Your mother's asses are perfectly safe provided I have access to your pretty posterior. Shall we meet at six by the path through the orchard?'

'You bastard,' she whispered, all resistance gone.

'Don't forget to leave your knickers off. You won't be needing them.'

Julia replaced the receiver in despair. Perhaps she should throw herself on Monk's mercy right away. If she were in jail at least Rodney would have no hold on her. But then the swine would be sure to sell the land and her mother's donkey refuge would cease to exist!

'What am I going to do?' she wailed as her sisters entered the room.

She had intended to shout at them, to vent her fury at their duplicity and selfishness. But her anger had gone. All she felt was fear.

'It's your fault,' she said through her tears. 'I'm going to jail and mummy's going to lose her donkey sanctuary and you two are waltzing around in my car stealing money.'

'Your car?' said Melanie.

'It was seen at the robbery yesterday and you borrowed it. Just like you borrowed it all those other times.'

'We're sorry, Jules,' said Mercy.

'That policeman handed me a list of dates and, when I looked in my diary, I saw that one of you had borrowed the car every time.'

'What did you tell him?'

'I didn't tell him about you two, if that's what you mean. You're in the clear – and I'll end up in jail!' She began to sob in agonising, gut-wrenching heaves.

'Don't be silly,' said Mercy, her arm around her sister's shoulders. 'There are thousands of cars like yours in the country and you must have an alibi for some of those days.'

Julia dabbed her eyes with a bundle of paper tissues. 'I was with Rodney Holmdale at least three times but he'll deny it, I know he will.'

'Don't panic, Julia,' said Melanie. 'We can fix Rodney Holmdale, can't we, Mercy? In fact, that's what this whole lark is all about.'

Julia looked at her sisters in amazement. Could there really be a way out of this?

'When's your next little rendezvous with Hot Rod?'

'This evening at six.'

'Perfect. We'll sort him out so everyone will be happy.'

'Oh, Melanie, could you?'

'You bet. It'll be a nice little warm-up for tonight.'

Julia looked puzzled and the twins began to giggle.

'Julia,' said Mercy, 'it's Midsummer's Eve. Surely you haven't forgotten the orgy?'

Five

LUST BY LIGHTNING

56

Josie was bored – and horny. What was it about this place? All she could think about was fucking.

She slipped quietly into Robyn's room. The curtains were drawn but the brilliant afternoon sunlight bathed the room in a golden glow. Robyn's long slim form was stretched across the counterpane. She lay on her stomach, her face obscured by a tangle of hair that spread in a black shadow across the pillow. Like Josie herself, she wore just a pair of bikini panties. The white cotton was taut over the firm apple cheeks of Robyn's bottom. The air was humid and stifling.

'Robyn, are you awake?'

There was no sound from the bed. Josie knew she should leave. She stepped closer.

'Robyn?'

It was not surprising she slept, she must have killed off several glasses of champagne and an entire bottle of Burgundy at lunch. Josie had been uncertain whether the occasion was a celebration or a wake, the morning a triumph or a failure. One thing was certain, alcohol had been called for.

She was standing by the bed now, at the head, looking down the length of Robyn's naked spine, admiring the dips and hollows in the firm pale flesh. Was this how a man felt? She was entranced by the perfection of skin and bone, of fleshy swell and curve and thrust and spread . . .

'Robyn,' she whispered again, dropping her hand to the mass of thick dark curls and twining a ringlet round her fingers. She knew she ought to go back to her room.

A long arm snaked around her hips and pulled her close to the bed. Without looking up, Robyn lifted her head and pressed her face into the flat delta of Josie's belly.

'No, Robyn,' said Josie as she felt the other woman's breath through the thin cotton of her panties. 'No,' she repeated as Robyn's mouth closed over her vulva and began to suck.

The small room at the top of the hotel was airless even though the window had been flung wide open. The twin beds were so close they almost touched but Maxwell Shaftesbury and his invaluable photographer-cum-assistant, Adriana, tried hard not to trespass on each other's space.

Max dozed, recovering from his early start and Margot Scallion, not to mention lunch. The pressure was off, his copy was written and despatched, the feud with the *Bunny* had been patched up – temporarily at least – by a few bottles of champagne.

He didn't mind that the hotel only had one poky room left. If he had to share he couldn't imagine a more agreeable companion. He woke from his slumbers and gazed at Adriana, just a few inches away on her own bed. She read her book with fierce concentration, chewing her lip like a little girl. She sat cross-legged and her thigh thrust towards Max, the soft denim of her jeans drawn tight across the skin. If he reached out a hand, he thought, he could touch . . .

There was a knock at the door. Both of them looked up. The knock came again and a voice said, 'Coo-ee, Mr Shaftesbury. Are you in there?'

'Who the hell is that?' said Max but Adriana did not reply, she was already on her way to open the door.

A top-heavy blonde with a frizzy mane of curls stepped timidly into the room. Marilyn.

'So you're still here,' said Adriana.

'And a good thing too,' said the girl. 'Somebody had to care for that poor Mr Rush after Franny went bananas. I used to be a nurse, you know.'

'A wet one?' asked Maxwell, his eyes on the swollen globes barely compressed beneath her tiny top. Maybe it was the booze but they appeared to have got bigger since the morning.

'Eeh, you are a card, Mr Shaftesbury,' she said. 'That's

why I've come. Now I've made that poor Mr Rush comfortable I thought I'd ask what I could do for you.'

'It's kind of you, Marilyn, but—'

'You promised.' She looked at Adriana reproachfully. 'You said he'd love it if I did things for him.'

'And so he will,' said Adriana, picking up her book and striding to the door. 'I'll leave you in his capable hands.'

'Adriana—' Max called but she was gone and the bright-eyed Marilyn was standing over him, bristling with eagerness to do his bidding. From his supine position, the hills of her chest loomed like a mountain range.

'Where do we begin, Max?' she said, her voice suddenly softer and not so harsh on the ear.

'Look, Marilyn, I've finished work for the day. I started early and it hasn't been plain sailing. Now I'm relaxing.'

'I'm good at that.'

'Marilyn, please. I need to sleep.'

'Let me help. If I just push these beds together like this . . .'

'What are you doing?'

It was no use. Max knew a determined woman when he saw one and this part of the country seemed to specialise in them. Marilyn had the beds together in a flash and was lying by his side, her cheap sweet perfume making his head spin. She turned on her side towards him and her huge breasts shifted in his direction.

He told himself he didn't feel like it. That he was too tired. That over-endowed chippies in tight shirts with curly hair and dimples were not to his taste. That what he required was the quiet companionship of the beautiful and distant Adriana.

But Adriana was too distant right now and his pulsing cock didn't give a damn for all this rationalising. Marilyn stroked its length through the material of his summer slacks. And she sucked in her breath as his hand landed on the great mound of her right breast and began to squeeze.

She tasted of chewing gum and cigarettes, her thighs were plump and the mascara round her gleaming hazel eyes was smudged across her cheek. But when she bent over to fasten her pretty little mouth over the head of his penis and he filled his hands with her warm breasts – like big loaves fresh from the oven – he lasted no time at all.

'Eeh, Maxwell,' she said, her voice slick with his juices, 'is this what they call putting the paper to bed?'

In Robyn's bedroom the air was thick with sounds and smells of sex. Rude sticky sucky noises. Salty scents of passion like a sea breeze. The bed was in disarray. The light was subtly different than before, not so bright, more golden. Time had marched on and the two women had lost all vestiges of inhibition.

Robyn raised her face from Josie's loins and surveyed the puffy pink lips of the other's sex, now wet and spread wide to show the darker flesh within. She snaked the tip of her tongue up the exposed groove into the soft hair at the base of her belly.

'Please, no more,' said Josie as the tongue found her clit again.

'I wish I had a cock to do you justice,' said Robyn and applied her tongue.

Josie came again.

Later, she said, 'What happened to Cliff? He's missed the action.'

'He's *hors de combat*, I suppose. I told him to take it easy. He can get all the horny shots he wants tonight.'

'What happens tonight?'

'Pagan fertility rites. Bucolic bonking rituals. You name it. The girls doff their knickers and the lads jump aboard.'

'Sounds pretty crude.'

'I hope so. The *Bunny* feels no shame. How would you like to help me cover the event?'

'What would I have to do?'

'Everything, I expect. You'll be in your element.'

'Robyn!'

'Don't sound so shocked. You're the horniest bitch I've ever met.'

Josie rested her head on Robyn's thigh and succumbed to a perverse flush of pride.

Chantal, too, was enjoying a randy siesta. She had the elder

Garter where she wanted him now – on his knees between her legs, his gross body folded over so he could get at her. She reclined half on, half off the bed, her thighs spread wide to accommodate his homage to her loins.

'Ooh yes, *chéri*! How you tickle my little button! You exhaust me.'

Strictly speaking this was not true, Chantal's capacity for rude pleasures being extensive. In her experience, though, it was never a mistake to suggest that a man had given her almost more than she could take. On the other hand, she was about to come – again.

'*Ohhh!* That's fantastic! Don't stop!'

Gordon Garter had no intention of stopping. Uncomfortable though he was and desperate to seek his own satisfaction, he worshipped at this shrine with the zeal of a new convert. To bring this young French girl off with his mouth and tongue thrilled him more than he could ever have foreseen. Truly, he thought to himself, it was better to give than to receive. And if he gave enough then he might receive what he really desired.

Pleasure rippled through the French girl's belly as Garter rootled in her crack with his cunning tongue. His business excursions to the Far East had not been spent entirely in the pursuit of export orders. Gordon Garter knew how to suck pussy and he had learned the art from experts.

'Oh, *mon Dieu*,' she groaned and raised her knees to her chest, allowing him access to every millimetre of her pretty crack, from clit to bumhole and back. He seized his opportunity.

'GG, you naughty man – not there! Oooh!'

He rimmed her arsehole with the tip of his tongue, then infiltrated the tiny puckered breach ever so gently. She squealed and moaned but did not stop him.

Flick, flick, went his tongue on the forbidden whorl, wetting and enlarging the intoxicating opening. She bent her legs back further, thrusting her arse off the bed, pushing it into his face. Now he replaced his tongue with his forefinger, pressing against the moist brown spot. It yielded.

She bucked her hips off the bed, then tried to lower her legs and squirm away from his attentions. But his forearm was across her upturned thighs, pinning them to her chest.

'Chantal, you're driving me mad,' he gasped, pushing his finger into the ring of her anus. 'I must have you *here*.' And he drove his finger in to the hilt.

Chantal gasped with pain and surprise. 'No, no, GG. You know my rules. You cannot fuck me in the arse unless . . .'

Garter gave a howl of frustration and thrust another finger into the tight opening.

Chantal squirmed and panted, ensuring that his invasion was successful. She had worked hard to bring matters to this point. Now it was payoff time. What price would this fat roué pay for the jewel of her arse? Five thousand pounds? Ten?

'All right, you French minx, you win,' he bellowed, pulling his hand roughly from her tender bottom to drag his engorged penis from his pants. 'I love you, Chantal, I swear it. Will you bloody marry me?'

Chantal could have said lots of things to this proposition. Now was the time to laugh in his face or open serious negotiations as to cash terms or even remark that his son had earlier made a similar offer.

Instead she said, 'Yes.'

'You've made me a very happy man,' he said. And buggered her to their mutual satisfaction.

57

Julia's blonde hair danced upon her shoulders as she shook her head in agony. She couldn't move her arms, which were shackled to a beam above her head, or her legs, which were chained to the floor some eighteen inches apart. She could only thrash her big pink breasts from side to side, wobble her gorgeous buttocks and undulate the delicious dome of her belly in an effort to escape from the fiery touch of Rodney's cane.

Things had not worked out as intended for Julia. Far from taking her to the paddock and the five-barred gate, Rodney had other plans. He had brought her here, to the old summer house by the river which had been used, in the days of George Holmdale's youth, as a schoolroom. It still contained a desk and chairs – and a cupboard that held a selection of instruments once used to correct errant children. From the whistle and whack of the bamboo cane now being applied to Julia's tender bottom, these implements had lost none of their power with the passage of time.

Thwack! Thin stripes criss-crossed the pale buttocks. Thwack! Thwack! Rodney laid on two more in quick succession, sending the pink and gold of Julia's ripe nudity into juddering convulsions. If she had not been gagged with her own panties, she would have howled for help and somebody might have come to rescue her. More to the point, the twins would surely have discovered where Rodney had taken her. As it was, she was at his mercy and she dreaded what was coming next. Dreaded it not just for the pain but for the shameful satisfaction she knew she would be forced to enjoy . . .

Lust at Large

Rodney's palm cupped the fleshy undercurve of her buttocks and delved into her defenceless pussy split. He pushed two fingers in as far as they would go, then spread her abundant juices over her labia and travelled to the top of her cleft, seeking the twitching bud of her clitoris. It was wonderful but it was hateful! She couldn't help herself. She howled a soundless orgasm into her panties as his fingers reamed her dripping honeypot.

Then she felt a familiar touch against the burning flesh of her throbbing buttocks – the touch of stiff male cock. She knew what that meant. Oh God – would her torture never end?

'That's enough, Rodney.' Melanie's voice cut through the delirium of Julia's next onrushing orgasm and, as Rodney stepped away from her trembling flesh, she felt the ecstasy of relief – and the emptiness of loss.

Rodney was thunderstruck. He felt frustration, embarrassment and anger. But there was no point in arguing with a gun.

Melanie aimed it below his waist at the rearing erection that thrust from his open trousers.

'That's what I call a tempting target,' she said. 'Even I couldn't miss.'

'Put that gun down,' screamed Rodney.

'No chance. Look what you've done to my poor sister's bum.'

'She likes it. It turns her on.'

'Says you. Take your clothes off, Rodney. I think it's your turn now.'

The twins strung Rodney up in Julia's place.

'I can see the attraction of this,' said Mercy as she surveyed his muscular torso stretched out naked before her. She gave his taut buns an experimental smack with the cane and his whole body jerked. She whacked again, harder this time, and a thin line of pink blossomed on the firm white curve of his left buttock. She matched it up with another on the right.

'For God's sake,' he hissed between his teeth.

'Now now, you know you like it really,' said Melanie. 'You can't deny it.' And he couldn't. His cock, which had shown signs of shyness when bracketed in Melanie's gunsight, now stood to attention, jutting proudly from the dark hair of his belly.

Mercy took a long birch rod from the cupboard and handed it to Julia. 'Go on, Jules, get some of your own back.'

'Oh no!' Julia shrank from the instrument in horror. 'I couldn't.'

'Never mind,' said Melanie, grabbing it in her sister's stead. 'I'll do it for you.'

When they'd tried out all the old instruments of torture and had decorated Rodney with a comprehensive selection of stripes and weals, they got out the camera.

'What's this? he shouted through a mist of sweat and pain. 'Blackmail?'

'Insurance,' said Melanie as she pointed the camera at his nude and inflamed body.

'Insurance for what? It won't bloody work, I tell you, whoever you show these to.'

Julia spoke for the first time. 'What about your Aunt Amy? And your godmother, Mrs Pinch? You're still her heir, aren't you?'

'How the hell do you know that?'

'Your father used to confide in me, Rodney. Melanie, don't you think it would make a good picture if Mercy got in the shot too, holding the whip.'

'Great idea,' said Melanie, 'but she'll have to strip. Leave on the suspenders and stockings, Mercy, and hold him by the prick.'

'You can't frighten me,' roared Rodney even as Mercy squeezed his rock-hard shaft, pointing the big purple glans squarely at the camera.

'Good. Then you won't mind missing your summer shooting in Scotland with the McFrosts of Stonemuir. Hamish McFrost still remembers you when you were a choirboy at St Pilchards, doesn't he? He'd cross you off his list, I bet, if he could see you now.'

'So what do you want, you horny bitches? *Oh my God!*'

'You'd better take your hand off his cock, Mercy. We don't want him to come just yet.'

Rodney was on the brink, it was true. Mercy's ministrations had brought him to the point where he was about to boil over. With reluctance, she took her fingers from his bulging tool and wiped them on the flat of his stomach. His lonely organ twitched and flexed in mid-air. Julia thought she had never seen it so big.

'Please,' he said. 'Just bring me off. I can't stand much more of this.'

'Too bad, Rodney,' said Melanie. 'It's business before pleasure. We want to buy that land.'

His eyes narrowed. His cock throbbed. 'Julia knows my price,' he said.

'Julia's no longer on her own. Mercy and I have a proposition for you and it's non-negotiable.'

Rodney nodded and so did his cock. Mercy put her hand between his legs.

'I'm listening. Oh, that's heaven,' he couldn't help adding as she began to stroke his balls.

'You sell us the freehold on the land and promise never to touch Julia again unless she's daft enough to ask you.'

Mercy's fingers crept upwards, dabbling and tickling at the base of his twitching shaft. She said, 'You will also tell the police, should they ask, that Julia was with you at any time they are curious about.'

'And?' He tried to sound firm but his voice shook. This was not the best position in which to horse-trade.

'And we offer you this.' Melanie turned a small green rucksack upside down and a cloud of banknotes fluttered onto the floor between his legs. There were fifties and twenties, fivers and tenners, some new, some worn – a carpet of crinkly Royal heads covering the dirty wooden floor.

'How much?' he croaked as Mercy's fingers danced oh-so-sweetly on the head of his cock.

'Twenty thousand pounds. In cash. It's double what it's worth. What do you say?'

Mercy's fingers wrapped around his aching shaft.

'Done,' he croaked.

'If you don't play fair, we'll use these photos.'

'It's a deal, I tell you. Just – *please* . . .'
Mercy's hands began to pump.
'*Ohhh!*'
The spunk sprayed all over the pile of banknotes.
Julia giggled happily. A weight had just been lifted from her shoulders.
'Why, Rodney,' she said, 'it looks like you've come into money.'

58

It was a hot and broody summer evening. On the village green the local youth, dressed in their finery, mingled with middle-aged tourists clutching cameras. Half a dozen venerable donkeys chomped listlessly at the grass and laid horsey turds. The air was thick with the smell of beast.

'This is hardly sin city,' said Josie, wrinkling her nose. 'Are you sure this is where the action is?'

'Have patience,' replied Robyn. 'You've got to realise that this is a traditional event. It starts slow and builds to a climax.'

'We hope.'

'First of all, the young married women who want to conceive ride to the barn on donkeys.'

'What's the point of that? If that's how they've been doing it all these years I'm surprised the community has survived.'

'It's tradition, Josie. Don't knock it till you've tried it – and you're going to. Miriam!'

Miriam Jarvis, looking eager for the fray in a well-filled peasant blouse, answered the call.

'Miriam's been giving me some background to this affair,' said Robyn, 'and she promised a ride on a donkey to the *Bunny*'s special reporter. That's you.'

'What!' cried Josie.

'Come on, honey, you promised you'd help me out. You can't go wrong on a cute little fellow like this.'

Robyn was indicating the small grey donkey that Miriam was holding by a rope halter. The beast fluttered a dark-lashed eye at Josie and swished its tail. It *was* cute.

'This isn't a boy,' said Miriam, 'this is Josephine. She's the tamest of my little lovelies.'

'OK, then,' Josie heard herself say and then yelped in surprise as the woman suddenly thrust her hand up her frock.

'I'm sorry,' said Miriam, her hand exploring without embarrassment, 'but I must check to see if you are properly dressed. It's just as well I did, isn't it?'

Josie stood stock-still in shock as her panties were slipped down her legs, leaving her naked beneath the thin cotton.

'That's better,' said Miram, tucking the knickers into her pocket. 'Now, on you get.'

Josie did not protest; given what she hoped to be doing later, underwear would doubtless prove an encumbrance. It was not until her leg was half over the donkey that she noticed that its hairy grey back was bare – and covered in a creamy ointment.

'Hey!' she cried as she realised that her private parts were about to sink into an unsavoury mixture of fur and goo. But it was too late to back off, for Miriam had placed her hands on her shoulders and firmly plunged her downwards. Her bare bottom met the soggy mat beneath her and stuck.

'Yuk,' she said. 'That feels disgusting. What the hell is it?'

But Miriam was gone, leaving the rope halter in Robyn's hands, and Josie became aware that she was now part of a group of mounted women.

'I've got gunge all over my fanny,' she hissed at Robyn. 'Did you know about this?'

The tall American grinned. 'No one else is complaining.'

That was true. A pretty redhead with a freckled cleavage was squealing with glee as she rubbed herself backwards and forwards on the donkey next to Josie. The chubby blonde beside her had her eyes closed and a dreamy smile on her face.

'Besides,' said Robyn, 'you'll find someone to lick it all off later.'

'You bitch.'

'Just don't forget to give the *Daily Rabbit* all the juicy details.'

It was not much more than half a mile to the barn but the donkeys took their time. The group set off from the green at a sedate pace, the spectators falling in behind the riders. Cameras clicked and voices were raised in boisterous cheer. Bottles began to be passed from hand to hand.

Josie found the sensation of riding very pleasant. Unlike those around her, she suspected, she was no horsewoman but Josephine was a kindly mount, solid and sure-footed. Suddenly, as she swayed along, her eyes fixed on the back of the blonde girl in front, she became aware of the heat rising from between her legs. She pictured the rough hairs abrading the tender skin of her bum cheeks and the pouting lips of her pussy slicking back and forth in that white ooze. This time the thought did not repulse her. Her mind revolved around primal images. Coarse hair. Hot skin. Honeyed body fluids.

'Oooh!' She sucked in her breath. She was fiercely on heat.

The girl in front turned and grinned over her shoulder.

'It's got to you now, has it?'

'God, yes!'

'Set your clock ticking, I bet. Look under the trees – see anyone you fancy?'

Josie was puzzled at first. She was so absorbed in her own feelings that she couldn't grasp what was said to her. Then she noticed the men. They lined the route under the trees along the river bank. They looked like farm lads, most of them, young and bronzed and strong. Some were dressed up, with jackets and ties, but most wore jeans and open-necked shirts; others were in shorts and many were stripped to the waist, their muscles gleaming in the low slanting light. They looked delicious.

'I want one,' said Josie to the blonde who had dropped back to ride beside her.

'Take your pick. They're all available.'

'But I don't know which one. It's like opening a big box of chocolates – you don't know where to start.'

'I do,' said her companion. 'I want that big fellow there in the cut-off jeans with the earring.'

'Good choice,' said Josie as her new friend waved at the boy. 'I bet he's no soft centre.'

The lad needed no encouragement. He approached the

blonde with a white-toothed grin, brown eyes flashing. He took hold of the donkey's halter and led it out of the parade, his other hand in the girl's golden hair. As they disappeared out of sight into the woods Josie saw the girl pulling the boy's shirt from his waistband.

She noticed other couples embracing on the parched grass. Two boys lay on either side of a girl, her body almost obscured by their attentions. Only her long bare legs were visible, scissoring open beneath their prying hands.

Without realising it, Josie had steered Josephine towards the verge and a black-haired youth in a starched white shirt and faded blue jeans had hold of the donkey's head.

'Whoa there,' he said, 'you're running out of control.'

'I'm not,' she cried, mesmerised by his muscular forearms and the cut of the tight denim on his thigh. She hadn't intended to stop. She knew if she joined this youth beneath the trees she may never get to the dance at all. But a tide of lust was rising in her belly and a fire was raging in her pussy. Out of control scarcely covered it.

'My name's Martin,' he said as he led her off the road to the knowing cheers of the pack of spectators.

'Have you got a big cock, Martin?' she whispered.

'Enormous,' he replied, hurrying her away, one hand already high up on her thigh under her skirt.

'And is it stiff?'

His fingers had found their way into her groin. The motion of the donkey seemed to wedge them into the opening of her vagina.

'Rock hard, I promise.'

They had passed under the fringe of trees now and he was hurrying them along fast. Josephine responded happily, as if she recognised the urgency.

He picked her up in one movement, holding her up in the air as he pressed his mouth to hers. She devoured him, hooking her legs around his waist and bearing him to the ground, her tongue halfway down his throat.

He pulled her dress to her waist and palmed and squeezed the firm flesh of her buttocks in a fever. Kneeling like that, with the evening air fresh on the wet mouth of her empty vagina, she felt ablaze. She scrabbled at his fly with both

Lust at Large

hands and had his cock out in a flash.

'Thank God you weren't lying,' she whispered, clasping it in both hands. 'You're huge.'

He said nothing as he pushed her onto her back and knelt between her thighs.

'You're hung like a horse,' she continued, weighing his big balls in one hand and skinning his satiny knob with the other. She placed the broad red head of his glans between the slippery lips of her pussy. 'Or like a donkey. That's more appropriate given the circ —'

He drove his outsized member home in one relentless thrust, cutting off her words.

Josie cried out with pleasure and clasped his tight buttocks, digging her nails in to spur him on.

'Come on, stuff me then,' she yelled. 'Stuff me as hard as you can! Fuck me with that big thing! Oh yes! Oh yes! OH!'

He thrust his pile-driver into her without finesse, as if she were a block of wood and he were hammering home a nail with thunderous strokes. And at each blow she cried out until the woods around her echoed with her squeals of pleasure. It was the most brutal fucking she had ever had and when it was done she felt as if she had been run over by a truck.

As she caught her breath, lying on her back with him sprawled across her, she caught sight of Josephine calmly munching at a bush.

She mustn't forget she was on an assignment. There was a lot more riding ahead of her on this Midsummer's night.

59

The barn dance was not a sophisticated affair yet, to her surprise, Mitzi Bluitt was enjoying herself. There was sawdust on the floor and the band was a rustic ensemble of banjo and squeezebox and country fiddle. Nevertheless the dancers swung into complicated routines with gusto. The large barn was already as hot as a furnace and outside it was hardly any cooler. The evening sun was sinking but the heat was fierce and the atmosphere airless.

'You're looking pretty spiffing tonight,' said Tony from Wales.

Mitzi took the compliment as no more than her due for she *was* looking pretty damn good in a lightweight cream jacket and black culottes. Her rich chestnut hair was pinned up, exposing the elegant sweep of her long neck. The jacket was held in place by one button and beneath it she wore a Louche Lingerie classic bra which lifted and separated her big brown melons to considerable effect.

'I thought I'd make an effort,' she said. 'The competition's pretty hot.'

'You're not kidding.' Tony stared at the knot of dancers with their whirling skirts and flashing thighs. Mandy was prominent amongst them, her breasts fighting to escape from her low-cut blouse as she wiggled to the music. Tony tore his eyes from the tempting sight and gazed at the no-less delicious vista of flesh exposed in Mitzi's gaping cleavage. 'Fancy a dance?'

Mitzi would have said no but she had just spotted Don the Marketing Director jumping about on the floor with a buxom blonde. Sod him. She sank her gin in one gulp and gave Tony her sexiest smile. 'I'm game,' she replied.

Max Shaftesbury was feeling far from game but he wasn't going to yield exclusive coverage of a genuine pagan fertility festival to Robyn Chestnut and the *Bunny*. Not that it looked much more than a bucolic knees-up to him. He was feeling exhausted and the reason was right by his side, clinging to his arm, her big liquid eyes blazing with excitement.

'Ooh, Maxwell, isn't this fabulous? I love dancing.'

'Well, you'll have to find someone else to do it with, Marilyn. I'm one of life's observers at this kind of shindig.'

'Yer what?'

'Go and find a man your own age. Just fetch me a decent glass of claret first.'

'They have beer, cider, whisky and gin.'

'I might have known. Get me something strong. A lot of it.' And he slumped into a chair leaving Marilyn to battle her way to the bar. As she retreated he watched her capacious bottom, like two plump cushions squeezed into red velvet hotpants a size too small, and his penis gave a reflexive twitch in his trousers. *No more big women*, he said to himself. In this one day he'd had enough outsized loving to last him a lifetime. He needed a tall slim girl with less violent desires.

'Hiya, Max, you look pooped.'

He lifted his eyes to a woman in a peacock-blue silk shirt and black leggings that seemed to go on forever. They didn't come much taller or slimmer than Robyn Chestnut.

'Have a seat, Robyn. I haven't the energy to stand.'

'That's a shame. I thought we might bury the hatchet with a ceremonial dance.'

' "The *Bunny* and the *Dog* trip the light fantastic at rustic love rite" – it has a certain ring to it, I admit.'

'Here you are, Maxwell,' said a shrill voice and Marilyn thrust a dripping pint glass in his direction. She took one look at Robyn and retreated with a sniff.

Robyn watched her depart. 'Isn't that the tender-hearted nurse who ministered to my photographer this morning?'

'Poor fellow.'

'She got him back on his feet. Thanks to her, the swelling went down.'

'Really? She had quite the opposite effect on me.' Maxwell had drained the rancid brown liquid to the dregs and was suddenly feeling very much better. 'Come on then, Robyn Rabbit, let's dance.'

Monk had emptied the mini-bar in his room of Scotch and was considering starting on the vodka. No, what he needed was company, friendly faces and jollity – and more whisky, of course. Wasn't tonight meant to be some local celebration?

He left his room and wandered along the corridor. He descended the stairs and found himself outside Julia Jarvis's office. He knocked. There was no reply. He went in.

Though the room was empty it was full of her. Of her scent and her presence and the memory of her upturned face as she boldly defied him that morning. And the feel of her soft lips on his and the warm weight of her bare breasts in his hands as she lay down on the desk for him. It was funny to think he had turned his face steadfastly from sex for fifteen years and all it took was one embrace and his abstinence meant nothing – except a string of missed opportunities, of course.

He closed the door behind him and descended to the lobby. It was deserted. A lone barman read the paper behind the counter. Monk went out onto the terrace in the hot evening sunshine and heard the sound of laughter and music from across the fields. He began to walk towards it, turning his predicament over in his mind.

His job was to assemble the evidence to convict Julia of the Brenda robberies. It was a serious crime and she faced serious punishment but he couldn't help that. One intense and passionate encounter meant nothing. It was his duty to arrest her.

He was close to the barn now. He could see the clearing outside where people milled around a barbecue. He smelt smoke and charcoal and hamburger and realised he was famished. The music was loud and tuneful. He couldn't remember when he had last had a dance.

As he opened the gate which led to the field by the barn there was a flurry of movement to his left and a gurgle of laughter, smartly cut off. A couple lay in the grass, their mouths glued together. Their hands were tussling while she fought to hold her dress down over a slim brown thigh.

As Monk closed the gate behind him he had a vision of a new future. One free from cynicism and distrust, from police politics and self-serving fools like Hatter, from forever seeking the worst in his fellow man. It was a vision with a warm curvaceous body in his bed every night. *Dream on, Archie*, he said to himself. It was a dream that would haunt him, he knew, if he arrested Julia Jarvis.

He bought a sausage and ate it, dripping grease down his front. He bought another and a can of warm lemonade. As the last sweet and sticky mouthful disappeared down his throat he felt a sudden glow of happiness and found himself grinning stupidly at the people around.

One of them returned his gaze.

'Hello, Inspector.'

'Ms Jarvis!' He spoke the name with reverence. 'I've been looking for you.' It was true, he realised.

She looked startled. 'Surely you aren't going to subject me to further interrogation here?'

'Just one question.'

'Yes?' Her lower lip was trembling, her clear blue eyes were enormous.

'Will you dance with me?'

60

Stephen Fantail watched with admiration as his boss led Julia Jarvis onto the dance floor. By God, Monk was a cunning bugger. All that stuff about resigning had to be his idea of a joke. Poetry indeed! Mad Monk was obviously going in for the kill.

A hand took hold of his upper arm, just above the rolled sleeve of his pale blue shirt.

'Excuse me, officer.' A tall blonde with a kiss-me mouth looked at him out of sky-blue eyes.

'We'd like your assistance.' The voice came from his other side, from a second blonde with cloudless eyes and pouting pink lips. He looked from one to the other. They were beautiful, stunning – and identical.

'How do you know I'm a policeman?' he said.

'We work at the hotel,' said one. 'You're DC Fantail, aren't you? Room 31.'

'And we need help. I've lost a ring.'

'Has it been stolen?'

'I don't think so but I might need to report its loss officially. For the insurance.'

'It's over here in the bushes,' said the other. 'Please come and help us.'

What else could he do? Police officer or not, a red-blooded young man with no current attachments does not refuse to go into the bushes with two horny-looking blondes. And they were decidedly horny-looking . . .

One walked beside him, her hand now burning a hole in his shirt. The other strode ahead, the pert halves of her bottom swelling the skintight denim of her jeans. Her hips swivelled as she walked and the cleft between her cheeks winked and tightened with each step.

'She's a peach, isn't she?' said the girl by his side.

'You both are.'

Twin peaches ripe for plucking, he said to himself and wished he could adjust his trousers without attracting attention.

They led him into the next field and the first girl turned and pointed to the far corner. 'Over there,' she said.

They searched for fifteen minutes. Fifteen minutes in which Stephen was treated to their lithe and nubile bodies bending and leaning and rubbing against his in a cock-stretching selection of poses. The girl in jeans doubled over before him, thrusting her rear into his crotch as she meticulously searched the grass. Her twin leant on his shoulder as he looked for the ring, her long blonde hair brushing against the side of his face in a golden curtain. She turned to face him on her knees and he found himself gazing down the front of her blouse into a deep ravine of creamy breast flesh.

'You won't find it down there,' she said, making no attempt to cover herself. He blushed to the tips of his ears.

'You know,' said the first girl, 'maybe I never put it on at all. Maybe it's still at home.'

'Oh dear,' said the other, 'now we're in trouble. He'll have us for wasting police time.'

'Will you?' said girl number one, putting her hand on Stephen's knee as he squatted on his haunches among the weeds. 'I think it's all her fault, she suggested we ask you to help. You should smack her bottom.'

'I, er . . .' Stephen gulped, bewildered by the turn of events.

'Go on,' the girl said. 'Take her jeans down and smack her bum. She deserves it.'

'Yes, it's true,' said the other, unbuckling her belt and hooking the flaps of her denims over her hip.

'Turn around,' commanded her twin. 'Take them down slowly and show him your arse.'

Stephen's eyes bulged from his head as the girl did as she was told, thrusting her bum back almost into his face as she lowered her jeans. Her bottom glowed white in the

Lust at Large

thickening light. Her panties, caught in the divide between the cheeks, provided little protection from his prurient gaze. Without being asked, she peeled the scarlet scrap of material down her legs as well and tossed it aside.

'How do you want me?' she asked over her shoulder, her pale satiny behind fully revealed beneath the hem of her pink T-shirt.

Stephen was struck dumb. He had the urge to plunge forward and bury his head between those plump curvaceous cushions, to lick her from the golden beard of her pussy, right up the crease of her arse to the base of her spine.

'Get over his lap, of course,' said her sister, pushing the half-naked girl towards Stephen.

He sat in rigid disbelief as she arranged her nude loins across his lap, compressing his mighty erection into his belly. She wriggled her warm weight against it. 'Ooh, officer,' she said, 'I can feel your truncheon.'

'Go on,' said the other girl, kneeling by his side, her eyes big with excitement. 'Slap her arse hard. Make her cheeks wobble. You're dying to do it, I bet.'

Stephen didn't believe in physical violence and he didn't believe in corporal punishment. He was revolted by the thought of sadistic practices and repulsed by masochism. That was the theory. But he discovered, as he brought his hand down hard on the firm rounded bum flesh spread across his lap, that theory and practice were two different things. Before he had laid on two solid smacks and set the smooth white flesh in motion he knew that he believed in spanking a girl's naked bottom when she asked for it.

And this one was asking for it all right.

'Harder,' she cried. 'Do it harder! Oh yes, please! Do it again!'

The sounds of the spanking and the moans and squeals of the spankee echoed across the fields. There were whoops and coarse shouts from the barbecue as connoisseurs of the art recognised what was taking place.

'That's enough,' said the first sister, 'any more and you'll have to fuck her straight away.'

'What!'

'Don't worry, you can fuck her soon enough but you've

got to spank me first. It's my turn now.'

She was serious. She was stepping out of her black miniskirt, revealing long slim thighs in stockings and suspenders. She wore no knickers and a blonde bush sprang from the base of her belly, the pink stripe of her slit fully revealed beneath. She laid herself across his thighs in place of her sister, her glorious white bum cheeks framed by the black silk of her suspenders and stockings.

'Go on, smack me. Take your revenge.'

'I don't understand.'

'Melanie,' said the other blonde in worried tones.

'Don't worry, sis, he'd never tell. Besides I'm sure he's already worked out who tied him to the garden roller this morning.'

'You!' exclaimed Stephen.

'Well done, Sherlock. Why don't you warm my bum and even the score?'

'It's a deal,' said DC Fantail and set her pretty buttocks dancing.

61

In the barn, the action was hotting up. The local girls had cleared a space on the sawdust-strewn floor and were performing a dance unknown to outsiders. It involved a lot of hand-clapping and whooping and skirt-flipping – an action that soon turned the male revellers into bug-eyed spectators.

'Did I see what I thought I saw?' said Tony from Wales.

'You did,' replied Mitzi. 'None of these sluts are wearing knickers.'

'Good Lord,' muttered Ray from Humberside as a small brunette lifted her frock to her waist and, for a split second, bared brown thighs and a triangle of black pussy curls.

'Fantastic!' cried Barry from Scotland who had his eye on a strapping blonde pirouetting in front of him. He could not be certain but he'd bet money she had a shaven fanny. Any second now he'd find out . . .

'Hey!' he cried in protest as a small but determined hand spun him round.

'That's enough,' said Mitzi, pushing and pummelling her Gartertex colleagues into a line with their backs to the dance. 'If you guys want to keep me company then you can take your eyes off other women. Don't I look good enough for you?'

Certainly she looked good enough, they agreed. She looked quite splendid. In fact, they had never seen her look so mouthwatering. Particularly in that brassiere.

'Would that be a Raquel you're wearing?' asked Tony as he gazed with fascination at the inner curve of her golden left breast, enticingly exposed in the deep vee of her jacket.

'Looks like a Cleopatra to me,' said Ray. 'Lifts and

separates as if by magic. My year-in, year-out stock line.'

Mitzi smiled. This was more like it. 'What's your guess, Barry?' She leaned towards him and gave him the benefit of both barrels, as it were.

He considered the problem. His professional judgement was on the line. 'It's a Samantha,' he pronounced. 'Enhances as it entrances. Only the biggest and the best can get away with it.'

'Correct,' said Mitzi and undid the button holding her jacket over the glories of her chest. 'Look,' she said, and they did.

The big beautiful balloons of her breasts were supported by the flimsiest of scalloped black brassieres. A transparent veil moulded her bosom into twin thrusting peaks whose upper curves were completely bare. The dark brown thimbles of her nipples pointed at them, just begging to be thumbed and tickled and sucked.

'I think Barry deserves a prize,' said Tony.

'Too right,' said Ray. 'Let him take it off.'

Mitzi hesitated. Over Ray's broad shoulder she saw Don. He was dancing in a clinch with that fat blonde and he had his tongue down her throat.

'OK,' she said hoarsely, wondering where this might lead. 'Take my tits out, Barry. You can all have a good look.'

'Which one do you fancy most?'

Max gave Robyn a surprised glance. The pair of them were sitting on a wooden bench watching the dancers.

'What makes you think I fancy any of them? This set-up is rather too provincial for my taste.'

'Come off it, Max. You're known as the horniest newshound on the *Dog*. Which one of those birds would you like to flush into the open?'

Max surveyed the swirling crowd of girls cheerfully showing off their plump thighs and pouting pussies. A flash of light drew his eye to a slim figure in cool silk whose copper-coloured hair was pushed back off her face as she aimed her camera. Adriana was taking the sensational shots which, suitably censored, would soon adorn Max's shock-horror exposé of naughty nights in the North Grinding.

'Robyn, even if I did fancy one of those fair maids do

you think I'd tell you? You'd claim I was about to sell her into white slavery in tomorrow's *Bunny*.'

Robyn smiled. Something of the sort had crossed her mind.

'More to the point,' Max continued, 'why don't you tell me which one you fancy? What about that small dark one with the brown legs who looks Spanish? I understand you have a penchant for Latin girls.'

Robyn forced a laugh but couldn't keep the shock off her face. How the hell did he know about Mercedes?

'It's OK, Robyn, I won't say a word in print. Alistair told me in strictest confidence.'

'He's a bastard. You don't want to believe anything he tells you about me.'

'Quite.' Max appreciated the unobtrusive way Adriana skirted the leering lurching crowd, crouching gracefully to get her shots. 'Did you know that they mix specially prepared seeds and grasses with sawdust and spread it on the floor? That's why the girls leave their knickers off. The seeds fly up and stick to their pubic hair and sexual parts creating in them a furious desire to copulate.'

Adriana was down on one knee in front of him, the thin peach silk of her loose trousers pulled taut across the full rounds of her buttocks. Max admired her professionalism. He reminded himself that he did not lust after her in the least.

'So?' said Robyn.

'So if you slipped your panties down your delectable legs and stamped around on the floor for a bit we might be able to verify the existence of this aphrodisiacal phenomenon.'

'Are you saying you want to screw me, Max?'

'You bet. DOG SHAFTS RABBIT – it would make a great headline. Let's go for it.'

'OK but I don't fancy getting a load of grass and seeds up my snatch, thanks very much.'

'Don't worry. I can provide something much more satisfactory.' And he grabbed her hand and led her out of the door, making sure not to catch his photographer's eye on the way.

Miriam high-kicked with gusto. As she did so she searched

Lust at Large

the cheerful throng for one face in particular. She had set her sights on a certain man. If he was here tonight, she meant to have him. It would crown a most successful day.

Her mind was still buzzing with the achievements of her three daughters. Just before they had set off for the evening the girls had sprung their surprise – through a lucky sequence of bets on the Lark Hill races they had won enough money to buy her the freehold of the donkey sanctuary! Rodney Holmdale had confirmed it by phone and congratulated her on having such enterprising girls! Miriam had been a little surprised to hear that Julia was resigning from the hotel but, since Melanie and Mercy were being promoted to Joint Manager, what did it matter? She'd long harboured the hope that Julia and Rodney might forge a romance but perhaps one of the others would catch his eye . . .

Suddenly she spotted her quarry. Like all the other lusty lads he was in the crowd, transfixed by the twinkling limbs of the dancing girls. Maybe Miriam was a little old to be part of the fertility dance but she was not the only matron in the throng and she knew she still had what it took to get her man.

The atmosphere was thick with smoke and wood shavings. There was an itch in her loins, fired by a recent memory and fanned by the warm air bathing her naked pussy under her skirt. She moved closer to her quarry, the blond boy from London, the one she had seen pleasuring Lucy Salmon in this very barn just a few days ago. Any minute now the dancers would break ranks, no one could hold out much longer. Then it would be every woman for herself and Miriam knew just what she wanted – the long white cock of Gavin Bird.

Julia Jarvis did not feel a part of the hysteria all around her. She observed the girls in their ritual dance as if from afar – to think she had been part of the obscene exhibition last year! She saw her mother cavorting in the crowd, her eyes alight with happiness and lust. Somehow, cocooned in Archie Monk's arms, it did not seem real.

The pair of them swayed together on the fringe of the

festivities, like a pair of waltzing pensioners. Julia loved the firm shackle of his arms around her, his lean body pressing into hers, the soft burr of his voice in her ear.

'You've led me a fine dance,' he said. 'You've fooled the entire country, you cunning witch.'

Julia's heart was thumping – surely he wasn't going to arrest her like this? She had the security of Rodney's alibi now, but it was still a frightening prospect.

As if guessing her thoughts, he said, 'Don't worry, I'm no threat to you any longer. I've resigned.'

'I've resigned too,' she blurted.

'I should hope so, you've done enough damage.'

'From the hotel, I mean. I've had enough of it all.'

'What are you going to do?'

'I don't know yet. Find another hotel job, I suppose.'

'How about Scotland? Come with me and we'll open a place in the Highlands. Somewhere miles away where I can keep an eye on you.'

It was an extraordinary thought.

Bedlam erupted around them as one lad threw himself on the small dark dancer who had been taunting him by wiggling her bare belly under his nose. The boy hoisted her over his shoulder and carried her off through the throng, her pert brown buttocks uppermost, a black wedge of hair clearly visible in the crevice between. It was the cue for a free-for-all, as men and women made a grab for one another, some falling to the floor, others surging for the door and the fields outside.

Julia watched her mother exit into the open air, her arms locked fast around a tall blond youth half her age.

The soft Scots voice was still purring into her ear. 'Come on, Brenda, what do you say? Give up your life of crime and come away with me. I'll make an honest citizen of you.'

Julia giggled. 'What if you don't succeed?'

'I've got a very firm hand. I'll teach you some real discipline.'

'Ooh.' Julia snuggled tighter, pushing her full bosom into his chest. 'I like the sound of that.'

They kissed, a deep-throated clinch that sucked the breath from their bodies. His fingers found the hard bud of a nipple through her clothes and she swooned against him.

'What makes you think I'm Brenda?' she asked.

'I examined you, didn't I? I'm sure you're the one.'

'No doubts at all?'

'Well . . .'

'I think you'd better make certain, Inspector. Take me outside and examine me again.'

62

The sun had gone down but it was no cooler despite a wind that gusted from the south. The breeze blew hot, like dog's breath, propelling big low clouds across the face of the moon. A storm was approaching and the pressure was rising – particularly in the fields surrounding the barn.

In the weird blue light cast by the moon, Stephen Fantail examined every inch of the two glorious sisters who cradled him between their naked bodies.

'We're not absolutely identical, you know,' said one, running her fingers along the rigid barrel of his tool.

'But only our very best friends can tell us apart,' said the other, grazing the tips of her breasts across his chest.

Stephen licked a patch of tender skin high on one girl's inner thigh. He knew, at least he thought he knew, where he would find the mark that would distinguish one from the other. He advanced his tongue and teased open the outer lips of the girl's pouting honeypot. Above him, he heard the hiss of indrawn breath; below, between his legs, he felt the lap of a prying tongue on his balls. Gently he began to suck. He was in no hurry.

Mitzi Bluitt was in the dark in every sense. With one of Ray's big red handkerchiefs tied across her eyes, she could not see a thing. But she could feel and that was the name of the game. From titty-ogling and nipple-pinching and three-way snogging, Mitzi and her admirers had progressed to cock-fondling in the field. As she knelt in the grass, naked to the waist, the men were grouped around her. Their erections were bared to the night air and Mitzi was trying to identify their owners. It was a new diversion for her and she was taking it seriously.

'Circumcised,' she said as she examined the cock on her right. 'Big broad head, fat shaft and – mmm – I can hardly get my lips round it. That's got to be Ray.'

'By gum, she's good,' said a thick northern voice.

'Don't put it away, Ray. I'm going to need it in a moment. Now, this one . . .'

From across the meadow came a harsh, bull-like grunting. Mitzi recognised it at once. It was Don reaching his short strokes with the over-endowed blonde. For a fleeting second she felt sorry for the girl, Don always came too soon. With three men of her own at hand, for once Mitzi was confident she was not going to go short of cock.

'This one's very long. Sweet, too. It's like a stick of rock. I bet it says "Barry" all the way through it.'

'Fantastic!' they cried.

'So this big juicy prick must belong to Tony. It's so smooth, like hot velvet. Let me just rub along here and suck this—'

'Mitzi, be careful! I don't think I can – OH!'

'Wow, Tony, you've gone off like a fire extinguisher! Look, boys, he's shot a gallon all over me.' She pulled the blindfold from her face and grinned at them in triumph. Then she began to rub the come into her tits. The sleek rounds of flesh glistened in the moonlight, the nipples shining like wet pebbles.

'God, Mitzi, you're the sexiest woman I've ever met,' said Barry, awestruck. The others murmured hoarse agreement.

Mitzi smiled and took hold of the two remaining erections that pulsed and throbbed inches from her face.

'Thanks, boys, you say the sweetest things. Now who's going to have my mouth and who's going to fuck my cunt? You choose.'

Outside the barn, with the sticky sounds of love and breathless cries of pleasure echoing all around, an earnest conversation was taking place.

'What are you doing here, Chantal? I thought my father had you under lock and key.' Graham knew he sounded callow and petulant but he couldn't help himself.

Lust at Large

'I came to find you, Graham, though I don't intend to spoil your fun. You should go with that Mandy, I can see you are longing to play with her big tits.'

'Don't be ridiculous. I only want you.'

'Maybe, but I saw you watching Mandy dancing just now and your penis was sticking out like a salami. Of course, now you have missed your chance. You will have to wait your turn with her.'

'Chantal, please!'

'She won't mind, I promise you. She's built like a cow, that one, she just loves having her udders squeezed. The man with her will be finished soon.'

'Shut up, Chantal.'

'Don't mind me, Graham. Go and join the queue. I'll wait until—'

He silenced her by placing his lips on hers. He invaded her small sweet mouth with his tongue and held her so tight she thought he would squeeze the life out of her. The kiss went on for a long time. When they came up for air, they were lying full length on a bank of grass and her hand was inside his shirt, toying with the tangle of hair on his chest.

'You mustn't tease me, Chantal,' he said.

'OK,' she said, moving her hand down his body, inside his waistband, to take hold of his rigid tool. 'I came to tell you I'm going to marry your father.'

'That's not funny, Chantal.'

'This is no joke.'

'I don't believe it. You can't do this to me!' He struggled to push her away but she was doing such delicious things to his cock that all resistance soon ceased. Her thumb and forefinger ringed his thick penis, sending waves of sensation down that unthinking limb.

'You're a tart,' he sobbed. 'A cruel gold-digger. You know I love you!'

'Don't be silly, Graham. I'm just the first woman you've slept with who knows how to please a man. You're too young to look further than between my legs.'

'We're the same age!'

'Maybe, but you're a provincial English boy who carries

his rich daddy's bags. I'm a French peasant who's never had anything she hasn't earned for herself. There's a world between us.'

'You're a heartless bitch.'

'Drop the self-pity, Graham, and listen to me.' She slowed down the rhythm on his tool and ran her thumbnail gently across the head. The big organ leapt at her touch. He was well under control. She whispered into his ear.

'I'm offering you a deal, Graham. I want us to be friends while I learn about your father's business. A firm like Louche Lingerie is made for me. I know about sex. I know what makes women desirable and I know just how to sell it to them. But all those other deadbeats won't see it that way. They'll hate me. That's why I need you on my side.'

There was a silence. Chantal undid Graham's trousers and pulled his throbbing member into the open.

'What's in it for me?' he said at last. 'The firm will be mine anyway.'

'When? If GG dropped dead tomorrow you wouldn't have a clue what to do. And if he lasts ten years he'll have run it into the ground and you'll have been pushed around for all that time for no reward.'

She pulled her top over her head and threw it into the darkness. Her little breasts jiggled with the movement and she leaned over him to brush their stiff points across his cheek.

'I can manage your father, Graham, and I can manage the business. I'll cut out the dead wood. All those clots like Jason Quiff will be out of work by Christmas. There will be plenty for you and me to do. Apart from the kinky sex, that is.'

She had pulled off her wrap-round skirt and now she was nude. The moonlight gleamed on her pale perfection. She knelt up over him and held the stiff pole of his penis between her thighs.

'What do you mean, kinky sex?' he said, panting.

She spat daintily on her fingers and began to rub the juice into the swollen head of his cock.

'You know, Graham. Sex. Fucking and sucking and wanking whenever your father's back is turned. He's too old, he'll never satisfy me. I need a young cock. Yours.'

'You said kinky sex.'

'You don't think fucking your mother is kinky?'

She surveyed his glistening tool with satisfaction. She could barely contain it in her two small hands.

'Your father is marrying my arsehole, Graham, did you know that? Would you like to bugger me too? Would that be kinky enough for you?'

'Chantal, I—'

'Go on, Graham, admit it. You'd like to stick your big cock in my special place. Of course you would.'

'Oh, Chantal—'

'Mmm, I'd better let you right now, I can see. I like it in my *derrière*. I'll need it regularly once I'm running Louche Lingerie. Suppose I bend down and stick my bottom up like this?'

'Chantal, you're so beautiful!'

'Before you put it in, Graham—'

'Yes?'

'Tell me I can count on your support.'

'I'll do anything you want, Chantal, I promise.'

'Then hurry up and fuck my arse.'

Robyn had a mouth full of cock or she would have said something to Josie as she passed by in the half dark. The *Bunny*'s special reporter looked as if she had spent a week in the undergrowth with an Under–21 football team. She was naked but for the tattered remains of a torn T-shirt and her buttocks gleamed in the fitful light of the moon. There were leaves and dust on her back, her hair was wild and a river of spunk ran down her legs. For all that, there was a spring in her step as she picked her way between the writhing bodies in search of further conquests. Obviously she was taking her assignment seriously.

Robyn watched her go with half an eye. Her hands were wrapped round Max Shaftesbury's mighty genitals and she was pumping on his shaft as she gummed and sucked the big, mushroom-shaped knob. Between her legs a rasping tongue reamed her dripping honeypot and a lurch in her stomach told her she was approaching orgasm again.

Lust at Large

This epic clash of the tabloids might be going the *Dog*'s way – so far he'd brought her off four times and she'd milked him dry only twice – but there were some battles well worth losing. What's more, she felt a remarkable appetite for the fray. After this episode of *soixante-neuf* had run its course, she resolved to get down on her hands and knees and put him through his paces – the thought was amusing – doggie-fashion.

A finger found her clit and she pressed her hungry vagina against his lips. He might be winning a few battles, she told herself, but at the final shot he'd discover he'd lost this particular circulation war.

The storm clouds were racing in fast and the moonlight flickered across the field of heaving bodies. In the distance could be heard the rumble of thunder.

Miriam cried out in ecstasy as Gavin emptied his balls into her with a shout that matched her own. Plunging forward onto the soft cushions of her chest, he fastened his lips around a big ridged nipple. She let him toy with her sumptuous breasts for a moment then impatiently turned him onto his back. Slithering down his lean body, she buried her face in the hair of his belly and sucked his limp cock into the warmth of her mouth.

Gavin lay on his back and allowed Miriam to do as she wished. He heard a whisper behind him and reached his hands above his head. There he encountered flesh – soft female flesh that answered his curiosity with explorations of its own. An unknown mouth descended on his in the dark. A sly tongue slipped between his lips. He found the curve of a firm buttock and squeezed. Between his legs Miriam had no trouble in restoring his erection.

Across the fields, hands traversed and prospected, mouths solicited and tongues probed, thighs opened and legs entwined. Couples parted and reformed in more interesting configurations, exclusive friendships were shared out, groups evolved and were reshaped afresh. Rampant and naked, men and women set about fucking as if the world was due to end the next morning.

The annual Blisswood Midsummer's orgy was approaching its climax.

63

Josie picked her way across the field by flashes of lightning, the sudden light illuminating lustful tableaux at every step. A woman rode, squealing, on a prone male, her gargantuan breasts rolling on her chest like medicine balls. A man's broad hairy buttocks were frozen before Josie's eyes, the dark plums of his testes dangling in the vee of his thighs. Two girls sat giggling on one lover, one on his stomach, the other rubbing the gash of her pussy across his face.

Josie walked on, stepping carefully between the groups of naked people, avoiding the hands that reached out to detain her.

Her adventures of the evening had been torrid. As she had guessed, her games with the boys in the wood had not been easy to conclude. First had been Martin with his donkey-sized cock, then a thin and beautiful youth who had played on the guitar and then on her clit with a similar dexterity. He had introduced her to two hippies with long hair, enthusiastic tools and inventive minds. She had missed the dance in the barn. She had lost her clothes. And still, despite being ravaged in every orifice big enough to welcome a penis or a tongue or a finger, there was an itch inside her she had still not satisfied.

She stumbled against a soft form on the ground and fell. Hands caught her and she found herself held fast against a broad and hairy chest. He smelt like seasoned wood and felt hard like teak. Without thinking she cuddled into his arms and pushed her soft belly against his groin. He was hard there too. How satisfactory.

Gavin cupped the big breasts in his hands, fondling and

stroking their satiny mass. If only he could see!

A flash of lightning answered his prayers and for a split second he held in his hands the object of his quest – the fabulous tits of Bra-less Brenda. Then the girl was pried from his grasp by another man and borne to the ground in front of him where, in another flash, he saw her spreading her legs for her new admirer. He sat on his haunches and listened to them, just a few feet away, as the man drove into her with a grunt and they began the steady see-saw of a fuck.

'Come on, baby,' whispered a soft voice in his ear and a slender arm curled around his neck, pulling him into a perfumed embrace that was impossible to resist. He answered her kiss and ran his hands over a pneumatic form as perfect as any he had ever embraced. On a rising tide of lust he dipped his head to her bosom and the lightning cracked again.

It was only then that he realised his search was over, his crazy and ridiculous quest to find the woman who had robbed him at breast-point and sent his life spinning off the rails. By God, he was grateful to her for rescuing him from his former existence. But now, as he kissed and fondled these new breasts in the darkness, he knew he must call a halt to his journey. For these tits, too, were the pair he sought – the warm and weighty, strawberry-tipped globes of the Topless Raider. To be sure, it was a wonderful way to be driven mad but unless he returned to reality they'd be locking him up for good.

There was a collective cry of joy as the first drops of rain fell on the parched earth and on the sweating bodies locked in their lewd embraces. The sky opened with the roll and crash of thunder and the water fell like waves breaking on a beach.

Cliff Rush, the only abstainer at the feast, leapt like a demented leprechaun to take the weird and wonderful shots of the orgy in the storm that were to make his name. His uncanny eye led him to capture remarkable scenes of sexual license lit by lightning. Of Marilyn the former nurse, hosing two ejaculating cocks over her vast wet breasts. Of Mario the waiter, holding Lucy Salmon back to front on his shoulders, his nose in her muff, her face upturned in ecstasy to the turbulent sky. Of Mandy, the would-be model, taking it simultaneously in her bum and in her mouth from two Gartertex salesmen while kneeling in a puddle the size of a small duckpond.

But Cliff failed to capture the one encounter that Robyn Chestnut really wanted – even if it was only suitable for her private scrapbook. . .

At the first drop of rain Gavin stood up and ran, his arms held high, his face turned to the storm. He collided with a woman and they stuck together, arm in arm, shouting and laughing. She was smaller than him and he bent to kiss her unseen face. She gave him her lips and flung her arms round his neck. It felt wonderful.

Gavin was tired but the rain was rejuvenating, like this girl. He hoisted her up and her legs curled around his waist. He held her by the buttocks. They were firm yet full and fitted into his hands as if made to measure. He slipped his little finger into the soft folds of her cunt and she mewed with pleasure, sinking her teeth into his neck.

As if by magic, the swollen head of his penis butted against the spread mouth of her vagina and lodged there.

'Oh yes,' she breathed into his ear. 'Do it to me please! Fuck me standing up in the rain, whoever you are.'

Gavin froze, the voice as familiar yet unexpected as bad news. But this, he realised as she wriggled the tight sheath of her pussy over the head of his trembling tool, was the most miraculous news he had ever heard.

The lightning flashed again and confirmed his happy fate.

'Josie!' he cried and drove his cock up into the depths of her.

64

Maxwell Shaftesbury lurched into his hotel bedroom drunk with exhaustion. The exhilaration of the orgy in the rain had already disappeared, leaving him as feeble as a day-old pup. He crashed onto his bed like a felled tree.

A light snapped on. It speared into his head through the membrane of his closed eyelids. He cried into the pillow, he didn't have the energy to speak.

'Get up,' said a soft voice.

Adriana. Of course. It came back to him that at some point during his marathon with Robyn – after his fourth come into that insatiable suction valve she kept between her legs – he had resolved to talk to Adriana about a live-in relationship. A relaxing, platonic, no-strings relationship. For the moment, however, he simply moaned. It was the best he could do.

A hand shook his shoulder through the sodden material of his shirt. He did not respond to its prodding. He heard the sound of the bathroom door opening and of water running.

Adriana returned and, to his complete surprise, rolled him off the bed and onto the floor. He landed on his back. Mercifully the carpet was soft. He did not open his eyes.

She stripped him of his clothes. There weren't many of them: a blue silk shirt spoilt beyond repair, soft denim designer jeans stained with spunk and one calfskin moccasin with a second skin of mud.

It wasn't easy for Adriana to undress a comatose man of six foot two who weighed nearly fourteen stone but she managed it with the skill of someone who had done it many times before. Max did not move a muscle to help. He couldn't.

She raised his head and pressed a glass to his lips. He opened one eye.

'Drink it,' she said.

He saw she was wearing a man's shirt. It was unbuttoned to the tops of her breasts and looked like one of his. A copper-coloured lock of her hair brushed his face and he caught the faint aroma of her perfume, clean and lemony. He began to feel more human.

'Drink,' she repeated.

He did so. It was brandy. The first sip scorched his gullet. The second lit a fire in his stomach.

'Oh God,' he said.

'Don't tell me,' she said, 'the things you frontline reporters have to do.'

He looked at her keenly, he wasn't in a fit state to cope with irony.

'Get in the bath,' she commanded and helped him to his feet.

The warm soapy water cleansed and revived. She brought him tea with sugar.

'Ugh,' he said.

'Drink it up,' she told him, so he did.

'Adriana, I want to talk to you seriously.'

She took the cup from his hands.

'I think you're a wonderful woman. I want you to come and live with me.'

Her mouth fell open.

'Don't say anything. Let me finish. We see eye to eye, we share the same kind of professional commitment and I'd be lost without you. I'm not talking about sex, though.'

'You're not.' It was a statement of fact.

'Oh no, I wouldn't expect that of you. Frankly, my work demands that I spend so much time in the intimate company of women that it's the last thing I need when I get home. We could have a close, mutually dependent, platonic union. Like our working relationship extended into our personal lives.'

The dregs of the tea hit him in the face as she flung the cup at him.

Lust at Large

'You despicable rat,' she spat. 'I spend the night sitting out the best orgy in the Western hemisphere while you fuck that skinny nympho on the *Rabbit* and you offer me a platonic union!'

'Adriana, believe me, I was just doing my job tonight.'

'I see. Screwing Robyn Chestnut was part of your professional duties.'

'It was one of the toughest assignments I've ever had. Honestly.'

She got to her feet. Her wide lush mouth for once set in a forbidding line. He couldn't help noticing that his shirt ended high up on her pale-skinned thigh, just an inch or so below her groin. Would the hair there, he wondered, be the same magical copper colour as on her head?

'Why don't you team up with her permanently? You deserve each other. For a pair of hotshot reporters neither of you are exactly exclusive.'

The door slammed behind her with such force that all the towels slithered off the rail onto the floor.

Max clambered out of the bath and picked one up. As he dried himself he had time for reflection. He knew what the situation required. Unfortunately, after his epic encounter in the fields with La Chestnut, he wasn't sure that he was up to it. But if he didn't take action now he would lose Adriana for good.

He pulled experimentally at the dangling member between his thighs and found to his amazement that, despite its red raw appearance, there remained a certain resilience. The image of the shirt-tail clinging to Adriana's retreating bottom sprang to mind. In his fist, his cock sprang to attention.

All the lights were off in the bedroom but he left the bathroom door open. Adriana lay on her back on the covers, stark naked. Her legs were bent, her feet planted wide apart. A shaft of light fell across her loins, on the shallow bowl of her belly, on the arch of her slender thighs – and on the silky fleece of her pussy mound. It was as he had hoped. Copper-coloured.

He slid to his knees and placed his lips on the inside of one thigh. He moved to kiss the opposite leg, just a little higher up. He leant over further and inserted the tip of his tongue in the dark dimple of her belly button.

'Oh,' she sighed.

He trailed his tongue downwards. Very slowly.

'Ah,' she muttered.

He placed his mouth over her vulva without touching it and blew hot breath over her sex.

'You bastard,' she said.

'Yes,' he said and applied his lips.

'Oh yes,' she said in turn and buried her small hands in his mop of dark curls.

The juice was running from her like a river. He drank it down like nectar. She came for the first time.

'You do forgive me, darling, don't you?' he said later.

'I don't know. Lick me out again, please.'

Still later, he said, 'Move in with me.'

'I'll think about it. Are you going to put your cock in now? Or are you past it?'

He wasn't going to stand for that.

'Ooh, you *are* big. The girls all said you were.'

'Marry me, Adriana.'

'Shut up, Max, and concentrate. Stuff me with your thing.'

She came again. He made to remove his abused penis but she wouldn't let him.

'I love you, Adriana. You're my ideal woman. You mean more to me than all those casual fucks. Believe me, sex isn't important.'

She stopped agitating her belly against his for a moment and pushed her face into his. There was no trace of serene composure in her features now. The light caught the blaze in her eyes and the rictus of determination in her open mouth as she hissed, 'Don't give me that, Max. If you ever tell me again that sex doesn't matter I'll cut off your balls!'

Max stared at her in disbelief. Somewhere in the back of his head a little voice reminded him that Adriana was Italian. From Sicily.

She beat a tattoo on his buttocks with her fists.

'Come on, Max, it's my turn now. I expect you to keep it up till dawn.'

65

Stephen Fantail sat on the terrace in the cool night air. The rain had stopped as suddenly as it had started and the water had already disappeared into the parched earth. If it weren't for the fatigue in his bones and the lurid images in his head, Stephen could almost believe that the wild events of the evening had not taken place. But they had and now he didn't know what to do.

He reread the crumpled letter in his hands.

Dear Stephen
I am sorry not to be telling you this to your face but, as I indicated to you earlier, I am resigning from the force. I am leaving at once to go back to Scotland and embark on a different kind of life. As far as I am concerned the Brenda investigation has come to a dead end. Between you and me, I can guarantee that there will be no more topless robberies. Officially, I suppose they will simply have to mark the case 'unsolved'.

Yours aye,
Archie Monk

When Stephen had discovered the letter beneath his door he had rushed to Monk's room. There had been no reply to his urgent knocking. It looked as if Monk had already gone. It was a mystery.

The cause of Stephen's discomfort was that he knew Julia Jarvis was not the Topless Raider. He could prove to Monk that Julia's twin sisters were the culprits, that they had shared the robberies between them so that, being virtually identical, they could alibi each other. But Stephen now knew how to tell them apart. He knew that one had a flat mole the size of a chocolate button on the underside of her left breast, while her twin had the same mole on her right; and that they covered these distinguishing marks for the robberies with butterfly transfers – like those he had found at their mother's house.

He felt sure that if he went back to the security photos and rounded up the evidence at Miriam's he would be able to solve the case of Bra-less Brenda. More to the point, he could save Monk's career – if that was what he wanted. But was it? It looked like the man had done a runner.

In any case, it was all academic. He knew he wasn't prepared to turn in the two unbelievably sexy creatures who had just taken him to paradise and back. How could he? Maybe he wasn't cut out for life as a policeman.

'Hello, my little virgin,' said a warm voice in his ear, 'I've been searching for you.'

Stephen looked up, startled, and found himself gazing into the delectable toffee-coloured eyes of Fliss Dodge.

'Don't look so pleased to see me,' she said as she slid into the seat next to him, her musky perfume enveloping him like a cloud. 'Or have you forgotten me so soon?'

Her heart-shaped face and curling lips rendered him speechless. So did her large round breasts outlined beneath her pale blue scoop-necked shirt. Had it only been the evening before when he had buried his face in their pink perfection? He could almost feel the pressure of their soft mass in his hands.

'Have you been out on the tiles?' she asked.

He nodded.

'I haven't, I've kept myself pure for you.'

This wasn't entirely true. Fliss had spent the evening scheming and packing her things surreptitiously so Cliff wouldn't notice. Now she needed Stephen in more ways than one.

'On the moors with you,' gulped Stephen, 'was wonderful.' It seemed so long ago, and he had had so many adventures since, that the memory of Fliss had already taken on the misty glow of nostalgia.

'You were an eager little virgin,' she said. 'So hot for me.'

'Yes.'
'Do you still want me?'
'Oh yes!'
'You'd like to stroke and fondle my tits? To put your big weapon into my pussy and ride?'
'Yes, yes!'
'Shall I teach you the San Francisco Suck-Off?'
'What's that?'
She told him. She explained that they needed a room with mirrors and she would get on all fours for him with his prick in her mouth and her big boobs dangling and her arse cocked so he could watch the reflection of her winking vagina . . .
'Oh God, yes please,' he cried. 'I must do it!'
'OK, but we have to go to San Francisco.'
'What!'
'Listen. You go upstairs to my room. Here's the key. You take the wallet and the car key that's on the bedside table of the man who is sleeping up there. Don't wake him.'
'I don't understand.'
Fliss smiled at him and slid her hand up his thigh to where his penis tented his trousers. She squeezed it gently.
'I'm leaving my lover for you, Stephen, and we're taking his money and his Porsche and going to San Francisco. That's if you've got the guts to be my partner-in-crime, Mr Policeman. Have you?'
And, with her fingers gently titillating his cock and her heavy breasts outlined through the cotton of her thin shirt, Stephen decided that he had.